"DO YOU INTEND TO KEEP YOUR PROMISE TO BECOME BLACK BEAR'S BRIDE?"

Then tenderly he asked, "Did you ever yearn for me these past years?"

He smiled, and Estrela suddenly felt alive with feeling. Every nerve, every sense she possessed awakened, cried out to him to touch her, to possess her, to . . . Estrela pulled her thoughts up short.

She could not have him.

"Black Bear, we should not be speaking this way. I have no future with you. You must return to your home. I must stay here—"

"Enough!" He reached for her and enfolded her into his arms. As his head drew closer to her own, Estrela felt the air between them spark as if set with lightning until at last his lips touched hers . . .

Praise for Karen Kay's
LAKOTA SURRENDER
"Bittersweet, entrancing and immensely gratifying. Karen Kay cannot fail to carve a special niche."
Romantic Times

"A potent tale . . . an unforgettable story"
Rendezvous

Other **AVON ROMANCES**

AWAKEN, MY LOVE *by Robin Schone*
CAPTURED *by Victoria Lynne*
CONQUER THE NIGHT *by Selina MacPherson*
THE HEART AND THE ROSE *by Nancy Richards-Akers*
MAGGIE AND THE GAMBLER *by Ann Carberry*
TAKEN BY STORM *by Danelle Harmon*
TEMPT ME NOT *by Eve Byron*

Coming Soon

HEART'S HONOR *by Susan Weldon*
REBELLIOUS BRIDE *by Adrienne Day*

And Don't Miss These
ROMANTIC TREASURES
from Avon Books

A KISS IN THE NIGHT *by Jennifer Horsman*
LADY OF SUMMER *by Emma Merritt*
TIMESWEPT BRIDE *by Eugenia Riley*

LAKOTA PRINCESS

KAREN KAY

AVON BOOKS ◆ NEW YORK

LAKOTA PRINCESS is an original publication of Avon Books. This
work has never before appeared in book form. This work is a novel. Any
similarity to actual persons or events is purely coincidental.

AVON BOOKS
A division of
The Hearst Corporation
1350 Avenue of the Americas
New York, New York 10019

Copyright © 1995 by Karen Kay Elstner
Published by arrangement with the author
Library of Congress Catalog Card Number: 95-94149
ISBN: 0-380-77996-X

First Avon Books Printing: September 1995

AVON TRADEMARK REG. U.S. PAT. OFF. AND IN OTHER COUNTRIES, MARCA
REGISTRADA, HECHO EN U.S.A.

Printed in the U.S.A.

RA 10 9 8 7 6 5 4 3 2 1

To my best buddy, Esther Lotz.
Thank you for the inspiration.

And to all those who helped:

Jeanne Miller, whose continued assistance
is completely invaluable to me;

Dan Stover, Jr., for all his suggestions
and well-thought-out input;

Lyssa Keusch, my editor, for her delicate
touch and wisdom;

Trina Elstner, for her wonderfully creative
artistry and suggestions;

and to Dan, for all his
magical influence in my life.

ACTUAL HISTORIC EVENTS

1810 King George III goes insane

1811–1820 George IV rules England as Prince Regent

1817 Charlotte, only daughter of the Prince Regent, dies, giving birth to a stillborn baby boy

1820 King George III dies

1820–1830 George IV rules England as Sovereign

1830 King George IV dies

1830–1837 William IV rules England

1837 King William dies

1837 Victoria becomes Queen of England

The British

King George III
(1738–1820)

George IV
Prince Regent
(1762–1830)
M
Caroline of
Brunswick
(1768–1821)

Fredrick,
Duke of
York

William IV
(1765–1837)
M
Adelaide of
Saxe-Meiningen
(1792–1849)

Charlotte
(1796–1817)
M
Leopold
of
Saxe-Coburg-
Saarfeld
(1790–1865)

Baby Boy
Stillborn

***Estrela
1817**

Royal Family Tree

M

Charlotte Sophia
Meckleburg-Strelitz
(1744–1818)

| Edward,
Duke of Kent
(1767–1820)
M
Victoire of
Saxe-Coburg-
Saarfeld
(1786–1861) | Ernest,
Duke of
Cumberland
(1771–1851)
King of
Hanover | Adolphus,
Duke of
Cambridge
(1774–1850) | Three Sons
& Six
Daughters
*Duke of
Colchester is
the son of one
of these
daughters |

Queen
Victoria
(1819–1901)
M
Albert of
Saxe-Coburg-
Gotha
(1819–1861)

*Fictional Characters

Note:
William IV and Queen
Adelaide were ruling
when story takes place.

LAKOTA PRINCESS

Preface

A FABLE

This story has been told and retold around many a Lakota campfire; it's a simple story, a mere fable, with nothing to base it on but the whim of fantasy—or so we are told. But there are some who believe this story to be true, some who believe in the force and power of love. And it is to those believers that the following story is dedicated . . .

Terrified, the Earl from a country across a vast sea, pushed the lone horse into a run over a wide, Lakota prairie, a young princess asleep in his arms. From the shores of a country called England, to the American Colonies, into what the white man called the Canadian Providence, the Earl fled, and never far from his mind was a promise he had made to his heartfelt love in that land far away.

The Earl had thought to escape his and the Princess's enemies in America and, failing this, in the Canadian Providence. In these places he had hoped to fade into anonymity.

But it was not to be. The man had barely escaped this time with his life—and hers, the Princess.

The Earl knew he couldn't fail now, he being the last hope of his King; he being the last protector of the Princess. The King's power was gone now. The monarch's daughter, the Earl's own dearest love, lay dead. Neither the King nor his daughter was able to protect their heir, the young Princess, from an unscrupulous enemy who lay unseen and unknown.

A king's position must be powerful, indeed, for so many to lust after it; yet, the King could do nothing to save his granddaughter, since he could not fight a hidden enemy. We did not understand such unwarranted ambition, since we of the Lakota Nation have no monarchy, no kings or queens, no princesses. And no ethics it would seem, no compassion, not even the voice from their own god would hinder the Princess' unseen enemy. In consequence, this Earl sought the safety of the Princess, for she and only she could dispute the right of accession to the throne of England.

She had little protection, few people even knowing she existed. The facts of her birth, the mystery surrounding that event, were so little known, even we did not understand it all until later . . . much, much later. At first, all we knew was what we could see: the extreme danger to the Earl and to the child. And so it is that we learned this Earl, the child's last hope, had no choice but to run, rarely stopping to eat, barely even sleeping. These enemies of the King, and of the young child, would never relent, never end the pursuit; not until their goal was accomplished—the Princess breathing no more.

The Earl fled on into the west, the enemy never far behind. Through forests, over prairie, down waterways, he fled, terrified, never sure how far behind the enemy followed—never losing sight of the danger.

Then one night, exhausted, both the Earl and the Princess slept, unable to deny the toll their flight had exacted from them, unable to press forward.

And that is how our Lakota men found them. At first they had appeared more animal than human, their clothing tattered rags, their hair knotted and unkempt, their bodies dirty. And certainly when they awakened to find themselves being watched by three of our men, they had known fear. But we showed them kindness, not torture or worse, and soon this Earl and his young Princess, became our friends.

To our men's surprise, both the Princess and the Earl wept, explaining that it had been so long since either had received friendship, that they were overcome with grief. And the Earl tried to warn our men of the danger that followed them, but it made no sense to us since we were in our own territory and could disappear without a trace. So our men laughed at the danger, took these two people into our care, treated them with kindness, and gave them our protection.

A few years passed within our village. Good years. Peaceful years. Under our guardianship, the Princess, a child of no more than nine years of age, became more considerate of others.

Yet, despite all the good with us, the Earl grew unsettled and anxious to know what had happened to the affairs of a country so far away.

And so the Earl left us, leaving the girl within our care.

More years passed and the girl blossomed and flourished, learning to cherish our four Lakota virtues for women: truthfulness, bravery, generosity, and childbearing. We showered her with love, we treated her as though she were one of our own, we tolerated her outbursts and taught her the art of listening. And gradually, so slowly we at first didn't notice, a change came over this Princess and it appeared to us that love itself had dissolved the young girl's selfishness until she, in turn, began to love us.

And though her hair gleamed pale in the light of day, she came to bear more likeness to us than to any other people.

Then one day the Earl returned, insisting that the Princess must leave us, must accompany him to this place across the vast sea. He insisted that her position in this far-off place was now safe.

We knew not of this land, nor did the Princess recall it well, and the Earl soon found he had to reckon with the spirit of the young girl, for she did not wish to return.

She refused to listen to her old guardian, reasoning that we were her people now—not some other people across a great sea. Besides, something else had happened, something more precious than all the peoples in the world. She had fallen in love; a rare, nourishing love it was, as fresh and as beautiful as the prairie under a rising sun. And she cherished this one she loved above all else.

But the Earl, her old guardian, refused to listen, refused to compromise. She, the Earl said, had urgent responsibilities. Others depended upon her.

The girl despaired, for even our oldest chiefs, much as they loved her, agreed with the Earl. And soon these chiefs, as well as the Earl convinced her that she must return to her "home" across the sea.

A dismal gloom of gray clouds hung over our

land the day that she left; the misty rain, the rumble of thunder unsettling, foretelling of dangers and troubles yet to come. We knew she struggled to keep her composure; none of her feelings were witnessed in her bearing, and we looked upon her with pride.

Bidding us good-bye, she cried, promising to return, and we saw her gaze seek out that one special person: he who would have been her husband, her love.

We saw their eyes meet; we knew their hearts touched, saw hers silently breaking. And we knew that she would never forget him.

And he in turn, this young Indian brave, made a silent promise as he watched her leave: a vow to protect her, to love her, and never to leave her in thought, in deed, in fact, forever.

Prologue

England, November 3, 1817
Midnight

The scream shook the villa at Claremont.

The tall, handsome man hesitated for only a second, then darted up the stairs as though suddenly fired from hell. Once at the landing he raced down the hall, reaching out for the door at the same time the door opened from within.

He ran straight into one of the doctors. Though stunned, the royal physician recovered at once. "It is good you are here, my friend," the doctor said without preamble, clasping the other man's shoulders.

"Is she—"

"She still lives."

The tall man sighed, looking up. Only then did he notice the tears still raw on the doctor's cheeks, only then did he see the fatigue etched into a face that was itself a testimony of the struggle for life that had occurred these past fifty hours. Only then did he know.

"No!" The word hung in the air as though sworn. The tall man shook off the physician's hold.

"No! Surely the Lord would not take her from us so soon! This cannot be!"

"Come." The physician, too weary to argue, simply ushered the Earl of Langsford toward the inner chamber. "There is little time. Hurry, for I must summon her husband."

"No!"

But the man's protest was in vain. He realized it as soon as he entered her chambers.

His beautiful love, Charlotte, lay pale against the pillows, looking more shadow than real flesh. Her eyes were sunken and closed, her breathing shallow. The silken sheets, the woolen blankets, even the coverlet of the finest linen were all stained in blood—birthing blood.

He rushed forward, kneeling at the bed, wishing he could endow her with his own energy, and as his larger hand encompassed hers, he saw it—the babe, the dead baby boy. A stillborn birth. It lay beside her and she hugged it as though it were a living thing.

"Isn't she sweet?"

In that moment he knew she was delirious. He looked at the only woman he had ever loved, a woman he had never known physically, yet a woman he still loved beyond all reasoning. And he realized then that the physician had plied her with too much wine in an effort to ease her pain, the long birthing hours now behind her. And so the Earl smiled at her tolerantly, the way he always did when she had been too willful, saying merely, "Beautiful."

He knew it as soon as he'd spoken. These moments were all he had left with her. His beautiful, spoiled, dear Princess would not live to see the morning sun. He wished for a few more hours out of time. Just a few. Enough to tell her he had always enjoyed her outbursts, her ill-manneredly, wild, behavior. *This*, he swore, a few more hours with her, he deserved, he craved.

Her lips were pale, almost purple, as she looked at him, but still she smiled.

"It's a girl," she whispered, then coughed.

"Do not strain yourself with speech, my dearest Charlotte," he said, wishing she were not delirious in these, her last few minutes on earth.

She smiled again, then said simply, "I must."

"No, tomorrow. We will talk tomorrow."

"You must know that I will not be here on the morrow—"

"No!"

She sighed, closed her eyes and seemed to drop away.

And the man, barely daring to breathe, squeezed her hand.

She took a strained breath and with eyes still closed said, "Keep her safe, my dear Earl. Promise me this. This is all I will ask of you."

She opened her eyes, staring straight at him, and the Earl of Langsford swallowed hard. What could he say to a being whose dreams were dying? Did he tell her truthfully that such a babe did not exist? But then his beautiful, sweet love smiled at him, and the Earl knew he would say anything, anything to ease her mind.

"Keep her safe. She is a part of me, my good Earl," Charlotte said. "Remember this."

"I promise," was all he managed to say.

Again, she smiled before whispering, "You will always be my dearest, best friend."

He could barely speak, but at last, drawing her

hand to his lips, he whispered, "And I, my dear Charlotte, will be your friend always—beyond the flesh. And you," he said, "remember this."

She seemed to smile, the gesture faint, just as Leopold, her husband rushed into the room.

"Leo," she whispered, "my love."

Her husband hurried toward her, taking her hand and as he did so, the Earl arose, stepping back, off to the side.

She smiled at Leopold then, one last time, and as she sank back into the pillows, the life force, the essence of who and what she was, took wing, departing this, its worldly flesh.

And Leopold, with one final kiss, relinquished his beloved's hand.

"Take it!" Leopold told the physician, who had just touched his shoulder. "Take the dead baby from my sight."

"Yes, Your Highness."

At that moment Leopold, minor Prince of a petty German duchy, looked to his wife. He frowned, then said, "With you, my dear wife, go all my love; with you dies all my ambition. I regret the babe did not live. For through it I would have been reminded always of your stubborn, free spirit. Through it, I would have ruled England. But now, my love, I am a conquered man."

Prince Leopold, who had only recently, and by marriage, become an English subject, didn't look up, didn't notice the doctor's departure, didn't observe the physician's discreet handling of the baby, didn't see him sneak into and out of the Princess's adjoining chamber, and certainly never dreamed that the court's physician had heard his every word.

Chapter 1

England, August, 1836

The faint wind wafted in through the open doors, the young lady, with hair the color of pale, yellow sunlight, leaned against one of those doors, sniffing at the air appreciatively.

She listened to the wind; its only sound the dim rustle of the curtains against the draft.

Below her lay the Colchester townhouse's ponds and gardens, the grounds so richly manicured that not a single branch of any one bush lay out of place. Despite the lateness in the year, flowers still bloomed here, carefully cultivated. There were late-year roses, mums of all different colors, daisies, coreopsis. But it was the scent of the wild rose that drifted up to her now. Closing her eyes, she inhaled slowly, deeply.

Ah, it reminded her of other times, other places, other people . . . She moaned. It brought back to mind images of the American West; the wild, beloved, American West. It caused her to remember *him*.

She pulled up her thoughts quickly, as though she had committed a terrible faux pas. She hadn't allowed herself to think of him in years. *Why now?*

"Excuse me, M'lady—"

"Anna!"

The Lady Estrela turned around quickly, catching the young servant's grin, but as though the maid suddenly remembered herself, she stifled the gesture. "Estrela?" And then the maid stumbled, "I mean Lady—Mistress—Estrela—"

Lady Estrela laughed. "They've told you then," she said.

"Yes, M'lady."

"I tried to send word to you."

"Yes, M'lady."

"I didn't want you to be shocked."

"Yes, M'lady."

"What is this, yes, M'lady? Do you know no other phrases?"

The young servant thought a moment and then, grinning, said, "No, M'lady."

Estrela smiled and shaking her head, said, "Oh, Anna, how I've missed you." Blond ringlets of springy curls fell to her ladyship's shoulders as she spoke. "I've missed your friendship. It's been most . . . overwhelming here."

"Yes, Mistress, I kin imagine."

"In the armoire is the blue gown I've been told would be suitable for the parade today," Estrela said. "If you can get it for me, I'll tell you what happened while you were gone. Would you like to hear it?"

Anna grinned. "Yes, M'lady."

Estrela twisted back around to gaze outside once more. The day was overcast and cloudy, but the sight of the flowers below, the fresh smell of cut bushes and drying grasses, the unmistakable scent of fall in the air, all conspired to enhance and brighten what would have been an otherwise gloomy day. The wind rushed by her. It seemed to moan, as though it tried to speak to her, but—

"You know it happened in the dining hall, don't you?"

"Did it, now?"

Lady Estrela stood up a little straighter as she glanced outside. But in her stockinged feet she had to stand on tiptoe to gaze beyond the balcony railing. She was just too petite, but she wished to show Anna where it had all taken place, so she had to step out onto the balcony. She did so now and at once, the wind whipped around her, blowing her hair back from her face, whispering to her in her ear.

Had it spoken to her? She listened: nothing.

"Is this the one?"

Estrela twirled around to face Anna. Startled, Estrela stared, but the maid merely held up a blue gown for her mistress's inspection and Estrela, after a quick glance, said, "Yes. But, Anna," Estrela motioned to her servant. "Come here, won't you?"

"Yes, M'lady," Anna lay the gown over a chair and, picking up her own skirts paced toward the balcony.

"It was there," Estrela drew her arm through Anna's and pointed to the dining hall, toward the northern wing, which was directly to the left of the balcony. Estrela's light-blue eyes gazed over to it now. "It was over a month ago." As she spoke, she turned and tread back into the room, bringing Anna with her. "The Housekeeper had sent me into the dining hall to attend to the Duchess. You know I had never been there before, being a kitchen maid. It all happened so quickly, I was never sure what . . . She screamed when she saw me."

"She screamed?" Anna asked. "Who? T' Duc'ess of Colchester?"

Estrela nodded. "The same. And I almost fainted. The housekeeper burst back into the dining hall. She grabbed me, was marching me out of the room when the Duchess recovered enough to order her to stop, turn around and bring me back."

Anna gasped. "What 'appened then?"

"*She* fainted."

"Fainted? The housekeeper or t' Duchess?"

"The Duchess."

"If she fainted then 'ow did ye—"

"It was the Duke. He had come around the table to see what all the commotion was, and then he spotted me. And Anna, he went white. The Duke looked as though he had seen a ghost. It was the strangest feeling, standing there, watching him look at me as though I were a phantom."

Anna gazed at her mistress and friend as they tread across the room. "I 'ave seen t' painting of 'is mother. Ye look jest like 'er. I should 'ave seen it meself."

Estrela smiled. "The Duke told me then that it was like looking at his mother as she had been at nineteen. He took me aside, he asked me how I had come to be in his household as a servant and when I told him a friend had sent me, the Earl of Langsford, the Duke had looked distant. He had known the Earl from their youth. And the Duke told me that he could tell, just from my likeness to his mother that I was related to the Colchester family—and that he intended to find out just how I

had been lost from the family. That was the beginning of this whole thing. In truth, he and his wife
have been most kind to me, have lavished me with
all sorts of gowns and pretty things, given me my
own rooms, my own chamber—made me a part of
their home. I only wish . . ."

"What?"

"I only wish other things could turn out so well."

"Other things? There's more?"

"No. Yes, Anna," Estrela glanced away, toward
the doors. "Did I ever tell you of my Indian heritage?"

Anna paused. "No, not really. But I knew it was
t'ere."

Estrela looked back. "You did?"

"Was 'ard t' miss, M'lady. Ye 'ad some strange
ways when ye first came to us."

Estrela smiled. Yes, she supposed she'd had
some "strange ways" when she'd reached England,
almost five years ago.

Anna bent over to pick up the blue gown, holding it out toward her mistress. But Estrela, caught
up in her own thoughts, turned slowly away, striding back toward the windows. She laid a hand on
the door at the same time a breeze blew in, bringing with it something else . . . an effusive fragrance . . . *his* scent.

A memory stirred, a vision; without her willing
it, the sweet image of *him* swept before her. And
as though caught in a dream she could neither
change nor control, she remembered other things.
His touch. The taste of *his* lips. The feel of *his* body
against hers. She inhaled sharply. She swayed. And
all at once the fragrance from the garden was her

undoing. It was the same scent, the same rosy fragrance that had been there that last day. The last day she had seen *him*.

Estrela closed her eyes and for just a moment, one delicate instant in time, she allowed herself to remember.

She moaned. She shouldn't. Estrela tried to pull up her thoughts, but it was useless. She could not keep them at bay.

It was a warm spring day, and the Earl of Langsford waited for her as she and Mato Sapa returned to camp, the two young people's moccasined feet making little sound over the newly washed, green grasses. Estrela sniffed at the air appreciatively, noting the fragrance of the wild rose and of the welcoming campfires that scented the moist air. They strode into camp, the Indian brave in front, Estrela following. Both she and Mato Sapa were trying to restrain their joy. Estrela was looking down so she didn't see the Earl until she was almost upon him.

"Ma!" she exclaimed, the Indian interjection proclaiming her surprise. She hadn't known the Earl had returned and, at first, all she registered was astonishment, though her shock gradually subsided into a shy smile. Still she dared not look up at the Earl, observing a form of Lakota courtesy.

Four years. Four years the Earl had been gone. It was a long time for the man to be away. A long time to wait. And so much had happened during that time. Why, she was thirteen winters now, marriageable age by Indian standards, having passed into womanhood almost one year ago today.

Estrela smiled and darted a glance upward at last. It was perfect. The Earl had returned and would soon learn of her good fortune. Mato Sapa, Black Bear, had at last asked her to become as one with him; to share his sleeping robes, his adventures, his very life. And she had told him she would accept his hand in marriage. It was wonderful. And her old friend, the Earl, would be here to witness her happiness. After all, wasn't Mato Sapa going to offer his two new ponies to her Indian parents today? And wouldn't her parents accept his proposal? Hadn't she already spoken to her father and mother?

Estrela, her blond hair gathered in two neat braids at each side of her head, waited the required time that good manners dictated she wait, until at length, she said in Lakota, almost under her breath, "Ma! Cokanhiyuciya. Welcome home."

"Ah, Estrela," the Earl spoke to her in a foreign language that Estrela had not heard for so long, she at first barely understood.

She gulped. "Es-tre-la?" And though she easily spoke the words, they still sounded strained—and so foreign.

"Do you not remember your own language, my girl? Has it been so long?" the Earl asked.

She understood what he said. Strange. Though his speech was odd, she could comprehend him. She answered, however, in Lakota.

"Wa-ksuya. I remember," she said. "And yes, it has been a long time.

"I've come to bring you home."

"Waglapi?"

"Yes," the Earl said. "I have come to take you home."

She looked up at the Earl then, catching his glance and gazing straight into his eyes.

"I am home," she said.

"No, my girl," the Earl said, still in English, "this is not your home."

Mato Sapa stepped between the two of them. He glanced at Estrela, then at the Earl. His eyes narrowed.

"*You are upsetting her and I do not understand what you have said that would make her nervous. Speak in a language I understand,*" he demanded, "*so that I, too, can know what it is that distresses her.*"

"*You,*" the Earl accused, speaking in Lakota, "*have no right to speak to me like this.*"

Mato Sapa raised his chin. "*I am her husband.*"

"*Her husband?*"

He nodded. "*Soon.*"

The Earl's gaze flicked over the young man, down once, back up, inspecting Mato Sapa as though the old Englishman had never before seen an Indian. At length the Earl asked, "*Soon?*"

Mato Sapa folded his arms over his chest. "*Today, I will give her parents my ponies and all that I own. Today, she will be mine. Tonight we will celebrate. You may join us in celebration.*"

"*Then you are not yet married?*"

"*Whether we are joined now or not is immaterial. We are as good as married. You will have to speak with me.*"

The old Earl raised one eyebrow. He smiled. "*We will see,*" he said in English, making Mato Sapa frown. And before the young Indian could say another word, the Earl spun around, catching one of the Brulé band chiefs by the arm and speaking to him in Lakota. Both men disappeared into the chief's tepee.

Mato Sapa turned to Estrela. "*What did he say to you?*"

Estrela didn't answer at first, instead looking down. At last, though, she spoke, her voice barely over a whisper. "*He said he is taking me home.*"

"*You are home.*"

"*Back over the sea.*"

"*Hiya! No! He cannot do this. I will not allow it.*"

"*Mato Sapa,*" Estrela actually looked up at him, gazing directly into his eyes, unaware that her gaze held a plea. "I sense that you should offer for me now to my parents, before the Earl speaks with all the chiefs. Something is wrong. I fear it."

Mato Sapa set his lips firmly closed. "I do not take orders from a woman," he said and as Estrela sighed, he continued, "but I think I should listen beneath the tepee flap where our chief and your guardian speak. I agree with you. Something is wrong." He smiled at her then. "Do not worry. Am I not already a great warrior? Have I not already taken many coups? Can I not defend your honor? I swear to you, you are mine. Let him try to take you from me. He will not be successful. And if he does succeed in taking you from me, I will follow. This," he raised his chin, "I promise you."

But in the end he could not keep her old guardian from taking her away. Mato Sapa did listen to the conversation between the Earl and the chief, but before the young Indian had the opportunity to gather his horses all together and confront Estrela's parents, a counsel had already been held—the chiefs all in agreement. Estrela was to leave, was to return to her "home" across the great water. And no matter her protest, no matter the anger, the speeches, the demands of Mato Sapa, by evening Estrela was packed and sitting atop one of her Indian father's prized ponies.

Her gaze sought out Mato Sapa, lingered there. She would not lower her eyes as was Indian custom; she would remember him, her love, now, forever; his solemn face, his long, dark hair rushing back against the wind, his chin jutting forward in anger. And using her hands in the age-old language of sign, she promised him, "I will return to you. Wait for me." It was all she could say, all she could permit herself to communicate, for with one more gesture, one more sign, she knew she would break down, embarrassing not only herself, but all her friends and her parents.

And so she looked away, not seeing that Mato Sapa, Black Bear, brave warrior of the Teton Brulé Tribe, signed back, vowing to love her, to protect her, to honor her always; in word, in thought, in deed.

But she didn't see, she didn't hear his shouted words above the noise of the crowd. She turned away instead, just as a storm wind blew up behind her.

As she left, she almost swore that the wind spoke to her and if she listened closely, she could hear it speak as though it were Black Bear, saying, "You are mine. It is so now. It will always be so. Do not forget it."

"M'lady?"

Estrela shook her head, pulling herself back to the present. What had come over her? How could she have let herself reminisce? It was useless now. She had nothing to gain from indulging in memory. Nothing. Not anymore. Once though, she . . .

She drew her hand over her heart, as though this action alone could erase the ache. If only it could be different. What would it have been like if the Earl hadn't found her again, hadn't demanded she return to England? If the Earl hadn't forced her on his deathbed to vow—

She drew a deep breath. It was pointless to remember. Black Bear was not here. And she could not return—ever. Why torture herself?

Glancing around, Estrela saw the soft rays of light filtering into the room, and she looked out to catch a momentary glimpse of sunshine.

"Anna, what is wrong with me?" Her voice was so low it caused Anna to strain forward.

The maid paused. "I . . . er ye . . . per'aps . . ."

"I cannot rid myself of *his* memory. I try. And yet it's always there, and each time I think of *him*, the feelings are a little stronger, not less."

" 'im? I . . . are ye in love?"

"Yes, I . . . no . . . perhaps. I . . . yes." She stopped, and staring down into the fragrant beauty of the stately garden below, she felt again the bitterness of something she could not change.

It had been sudden. The Earl of Langsford hadn't expected to die on the return voyage to England, hadn't expected his heart to fail him. And yet it had.

He'd had to act quickly; there hadn't been time. And he'd had to convince his young charge; persuading her so thoroughly to do as he'd wanted that she'd had no choice but to break a vow; a vow she had made to Black Bear, a man she had loved— loved even still today.

A small sound escaped Estrela's throat.

Why did she torture herself with this?

It had been so long ago. What did it matter now? It was all a part of the past she could not change.

Perhaps if the Earl had taken the time to explain things to her, she wouldn't now feel this ache, wouldn't now yearn for something she could never have.

It was not to be.

The Earl had been desperate. He'd shown her papers—legal papers giving him the right to do what he asked of her. He had reasoned with her, pleading with her. He'd summoned the captain of their ship to his bedside.

But Estrela had remained adamant. She'd made a vow to her love, to Mato Sapa, Black Bear, and she couldn't, she wouldn't break it.

In the end, though, she had realized this was the Earl's last request. He lay dying before her. He lay in pain. He'd pleaded with her. And Estrela, looking at him then, could not continue her argument. The Earl's need had been more than hers.

And so she had done as he'd asked.

She had married.

Married a man by proxy. A man she had never met; a man she knew nothing about; a man she could not find.

She stood at the doors now and sighed.

She shouldn't have thought about *him*. Hadn't she learned, long ago, that thoughts of the American West, *his* memory brought pain? Hadn't she taught herself to keep away from *his* memory? It was the wind that had done it today. It was the wind that had brought *him* back to her after so many years, carrying *his* scent to her. It was the breeze, which even now, seemed to whisper *his* name.

And though the Indians believed one should always listen to the wind, Estrela balked at doing so.

"M'lady? Please forgive me. I shouldna 'ave asked ye if ye still loved the man."

Estrela felt Anna's hand on her shoulder. "I'm sorry. It's not your fault," Estrela said. "I don't know why, but I can't seem to stop thinking of *him*. I can't stop thinking of my home on the plains. And this after all these years of carefully burying those memories." She paused. "Yes, Anna," she said. "I fell in love."

Anna was quiet for several moments. At last, clearing her throat, she ventured, "Ye could return."

Estrela might have cried. How many times had she wished that? But it was not to be. "I can never return," she said. "I can never go back."

"And why could ye not?"

"I broke a promise I'd made to someone there."

" 'Tis not a sin. Ye could still go back."

"Anna," Estrela squeezed the hand that still lay on her shoulder. "I made a vow to a man there to marry him. If I go back, I would have to marry him, and I can't."

"I still dunna understand. Did ye love t'is man?"

"Yes."

"Then—"

"Anna," Estrela cried, turning around. "I am married to another."

Anna said nothing—not even a murmur.

" 'Tis a long story."

"I 'ave time."

Estrela glanced at her friend briefly before setting her gaze onto something else. "You must swear to me," Estrela said, "that you will not repeat what I am to tell you. I was once told by a trusted friend that if anyone else knew of this, my life would be in grave danger."

Anna nodded. "I swear. I am 'onored t'at ye would trust me so."

Estrela, her glance focused elsewhere, hesitated only a moment, before saying, "The Earl of Langsford—have you ever heard of him?"

"No, Mistress."

Estrela sighed. "He was a friend of my grandfather and my mother, though I have no knowledge, or memory, of either. But my grandfather had enemies who forced the Earl to flee the country with me—to save my life. Why, I do not know—nor do I remember. The Earl, a true friend to me, died on the voyage back to England and whatever knowledge he had died with him. He was not ill, you understand. And perhaps he meant to tell me about my early life and my family, about the man he insisted I marry, but he was unable to; his heart failed him, his final appeal to me being that I was to seek out the Duke of Colchester when I arrived in England if I could not find the man he forced me to marry."

"I still dunna understand. Who did ye marry? Why?"

Estrela looked over her shoulder to the garden below. "I married someone named 'Sir Connie' as the Earl called him. I married him because the Earl insisted upon it. Insisted that if I did not do this, I would die when I reached England. I married him by proxy—the Earl having papers giving him this right."

"And ye canna find this man 'ere in England? What is 'is full name?"

"I don't know."

Anna remained silent.

"I should have asked for the papers the Earl carried. I should have paid more attention to the marriage papers I signed. I was distraught at the time. Not only had my friend died, but I was married to a man I did not love, a man I do not know. Plus, I had broken a vow to a man back in the American West to whom I had promised to return, to marry. I should have paid more attention to the names, to the Earl. I didn't. I thought I would have no trouble finding this 'Sir Connie.' The Earl made it appear as though this man would be waiting for me when I arrived in England. But this, too, was not to be. When I arrived here, no one met me at the docks, no one knew me or was there to help me."

Anna gasped. "Why did ye never tell me this?"

"The Earl swore me to silence," Estrela said. "He begged me to trust no one; only Sir Connie and the Duke of Colchester. I could not find Sir Connie and so I came to the Duke of Colchester's home. And you know the rest of the story. No one here knew me and I was pressed into service for these past five years in order to survive. In truth, I didn't mind it. The work kept me from thinking, kept me from the pain of remembering."

"Did ye ever return to t' ship? Would not t' captain there 'ave knowledge of t' man ye married?"

Estrela smiled, though the gesture contained no humor. "A servant has little free time, as you know. As soon as I could, I sought out the ship, the captain of the ship, but I was too late. The ship had sailed and I could find no trace of the captain, the papers, the marriage."

"Per'aps ye are not truly married. T' marriage is not consummated. Ye could still—"

"Perhaps. Yet I am still bound. The Earl made me promise to find Sir Connie. Made me promise to tell him all that had happened; made me vow before God to honor the marriage. No, I am truly bound; bound by my promise to a friend—unable to fulfill a vow made to another."

Anna stood before her friend, her silence encouraging Estrela to continue.

" 'Tis all I know," Estrela said, "except one other thing. I possess dim memories of a childhood where it appears I played amidst great wealth. Only since I have been here in England do these memories haunt me. Before this, they were hidden to me."

Anna gasped. "Estrela, ye 'ave spoken of danger. I fear fer ye. 'Tis odd. From t' first moment I met ye, I 'ave felt there was menace for ye. But until now I 'ave thought it was only my own fears."

Estrela stared at her friend. "I did not tell you this for you to worry. I do know that as long as I remain with the Duke of Colchester, I am safe. But safe from what? If only I could remember. Perhaps the answer lies in Sir Connie. The man I cannot find. The man I married."

Neither Lady nor maid spoke, letting those final words fade into the room as though never voiced.

At length, Anna reached out and squeezed her mistress's hand. " 'Ave ye asked the Duke of Colchester about this Sir Connie?"

"Yes," Estrela said. "But the Duke looked vague, thought it over and said no. He told me the name sounded as though it were a nickname. A nickname! He could be anybody—or he might not even be in England and I . . ." Estrela released her hand from that of her friend's and looked away. "It doesn't matter, anymore. By not returning to the Americas at once, the man I love will probably be married by now. And I must learn to live with nothing but my memories of him. 'Tis not so difficult. Besides, as I have said, through the Duke, I have learned that I may yet have family here. I know that the Duke is determined to discover just how it is that I am related to his family. And this, perhaps only this, gives me reason to live, reason to stay here, reason to keep looking for—Sir Connie."

"I dunna know, m' friend," Anna said. "If ye still carry these feelings fer this man back in t' Colonies, per'aps 'e still cares fer ye, too. Per'aps ye should go back there if that is where yer 'eart is."

"No, Anna. I cannot. I cannot follow my heart. I

cannot return. I cannot face *him*." Estrela hesitated. "I made a vow to one man, Anna. I broke a vow to another. But what was I to do? It was the Earl's dying request. I could not say no. And now, I could no more end my pledge to the Earl than I could . . ."

Estrela didn't finish and Anna didn't speak out at once. At length, Anna said, "Ye will look fer yer family 'ere, then, look for this Sir Connie?"

"Yes," Estrela nodded. "In truth, it may be all that I have or will ever have. For I cannot marry the man of my own choosing, the man I promised to marry, the man who probably hates me now."

Anna remained silent for several moments before she at last said, "Yes, M'lady."

Estrela suddenly looked to her friend. "Why do you call me, M'lady?" she asked. "Anna, you are my best friend. It has been so ever since I arrived in England. You are my lady's maid because I've asked for you. In public, you are my maid, if need be, but in private, you are my friend."

"Yes, M'lady," Anna said, staring away. "It will be 'ard. Ye must realize that ye are a lady of position now. 'Tis not done to 'ave a friend from the lower classes. Please forgive me, M'lady, but 'tis best that ye understand this now. We were," Anna gazed back at her mistress, "best friends. Once we were t' grandest of friends."

"The best," Lady Estrela said. "And friends we are still. Good friends. This will not change. I will not allow it."

Anna paused, then, looking into Estrela's eyes, she said, "I dunna think so. But I appreciate yer loyalty to me. Ye may 'ave a change of 'eart. Ye are still too new to t' ways of t' court."

Estrela kept her gaze steady as she said, "And if these 'ways' insist that I break a friendship, then may I never learn them."

A moment passed, another, as both girls stared at one another until at last Anna grasped her friend's hand firmly in her own.

Estrela drew a deep breath. "Come, Anna. I linger here a little too long, I think. The royal parade will not wait for me and I cannot keep His Grace waiting. He has been too kind to me. Will you help me with the dress? I do not understand these styles."

Anna smiled, saying, "Yes, M'lady." Then she picked up the pale blue gown, but before she explained the latest styles of the English court, she said, "Do not give up 'ope, m'friend. There may yet be a way out. 'Tis always 'ope."

Estrela shrugged and though she couldn't fully share Anna's optimism, she repeated, "Yes, Anna. 'Tis always hope."

And as Estrela dressed, she forced her attention into the present; her movements, her actions intended to sweep all thoughts of *him* from her mind.

But Estrela, completely honest with herself, admitted total and utter defeat.

The tall, dark man with long, black hair and Indian dress stared out into the foreign, English port, while above him gray clouds hung in a dreary sort of welcome. The town that he observed from this, his prime, vantage point, with its bustling occupants and horse-pulled carriages, looked much the same as the town they had departed by ship so many months ago. Looked the same, yes, but this town certainly did not smell the same. The man resisted the urge to hold his nose, instead he sniffed at the air, heavy with moisture. He coughed and made a pledge at that moment to stay away from the water in this place.

Still, he looked out at the town with interest. At last, he had arrived. At last he would be able to lay claim to that which was his.

It had been a long trip across the sea; a trip filled with strange sights, strange sea animals, new ideas from a foreign race, odd languages and different cultures. But the man had learned it all solemnly; practicing, watching, taking careful note of all around him. He would need it all if he were to succeed in this place. And this man had every intention of success. After all, he'd secured one of the best teachers, a German Prince who had been willing to instruct him, a foreigner, in the intricacies of Continental manners during the endless days at sea.

Yes, it had gone well and now he, this tall, dark man, stood prepared to enter the English society, as he must in order to search for that which filled his dreams, his nightmares. He only hoped he would find all that he desired soon, for already his heart longed for the familiarity of home.

The man continued to gaze out at the strange-looking town, smelling the stench of filthy water and rotten fish. Not a pleasant way to start his search. Not a welcome greeting into this society.

But it didn't matter. He would find that which he sought—the one whom he sought. And when he found her . . .

His dark hair shifted in the wind, accentuating his high cheekbones, exposing the bronze color of his face, and all at once the man, an American Indian, knew where he should be, where he would see her, the vision right before him.

He nodded, understanding the insight and turning around, he caught up with the Prince who, along with two other Lakota brothers, were in the process of departing the ship.

But this particular Indian glanced around him once more, feeling the moist freshness of the breeze upon him.

Yes, he knew how to find her, where he would find her.

So be it.

Chapter 2

"Waste Ho Win."

Estrela sat up straight and glanced into the crowd.

What was that? The wind blew by her and seemed to whisper. What? No. It could not be. It couldn't be her name—her Indian name.

She listened; nothing more. She gazed back around and stared at members of the Royal Guard as they lined the streets of Pall Mall. Dressed in red jackets and tall, black hats, the Guard reminded her that she was, indeed, in England. Crowds of the English populous had lined up behind the military for a view of their royalty, the parade being in honor of the adjournment of Parliament. There was nothing here to make her think of the American West. Nothing Indian. Nothing at all.

"Waste Ho Win, where are you?"

Estrela caught her breath. She'd heard Lakota words. There in the wind. It wasn't possible and yet . . .

She stared around her. She sat alone, perched up high in the back of a grand, mahogany coach. The Duke and Duchess of Colchester, along with their two daughters, reclined in the main coach, their seats facing one another. Two drivers, dressed in red jackets and black hats, sat in front, controlling a team of four horses.

A faint breeze of humid air rushed past her and Estrela strained to hear more words the wind might carry to her, for any sort of explanation.

Yet there was nothing more. No scent. No memories.

She brushed a hand over her forehead.

Did the breeze know something?

She thought she'd heard *him*. His whispered words, carried on the wind. She shook her head as though to clear it.

At that same moment the drums began to beat, fifes to play, the Guard, straight ahead of her, began to march. And as her own coach pulled out into the street, behind the Guard, the noise of the horses, the crowd, the military should have blocked out any further sound.

"I look for you."

Estrela gasped. It was *him*. She would recognize his deep, baritone voice even a thousand years into the future; she would recognize him. How was this possible?

Could it be that the wind carried his voice all the way from the Americas?

It is said in Indian culture that wind goes everywhere, sees everything. And spirit wind, she remembered, will speak to you.

"Mato Sapa?" she thought to herself.

"It is I," the voice returned.

"Are you comfortable, Lady Estrela?"

Estrela's eyelids flew open and she gaped at the Duke, who had just spoken to her. She smiled, though surprise kept her silent, until at last she managed to say, "I am fine."

The Duke smiled back at her and she sighed.

The Duke of Colchester had been kind to her, going so far as to present her to King William even though the King, being ill, had barely noticed her, leaving it to Queen Adelaide to smile a welcome to her.

There was something odd there, Estrela thought as she remembered it now. The Queen had stood surrounded by her court, and Estrela remembered feeling as though eyes watched her, followed her, too closely . . .

"Waste Ho."

Why wouldn't the wind leave her alone? Not only did she hear his voice, now an image caught at the corner of her vision—there in the crowd.

It couldn't be.

It was impossible . . . and yet . . .

She shouldn't have thought of him today. She should have left his memory in the past. Wasn't that where it belonged? This was no good. She seemed to hear him, see him everywhere. She must not think of him, she . . .

She strained forward in her seat despite her thoughts, and peered into the crowd, around the people, to the right, to the left. She saw nothing more.

What was that? She shifted in her seat, but whatever had caught her eye was gone as surely as if it had been a phantom.

Was she losing her mind? Or had she really seen a buckskin jacket? A jacket with beaded designs and porcupine quills? A jacket that only an Indian would wear?

She muttered a curse, deciding the winds, the very spirits themselves were conspiring against her.

What good was this doing her?

She brought her head up, refusing to look anywhere but straight ahead, unaware that a man dressed in colorfully designed buckskin shirt and leggings with a buffalo robe thrown over his shoulder followed her, followed her carriage.

A cool, humid breeze brushed at her hair, releasing blond tendrils from her coiffure.

"Look at me."

Estrela bit her lip. Don't listen to it, she told herself. Don't look. Don't . . . She moaned, glancing into the crowd despite herself, catching a glimpse of long, black hair flowing back against the wind.

No! It couldn't be. And yet . . . She saw him there in the crowd.

She gasped.

A shot split the air.

Estrela screamed, instinctively ducking down, realizing with horror that blood streamed down her own arm.

Was someone shooting at her or . . . ?

Another shot exploded, barely missing her. Another.

She fell to her knees then, her head down, her hands sheltering her face. Bells rang outside, women on the street screamed and men yelled. The Duchess of Colchester cried, the Duke shouted orders to the driver, the horses reared. So much noise was there, that she didn't hear the high-pitched whooping of a warrior's voice; she didn't see the flash of bronzed skin as a man ran toward her, didn't even feel the carriage tip as it gave under the weight of a lone, single man who had leaped from the streets, to her side.

She sobbed, she cried, making so much noise herself, that she didn't hear anything, didn't sense anything until strong arms encircled her, lifting her out of the carriage. Only then did she catch a faint scent of familiar masculinity, but with so much motion bursting around her, she only registered confusion.

Another shot fired.

Horses reared, more people screamed and scattered. Soldiers fell out of order and were suddenly everywhere. Another shot exploded and Estrela felt her rescuer dodge the deadly bullet. Estrela opened her eyes and looking up, saw for the first time the man who held her. And had she been at all faint-hearted, she would have swooned.

Had the wind been foreshadowing his presence, or was she delirious? Not only was this man Indian, he was ... Her mind swam and her senses spun.

What was happening?

Another gunshot fired and Estrela abandoned all conscious thought, reacting in league with her rescuer. The Indian, however, remained in control, and dodging between people, he ran, Estrela held in his arms. No one stopped him, she noted, and he paused now and again in the crowd, looking around, as though hunting for sanctuary. Estrela, glancing up at him, understood, despite her confusion, that his only defense lay in taking shelter among the crowd, until he had either outrun his assailant or found safe refuge. Estrela wondered at her own encumbrance to him in his flight, then dismissed the thought, remembering that the American Indian was accustomed to such maneuvers.

The Royal Guard, with their red jackets glaring within the crowd, burst forward, dispersing the people everywhere, and oddly enough pursuing the Indian as though he were the one who had fired the shots. They raced after him through the crowd, shouting at him, ordering him to stop. But the Indian refused to relent and without seeming to exert much effort, he outmaneuvered the guards, changing directions without breaking stride, running between people, animals, buildings; he carried his charge as though she weighed no more than the quiver full of arrows upon his back.

Still, it was only a matter of time before the Royal Guard caught him, greatly outnumbering him and being themselves on their own territory; soon, caught, cornered, nowhere to go, the Indian stopped before a building. Penned in he took up a stance, determined, it would seem, to fight the entire Guard.

The Indian, a knife his only weapon, set Estrela behind him, protecting her with his body, while he faced his opponents, crouched, ready to respond.

And she noted, even though she wasn't fully convinced this was more than a dream, that he stood before the Guard, outmanned, only one against many. Yet he stood, proudly, his prize held behind him, his body her shield.

That's when she heard them, his growls and she wondered: Was this real or was spirit wind playing tricks on her still, bringing visions to her?

As if in answer, she heard his war cry—the sound terrible. And she realized, as she reached a hand out to touch the long mass of his hair that this was real. He was real. He was here. He had saved her life.

She almost collapsed.

Except that he held her with one arm behind him and she had no choice but to watch as Mato Sapa,

Lakota warrior, held off a hundred, red-coated Royal Guard.

Besides his bow and quiver full of arrows, he possessed only his knife, she noted again, realizing at the same time that it would be ineffective against the Guard's long swords. Still she took pride in him, much pride. For he showed nothing but courage, and he would not relinquish his position. Instead, he shrieked, he snarled at the Guard, challenging them to do their worst.

No one moved. And whether it was because no one dared to go up against the Indian, or because all stood shocked that he would not surrender, it mattered little. The effect was the same. A standoff, the Indian crouching low, his demeanor one of pure confidence, a low growl sounding in his throat amid horrible war cries and the Guard wary, uncertain, holding him back, reluctant to advance.

All at once one of the Guard broke away and rushed forward, his sword drawn, held high above his head.

"Halt!"

The well-trained Guard stopped, sword still raised.

"Go no further." The order resounded from within the Guard. "What are you doing here? Are you men mad? Who has ordered this?" The voice came through the crowd of guards who dispersed as one man pushed his way through them. "This man," the voice said, "is the only one who has acted to avert disaster, and you challenge him?" It was then that the Duke of Colchester broke through the men, and advancing forward, waved the Guard away. "Have you no sense at all? Why do you detain this man when you should be seeking the person responsible for all this shooting? Do you see this man armed with a gun? Of course not. Cease detaining him at once. Now! Go!"

Each member of the Guard hurled a look toward their Captain who, giving the order, withdrew the entire command.

Still, even as the soldiers left the scene, the Indian didn't relent. With one arm held behind him, protecting Estrela, he still crouched, poised, ready to fight.

Estrela, peeking around her rescuer, saw the Duke of Colchester approach them.

"Are you harmed, Lady Estrela?" the Duke asked.

Estrela swallowed, unable to make herself speak.

"You do not have to answer him," the Indian pronounced in distinct English, though the accent was purely American—and Indian.

"I . . ." Estrela could say no more. Emotion overcame her. But not the emotion of pain. Nor that of shock. Her arm, its wound, the blood staining her dress, even the Duke himself paled into insignificance beside what she felt at this moment.

He was here—here in England. When she'd needed him most, he was here.

Blood rushed to her head and her knees suddenly buckled.

She felt the Indian's grip on her strengthen as he held her with one arm, and she knew she stood now simply because he clutched her.

His wild scent reached back to her, another reminder that he was real flesh.

"*Mato Sapa*?" she asked. She grabbed a handful of his long hair and held it between her fingers. She twined the dark mass of it around and around her fingers as though only in this way could she believe what she now knew to be true.

"It is I."

"Lady Estrela." The Duke of Colchester was not to be put off. "There is blood on your dress, on your arm. If you are injured, we will need to see to the wound." Then to the Indian. "I am a friend. I will not harm her."

The Indian chanced a glance behind him, and Estrela stared back.

The look he gave her took a mere second, yet in his eyes she noted that his gaze took in everything around him. The people, the buildings, herself, her dress, the blood.

"Is he friend?" the Indian asked Estrela, though she saw that his gaze held onto the Duke. The Indian asked her as though five years had never elapsed, as though she were still his woman, he her man. And Estrela felt quite shaky.

"Yes, he is my friend," she whispered, at last finding her voice.

Only then did Mato Sapa, Black Bear, brave warrior of the Teton Lakota, Brulé Tribe, relax his position, rising to his full height of six feet, a few inches taller than the Duke, himself.

"You may take her to mend her wounds," she heard him say to the Duke. "But she will not leave my sight until I am certain of her safety."

"Yes, my friend," the Duke spoke back, moving forward and extending a hand in welcome to the Indian.

Mato Sapa drew back, she felt it, felt him reach for his knife with his free hand, though she saw that he didn't draw it. Estrela could see the Indian's chin rise and she knew that he was looking down his nose at the Duke at this moment, his glance unwavering. "I only allow this," Mato Sapa said, "because she says you are friend. I will reserve judgment myself until I know you better. She rode in your travoi-on-wheels. You did not protect her well."

The Duke actually smiled, then said, "You are wise for such a young man. So be it."

The Indian nodded before turning to sweep Estrela into his arms, taking her full weight upon himself. His steps followed behind the Duke, and though his glance swept over her briefly, he kept his gaze on the Duke as he said to her, not even a smile on his face, "Was easy to find you."

Chapter 3

~~~ഗ⦿ഗ~~~

E strela sat poised in a grand room, her arm resting on the polished wood table. Carvings of flowers and angels adorned the table's legs and fine trim, each of the ten matching chairs echoing the same ornate designs. Fresh flowers in the center of the table scented the air with delicate fragrance while their beauty brightened the room. Two tall candles stood on each side of the flowers, their silver casings polished until they glowed almost as brightly as the few rays of sunlight sneaking into the room from the five-foot windows.

An intricately woven, multicolored Chinese rug spread over the floor from one end of the room to the other and Estrela watched as Mato Sapa, Black Bear, examined first it, the table, then each painting that nearly covered each wall.

Estrela sighed and tried to take her gaze away from him, but she couldn't. And though she knew it was impolite to stare in both the Indian and the English societies, it mattered little. He looked too handsome, too potent, too . . .

She hadn't seen the wild, Indian garb for years and, as though she were starved, she stared and she stared.

He looked magnificent, dressed in buckskin

shirt, leggings and breechcloth, each one beaded and quilled in designs of blue, red, yellow, and white. He stood erect and tall, his shoulders broad, his head thrown back. His hair was long and unencumbered, falling well below his shoulders. He wore two eagle feathers at the side of his head, tied with buckskin and hanging down, there to flow in with his hair. His eyes were black, his cheekbones high, and his nose bore all the traits of his pure American-Indian heritage. He looked exotic, handsome . . . and dear.

And she could not look away.

She watched him now as he paced back and forth before her. She knew, from being herself with the Indians, that in addition to memorizing every article in the room, Mato Sapa watched the physician who sat next to Estrela. He did not trust the man. It was plain to see.

"What does he do?" the Indian asked in Lakota.

Estrela paused only a moment. "He dresses the wound, though don't tell him," she spoke in Lakota, "but he mutters about this not being a physician's work."

"Then why is he here? I could do a better job of it." The Indian looked annoyed, but only for a moment. Quickly he masked the look before saying, "But we leave the point," again in Lakota. "I know he is 'dressing' the wound, but that is not what I need to know. What I am asking is what sort of poultice he applies, and why does he keep bleeding the wound? He looks to be doing you more harm than good."

"It is their way."

Mato Sapa cast a doubtful glance at the physician, then at his work over Estrela's arm. The Indian tread over to them, centered himself between them and glowered down at the doctor.

"Why do you allow this man to touch you like this?"

Estrela lowered her gaze, deferring at last to proper Indian etiquette. And though she longed to reach out and touch Mato Sapa, Black Bear, as he stood so closely to her, all she said was, "The sick and injured here in England are attended to by the men." She paused, then, "Women have no place in the sickroom."

Though she perceived that he listened to this statement with something akin to shock, his features revealed nothing. Instead he said, "Were I this man, I would have had this done and you wrapped in a buffalo robe, resting. You may yet grow warm with fever. Has he no concern for you?"

"He is doing the best that he can."

"Humph," was the Indian's only response.

"Mato Sapa," Estrela said, not even daring to raise her gaze to his, knowing he would consider this action an insult. She sighed, then said in English, "Black Bear, though I know I should not speak it to you, I hope you will allow me to ask you a few questions. I am glad to see you. I thank you for your assistance to me. Because of you, I still live."

He didn't say a word, emitting only a grunt low in the back of his throat.

"But Black Bear, I am astounded that you are here. And I can't help wondering how you managed to come here. And I wonder, too"—she gulped and closed her eyes—"why have you come?"

"Do you forget your manners so easily?" Black

Bear answered her back in Lakota. "I am barely arrived here and already you ask me my purpose? Besides, I cannot believe that you cannot answer your own question. Or have you forgotten our vows so soon? The years since we have seen one another have not been that great."

"I . . ." she hesitated, then, "I am not ill-mannered," Estrela said, choosing to respond only to his first statement, ignoring the rest. "Customs are different here and—"

"But you know mine. And," he added, taking care to speak his language slowly, "you know my purpose in being here."

Estrela paused. She didn't dare look at him. She didn't dare speak. And Black Bear, realizing her dilemma, nodded, treading away from her to re-study each painting.

Still in Lakota he said, "I have been much disappointed that you have not returned home before now. And," he looked back at her, over his shoulder, "I had at one time considered your absence betrayal to me."

"I know."

"You know this?" He turned around in full, letting any anger he felt settle in upon her. "Then why did you not come back? Why did you not keep your vow to me?"

Estrela died a little inside, though outwardly she managed to look contrite, tilting her chin upward as was her way. Slowly she raised her gaze to look at him. "I had no means of getting there," she said, "until recently and then I worried that . . . Black Bear, I must know." She paused. "Have you . . . married?"

He didn't move. He didn't answer. He didn't even blink. Finally, after several moments, he turned, putting his back toward her, pacing to one of the huge, five-foot windows and Estrela thought she might have seen him shudder before he said, "I realize my coming here has been a shock. I will give you time to accustom yourself to me again. I will give you time to think more wisely. But I do not understand why you would believe I would marry. Did we not, you and I, make a promise? Do you think I would so easily break it? No, *Waste Ho Win*, I have not married. I have waited for you. Waited, perhaps for a phantom, a mere ghost of my imagination."

"I—"

"I am here to take you back. Or so I had thought. Your silence on this subject now makes me wonder if I have made a wasted trip." He turned away from the window, facing back into the room, his glance seeking her out. "Tell me, *Waste Ho Win*, Pretty Voice Woman," he said, his features revealing no emotion, "have you changed so much?"

"I—"

"Do not answer now. You are injured. My presence here is perhaps startling. I will allow you time to heal, time to become accustomed to me again. But know that I cannot stay here long. Even now, my heart longs to hear the voices of the prairie, of my grandfathers."

Estrela shivered, but whether from cold or pure reaction, she couldn't tell. She shut her eyes and inhaled sharply.

Tell him, a part of her demanded. *Tell him you are married to another, even though that marriage be a sham. Tell him and let him return to his people now before you become too attached to him again; and he, perhaps to you.*

"I . . . I . . . you," she started, then stopped. She glanced up at Black Bear to see him watching her intently. "I appreciate your kindness. I am glad you are here. It is only that I . . . thought you might have married."

"I have not, as you can see. I have kept my vow to you. I have even come to you. And what of you? There is a ship sailing within this next moon. We could be on it. We could journey back to our home. You, Waste Ho Win, have a chance to keep your vow to me. You have a chance to become my woman and return to the people, as we planned."

Estrela winced inside. She longed to cry out, to accept his proposal, to tell him that she had never forgotten him, that she never would. She couldn't. She was bound by a promise to another, bound by her own integrity. And so she looked away. It was all she could do.

"What is it?"

"I cannot leave here now." Her words, though soft, held a note of finality, a note she knew would not escape Black Bear's notice.

He didn't say anything in response. He didn't even move. And with his back toward the window, Estrela had a difficult time seeing the effect of her words, for the light encircled him, blocking out his features.

She swallowed hard, and had she been able, she would have gladly died at this instant. Her stomach twisted, her heart quietly cried and every part of who and what she was now demanded she run to him, that she put her arms around him and tell him that she loved him still, would always love him.

She didn't, however. Instead she began to speak,

softly, in Lakota, "Please believe me. My heart is
happy you are here. I have much longed to see you.
But I must tell you that I cannot return to the prairie with you. I . . ." *Tell him. Tell him and let him
leave.* "I . . . I cannot leave because . . . I am . . ." *Tell
him.* She closed her eyes, unable to voice what she
knew she must. "I have discovered that I may yet
have parents living here." She trembled and looked
up to him. "The Duke and Duchess of Colchester,"
she said, all at once in a hurry, "the people I am
staying with, have found I may be related to them
because I so closely resemble the Duke's mother."
She paused, studying him, straining to see the effect her words had on him.

"Humph!" Black Bear stood before her, in front
of the window, hands folded over his chest. "I fail
to understand"—he moved a little, pacing toward
her—"what this has to do with our vows."

"Don't you?"

He shrugged. *"Hiya,"* he said, still treading toward her. "No."

Estrela sighed. *Tell him now. Tell him the truth.* "I
have never known my mother and father," she said
instead. "Not those who gave me birth," Estrela
added. "I have never known who I truly am. I have
that chance now. The Duke of Colchester is tracing
our lineage. Don't you see?" she asked, glancing
up at Black Bear as he had come to stand over her.
"Until I discover who my parents are, I can go nowhere."

He said nothing for a long while, simply looking
down at her. At length, he spoke, saying, still in
Lakota, "You wish to stay here where people shoot
at you? Where there are enemies whom I cannot

follow, whom I cannot see? You already have a father and mother in my country. Why do you need another?"

"I . . ." What could she say? She *did* have parents in the American West, adopted parents she loved. Estrela groaned inwardly at the half-truths she was speaking, though outwardly all she did was sigh. She searched within herself for explanation and at length said, "Be it good or bad, right or wrong, Black Bear, now that I know my natural parents might still live, I cannot turn my back on finding them. How can I explain it to you? I have a need to discover them, if only to talk with them for a moment."

Black Bear stared down at her for a long while, as though debating between his need and his understanding of hers. She knew it would never occur to him that she told him only a partial truth. To him, she was Indian and no Indian ever lied—and certainly never withheld pertinent information.

At last he said, "So be it." Then spinning about, he stepped away from her, across the room, to begin pacing back and forth. "Then I, too, will stay until you meet these people, if they truly exist. For Waste Ho, I will keep my promise to you. I am keeping my promise, even now. And I wonder, will you be true to your own vow?"

Unbecoming warmth flushed her face. And it was several moments before she was able to respond, "I—"

"Do you know," Black Bear asked as though she hadn't been about to speak, "who might want to kill you? Do you know why? If I am to be here, I will protect you, but in order to do that, I must know where the danger lies."

"I . . . I don't. And Black Bear I—"

"Do you know that I have dreamed of you? Of danger? Do you realize that I might be the only one who can avert a disaster to you?"

"Black Bear, I am sorry."

It was odd, she was to think later. For at that very moment Black Bear looked as though he might have smiled at her. But instead, all he said was, "I know."

"Children, children." The Duchess of Colchester burst in upon her guests stepping lively into the room, followed by her two teenage daughters. And if she noticed the tension between Estrela and her Indian friend, she chose to ignore it. "Oh." She stopped, causing both daughters to collide with each other, then with her. "Lady Estrela, I had hoped your wound was dressed by now. I have so much for us to do, so much for us to see. But then, I doubt that you would be able to accompany us, anyway. Oh, you poor, dear girl. What are we to do? Oh, I know. You must rest. That's it, my dear. And don't you worry about your Indian friend." She led the party of three toward Black Bear, and stopping close to him, smiled up at him engagingly. Both daughters peered around her and giggled. "Why we'll take such good care of Black Bear, you'll be astounded. Don't you worry. Now Black Bear, have you met my two daughters?"

Estrela opened her mouth to speak while the introductions were made, but closed it as she watched the Duchess draw Black Bear's arm through her own, her two daughters surrounding him. Both girls were blond, pretty and were now flashing their eyes up at Black Bear.

"Oh, dear," the Duchess said, "you are so dark, not too dark, mind you, just nicely bronzed and so strong. Such a fine-looking fellow. Ha! Won't I be the envy of all my friends? Imagine, first we discover that you, Estrela, are related to our family and now because of you, we have a real Indian staying with us, a real Indian to escort. Bless me, but I am excited. No one will have more attention than I. No one. Come, girls. Come, Black Bear. No, no, dear boy, don't hold back. I will take you everywhere, show you everything. Since my husband has decided that you will stay with us, it is my duty to escort you everywhere. To introduce you to society. Oh, but there is so much to do. Come, girls." The trio of women surrounded the Indian, and without choice, Black Bear, after one last look at Estrela, followed the women out of the room.

Estrela sat still. She looked at the door, at the physician, then straight ahead. She closed her eyes, opened them. Finally, when she regained her ability to speak, she said, "What was that?"

The doctor could have smiled. It was hard for Estrela to tell. A corner of his mouth lifted before he said, "That was Her Grace, Lady Estrela. Have you never witnessed her prattle before now?"

"No, I . . ." Estrela gazed at the older gentleman who sat beside her. It was the first time she had looked at him fully since the Duchess had placed her here under his care. He was bent over her arm now and Estrela swallowed hard. *She knew him.* Shock waves ran through her at the knowledge. She knew him, but from where? How? Her brow furrowed briefly before she spoke, as softly as she could, saying, "It is most strange, sir, but I feel as though I should know you. Do I?"

He stopped and looked up at her. And in his face, which might at one time have been handsome, a muscle twitched. Finally he spoke, though he lowered his gaze again to her arm. "I do not believe, My Lady," he said, "that we have ever met until now."

Estrela sighed, raising her eyes to the ceiling. "Pray, do forgive me, sir. I fear that I am under a great deal of strain. And I am afraid that I have embarrassed you. Please, tell me again. What was it you asked me?"

"It was not important, M'lady."

Estrela sat for a moment in thought before asking, "Is there any reason, sir, why I can't follow the Duchess and her daughters?"

"None, except the limits that you place upon yourself. Your wound was only superficial."

"Will you hurry then, please? I can't allow Black Bear alone with them. He will not know what to do and he would never think to say no to anything they would suggest. It is his way."

The doctor nodded, and as his gaze met hers, Estrela thought he carefully masked something, some thought, though all he said was, "Do not strain yourself overly much. The wound may be minor, but you might still be weak from the excitement. Promise me that you will not exert yourself too much and will rest when you're tired."

"I promise," was all Lady Estrela said before rising. She curtsied to the doctor, and then in a flurry of motion, left the room.

And if she didn't see the physician's eyes narrow at her departure, so much the better.

She found them in the west wing. Black Bear stood, arms over his chest, surrounded by feminine laughter and wiles. The two girls chatted with him, taking turns trying to escort him along the corridor.

They were making little progress, however. Black Bear simply would not move along at the pace they desired, taking his time studying the portraits that lined the walls.

He towered over the women as they relentlessly shot questions up at him, but he paid them little attention. He scrutinized the portraits instead, striding up to them, touching one, then another. He would gaze at a painting, then step back. And all the while the women moved with him, pacing up, then back, constantly talking.

Finally, Black Bear shook his head, opened his mouth to speak, perhaps to ask a question, but he didn't get the chance. The demands for his attention were such that Black Bear, unable to do more than listen to the women, resorted back to his original stance, arms crossed over his chest, posture straight.

And Estrela couldn't take her eyes from him.

He looked magnificent. He had draped his buffalo robe over his shoulders, his hair fanned out behind him in one long mass; his stance with legs apart reminded Estrela of his stubbornness. She was caught up at once by the odd comparison between the Indian and a portrait of an English gentleman that Black Bear was studying. Black Bear was as well and richly dressed in his own culture as this representative was in his. Both the Indian and the Englishman boasted weapons, both mocked the world with an intelligent leer; but the most striking resemblance between the two was that in the portrait, as well as in Black Bear, Estrela noted an air of confidence. The Englishman's claim to it most likely stemmed from his title, the Indian's, more readily from his skill.

Estrela sighed and felt a pain and longing like

she had never known deep inside her.

It didn't matter how much she admired him; she could not have him.

He turned quickly at that moment to catch her study of him and, before she could drop her gaze, he frowned. "Why are you not resting? Surely the white medicine man has insisted upon this."

Perhaps it was because of all the excitement today. Perhaps it was her own shock over seeing Black Bear or maybe the stress was simply physical. Whatever the cause, Estrela suddenly felt quite faint. And she struggled with herself, determined to stay upright. She tried to think of something brilliant to say, but her mind was sluggish, her wit at rest, and all she managed to utter was, "I—"

"Oh, no, my dear, no," the Duchess interrupted. Her Grace broke away from the others, hurrying toward Estrela. "My dear girl, your Indian friend is right. You should not be worrying about us after your terrible ordeal today. I shall take good care of your Indian. You really should rest. It would be a pity if you took ill. Here, I will accompany you to your room while my girls entertain your Indian, won't you girls?"

The two girls didn't even acknowledge their mother, so rapt was their attention on the Indian. Both of them giggled.

"I'll be fine," Estrela said, her gaze flicking to Black Bear as she spoke. "The doctor said the wound is only superficial and that I can carry on as usual. So you see"—she tried to smile brightly— "there is no reason why I can't keep you company. I mean, you aren't going out, are you—at this hour?"

"I, well . . ." The Duchess of Colchester was

stunned speechless, an unusual circumstance. But she recovered quickly, saying, "I had hoped to visit one or two friends, but I believe you are right, my dear. It is too late and ha! I know what I shall do. I shall give a party myself, within the month. A party for you—a party for your Indian. Oh, my goodness, yes, what a simply grand idea. I imagine there won't be a person in the Royal Court who wouldn't come to my party—not with the Indian and all. Why, I daresay, it will be the most talked-about event of the year. Bless me, what an opportunity you and your Indian have given me. Come, my dear, come along with me. And as long as you are sure that you are feeling up to it, you may as well accompany us while we show your Indian the rest of our home."

Estrela nodded and allowed herself to be pulled along behind the party of three women and Black Bear as they set off down the long corridor of the Colchester mansion.

They made a magnificent sight, this foursome plus one, standing on the second floor of the hall with just a brass railing separating them from what could only be called a grand spectacle of a room below them. The entire hall stood bedecked with black and white marble floors, upstairs and down, along with lush, red carpet; spectacular paintings and sculptures hung everywhere; and Black Bear, instead of appearing the backwoods cousin, blended in with the rest, his stately manner as much at home here as the English treasures.

Estrela watched the images they presented with interest but soon she began to feel weaker and weaker, and she sincerely began to doubt her own ability to continue along the tour. Had she a chair, she would have sunk into it without the least excuse.

But there were no chairs, no excuses, and Estrela, somehow had to hold herself upright.

She stood, propped up with a hand on the second-floor railing, as she witnessed the butler approach the Duchess. And it was with tremendously mixed emotions that Estrela overheard their conversation: the Royal Duke of Windwright had arrived and was waiting for them in the drawing room, requesting specifically to meet the new Lady Estrela and Black Bear. Estrela grimaced. She did not feel up to the occasion.

Literally.

Nevertheless, the Duchess of Colchester ushered them all along the hall, hurrying them on toward the drawing room where the Royal Duke of Windwright stood, and as they drew near, it was clear he awaited them none too patiently.

"Oh, dear sir," the Duchess said even before they had come fully into the room. She hurried forward and met the Duke, offering him her hand. "I am delighted, simply delighted, you have come calling on us. And lucky man, we have not yet taken dinner. Won't you please stay?"

"Well," the Royal Duke began, "I thank you for the invitation, but so sorry I must decline. I have come here solely to meet the new lady in the house and her interesting friend. I must say I was quite impressed today by the young lad—what did you say now? Is he Indian? Whole town is talking, you know."

"Oh, my, but they are? How perfectly splendid. But you must stay for supper, Your Grace. At least there you can question our guests to satisfy your curiosity about them, and I'm sure these two lovely people will not mind this in the least. Will you?" She turned an engaging smile upon Black Bear, but the gesture was lost on him. He scowled at her, at the Royal Duke, and in answer to the Duchess's question, placed his arms back over his chest.

"Yes, well," the Duchess put her hand on the Royal Duke's arm. "Come along this way and we will sit down to dinner. Won't you please? I'm sure my husband is there already."

But the Royal Duke was not to be led away so easily. "I say," he said. "how has the Indian come to be here? Has he a sponsor?"

"Why, yes, Your Grace, I suppose we are. After all, he is here because of Lady Estrela, isn't he, my dear?"

All heads turned toward Estrela where she lagged behind the others, and though she would have loved to claim that she hadn't heard the exchange between the Royal Duke and the Duchess of Colchester, she knew it would do no good. All here expected her to answer.

She opened her mouth to speak, too tired and too weary to parry their interest.

"I can understand your language," Black Bear spoke up as Estrela entered the room. He glanced over to her quickly, examining her from top to bottom. "I can even speak English a little. Why do you question a mere girl when I can answer your questions myself?"

Estrela's eyes opened wide. She hadn't expected Black Bear to speak. She hadn't expected him to assert himself. She couldn't help the warm feeling it gave her to experience his care and concern.

Black Bear moved across the room so that he stood in front of her, a bit to the right; his countenance, his stance clearly stating his intention.

"Why, I . . . yes, old chap," the Royal Duke said. "I suppose that you can speak for yourself. No harm meant to the Lady, after all." The Royal Duke's laugh held a particular sort of nervousness. He cleared his throat. "I do believe that I can ask these questions of you personally," the Royal Duke said although he never repeated the inquiry, "but let me introduce myself first."

"Oh, dear me, I have forgotten my manners," the Duchess of Colchester said at last. "Let me introduce you to the Lady first." She led the Royal Duke toward Estrela. "Lady Estrela, the Royal Duke of Windwright. And my dear man, can you believe that she is related to our family? But of course you can see the resemblance yourself. However, we have only recently discovered her, and, bless me, but isn't my husband trying to research through our family tree to find her relation. And he will find it, my dear man. He will find it."

Estrela curtsied, her head low, her body bent.

Oh, dear.

Estrela grimaced, her worst fear realized. Her head reeled. *I'm going to faint.* She tried to straighten up, she tried to rise, but her body simply wouldn't obey her command and the ground suddenly loomed ever closer.

"But come along, my dear man, I know you are anxious to meet the Indian." The Duchess of Colchester, unaware of Estrela's plight turned away and moved the Duke along until they stood directly in front of Black Bear. "And this," she reached out and touched Black Bear's arm, which produced such a scowl from the Indian that she snatched her hand back at once. She cleared her throat. "Yes, as I said, this is the Indian, Black Bear, who so gallantly saved Estrela this afternoon and who is staying with us—"

"Ah, such a daring rescue," the Royal Duke interrupted, "I couldn't keep away. I had to come and meet you myself, old chap." He offered his hand to the Indian, but Black Bear held back, arms still positioned over his chest.

Estrela, with one last concerted effort, tried to straighten up. But blood rushed to her head and with dim awareness, she saw the room spin out of control and . . . she swayed, rocking without intending it. *Oh dear. I can't faint. I can't.*

But it was useless. She couldn't keep consciousness. She attempted to speak, perhaps to convey her predicament, but no words came to her. Without any warning to the others, Lady Estrela fell over, flopping onto the floor.

"What the . . . Oh, dear me," the Duchess looked to Estrela and gasped, clutching her throat. "I . . . ah . . . where are the servants . . . ah . . . I told the girl she shouldn't be up and about after her horrible afternoon . . . I . . . girls . . ."

"I say, are you quite all right?" the Duke asked from a distance, as though Estrela would immediately respond to his royal question.

No one made a move toward her.

The two daughters cried, looking faint themselves, and if it weren't for Black Bear, Estrela might have lain on the floor for a very long time, at least until a servant could be summoned to carry her.

But Black Bear was there. He bent down to her, lifting her into his arms, and had anyone looked closely, they might have seen the fleeting rush of pleasure come onto his face, a look that told of his feelings for this pale-haired beauty. But too soon it was gone, quickly masked.

"Where does she stay?" he asked.

"Oh, but my dear boy, I . . . why, you can't take her there. Wait and I will get a servant."

But Black Bear had already strolled away and was climbing the marble stairway, his gaze silently admiring the girl he held closely in his arms.

"I need no one else," he said. "I will see to her. Just tell me where she stays or take me there."

"I never . . . you can't . . . I wouldn't allow—"

"She needs her rest. Had she been in my home, I would have sent her to sleep long ago. Now if you will not tell me where it is that she stays, I will pick any room of my choosing."

"Third door on the right, up the stairs, dear boy. And do be quick about it. I couldn't allow you to stay there with her for any length of time. Beth, my daughter, will fetch a servant to help. Your Royal Grace, please come this way. I am truly sorry for all of this. I simply can't imagine what could have happened and I cannot believe that . . ."

Her words trailed into the distance as the three women and the Royal Duke left the drawing room, adjourning to the north wing, there to partake of dinner and to relate over the scandalous events of the day; and Beth, the prettier of the Colchester daughters, never thought to summon a servant.

He stared at her on the bed where he had placed her. She lay amid creamy, silken sheets, and he thought her the most beautiful creature he had ever seen.

He had risked much to come after her in this foreign place: his home, his friends, his life itself.

Yes, he had risked much. But as he looked at her now, he knew his decision to come after her had been the right one.

He touched her cheek. So soft—it rivaled the very texture of the wild rose. He bent down to inhale her sweet scent, a fragrance so uniquely her own, he had found himself unable to find its equal in nature. His senses reeled under the onslaught of that which she was.

He tried now to memorize her every feature, for he had discovered today that his recall of her had not been true to her beauty. Her unbound, blond hair flowed about her face and shoulders, the mane's wild profusion fanning out over the silken sheets, and the cast of the wild, red sunset filled her cheeks with color.

His gaze fell to her full breasts, which her gown did everything to emphasize, pushing them up and clinging scandalously to them. He had seen gowns such as this, on the eastern seaboard of the Americas, but none as exciting as this, and certainly none of the women had been as beautifully shaped as his own Waste Ho Win. How he longed to cup her breasts, to feel the creamy mounds in his hands as they rose and fell with her breath. But he dared not do it.

She had changed.

He closed his eyes against the longing to feel her, to claim her, to make her his own. He reminded himself that he could not pursue it. He had discovered in only a matter of moments that their relationship held a difference. Waste Ho kept herself distant from him as though she . . . he was unprepared to acknowledge it, but she held herself aloof as though she no longer desired him as husband.

His insides filled with raw emotion at his

thoughts and for just a short moment, he let his features mirror the inner struggle of his torment.

He had not expected this change in her. He had thought his pursuit of her would end once he had found her, that she would easily leave with him to return to the Western plains. Never had he dreamed that her feelings for him might have dimmed. Never had he thought that she would have found something else—perhaps someone else—more precious than their own love.

So much was different between them now. And though he tried to fault the English culture for the change in her, he could not. There was something else here, something more compelling, more commanding than just the difference in culture; and he did not know what it was.

True, she had found family here, family and a need to stay—something he had not considered and something he could not change.

But there was more to it. He sensed it, trusting his instincts on such things as readily as he did his sense of sight, smell, or taste.

Either she had changed or something was causing her to act in a way he did not understand, in a way that did not fit her character. For of one thing he was certain: she did not intend to keep her vow.

It was there in her demeanor, unspoken within her words.

Why?

Did she no longer desire him? Or was something else distracting her?

He brushed a delicate tendril of hair from her face, groaning at the effect she had on him. Desire leaped to life within him, and as he looked down on her, he could only hope that someone would come soon to help him put her to bed; for she needed her clothes removed and he doubted he would have the willpower to do it without . . . Not now. He wanted her too much.

"*Waste Ho*," he whispered just before he brushed his lips over hers. "*Waste Ho Win*, Pretty Voice Woman, Estrela. I have come for you and what do I find? A beautiful woman who is deeply entrenched in a life without me. And I wonder, when I came to you in thought these past years, did your heart beat faster at my memory? I did not think that I would have to win you again, but I see that I am wrong. You do not intend to keep your vow to me. Why? Has your love faded so much while mine has grown stronger? I am like a man demented. I want you and only you. No one else will do for me. And so I will try to understand. I ask that you do not test my patience for long, though. I am but a man with manly needs." This said, he gave her a lingering kiss, then slipped silently away to summon a servant.

Chapter 4

Strong arms held her, hugging her, endowing her with sweet, precious warmth. It reminded her of . . .

She dosed, she couldn't quite recall it. It reminded her of . . . ?

"We'll marry . . ." he'd said, his voice quiet, yet certain, filled with authority. "You will give me many sons. You will call me husband, and I shall love you, extend to you all my protection and care for you all of my life. I do not believe there is anything you could do that would make me love you less."

A picture flashed in her mind, and her body, already drowsy with exhaustion, let the past remind her, let her recall, if only for a moment in sleep, the sweet passion of first love . . .

The sun was warm upon her skin that day, the prairie alive with the new growth of spring flowers and wild, green grasses. Not one person, not one animal could remain outside and be unaffected by the renewal of spring, by the life all about them. Perhaps it was her imagination but the birds appeared to sing a little sweeter that day, the air seemed a little crisper, the warmth of sunshine felt a little kinder, gentler.

They had spent the day together so far, laughing at the squirrels, the prairie dogs, at that animal's incessant chatter. And now they lay under a tree, a gurgling stream beside them, rushing on its way to carry its waters into some bigger stream or perhaps even a river. But they paid it no mind, their attention only half aware of the budding nature all around them.

He held her in his arms then, closely, as if he never wished to relinquish her, and she smiled at him, barely daring to believe that this handsome warrior stared back at her, his passion, his love for her clear to see.

"Mato Sapa," she said, gathering a handful of his long, black hair in her hand. She lay on her back and he positioned himself on his side so that he lay half over her, staring down into her eyes. "Will your mother welcome me into her family? I am, after all, white and her father was killed by white trappers."

"She will love you as I do. She already does. She will welcome you into our family. It is not as though you are still white. Are you not a part of our tribe? Do you not have parents among our people? Will I not have to honor your father with many horses to make you mine?"

"Yes, but—"

"Shh," he touched a finger to her lips. "You worry over much. I love you. It is enough."

He kissed her then, and Estrela, or Waste Ho Win, Pretty Voice Woman, as she was called by the rest of her tribe, was lost to the consuming power of sweet passion.

She closed her eyes, his lips warm and responsive beneath hers. She let go of his hair to pull him closer to her, running her fingertips over the smooth expanse of his chest, glorying in the sensation that swept through her at his sharp intake of breath.

It was good, their love. It was sweet, wonderful. These were her last thoughts, for he was slipping his tongue into her mouth, letting her taste the heady flavor of his breath.

Rational thought ceased for her, replaced by raw feeling and when he untied the straps of her dress, pulling it down further and further, slipping it off her completely so that she lay naked beneath his touch, she didn't think once of protest. It was all she could do to keep up with the delicious sensation. His hand played over her skin, held her breasts, caressing them, his palm circling her nipples and a response began to build between her legs that demanded all her attention, demanded appeasement.

She gyrated her hips toward him, wanting . . . wanting more—but what?

Mato Sapa seemed to know. Gliding his hand down over her stomach, he reached that place between her legs, letting his fingers explore her most secret, feminine beauty.

"Open your legs, my love."

She did.

Ah, the feeling, the excitement, the sensuality. It was almost more than she could take, until . . .

Shuddering, he drew away, falling upon his back, away from her.

Estrela lay still for a long while, the shock of his withdrawal playing havoc with her own sense of propriety. She didn't bother to dress. She didn't cover herself. Unsure what to think, unsure what to say, she remained silent. And as the heat of passion grew less, she began to think, began to reason, and all at once she realized that by her actions today she brought shame to herself.

How could he possibly respect her now, want her for his wife? Wasn't it true what the grandfathers said? That a woman who let a man lay with her before marriage, was worthless? She berated herself silently before

*venturing to say, "You are ashamed of me. I have let
you go too far. I have lost my dignity. I—"*

*"Hiya! No!" He lay his hand on her then, on her
stomach, still bare. "It is I who have gone too far. It is
I who has lost control. We are not yet married and I
have taken too much liberty with you. But do not fear,
you still have your dignity. You have your virginity. I
would not take that from you until the day we marry. I
will not mar you. I know now why our grandfathers
insist a young man not be alone with his sweetheart
until after marriage. The temptation is too great. Come,"
he sat up then, rising onto his knees. "I will help you
dress and we will return to the village before I lose all
control."*

*She allowed him to help her, to dress her, to fix her
hair again into two neat braids. But she hadn't forgotten
his touch, his power over her, his sexuality. And most
of all she hadn't forgotten her own responses to him.*

*That had been her last day with him, for when they
returned to camp, the Earl was there, back from England
and insisting she leave the Indians, leave the one place
where she had found peace —had found love.*

"No, don't go," she cried aloud, twisting her
head back and forth, still lost to sleep, still held in
firm, strong arms. She felt a gentle touch upon her
cheek, the feel of full lips caressing her own. *Ah,
such a sweet dream.*

She settled down, her breathing returning to normal and content now, she smiled.

Estrela awoke to the fresh smell of dewy, morning air. She opened her eyes, looking around her.

Where was she?

She glanced up but instead of the lodge poles
and hide covering she half expected to see, her eyes
took in the ornate designs set in pink silk with gold

etchings. Her gaze dropping downward, Estrela hoped she might yet see the familiar buckskin articles of the American West, but all she saw were the bedposts from which hung more yards of the pink silk curtains, each lined in gold. The bed curtains were pulled back toward each post so that the bed lay open and exposed to casual view.

Ah, England.

Across the room, she noticed the heavy curtains that hung over the chamber's tall windows were billowing in and out, indicating that the windows must be open. The French doors stood open and Estrela saw that it was still dark outside, too dark to be overcast; she had awakened to the dark just before dawn.

She contemplated going back to sleep, but dismissed the idea. She had spent too much time in the service of others to lay abed when there was so much for her to think about, so much to do.

And so she groaned. She sighed. She stretched her uninjured arm over her head while she wiggled into a sitting position. She had slept well. At least she had done so after her dream. Her dream—she shut her eyes and brought the memories back to mind, marveling at the intensity of sensation that swept over her body. For a short space in time she'd been held in *his* strong arms; for an indefinite moment she'd breathed in the clean scent of masculine beauty—Black Bear.

If only it had been real.

It could be.

Estrela shook her head vigorously. It could not be.

She pushed her hair back from her face and breathed deeply. The movement pulled the soft, white nightgown across her breasts and she glanced down at the gown, trying to remember putting it on.

She had no memory of it.

Odd.

She brushed the covers aside, dropped her feet to the Persian rug that covered the floor, her toes finding and curling around her soft slippers.

That's when she saw him.

He sat on the floor across from her bed, his buffalo robe spread out beneath him. A sliver of light from the pale moon outside fell over his features and Estrela noted that he was wide awake and . . . he stared straight back at her.

He presented quite a picture, camped out as he was beneath an enormous tapestry that hung on the wall.

She didn't gasp at the sight of him; she didn't cry out. Shock, perhaps, kept her silent. She did nothing, as was proper Indian etiquette. Excitement raced through her, however, and her heartbeat pounded as though laced with fear. But Estrela knew the rapid beating of her heart had nothing to do with fear and everything to do with wonder, exhilaration, soul-stirring love and, Lord help her, blatant sexual appeal. Truly, she felt wicked.

She forced her gaze downward. What was she thinking? She was reacting to him as though she had every right to court him.

And she didn't.

"You slept well?" he asked at last.

Her stomach twisted at the rousing baritone of his voice, at the wanderings of her thoughts. But she merely nodded her head.

"How do you feel?"

"Well enough," she answered, her voice soft,

high-pitched, and she hoped, reflecting none of her inner turmoil. She glanced up at him. "Have you been here long?"

He nodded. Or at least she thought he did. Against the backdrop of darkness, it was difficult to tell. Silence fell between them until at last he asked, "Your arm? Is it sore?"

"Yes," she replied, "quite a bit . . . All night?"

Another nod of his head. "You should not be up yet. With an injury such as this, sleep is more beneficial than any medicine cure, white or Indian." He paused. "Will you rest again when I leave?"

"Perhaps," she said. "I should be up and about, seeing to my responsibilities and to you." She hesitated then, before saying, "I . . . I . . . your presence here in my room . . . I . . ."

"I am only here to protect you." He answered her unspoken question, "There is no other reason, except . . ."

Her gaze flew to his through the darkened room.

"Except," he continued, "to speak with you privately."

"Oh." She knew the sound of her voice conveyed a note of disappointment and Estrela gave herself a silent reprimand. What, after all, had she expected?

She glanced down at the thin nightgown she wore, her only covering, and she wondered if he could see beneath the white lace. True, the murky darkness in the room should have hid her from him, but she knew that he could see as well as the owl in the darkness, knew that if he desired, he could inspect her every feature, survey her every feminine attraction.

The thought was wildly exciting and she fought

with herself to keep her feelings, her thoughts to herself; she could not have him, for her sake, for his. And so she simply asked, "Protect me?" as though she weren't aware of the potency of his presence in her room.

"*Ho*, yes," he said, taking his time before he spoke again. "Does Waste Ho wish me to do more than protect her?"

Estrela sputtered. "I . . ." She had become accustomed to the English fondness for subtlety. She had forgotten that the Indian did not avoid confrontation.

"I have come to this land to see you, Waste Ho," Black Bear continued. "I have come in the belief that I would bring you back with me. I am not adverse to showing you how glad I am to see you."

Estrela swooned. More than anything she wished he would. But she couldn't tell him that, she couldn't even let him know how she felt about him. "Black Bear . . ."

"*Ho*? Yes?"

"I couldn't, Black Bear. Things are different between us now. I—"

"Enough!" He sighed. "I understand. You do not need to explain." He grinned. "But I wonder how things are different between us. Would you respond more to my touch now or would you—"

"Black Bear!"

He leered at her. "What?"

Her gaze shot to his, catching the capricious grin on his lips before she looked away.

"Black Bear, you flirt with me when you shouldn't."

He didn't answer right away. And Estrela strained forward to see if she had missed something, pulling back when she heard him ask,

"Are you married that I cannot court you? Do you belong to another that I cannot have you?"

"Me . . . married?"

"No," he carried on as though she hadn't spoken. "You are not. There is no other man here. No one to protect you, to comfort you—to see to your . . . needs . . ." He paused for effect. "So," he continued, "I fail to see why I cannot seek to persuade you into my life, into my sleeping robes."

Black Bear couldn't have had more effect on her had he speared her heart with his lance. And Estrela wondered, as her heartbeat picked up speed, if he knew about her, about her secret.

He couldn't.

And yet . . .

"Black Bear," she could barely whisper. "What makes you think I could be married? Why would you ask . . . ?"

He gave her an odd look she could not interpret. And when he said nothing, her stomach plunged.

"I am in your room to protect you," he changed the subject so quickly, Estrela's mind reeled. "I believe that you need my protection. But for now I want you to rest. You say you have other duties to attend to; they will have to wait. You need your sleep. Among other things, I am here to see that you rest."

She had been looking at the woven, patterned rug beneath her feet as he spoke; she raised her gaze to his now. "I appreciate your consideration, Black Bear, yet I must tell you—" She looked away from him. "Does anyone else know you are here?"

"No one," he said at once, his soft, baritone voice causing spasms of pleasure to run up and down her spine. And unable to help herself, she shivered under the spell of it, glancing back at him.

"Would I leave a trail someone else could follow? Would I have someone else know I have come to you when we are not pledged to one another yet?" A corner of his mouth turned upward. "No, Waste Ho, no one knows I am here. We are quite alone. We could—"

"Black Bear!"

He merely smiled.

And Estrela felt faint.

Was it the dream she'd had earlier? Was it that which was creating such warmth within her, such desire? Or was it simply Black Bear, himself, her love for him?

Whatever it was, Estrela felt suddenly alive with feeling; every nerve, every sense she possessed awakened, cried out to him to touch her, to possess her, to . . . Estrela pulled her thoughts up short.

She could not have him.

"Does Waste Ho wish me to love her despite her protest?"

Her eyes opened wide. Could he read her thoughts?

"No, Black Bear, I—"

"You confuse me, Waste Ho," he said. "Your body, your response to me tells me something that your words contradict. And I wonder why."

Suddenly he rose to his feet with a graceful movement that would have been lost to the staid, English society, he came to her and bending toward her, took her into his arms.

It was a heady sensation—it was naughty, it was sinful, it was—Lord, help her, it was wonderful. And all at once, she was swamped with his overpowering presence, as though the essence of who and what he was merged with and became a part of all that she was.

She shut her eyes, breathing deeply, glorying in the feel of him, in the musky scent of his body, the comfort of his arms and she knew in that moment that she could not let him go.

Yet, she also could not have him.

His fingers grazed her cheek and Estrela was instantly beyond thinking. She let her body melt into his, knowing that her response begged him to do more than simply hold her.

So it was with no surprise that she felt his fingers threading through her hair, his touch trailing further down her cheeks, her neck, the soft rise of her shoulders.

At last he whispered, "Holding you like this is sweet torture, Waste Ho, for I feel you will not let me have you. Not completely. And yet when you are like this in my arms, it is all I can do to keep my hands from you."

He kissed her then, but it was the tender kiss of exploration, not of passion.

And Estrela, unable to draw away, lay pliant in his arms, hoping for more, wishing him to—

He drew back, his gaze touching her everywhere as he said, "What has happened to you in these intervening years? When I hold you like this, I feel the woman I once knew. And I wonder, does Waste Ho wish me to consummate what we now feel for one another? Does she wish to become Black Bear's bride?"

Estrela died a little, right there in his arms. How she longed to say "yes" and forget England, the Earl, her promise . . . Sir Connie. She shut her eyes.

"Does Waste Ho wish to answer?"

"Black Bear," she said, her voice just over a whisper. "I can't. I—"

"Have a family to find," he finished for her. He stared into her eyes. "Has it never occurred to Waste Ho to ask if I might be willing to stay in England?"

"Would you?"

"No," he answered and Estrela breathed a sigh of relief. "But you could have asked."

She smiled.

"So beautiful," he said and Estrela gazed back at him in wonder. "Your smile," he said. "I believe that this is the first time I have seen you smile since I have arrived and I am happy to see it."

She laughed, just a little, and Black Bear sat back, kneeling beside her, gazing back at her.

She instantly missed his warmth and pushing herself up, she sat forward, following him. She regarded him in silence then, her glance surveying him, her look at him as potent as a caress.

"I am happy to see you," she said at last. "I have missed you. I have missed our laughter. I have missed our home."

"Our home?"

"No, I didn't mean . . . home . . . I mean that . . ."

"I dreamed of you, of danger to you," he said. "It is one reason why I am here, why I have taken such trouble to find you. I left our home because I became certain that if I did not come after you, you would die. And Waste Ho," he grinned at her, "I did not wish you to perish. Not perish—*hiya*, no, something else perhaps—not perish—"

"But I thought you came here to take me back with you."

He sighed. "What would you have me do?" He was serious all at once. "What would you have me

say? I have already asked you to become my bride.
You have remained silent. Would you have me
now tell you that I have never forgotten you?
Never forgotten my vow to you? That my life was
a mere shadow of existence without you?"

Estrela melted at his words, but the softness of
the bed hid her weakness.

"Would you have me get down on my knees and
plead with you to return?"

"I—"

"You seek to know about me, about my feelings
for you. I have not kept these from you. Tell me,
Waste Ho," he scrutinized her. "Did you ever think
of me in these intervening years? Did you ever intend to keep your vow to me?"

"I . . ." she hesitated, all her courage deserting
her in an instant. *Tell him*, she demanded of herself.
He deserves to know the truth. He is asking for the truth.
"I . . . you should not have come here."

He didn't say a word. And his gaze turned from
mere survey of her to sulking scowl.

"I . . . I can't," she said. "I . . . the Earl . . . the
ship . . . I . . ." *I am married to another*, she finished
silently, knowing that she would not say it aloud.
She couldn't. If she told him, he would leave. And
more than anything, she wanted him to stay,
needed him to stay. It was wrong, so very wrong
of her to keep him here, but despite her good intentions, she couldn't help it. "I have remembered
our vow, Black Bear. I have thought of you. How
could I ever forget my . . . ?" *love for you*, she admitted to herself. She cleared her throat, saying, "I
remember all that was between us, yet it changes
nothing," she said, gazing downward. "I cannot
leave this place now. I have responsibilities and a

family to find. Black Bear," she glanced up shyly, "how did you ever arrange to arrive here in England?"

He shrugged and she held her breath. Would he allow her to change the subject?

She saw the look in his eyes, saw that he understood what she did, observed his frustration. Still, at length, all he said was, "It was not so difficult as it would appear to come here. If the gold bars and powders of the white man are offered to him, and if an Indian has friends, it is easily accomplished."

She nodded. "I see," she said. "Then someone helped you to come here?"

"Yes." He smiled, then voiced, so very gently, "But we leave the subject. Can you tell me, Waste Ho, do you intend to keep your promise to me?"

"I gave the Earl my word that I . . . Black Bear, did you undress me?"

Anyone else might have snapped at her, at her so obvious evasion of the question. And if Black Bear felt that urge, he certainly suppressed it. For he merely grinned at her. "Yes, I did undress you," he said. "There was no one else to do it last night." Then tenderly, he asked, "Did you ever yearn for me these past years?"

"I . . . yes, maybe, I mean . . . Black Bear! All of my clothes?"

He nodded, sending her a lopsided grin before asking, "What did you promise the Earl?"

She glanced down. " 'Twas between us. The nightgown, too?"

"I had to dress you in something," he responded. He let his gaze settle in upon her before he finished, "Or risk lying with you—and more." Again he treated her to a heart-stopping grin, then said,

"Tell me, Waste Ho Win, did your heart ever beat faster when your memory brought me to you?"

Estrela shut her eyes; she inhaled sharply. "Black Bear, I . . . we should not be speaking this way."

He said nothing in response. Several moments passed before he at last spoke. "This you have said to me many times now. I do not understand it. I have come for you. How else am I to speak to you?" he asked at length, his voice low, revealing none of the tension that she could feel was beginning to enshroud him. "I have come to bring you home. Was I wrong to do this?"

"No. But my life is here now, Black Bear."

He stared at her, the soft silence of morning at odds with the friction between them. And Black Bear, not one to evade an issue said, "Like the clever coyote, Waste Ho Win has learned in the years separating us to elude the question as the coyote eludes the incautious hunter. And were I not skilled in the hunting and catching of something as tricky as the wily coyote, I might have long since lost all sense of what I ask you. But I learned long ago, Waste Ho, that only the patient hunter will at last catch the animal he stalks. He must, however, wait. And I," his gaze peered into hers, "have an abundance of patience."

Estrela watched Black Bear as he spoke, and as his glance pierced into hers, she closed her eyes, her only means of defense. It didn't help. She was more than aware of him; she was reacting to him, to the warm caress of his voice, to the logic of his mind, the aesthetics of his language, even to his choice of words. And though her mind, her innate sense of ethics cried out that she must turn him away, her body, as though in protest, begged for his touch. And Estrela grimaced as she felt her nipples harden, the soft peaks standing erect beneath her gown. There was more, too, more that she hoped he could not sense, for that place between her legs most secret, most feminine, felt moist and—

"Waste Ho . . ."

She gulped. She shouldn't say anything—nothing at all. She knew it; knew she shouldn't, and yet, "When my nightgown was off," she whispered, "and I lay beneath you, did you—"

He stared at her.

"I . . ." She stopped. She had to gain control over herself, over her body. She mustn't do this. She had no right; no right to flirt, no right to— "Touch me again, Black Bear," she pleaded. "Please."

It was all the prompting he needed.

He sat forward on his knees, he enfolded her into his arms and as his head drew closer and closer to her own, Estrela felt the air between them spark as though set with lightning until at last his lips touched hers.

Ah, the sensation, the power of the feeling that ran between them. It was right. It had to be right. Nothing this beautiful could be wrong. And as her pulse raced and her head spun, she knew she would do most anything, anything at all if he would only touch her like this forever.

"Waste Ho, do you feel it, too?"

"I . . . Black Bear, I . . ."

He didn't wait to hear what she said. He didn't wait for anything. He swept his tongue inside her mouth and if Estrela had been awash with feeling before, she was more than swamped with it now. She was alive, alive with the taste of him, the scent of him, the feel of him, and she thought to protest not in the least when he raised her arms one by one, discarding the gown she wore. And as she sat before him, naked, she knew that despite what the world around her might say, what was between them was right—was good. She couldn't have stopped it if she'd tried.

He felt her everywhere. Her breasts, her flat stomach, his fingers trailing over her moist flesh, dipping lower still.

He set his mouth more fully over hers and pushed her backward on the bed.

She parted her legs for him as naturally as if they'd been married for years.

He moaned and Estrela was uncertain that he even knew it.

"Waste Ho, I want you."

"I know," she said. "And I—"

"Shh—" He rose slightly away from her. "Do not say it. For if you do, I will never leave you. And you know that I must. At least, for now."

It took her awhile to realize that he had pulled himself away, that he stood by the bed and that he stared down at her.

She gazed back at him, unaware that passion still lit her eyes and that her lips, swollen, bore the silent testimony of her sweet surrender. He smiled.

She started to cover herself, but he quickly reached down to still her hands. "No," he said. "Do not cover yourself. Let me gaze upon you, upon your beauty. For you have made me very happy. Your actions here speak for you when I do not hear the words from you that I wish to hear. By your actions, my dear one, I know your heart. And I am happy to know it. For I have learned something very precious to me." He reached over to caress the hard nub of one ripened breast. "Your body, Waste Ho, still remembers me, still yearns for me."

Estrela blushed, yet she couldn't help her reactions to him. More than anything she wanted him to do more and she marveled at his control. She arched her back, inviting him with the unspoken lure of her response.

But Black Bear was not to be coerced. He straightened away. She looked up into his gaze, seeing the tight control he exhibited there, as he said to her, "Though I am happy with your response, you distract me from my purpose and I am afraid I must bring to an end the passion that has taken me so long to spark to life. For Waste Ho, I must speak to you."

She didn't know how to respond. Laid out naked before him, with his glance caressing her every curve, Estrela was beyond speech. And so she did the only thing natural to her. She brought her legs together.

"*Hiya*. No. Do not move."

"But I—"

"Do not hide your beauty from me," he said, kneeling at her bedside. "I have dreamed of this moment for so many years, do not take it from me yet."

She shut her eyes, but she allowed him to touch her, to mold her body as he wished.

"So beautiful."

"Black Bear . . ."

"I have decided to stay here."

A simple groan as he touched her was her only response.

"I will stay at least a moon, maybe two," he said. "I have discovered that you need protection." He raised a corner of his mouth, grinning at her. "I have examined what is occurring in this place called England, and I am not pleased with what I find. You are vulnerable and I cannot find the cause. But this I know. I will find the source of danger to you. I can only hope that I can also discover why you do not intend to keep your vow to me." He held her hands back when she would have shielded her body from him. "When you are like this, I know that you want me. What I fail to understand is why you do not become my bride."

She lay absolutely still. What had she done? What was she doing?

Estrela felt truly shamed. She shouldn't have let him touch her, she shouldn't have encouraged him, she shouldn't have . . .

"What is it, Waste Ho?"

"I'm sorry, Black Bear," she said, ignoring his hands and pulling the covers over her. "I have let you touch me when I shouldn't. I have flirted with you when I have no right. I have . . ."

He held up a hand. "Why do you say this?"

She drew away from him. "There is no reason," she said, "except that I cannot return to the Americas with you. I must stay here. I have a family to find. I have no future with you—with our—romance. You must return to your home. I must stay here. We cannot—"

"Enough!" He reached for her, drawing the covers away from her. He smiled. "Waste Ho is as prickly as the wild rose. And I wonder why." And though he smiled at her, his gaze searched over her features.

"Why can't you realize that I need to find my parents? I—"

He laughed. "Ah, Waste Ho has found her spiteful tongue." He shook his head. "I will speak of this no more this morning."

"And if I wish to talk more about it?"

He merely smiled at her before saying, "I am concerned for your safety. I questioned others about you last night. I have spoken to the Duke of Colchester. I am unhappy with what I find. Most here believe you were not shot at yesterday. Most contend that the shots were for someone else." He shook his head. "It would appear that only I was there to dodge their marksmanship. Only I was there to feel their danger. Only I seem to know that those shots were meant for you, Waste Ho Win. And I discovered, even before I came to your room this night, that no matter what is between us, I cannot let you go unprotected. This house should give more protection than a tepee, yet I find it is of easy access to anyone. I arrived here by your balcony. And so could someone else."

She didn't say anything. In truth, his closeness to her kept her silent, making her feel forbidden desires. And so she merely stared up at him.

He smiled. "Perhaps it is because this house is so solidly built that no one feels a sentry must be posted. Or perhaps all others in this household are blind to your danger. I tried to point out that someone tried to kill you. That the same person may seek to do it again. I have tried to communicate this. But no one will listen to my counsel. I am told by your sponsor, the Duke of Colchester, that it was a stray bullet, but he who tells me this forgets there were many bullets fired and that I had to dodge them. I am told that the matter is under investigation by English authorities. I do not know what this investigation is, but I do not like it. It leaves you unprotected when you need it most. And so, Estrela, Waste Ho Win, until I know where the danger lies, until I am assured that you are safe, I cannot stay away. I will have to assure your safety. I will have to sleep here every night—"

"Sleep here?" She sat forward, holding the covers up to her neck. "With me?"

"No, Waste Ho, you misunderstand." He leered at her. "I have made plans to protect you, not to make love to you. Although after this morning, I may revise my decision."

"Oh." It was all she could think to say.

He smiled, a self-conscious gesture that reminded her of the boy she had fallen in love with all those years ago. "Perhaps," he said, "Waste Ho wishes me to do more than guard her?" He flashed her his lopsided grin. "Perhaps Waste Ho is disappointed I plan to do no more than protect her?"

"I—"

"Do not worry," he said as he fingered the silken sheet Estrela held to her chin. "You will be safe with me. I only tease. I am not such a young man anymore, inexperienced in the ways of love that I cannot resist your allure. I will have to exert more control. Do not worry. You will be safe with me . . . until our marriage . . ."

"Until our . . . ?" Estrela closed her mouth.

She should have corrected him. Truly, she should have. But she couldn't, not when other things ran through her mind; like how Black Bear gained the sexual experience that he boasted of . . . and with whom?

She felt his touch upon her through the silken sheet and Estrela thought she had never felt more vulnerable.

"Black Bear." She looked up at him to find him watching her. She swallowed. "Black Bear, I . . . am not sure this is the best thing to do."

"*Ho*. Yes," he said, tugging at the sheet, pulling it away from her as her full breasts spilled out into his hands. It was a sensuous thing to do and Estrela arched her back, allowing him the freedom she knew she should deny him. He held each of her breasts before saying, "You are correct to doubt me. There is danger for you with me. The passion between us has never diminished. And I cannot assure you that I will not try to seduce you." He trailed his fingers over her stomach, lower still. "Ah, so beautiful."

"Black Bear," she said, her voice no more than a whisper. "Please."

He drew a deep breath. "Please, what?"

She didn't answer and Black Bear, watching her, withdrew his hand.

Estrela immediately felt bereft and experienced an odd disappointment, the feeling of something important remaining unfinished.

"I must go," Black Bear was saying. "Already the sun is rising and someone will be here soon to awaken you. I will not damage your reputation by being found here with you."

"No," she said without thinking. "Don't go."

He paused. He smiled down at her. "Come home with me."

"Black Bear, I can't."

"Why?"

"I must find my family."

He frowned. "I would caution you, Waste Ho. Do not forget what the elders have taught us," he said. "I think that you believe finding your family will show you who you are. But you may forget that a man is not his name. He is not even his family. These things are as birds are to a tree. The tree can shelter the bird, protect it, but the bird would never mistake itself for the tree. You are not a family—not even a name. You merely have these things. That is all."

Estrela gazed at Black Bear in the pale glow of dawn, his high cheekbones illuminated in the soft warmth of pinkish light, and she thought she had never seen anyone more handsome, had never known anyone so honest, so understanding or so brave.

And she wished she didn't have to do what she must. She pulled the covers up to her chin.

"Black Bear," she said, unable to look at him directly. "I must tell you something you do not wish to hear. I have tried to make excuses, I have tried to tell you in ways that you will understand, and still I fail. Hear me now." She refused to look at him, didn't see him frown at her. "I can never return to America. I can never return to the Indian camp." She drew a steadying breath before saying simply, "Black Bear . . . I am married."

Chapter 5

It was several moments before Black Bear regained movement again. And even then he merely shifted his weight from one foot to another.

He stared at the woman he loved, the woman for whom he had risked so much.

The woman he'd been so sure loved him.

"I can explain," she was saying, but he didn't even hear, couldn't hear. Shock kept him still but anger made him deaf, even to the turmoil of his own thoughts.

"You let me make love to you when you are married?" he asked at last.

"Yes, but I—"

"Where is your husband that he leaves you here unprotected?"

"Black Bear, it's not what it seems. The Earl on the return voyage—"

"You married the Earl?"

Estrela sighed. "No. I'm trying to tell you that the Earl forced me to—"

"Forced you as I did? Which is not at all? You gave the Earl your favors without marriage? How many others have you treated in such a way?"

She shook her head before replying, "Black Bear, you are making this worse than it is." She pulled the sheet more closely around her and Black Bear saw that she searched under it for more covering.

It shouldn't have created such an effect on him. It shouldn't have. But her movements suddenly infuriated him and Black Bear felt himself shaking under the force of uncontrollable emotion.

He jerked himself away from her and paced to the window, peering outside at the reddish glow of morning, at the sun peaking up through the clouds, at its deceptive beauty. He breathed deeply, cautioning himself to stop and to think.

He felt like thrashing her and he had to hold himself in check long enough to argue the foolishness of such an action if only within his own mind.

She had married.

Married!

How could she? Hadn't she vowed to return to him? To marry him?

She belonged to another. Had lain with another. Had . . .

He pulled this line of thought up short. He spun back into the room.

"I leave now," he said. "I will return to my home. I will leave you here to your . . . husband, who cannot even protect you in your own bedroom. And if anyone asks me about you, I will tell them the truth, especially about how a married woman lured me to her bed."

She gasped, just as he had intended her to do.

"Do not turn away," He stepped toward her. "Is the truth so unbearable? Did you learn nothing from living with the people that you must act the coward and lie? You are married. And I have made a wasted trip. Tell me"—he smirked at her—"why did you not inform me of your marriage when you lay naked beneath me? Does your husband know you give your favors so freely to others? Perhaps I have learned a valuable lesson, for I have discovered I do not wish to have such a wife as you, one that I would have to search through every tepee to find."

She swung her head away as though he had slapped her and Black Bear felt a moment of remorse—a very short moment.

He spun away toward the doors and the balcony. He stepped outside, then stepped back.

"Where is your husband?"

"I don't know." She didn't even look at him and her lack of action perhaps angered him more than anything else she could have done.

"You don't know? Is he hunting? Is he warring?"

"Black Bear," she turned a solemn gaze on him. "You do not understand. I don't even know who—"

"How could he leave you when there is so much danger to you? I would not do this."

She didn't say a thing—just gazed at him.

He tread back into the room, stalking around her as though he were a caged beast—not the least bit human.

"Does he know your life is in danger?"

"No and I'm not sure that—"

"Does he leave you because he is afraid of where that danger may lie? Does he tremble before an enemy?"

Estrela had pulled on her nightgown and Black Bear stared at her as she sat on the bed. The gown did little to hide her beauty from him and his stomach churned at the sight of her. He had been so certain that she loved him—not just loved him—adored him—and that the strength of her love was enough reason for her to return to Lakota land with him.

He had never felt more the fool.

Still, he stood before her, unable to leave. And he cursed himself for his feelings for her.

He could not leave her unprotected. He could not just walk away and leave her to her fate. And it was this knowledge, more than anything, that spurred on his anger.

"When will he return?"

"Who?"

Black Bear grunted. "Your husband. When will he come to this house to get you?"

Estrela paused. "Black Bear. I am trying to tell you something, if you will only listen."

"I do not listen to women. No more. I am here because I listened to you. I let the beauty of your voice, your words sway me. I believed you. I trusted you." He threw his head back and looked down his nose at her. "But no more. When does he return?"

"He doesn't."

Black Bear maintained his poise in front of her, his outward demeanor condescending, no trace to be read there of the trembling he felt within.

"He would leave you to your fate? What sort of man is this?"

"None. He is no man at all. I've been trying to tell you that—"

"You speak of your husband in this manner? It is good that I have learned this now. I would wish no wife of mine to speak of me in such a way."

"Black Bear. Listen to me . . ."

"No," he said, his features set, his jaw thrust forward. "I do not listen to you. You declared you loved me and look at what you have done. You have—"

"I did love you. I love you still. Listen—"

"Halt!" He said it, and with his hands he signed it. Black Bear stepped forward, scowling at her. Her words should have soothed him. Should have. They didn't. No. Rage surged through him at this moment and it was all Black Bear could do to keep his hands off her.

Had he been home, he wouldn't now be standing in front of her. Had he been home, he would not even argue with her. Had he been home, he would long ago have thrown her over his shoulder and stolen her away to his own camp.

Stolen her away . . .

Why not? What did he care for the white man's marriage? What, for that matter, did he care for the white man's civilization?

Any society, any man who could leave his wife so unprotected did not deserve to have her.

He stopped. He stood absolutely still, his demeanor challenging to her, to the whole world. And a look swept over his face that would have frightened even the most stalwart of men.

He raised his chin then, glaring at her. And slowly, so very slowly that the action wreaked of calm menace, he smiled.

Estrela saw the look and cringed. Of what was he thinking?

She drew back, clutching the covers more fully around her.

"Black Bear?" she ventured.

But he only grinned at her, the gesture at odds with any sort of humor.

"Come, *witoka*. We waste time."

Her eyes widened a fraction of an inch as she repeated, "*Witoka*?"

"Did you think I had come here alone, that I have no friends here? Did you think I couldn't return home at any time?"

"*Witoka*? You wouldn't."

Her answer was a mere grin. And with no further warning he swept forward, snatching her around the waist and throwing her over his shoulder.

She beat at him, she kicked, she struggled. She even screamed.

He remained, however, impervious to it all. He grabbed the sheet she had used as covering and throwing it over her, shot toward the balcony.

"You can't do this," she screamed at him in Lakota. "I am not *witoka*. I am one of the people."

He didn't say a thing, not even the obvious response that she was no longer one of the "people." Not when she had so obviously betrayed him.

She kicked him in the ribs and Black Bear stalled long enough to wrap her in the sheet, her efforts against him ineffective, her feet, hands and arms bound to her in the silken knots of the cloth.

"I am not *witoka*," she screamed again, her voice her only weapon. "I am not your 'captive.'"

"*Ho*! Yes! You are right," he said, leaping toward the edge of the balcony. "You are *wa-wici-mama*."

She screamed.

"Does the truth hurt?" he asked, no sympathy to be read in his tone. "Be glad I do not cut off the end of your nose. It is the least I should do for the offending adulteress you are. *Wa-wici-mama*. Adulteress. Now, quiet, before I throw you to the ground and, Waste Ho, we are as high as the bird soars. I do not think you would like the landing."

And with this said, he sprang over the balcony ledge to the stone walls of the house, using a figure head there to catch himself. With a plop they fell against the side of the building. Estrela knew the stone wall provided plenty of footholds for his moccasined feet as well as handholds, and she could feel Black Bear scaling down the vine-covered surface one story, two, as easily as he would climb down a cliff ledge.

It was probably not the wisest thing she did, yet Estrela struggled against him as he tore down the wall, her efforts completely ineffective against his expertise.

Slung over his back, she watched the ground come closer and closer until she felt his pattern of climbing change and she glanced over to the wall to see a section of the structure change from jutting stone to smooth brick. But even that didn't stop Black Bear. He scooted over to a nearby trellis, grabbing a hold of the oak handhold it provided.

He hadn't counted on its flimsiness, and Estrela almost laughed at the expression she glimpsed on his face when a section of the trellis came off in his hand.

He grabbed at another handhold, but it was too late. They fell backward through the air, Estrela face first. She screamed as she watched the ground come ever closer.

An awning caught their fall, yet still it didn't break the speed of their descent. With a bounce, they flew through the air, up, up and over the awning; down, down, closer and closer to the ground. Estrela screamed and tightly closed her eyes.

Thud! Splash! They crashed down into cold, cold

water over their heads, and unprepared for it, Estrela gulped water into her lungs.

But with a powerful kick, Black Bear swum up to the surface, still clutching his prize.

Only then did Estrela dare to peep her eyes open.

They were surrounded by water; dizzying, cold water. *The fish pond*, she thought, grimacing.

Still Black Bear didn't relinquish her. He tread water a moment before lashing out in a strong stroke toward the side of the pond, the ducks, the geese and swans quacking at his interference.

He pulled himself and her up onto the shore. And getting to his feet, he stood, the both of them sopping wet. He gave her an odd, amused glance before commenting, "Was easy to steal you."

And throwing her over his shoulder once again, he fled through the bushes and flowers, around another pond and straight into the manicured garden of tall bushes.

And so intent were they upon their own getaway that neither one heard the gardener's quiet applause as the Indian fled with his captive through the maze of the hedged labyrinth . . .

Chapter 6

"Ah! Children, children, there you are."
The Duchess of Colchester met the
Indian and his captive as they emerged from the
gardened labyrinth. Both were wet, haggard, and
Estrela's silken sheet lay in shreds around her as
she remained thrown over the Indian's scratched
body. Snatches of branches clung to Black Bear's
hair and to his clothing, and the Duchess frowned
at them.

"Old Indian game," Black Bear said by way of
explanation.

The Duchess looked skeptical. All she said, however, was, "What unusual games you play." Ignoring their appearance, the Duchess placed her hand
through the Indian's free arm. "And I daresay the
exercise must be good for you. What? Do you
agree?"

Black Bear would have cursed at this moment, if
there had been words for such a thing in his language. However, the Indian language allowed for
no such words and so all Black Bear said was,
"*Hau*, good morning."

"Why, bless me, yes, but it is a good morning."
The Duchess of Colchester chanced a glance at Estrela as she lay over Black Bear's shoulder, then

94

looking quickly away, said, "Why, my dear, I must
see to your maid at once. She must dress you more
properly in the morning or is this part of your
game? Well, no matter, I will see that she is sent to
your room at once. Oh, my, but what fun it is to
have you here. But come now, we've all been waiting for you in the breakfast parlor. Come along,
you must hurry and dress."

Estrela made a face of pure perplexity before saying, "Thank you, Your Grace."

And the Duchess, apparently unwilling to glance
in Estrela's direction again, said, "Yes, of course,
my dear." She pulled Black Bear along with her as
they strode toward the house. "Come now. I will
send servants to your room at once. You needn't
think I will give you no help. After all, we are your
sponsors now. We are responsible for you. Dear
me, but it is so delightful. Come now. Don't hold
back. I will walk you both to your rooms. Oh, we
will have such fun today. My, but I grow more and
more excited."

Estrela, her bottom swaying in the air, contemplated her lack of choice: Black Bear would carry
her into the house, accompanied all the while by
the Duchess of Colchester, who insisted on chatter-
ing the entire way.

And to her credit, though the Duchess might
have thought it unusual to see the Indian wet,
dirty, scratched, with various branches of several
different bushes and trees caught in his hair and
his clothing, and carrying Estrela over his shoulder
as though she were a deer he had shot for supper,
her Grace never said a word.

"Surely there must be a way to stay here. I am,
after all, injured."

"I'm afraid t' Duchess was specific," Anna said. "I am to get ye dressed and escort ye to t' breakfast parlor. 'Ave ye a dress that ye favor wearin' today?"

Estrela glowered at her reflection in the mirror and Anna almost laughed at the expression.

"Ye could wear that pale pink creation t' Duke and Duchess of Colchester gave ye. W' yer blond 'air and fair coloring, would go well w' it."

Estrela sighed. " 'Tis almost see-through."

Anna laughed. " 'Tis t' style."

"Just the same, I'll wear something else. He'll think me wanton if I come to breakfast in a transparent gown."

Anna paused while she studied her friend. At length, she said, "Is 'e t' one, then?"

Estrela lifted her gaze only briefly to her friend, then just as quickly looked away, saying simply, "Yes."

" 'E came after ye all t' way from t' Americas?"

"Yes."

"And 'e came to yer room last night?"

Estrela nodded her head.

"And . . . ?"

"I told him I was married."

"Ye told 'im ye were . . ." Anna paused a moment. "Do ye think that wise? Ye could 'ave waited a bit couldn't ye? Waited at least until t' man settled into 'is new 'ome?"

Estrela winced and lifted her blue-eyed gaze toward Anna. And in that glance blazed a wealth of emotion, raw with feeling.

Anna held her breath.

"He is leaving."

"I see." Anna said, studying her friend through

the looking glass, seeing things about Estrela that others might miss: from the stubborn set of her ladyship's chin to the perfection of her creamy complexion.

The maid shook her head. Some might mistake Estrela's soft-spoken manner for weakness or lack of strength, not realizing that only a strong person can afford to be kind. Some might see only her flawless beauty without looking beneath the surface to notice the loyalty, the truthfulness, the innocence of a true friend. And it was with no surprise that Anna realized that Estrela's allure had little to do with the physical, her outward beauty being a mere complement to all that she was.

"Did ye 'ave to tell 'im?"

"How could I not? To keep it to myself would not have been fair—to him. I have no right to keep him here. I have no right to . . ."

" 'E will be snatched up if 'e stays here."

Estrela gasped. "What do you mean?"

Anna sighed, wishing she were not the one to have to educate Estrela about the more unscrupulous aspects of the society in which she now found herself. "W' t' Duke and Duchess be'ind 'im now," Anna began, " 'e will become a sought-after 'catch.' 'Tis not one lady who will not want 'im for 'er own daughter . . . as a son-in-law. 'E is, after all, under the guardianship of t' Duke. 'E 'as become a valuable, matrimonial 'catch.' "

Estrela opened her eyes a tiny bit wider.

" 'Tis a shame ye 'ave told 'im of yer marriage. If ye 'adn't, 'e would not even look at another— now . . ."

Estrela shrugged. " 'Tis done. And I would do it again. I did not tell him for my sake, but for his."

"Still," Anna persisted, " 'e is a bachelor and 'andsome and I'm afraid many of t' young ladies will seek 'is favor. Besides, there is somethin' about 'im: a backwoods charm or some sort of wildness that t' ladies will find irresistible."

"But he is leaving. He told me so himself."

Anna shrugged. " 'E may change 'is mind, especially after 'e finds 'imself so popular. Ye did tell 'im t' truth of yer marriage, did ye not? That ye are not truly married in deed?"

"No. I wasn't somehow able to and then I thought maybe it was better this way. This way, he will leave. And Anna, I'm afraid that if he were to stay, I would somehow try to keep him with me."

"And why should ye not?"

"Anna, I am married."

"Forget it, I say. Ye kinnot even find t' man ye supposedly married."

Estrela sighed and Anna, looking at her, shook her head.

"T' staff will be talking about yer Indian for years to come. 'Twas quite an escape from yer balcony."

"They know? But that only happened a few moments ago."

Anna smiled. "Somethin' like this does not 'appen often, M'lady. Before t' morning is gone, t' whole of Mayfair will know of it. Yer Indian will be quite well known, M'lady. 'E will be well sought after. Be ye careful."

"I'm sorry, Anna. I know what you think I should do, but I can't. I gave my word to the Earl of Langsford."

"Why does t'at make so much difference?"

Estrela sighed. "Anna, until I met the Indians, the Earl was like a father to me, the only one I'd known. He raised me and he cared for me as though I were his own daughter. And this pledge I gave him, the commitment, was made on his deathbed. 'Tis not something I can ignore."

"But did ye not give yer vow to yer Indian, too?" Anna hesitated, and then continuing in a whisper, she added, "As I see it, ye must break one of yer vows. Why make it the one ye gave to yer Indian?"

"Because I owed the Earl, Anna. I owe him even still. And these debts include my life and my loyalty. When I made my pledge to Black Bear, I didn't know the Earl was coming back to take me away from the Indians. I was too young. I didn't know anything of life outside the Indian camp. And I never dreamed at the time that my marrying Black Bear would cause the Earl pain. When I did learn of it, when I came to understand that my pledge to Black Bear would hurt the Earl, what could I do? No, Anna, perhaps you do not understand my commitment to the Earl, to the man who cared for me, and to his dying wish. No matter my own feelings in the matter, I cannot break that pledge."

"I see," Anna said, breathing deeply. "I did not realize t' extent of yer devotion and I kin only admire yer courage in remaining true to yer own 'onor. I kin see t'at 'tis this which makes ye what ye are. Still for yer own 'appiness, I wish ye could . . ."

Anna let her words trail off, and as she stared at Estrela, she became cognizant of just what the indulged aristocracy would expect from Estrela, her budding innocence looked upon as a challenge to fight over and to take, rather than to nurture.

And with a shudder, Anna helped Estrela prepare for breakfast. And if Anna, herself, were devising a plan to help her friend keep the Indian . . . well, who would know? It wasn't as though any of Anna's peers had ever sought counsel with her.

Feeling a bit better, Anna slowly smiled.

She wore the pink, transparent creation into the breakfast parlor after all, and was rewarded for her efforts by a frown from Black Bear. The gown's lines trailed downward from an empire waist and Estrela smoothed the outer filmy material down with a self-conscious gesture of her hand. She hadn't wetted down the undergarments as was the current custom, it being thought by those who ruled fashion that if the material beneath looked wet, it would allude more to the feminine form; something which, it would appear, was most desirable.

Her shoes of soft, pink satin peeked out beneath the hemline of the dress as Estrela paced forward and all at once, she felt the heat of Black Bear's piercing scowl.

She peered down at herself. It didn't matter if she hadn't wetted down the undergarments; the dress still made her look practically nude. She looked up then, and away, her cheeks awash with unbecoming warmth; she felt suddenly inadequate.

It also didn't help, she realized, when she looked at the other women seated around the breakfast table and found them to be dressed in a much more risqué fashion than she. *They* didn't appear to bother Black Bear.

He scowled at her alone.

She advanced into the room.

"Ah, Lady Estrela." The Duke of Colchester arose from his seat and smiled at her. "So good to see you this morning. Did you enjoy your morning of exercise?"

"Yes, Sir, I did," she replied, sweeping her lashes down over her eyes to study the Duke without his knowledge. The man had been most kind to her. Did he mean more by his question? She couldn't tell.

"Ah," the Duke continued. "I must admit that I was concerned after that dreadful event yesterday. But I see that you have recovered most splendidly. Jolly good of you to join us, I say."

Estrela smiled. "Thank you, Sir," she said, and treading down the long length of the breakfast table, took the seat that a servant held out for her.

She smiled at the servant, then at the Duke as he, too, sat down.

She glanced around the table noting that the Duchess of Colchester chatted gaily with her daughters and with Black Bear, who after his initial glare at Estrela, hadn't looked again in her direction.

There were other people here, too, women she did not recognize and a few other men. The Royal Duke of Windwright must have spent the night, for he sat just opposite her at the table.

He glanced at her now, and clearing his throat, said, "So good of you to join us, Lady Estrela. I say, did you sleep well?"

Estrela smiled at him. "Yes," she said, "quite well, thank you."

Black Bear glowered at her down the length of

the table, but he said nothing and Estrela wondered if Black Bear intended to discipline her—and if he did, what form would it take?

Well, she wouldn't think of it now. She *had* done the right thing for him. In time, he would see this. She only wished that time would elapse quickly.

"I daresay, old man," the Duke of Windwright addressed the Duke of Colchester. "Must retire to the country soon, now that Parliament is out of session. Can't afford to miss the fox hunt, you know."

The Duke of Colchester chewed upon a long cigar, not daring to smoke it in the presence of ladies. As it was he bordered on commiting a social faux pas just by bringing a cigar into the same room as a lady.

He leaned forward across the table and leered at the other Duke. "I say," the Duke of Colchester said, "geese are in season now. Do you fancy hunting geese? Could make a trip to the country, we could. I say, there, Black Bear." He turned his attention to the Indian. "Have you ever hunted geese?"

Black Bear glanced down the table, glaring first at Estrela, then turning his solemn gaze upon the Duke. He didn't smile and his features revealed nothing at all. At length, he said, "Geese are many in my country. I have hunted them, yes."

"Well, I say, old chap," the Duke of Colchester said, "would you quite fancy taking to the country with us to hunt geese?"

Black Bear didn't scowl, but he didn't smile either. He stared at the Duke of Colchester, then at the Duke of Windwright. And as he studied the two men, his brows narrowed. At length he spoke, saying, "I would greatly honor the chance to hunt with you. But it is autumn, the season to make meat, and I think we would do better to hunt deer or elk so that the women can fill the food stores for the season when the babies cry for food. Does your country have—*tatanka*—buffalo?"

"Make meat?" It was the Duke of Windwright who spoke, "I daresay we have no buffalo, my fine fellow, but the deer are aplenty and we could hunt them, too; however, shooting geese or any fowl is more the sport this time of year."

The Indian nodded. "Then we will hunt geese," he said, returning his grimace once more to Estrela.

Estrela glanced away.

And Black Bear, after a quick survey of the people sitting around the table said into the quietness of the room, "There is old Indian legend told in my country about geese."

"Is there?" It was the Duchess of Colchester who spoke. "Oh, how exciting. Won't you tell it to us, please?"

"Yes, please."

"Oh, do tell us."

Black Bear smiled and, shooting Estrela one last glare, began, "It is said that—"

"I say, young fellow," the Duke of Windwright interrupted, "what is 'making meat'?"

Black Bear's gaze leaped to the Duke.

"Oh, do be quiet." the Duchess of Colchester said, perhaps without thinking first. "Can't you tell that . . ." She stopped, and glancing quickly at the Royal Duke, carried on, "Oh, so sorry, Your Grace. It's only that the Indian is telling us a story and I thought that you were my husband or that—I mean—perhaps I—"

"Making meat," Estrela spoke up, thereby "saving" the Duchess, "refers to the necessity in an Indian camp to ensure there is enough food in store to get the people through even the harshest of winters. Usually in the fall, there is one last buffalo hunt during which the women will take what meat they get and dry it and pound it into *wasna*, which is a mixture of pounded meat, fat, and chokecherries. It is an important venture since, if there is not enough food to get through the winter, the people will starve."

Estrela glanced at Black Bear and nodding, returned her attention to her breakfast.

The Duke of Windwright snorted.

The Duchess of Colchester fluttered her eyelashes and her husband, the Duke of Colchester, brought his attention onto the Indian.

"I say," the Duke of Colchester started, "I believe I would like you to tell that story you were about to begin—the one about the geese."

"Oh, by all means."

"Please do continue."

"We want to hear it."

Black Bear smiled. "There is a legend," he said, relaxing back into his chair, "about the geese in my camp. For you see, the geese tell us much." He gazed at the Duchess a moment before sweeping his attention around the table. And seemingly satisfied, he fixed his glance once more upon Estrela, his stare a sulky glower. "Those birds' habits announce the season change," he continued, "and we look upon the geese as good food when there is no buffalo to feed our women and children. But their meat has too much fat, though the taste—good." He paused, and with his glance clearly on Estrela, said, "It is well known that geese mate for life, something a wise person will study."

Estrela choked on the bit of sausage she had just

swallowed while the Duchess of Colchester exclaimed, "Oh, how endearing. Tell us more!"

"Yes, please, tell us," the women's enthusiastic voices re-echoed the plea around the table.

And Black Bear, ever ready to continue, said, "This story is about the female goose who could not select just one mate." He stared directly at Estrela, who, in turn, moaned, closing her eyes.

Obviously enjoying her reaction, he continued, "Once there was a family of geese."

"I say, young man," it was the Duke of Windwright speaking again. "Do you force your women to work, then? You have no servants, no slaves? You make your women—"

"Your Grace," the Duke of Colchester interjected. "This young man is trying to tell us a story. Perhaps you could ask your questions later."

"So sorry, I didn't mean to—it's only that—well, who would hear of it, after all? Forcing women into physical labor? I mean, after all, are all their women merely servants?"

"The women," Estrela spoke up, if for no other reason than to stall for time, "work, but the work is not great and there is much time to talk and to tease. Mayhap one could compare it to the fine ladies at work over needlepoint."

And although the Duke of Windwright merely "humphed," and scoffed, he said no more.

"Black Bear—please."

"Yes, do continue."

He smiled. "Most geese have many children," he said, satisfied, "all of them dedicated to the continuation of their race, and . . ."

Estrela glanced away, trying, in vain, to concentrate on something else besides Black Bear. The story was told for her benefit, she knew. He believed he spoke about her; this form of storytelling was probably one of the more severe forms of discipline he would administer. The Indian, regardless of Western belief, rarely punished his children. Estrela realized that most people who did not know the Indian in his own territory, did not understand Indian logic: that he did not scold his children, did not physically punish them in any way, and did not even raise his voice to a child, a mild look of disapproval sufficing to correct any bad behavior.

". . . but this female bird was beautiful, her feathers most fine, more colorful than any other, her squawk more pleasing to the ear," Black Bear was saying. "She did not want just one mate, it is said, and she did not feel she should be confined to just one husband. Nor did she have to. There were several young ganders who sought to have her under any condition."

Estrela moaned.

And Black Bear did not take his gaze from her.

"There was one gander, one male who loved her more than any other . . ."

"Why don't you," the Duke of Windwright cut in, "hunt for two or three years at a time, or raise the animals for slaughter, or . . ."

All the rest of the table groaned except for Estrela, who was only too glad for the interruption.

"The Indian does not wish to disturb the balance of nature," Estrela said. "And so he takes only what he needs and leaves the rest."

"Bad show, I say. Jolly bad show."

"Yes," she said, "we could discuss the economics of the Indians and—"

"Waste Ho," Black Bear snapped at her. "I am telling a story."

"Yes, well, I—"

"Please continue."

"I want to hear more."

"Yes, pray, finish your story."

Black Bear grinned, the gesture not sitting well with Estrela. "The goose," he carried on, "the beautiful goose could not decide on just one gander. And the one who loved her most of all was but one among the many and she wanted many. And so she took many to her, not realizing that the gander seeks only one mate."

He paused, and his focus on Estrela was such that he didn't even notice the gasps from around the table at so delicate a subject.

But no one stopped him. All, except the Duke of Windwright, seemed entranced with him. And whether it was his deep baritone or the unusual content of the story that mesmerized them, Estrela could not tell. She only knew that he held the attention of most all seated around the table.

"Yes, she had many," he continued.

"Bad show, I say," the Duke of Windwright spoke. "Jolly bad show, making your women work—actually work—why I've never heard of such a thing—except servants, of course, but then—"

"The gander," Black Bear continued as though the Duke weren't at that moment speaking, "will allow no competition with the mate that he seeks and so one by one the males vying for this beautiful goose's favor fought among themselves until not one male bird lived. And she looked in vain for the one gander who had loved her more than any other. But he had gone to seek his mate elsewhere believing that she, like the sparrow, could not be satisfied with only one mate. And so died out her race, not because of man hunting her, not because of the wolf or bear who would seek her meat, but only because the female goose sought to have more than one mate."

He paused and glanced around the table. "And so it is," he said to his entranced audience, "that we learn from the geese that a woman must seek only one mate. And the more beautiful the bird, the more careful she must be to ensure she chooses only one."

"Dare I ask, young man," the Duke of Windwright plowed right in, "are all your women servants?"

Black Bear ignored the Duke as did the others.

"Oh, that was lovely."

"Tell us more!"

"Yes, please, more!"

Black Bear held up a hand. "I will tell another tale tomorrow at the morning meal, if you are all here again."

And while exclamations of joy and wonder resounded around the table, Estrela groaned.

It would be the same story, told again, a bit differently, said over and over until Black Bear determined that she'd been suitably chastised.

And Estrela made a mental note to ensure she missed each breakfast meal in the future.

"Well, it is my belief," the Duke of Windwright carried on, "that the Indians must be saved from themselves. Yes, I believe that—"

"I think the gander acted most irrationally." Estrela's quiet statement, said amid the Duke's meanderings, had the effect of silencing all other chatter at the table, including the Duke's and as Estrela glanced down the table's length to peer at Black

Bear, she noted that every single pair of eyes were turned on her.

"And what would you have him do?" Black Bear asked, each person at the table looking to him. "Wait until the silly goose decided she wanted him more than any other?"

"He could have waited," Estrela countered, recapturing the attention of everyone present. "Had he truly loved her, he would have waited."

"Waited for what? She was taken. Before he even had a chance to take her, she was taken."

"Who was taken?" the Duchess of Colchester intervened. "Did I miss something in the story?"

"He could have understood," Estrela replied.

"Understood what?" The Duchess interrupted.

Black Bear nodded his head in agreement, repeating, "Understood what?"

Estrela snorted. "If he believed in her, he would have known—he just would have known."

"He's a bird," Black Bear said. "He's incapable of thinking."

"Known what?" It was the Duchess who spoke.

"Then why tell the story if the gander is such a fool?" Estrela asked.

All heads turned back toward Black Bear.

"Because the story has a moral," Black Bear said, each word clipped. "We are supposed to *learn* from such a story. Most people do unless they have the morals of a sparrow."

Estrela flushed and looking down the length of the table, she saw that each person present gazed at her as though they watched a fox surrounded by hounds.

"Well," she said, "I think you should pick a more intelligent bird in the future, unless you want your characters to act so . . . so . . . stupidly."

And with this said, she jumped from the table, upsetting her plate and knocking over her cup of tea.

"Oh! See what you've done?" She addressed Black Bear.

"I've done . . . You are the one who—"

"How could you?" Estrela threw down her napkin just as a servant came up behind her. "Why don't you use swans next time, or wolves—at least they have a certain intelligence that I find sadly lacking in the gander."

She spun about, upsetting the servant, his tray of food, and the tea. But the servant was well-trained and caught the tray before any damage could be done.

Black Bear watched her leave but only for a moment before he, too, arose. And though his movements were slower than Estrela's, he still moved quickly to follow her.

Too quickly.

The servant stood behind him. The tray of food and tea crashed to the floor, most of its contents spilling innocently, except for the tea, of course, which landed on the Duchess of Colchester.

And as she, too, jumped to her feet, wiping at her dress and holding it away from her, one could hear her say to an oddly silent room, "Oh my, oh my, did I miss something from that story?"

The only response to her question was complete and utter silence.

Chapter 7

Black Bear took to the streets. He had to get away.

Grabbing his bow and quiver full of arrows, he dashed out of the Colchester House at a fast trot that, if he chose to, he could continue for days.

He had no intention, however, of running for days. He just needed to clear his mind, and running provided the means.

He fled through the streets of Mayfair, past the manicured lawns of the aristocratic town homes, past Berkeley Square, onward until he reached the iron gates of Hyde Park; there, once inside, he found the solitude and peace he was after.

It was late morning, the dew still clinging stubbornly to the newly mowed grasses and, as he sprinted over pathways and around late-year flower gardens, he experienced the sensation of his troubles being shed with his exertion. The park looked foreign to him with its sedate, carefully controlled flower beds and neat ponds, but it didn't matter. It was still nature and Black Bear breathed in deeply, the scent of flowers and the unmistakable feel of crisp, autumn air acting as a soothing balm to the turbulence of his thoughts.

Suddenly it was too much. The wild scents, the

feel in the air, even the gray sky overhead reminded him of home, and without willing it, he saw the faces of his friends and family before him.

Had Black Bear been able, he would have cried at that moment, so great was his distress.

But he didn't, he wouldn't—not in public. And so he stoically masked all feeling.

He sighed. *Home.* How he longed for the familiarity of the faces of his relatives, of his grandfathers. How he longed to return there, to hear the wisdom of the elders, the quiet reassurance of his mother.

But it was not to be.

He had to fight his own war here in this foreign land. And all he had to rely on were his own senses, his own observations and knowledge.

He quickened the pace of his run, oblivious to the stares he received from passersby.

Estrela—Waste Ho Win—Pretty Voice Woman. What was he to do *about* her?

He didn't know, and, where he was usually quite decisive, he suddenly found himself wavering over the decisions he must make.

Should he snub her and return home as his pride demanded of him? Should he attempt to reason with her?

Should he steal her?

He had little enough love for the white society in which he found himself and no respect whatsoever for their laws, which hindered a man's freedom. The more he thought of it, the more he liked the idea. Why not steal her as he had intended this morning? It would be talked about, sung about in his camp for years to come. Such an act would bring honor to him, to his family.

However, such an act would alienate Waste Ho and make her captive, something he hesitated to do.

Despite her betrayal, despite her reluctance to tell him at once of her situation, he still respected her right to her own freedom, and he hesitated doing something that would overthrow her own power of choice.

Besides, she must care for him, otherwise she wouldn't have given herself so freely—

He couldn't think of it. He couldn't allow himself to consider how she had responded to him . . .

Where was her husband? Why was he not here protecting her? From gunshots? From other men?

Black Bear sprung forward, quickening his pace even more.

He fled over a path directly parallel to the Serpentine River, watching the ducks, the swans, and other fowl in his peripheral vision. At last he sighed.

He must come to some decision. This he knew; this he must confront, yet still he hesitated. He could not fathom it all.

She was married. *Married!*

Were all his efforts wasted, then? Were all these years spent waiting and planning for her return to come to nothing? He had invested so much time, so much energy in this, his search for her. And for what? To discover it had all been unnecessary?

She had broken her own vow to him, something he had never considered she would do.

He could make no sense of it. This was not the woman he knew. The Waste Ho of his experience would never dishonor herself in such a way. Had she changed so much?

Lost in his thoughts, Black Bear squinted his eyes as he tore over the paths of Hyde Park, bringing to mind the Waste Ho he had known back in their own country, recalling again his vow to her.

Her hair, caught in two braids at the side of her head and held there with blue and red strips of rawhide, had sparkled beneath the sun. And though her hair gleamed pale in the light and her eyes shimmered like the pure blue of morning sky, she had been the epitome of Indian beauty—her looks renown, even within the entire Lakota Nation, her manner properly shy, her lashes lowered to show respect and her melodic voice, soft, never harsh upon the ears.

It was this memory of her that Black Bear carried with him as he sought out his father on this day almost three years ago.

"I must go after her," Black Bear said to his father as the two men sat within their family's tepee.

"My son," his father responded, "why do you say this?"

"She is mine. We made the vows, I just hadn't spoken to her parents yet. I promised her that I would come after her, that I would find her and so I must. Besides"—here Black Bear lowered his voice, speaking so that his mother would not hear him and become concerned—"I have received a message from Wakan Tanka. I dreamed a vision of her. In this vision, I saw Waste Ho's death, but also within the same vision I dreamed of her life—with me. I have spoken of this to Two Eagles, whom we know carries much medicine, and he has told me that I must go to her if I wish her to stay alive. He told me that I, and I alone, have the power to save her. She is my responsibility. I must go to her."

*His father listened in silence, then he nodded his head,
thereby giving his approval. And Black Bear, looking at
the older man, saw the spark of admiration there within
his father's eyes. And though his father would never
speak it, Black Bear could feel his father's pride, the older
man's confidence in his son. It was a good thing. It gave
Black Bear much courage, a welcome commodity in this,
his struggle to locate Waste Ho Win. It provided him
with the strength and the will he would need in the years
to come.*

And so the quest had begun. Black Bear had
started to listen to the white man, to observe him
interacting with the environment.

Why did the white man trade? For what? Not
food. Not beads. Not cooking utensils. No,
something that Black Bear had been hard pressed
to comprehend: gold, a substance that the white
man appeared to value above all else, above even
his life. Why?

Black Bear hadn't understood, couldn't understand, seeing no practical use for the stones; still,
he'd begun to imitate the white man's trade and
within a short period had accumulated so much of
the white man's strange wealth, he knew he could
begin his long trek to the east.

What a fool he had been, he realized now, thinking back on it all. He hadn't known there were different values on each of the nuggets, hadn't known
nor understood the system of the white man's
money and he had discovered soon enough that he
had been cheated. Cheated by the traders in his
own country.

Those nuggets he had traded for, the gold the
traders had given him were worthless. Fool's gold,

they had called them. Fools gold—aptly named, Black Bear decided, since he had certainly felt the fool.

But there had been something far worse than being made the fool, something Black Bear couldn't even now understand; that first excursion into the white man's world revealed one other point he had overlooked: he, as an Indian, was not permitted to travel within the white man's world without escort—escort by a white man.

The concept was incomprehensible to the Indian. To his own thinking Black Bear was free, as free as the air, as free as the stars in a midnight sky.

He was a man of the earth; never had his freedom of movement been questioned, let alone checked. As long as he obeyed the laws of his tribe and the laws of nature, Black Bear had always been able to do anything, traveling anywhere, sometimes covering hundreds, even thousands of miles to attend a trade, or to investigate a disturbance.

It was this white man's arbitrary law, this demand that an Indian could not go anywhere he should choose, alone, that had stopped Black Bear. And it had seemed for a while that it had stopped him completely.

A full year had passed, a full year with Black Bear trying to solve something incomprehensible.

Then it had happened.

It had been during a summer trade. That year the summer had been warm, too warm; tempers at this time had been as fire on the prairie, needing only a spark to ignite them into flames of full destruction.

But it was then that Black Bear had seen him, a

white man with short, dark hair, a man he had learned was living with a far distant tribe. And though the man had worn elaborate, Indian clothing, he couldn't have understood the Indian well, for he was trying to trade with gold; something an Indian did not understand, or value.

Black Bear had watched, waiting, hoping for a moment when he could talk with the man, awaiting the chance to trade—something he had for the white man's gold.

He hadn't expected the fight. He hadn't expected to have to intervene. But then who would have thought that the white man would cheat?

The white man had been playing the moccasin game with a Chippewa Indian, a game in which one warrior hides a stick in his hand, leaving the other man to guess which hand holds the stick. The game eventually passes into magic, sticks appearing within a moccasin.

Black Bear had decided then, watching the game, that the white man did not realize how warlike an opponent he had chosen, for the stranger joked with his opponent, something no man did to a Chippewa warrior . . . and lived to tell of it.

Black Bear had known the moment when the other Indian could take no more, had watched as the Indian stood to challenge the white man. Black Bear had marked the moment the Chippewa drew his knife; he had watched as the white man nearly fainted before the Chippewa. Black Bear had acted quickly, running forward and leaping into their midst. And before anyone could see what he was about, Black Bear had disarmed the Indian, turning to the white man to signal him into silence.

* * *

"Do you forget, brother," Black Bear pivoted around, addressing the other Indian with the hand motions of Indian sign language, "that we trade here in peace?"

"You are no brother," the Chippewa replied, using the same mode of address. "You are Sioux, mine own enemy, and I will have your scalp now as well as this white man's."

"Unless you are Chippewa chief," Black Bear had signed, his gestures fast and brief, "you will do no such thing. We trade here in peace. Has it not been so through the ages?"

The Chippewa clearly hesitated. "You do not understand," he signed. "This man has cheated me. He has asked for my four horses in the moccasin game. He had guessed where all the sticks were correctly and I would have given him all that I own until I discovered that there was another at my back watching my hands, flashing signs to the white man. That Indian fled who helped him, probably never to be seen again, but this man here is a liar and a cheat. By the laws of our grandfathers, he does not deserve to live."

"Did you do this?" Black Bear turned toward the white man, watching that man nod his head.

"Why?" Black Bear asked, himself at a loss to understand such stupidity.

The white man shrugged. "I have not been long in your country," he signed in gestures. "Though I know that cheating is not good, I did not know the penalty for it was death."

"And why should it not be?" Black Bear tried to reason. "If one lies, will he not do it again? Is it not true that it is only the coward who lies? Is it not true that the liar will only run from a battle, leaving his friends to fight alone?"

"No more talk. He dies," the Chippewa yelled at that moment, raising his knife.

Black Bear swung around, facing the Chippewa once more.

"This man does not know our customs," Black Bear's gestures were crisp, his hands cutting through the air. "Do you see that he is white? He is a foreigner. He admits that he cheated. It is no crime in his country and he did not know better, though he should. He is willing to make it good to you and will give you all that he has to show you he has seen his mistake and will not do it again."

Black Bear watched the other Indians who had crowded around grunting and groaning as they debated among themselves. Then, finally they turned back toward the white man, toward Black Bear.

"What have you to give him and his people?" Black Bear quickly signed in gestures to the white man.

"Nothing," the man signed. "I'd rather fight him."

"And lose your life?" Black Bear let his disdain for the white man show by snorting. "Do you see any other white man here? Every Indian present will fight you. Do you not realize how severe cheating is and that no one will support you? Who are your sponsors, that you are let loose among us with so little knowledge of us? You will surely die if you do not do as I say. No Indian lies and cheats . . ."

The man looked contrite, but only for a moment. Digging into his pockets, the white man produced several nuggets of gold, their value meaning nothing to the Indians, yet everything to Black Bear.

"That is all that you have?" Black Bear asked poker-faced, watching the white man nod. At length Black Bear signed, "You will surely die."

A moment passed. Another.

"What can I do?" the man asked at last. "Will you help me?"

Black Bear took his time, looking at the gold, then at the man. "I will help you," he said at length. "I will save your life, if I can. And in exchange, I would ask that you pay me your golden rocks."

"Anything."

Black Bear nodded, turning back toward the other Indians and in the descriptive gestures of sign language, began his story, telling the others that the white man possessed only gold to exchange for his life. Black Bear, however, would take pity upon the man and would bargain with the Indians, himself, for the white man's life.

But the others were not appeased so easily and it took everything Black Bear possessed to rescue the man: Black Bear exchanging all four of his horses, his buffalo robe, the shirt upon his back, his bear's claw necklace, and a wampum shell pouch that had been passed down from his grandfather. It all went into the bargain for the white man's life.

Finally, the other Indians left, satisfied, though each one shook his hand toward the white man, indicating no one in Indian country would ever trust the man again.

The white man breathed a sigh of relief and approached Black Bear, signing in gestures, "Thank you, my friend."

But Black Bear withdrew from the man, insulted, gesturing, "I am no friend to a liar. I do this only for your gold, not for you. I have need of the golden nuggets."

"You do? An Indian?"

Black Bear nodded, which caused the white man to laugh, and Black Bear to frown.

"Why do you laugh?" Black Bear asked. "You do this as though you know an Indian does not value this gold."

"Yes, you are right. I know that the Indian has no use for these rocks."

"Then why," Black Bear asked, *"do you trade with them among us?"*

"Because," the other man signed, *"it is a symbol of wealth in my country and it is all that I have. My Indian wealth is limited. Now come, my friend."* The man slung his arm around Black Bear's shoulders. *"No matter what you say, you have saved my life and I will call you friend. But let it not stop at the golden nuggets. Tell me how an Indian has come to 'need' these pretty rocks."*

That had been the beginning.

True to his word, the man had listened to Black Bear's plight; and without hesitation, he had offered Black Bear not only gold, but companionship.

He would escort the Indian abroad.

Plans were made; two of Black Bear's closest friends demanding to accompany him on the long trip, to share in the adventures and to protect their friend.

And within only a few months, the foursome of three Indians and one white man had boarded a ship, headed for the English coast.

Black Bear, thinking it over now, could not have hoped for anything better. The white man had been a German Prince and had taught the Indian, on the long sea voyage, not only what a German Prince was, but had shown the Indian some of the impossible intricacies of Continental manners and society.

"No, no," Prince Frederick said. *"Don't eat the food with your hands. Here,"* the Prince pointed out a utensil. *"This is a fork,"* he explained to Black Bear. *"You hold it thusly and you pick up your food like this."* He demonstrated.

"Why?"

"Well, I . . . it's because . . . well," Prince Frederick looked flustered. "Never mind. It's simply the way it is done. Just try it." And Black Bear, smiling, complied . . . this time.

And it continued in much the same vein, not only with table manners, but with the English language itself, including the complicated forms of address. The Prince explained that just as the Lakota had a system of manners, so too, did the English, Continental manners being just a little more complex. The Prince even tried to explain the system of class, but this was something the Indian could not grasp, seeing no reason why a man could wield influence simply by reason of birth. Did the white man not realize that the worth of a being came from his own contribution? Not by that of his fathers? No, he could not comprehend this.

Still the lessons went on each day. The Prince taught the Indians Continental culture; Black Bear instructed the Prince on Indian society and lore.

"How is it," Black Bear asked of the Prince one day, "that you came to be in such a grave situation with a Chippewa Indian? Did you truly not know how warlike that tribe is?"

Prince Frederick grinned at his friend. "I gambled," he said. "And I found I routinely lost to the Indians, who hide their thoughts behind a stoic mask. So I devised a system of cheating. It seemed harmless at the time. And no, I did not know how warlike the Chippewa are. I did not realize how much I had to learn. I had come to visit your tribes, you see, to hunt strange animals, to rid myself of utter boredom, and to feel what it is like to be wild and savage."

Black Bear grunted, but Prince Frederick ignored him, continuing, "I had no idea," the Prince said, "that

*there was such a civilization and I certainly had no idea
what this society considered wealthy. You see"—he
leaned in toward his friend—"I had no Indian wealth
and I wished to buy a maiden's favor. Needless to say I
found out the hard way that Indians have no use for my
gold. Imagine my distress when I found myself unable
to buy even one night with a maiden?"*

*Black Bear glanced at the Prince and smiled. "Did no
one tell you," Black Bear emphasized each word with
descriptive gestures, "that Indians have been known to
share when the need is great?"*

*"No, they did not." Prince Frederick sighed. "Well,
it doesn't matter now. I found myself poor for the first
time in my life, unable to bargain or buy anything. And,
pray, believe me this was more intolerable to me than
anything else I have yet to endure. I am a prince, you
see. I have breeding, status, and wealth, all mine to command. I couldn't . . . why do you laugh?"*

*"It would have been so simple," Black Bear said, "to
make your need known. I imagine there were many a
widow only too willing to share her blanket with you."*

"I wanted a maiden, a particular maiden . . ."

"Before marriage?"

*Prince Frederick shrugged. "Yes. How was I to know
such things are not done? As you can see," he said, "I
had much to learn about your society. A mistake I will
not allow you to commit. Come now, let us review again
the proper utensil one uses for soup . . . no, no the bigger
spoon. See . . ."*

And so it had continued, lesson after lesson,
some more tedious than others, until at last they
arrived in England.

Black Bear wondered again as to the whereabouts of his two friends and the German Prince. The four of them had been separated at the parade.

Slowing his pace, Black Bear spared it no more thought. His friends would find him.

Black Bear glanced over to his right. The river here in the park had become narrower and as he glanced around, he noticed a horse path to his left. He trod toward it.

The path was tree-lined and sandy, and upon it rode a steady traffic of fancy-dressed ladies and gents sitting atop fine-looking animals. The women rode their horses strangely in this country and Black Bear sat for a while pondering the why of it.

That's when he saw her, leading a procession of her lady's maid and a stable boy, who followed discreetly.

She wore a green outfit that rivaled the very tree-tops in color. She had tied her blond hair back with ribbons of the same color and placed a hat upon her head. She, too, sat sidesaddle and Black Bear almost laughed at the incongruity of it, for she had been taught to ride Indian-style, upon Indian po-nies.

But he didn't laugh. She looked too beautiful.

And *he* couldn't have her.

Black Bear snorted, angry all at once.

That was that, then, he decided, a bit too quickly. He would leave. Before the day was out, he would arrange passage back home, whether he found the Prince and his two friends or not.

He would not stay here a moment longer and watch the woman he loved become slowly trans-formed by another man.

He would not do it.

No more.

He turned to go.

But something caught his attention. Not a sound, not something he could see or even feel. No, it was a sense that all was not right.

He glanced around him, at the trees, the bushes, finding nothing that could account for the premonition.

A bush shook.

Black Bear stood poised, not making a sound, not making a single movement.

No wind. The bush moved again.

He crept toward it, his moccasined feet making no sound on the dewy grass, his toes turned inward for control.

Slowly, cautiously, soundlessly, he crept forward.

He caught an image of a man, of the barrel of a gun, pointed—he glanced toward the road.

His stomach dropped.

Waste Ho . . .

Chapter 8

$\sim\!\!\mathcal{S}\mathcal{S}\!\!\sim$

Estrela had gone to her room directly after breakfast. She'd seen Black Bear leave the house, but she would not follow. What she did was for the best. It had to be.

She stood now at the doors in her room, too angry to have stayed in the breakfast parlor, too embarrassed to return.

She should never have said anything to Black Bear.

She should have taken his scolding without reaction. She should have just smiled at him demurely, as though nothing he said bothered her. She should have.

This wasn't, however, what was.

How could he? How could he have chastised her? In front of the others, no less? It did occur to Estrela, though, that no one else appeared to have noticed the chide. Estrela was still uncertain of her welcome within the Colchester household and Black Bear's criticism, along with his chastisement of her did not endear him to her.

"Oh!" It was all she could think to say as she began to pace, up and down, back and forth.

"Mistress?" Anna called out, knocking quietly on the door.

"Come in, Anna."

Anna entered the room, although she didn't advance into it. She closed the door and leaned against it.

"I 'eard."

"You did?"

"Yes, Mistress."

"Estrela."

"Estrela, then," Anna said, smiling. "It would be my guess t'at geese are not t' be discussed?"

Estrela flicked her gaze upward, wishing she had not confided her humiliation at the incident to her friend. The maid saw too much. " 'Tis not funny," she said, glancing at Anna.

"If ye say so, Mistress."

Estrela spun away, tossing her head back as she gazed outside. "Why does he torture me?" she asked softly, causing Anna to strain forward to hear her. "I have provided him with the perfect excuse to leave. And believe me, Anna, I do this for him, not for me. Were I to have my way, I would never let him go again."

"Then don't."

Estrela twisted back around. "What do you mean?"

Anna shrugged. "Don't let 'im go. Keep 'im 'ere as an . . . escort . . . or a—"

Estrela gasped.

"What? 'Tis done all t' time. Many a lady from t' aristocracy whose 'usband ignores 'er 'as taken a . . . another from time to time. 'Tis only necessary t' be discreet. And in this case, ye don't even know yer 'usband. It would be easy."

"Anna, 'tis exactly what I fear. 'Tis what I am trying to prevent. Black Bear already thinks me no better than an adulteress. And if he remains in England, close to me . . . Anna, I am not immune to him. If I give in to him, what then? I cannot marry him. I cannot return with him. I cannot give him what he wants. I am bound by a promise; a vow that does not include Black Bear in my life." Estrela stared solemnly at her maid. "No, if I would ever make love with him, I would earn no more than his contempt."

Anna paused. She looked at her friend and mistress, then away. At last, with a deep sigh, she said, "Pardon M'lady," she averted her eyes, gazing downward. "But 'ave ye not already succeeded in gathering just t'at? What 'arm would it be t'—"

Estrela groaned.

And Anna glanced up quickly. "I should not speak t' ye as such. Forgive me and me wayward tongue. Ye 'ave been kind to me and I only meant that ye 'ave nothin' to lose if ye—"

Suddenly it was too much. Estrela turned away from the doors, stepped across the room, and threw herself onto her bed. As she cradled her head in her arms, the Earl of Langsford's image swept into her mind, unbidden, unwanted.

"Come here, child."

The ship lunged at that moment and Estrela was forced to brace herself on a handrail, making her way unsteadily toward where the Earl lay.

Hearing the Earl gasp in air, Estrela grew annoyed, thinking this another ploy of the Earl's to try to bring her under control. She did not believe him to be in danger when he grabbed his heart. Hadn't he done much the same thing, play-acting, only yesterday?

And so she just stood there, her chin thrust forward, her arms folded over her chest, her temper flaring. How she wanted to scream at him, stamp her feet, rave at him, anything. But she didn't. She stood, unflinching, glaring.

So far she had bickered and argued with the Earl the entire trip. She didn't want to return to England. She didn't want to be on this sea voyage. And she grew tired of the Earl's evasions to her questions.

"I haven't much time," he said again.

Still Estrela did nothing, just glared at him.

"Child," he pleaded and this time, Estrela noted that there was about him a strained quality. Slowly she moved forward until she came to him, kneeling at his bed, gazing at him, studying him.

"I must ensure your safety," he said and she snorted, sure now this was simply another ploy.

"Don't worry yourself over me," Estrela said, waving her hand. "My future is already assured. After we arrive in England, I intend to book passage back to the Americas immediately. And there is little you can do about it. Now come, my friend," she said, moving to help him. "Sit up. You are well now. I will it."

But the Earl didn't responded in kind, as she had expected. Instead he smiled at her.

"Ah," he said to her. "You are just like your dear mother. She, too, thought she could change things simply by willing them to be different." He coughed then, but Estrela was not to be put off. And so she remained seated at his bedside, staring at him. "But it cannot be this time," he continued. "I have little time left. Augh! Come closer, child."

She did as he asked, and as she did so he clutched at his chest, whispering, "I must see that you marry . . . now—"

"Marry?" she asked and it took every bit of will she possessed not to laugh at him. But she didn't, asking *him instead, as though she believed he were entirely serious, "What do you mean marry?"*

"Child," he gazed at her, and Estrela saw a look in his eyes then that should have alerted her as to what was to come. But it didn't. All she noted was that his eyes beseeched her. " 'Tis my duty," he said. "I must see you married. I must ensure your safety. Quickly, now. Go get the Captain."

Estrela wasn't startled by the unusual request. It was what she expected from the Earl. But she didn't move, she wouldn't, asking simply, "Now?"

"Yes," he whispered in return. "It must be."

"But Uncle," she said to him, her tone flippant, "how can I marry Black Bear now? We are at sea and I—"

"My child," he took her hand in his own then, and had Estrela not been so convinced that the Earl played with her, she would have seen the truth to be witnessed there in his eyes. She didn't, however, and so when he said, "I know you love the Indian brave. But duty demands that a marriage between the two of you can never be," Estrela didn't really hear. But he continued talking, saying, "My child, you are—" he coughed. "Quickly, go fetch the Captain."

But Estrela merely shook her head.

"You must marry another—" he said, "—and now."

"I will not," she responded at once, reacting instead of thinking, pulling her hand away from the Earl's and jumping to her feet. She turned her back on him. "I think the joke has gone on too long. I know you play with me and I cannot understand what game you are about now. You must know that I cannot, will not do as you ask. This time you have gone too far." She swung back around to face him, venting the full force of her fury on the Earl, saying, "How would you know what I feel? How can you seek to dictate to me what I should do? You," she went on, "who can never stay in one place

long enough even to know love. You, who even now can speak of love with great detachment. You must know that what you ask me to do is ridiculous and that I will not do it. I do not know why you seek to control me in this manner. I don't understand what it is you have to gain from it. But know this. I love Black Bear. I will love no other—ever. I have promised to marry Black Bear and—I will marry only him, because I love him, because I promised I will marry him, because I will not break my vow."

She stuck her chin up in the air and looking down upon the Earl, knew her mistake at once. He was not play-acting, he was not using a ploy. Had she been doing anything but reacting, she would have seen it long before now. It was there in the dull grayness of his facial coloring, in the dilated fullness of his eyes, the listlessness of his manner. She knew it then with full certainty. The Earl lay dying before her.

Sudden realization made her weak.

She moaned deep in her throat and rushing back to his side, she knelt down beside him.

"I'm sorry," she cried. "I did not realize . . . I . . . You have been my friend ever since I can remember. You have been my family when I had no other, my father. I thought that you . . ." She gazed at him while tears threatened at the back of her eyes. " 'Tis not important. Can you ever forgive me my wayward tongue?"

"Child," he said, smiling up at her. "I would most likely forgive you anything. But you're wrong, you know." He reached out for her hand then, his fingers, his arms shaking. "You," he said, "never knew your mother, did you? Of course not," he answered for her. "But my child, I loved your mother as I have never loved another. She was willful, she was"—he glanced away— "perfect. No, child, you're wrong. I have loved well. And

I have loved you, her own child, as though you were mine. All my life I have devoted to her, to your grandfather, to you. And child," he turned his gaze once more to Estrela, "do not fret that you break your promise. It is not the same thing. You simply don't know who you are. But —" he gasped, his every word strained. "I have no time left. All I can ask is that you trust me, the faithful servant who has never had anything but your best interests in my heart. Trust what I ask you to do. It is my final request. For child, even if I were not so anxious to settle your future, you could never marry the Indian." He was racked with pain now and, unable to speak fully, he signed his next words in the Indian sign language they both understood. "Please, I have little time left."

"No!"

"Estrela," he managed to whisper. "Listen to me. I must settle your future. Please believe that I am only holding onto life so that I can do this for you." He was unable to speak any further. And again, he resorted to Indian sign language, saying with his hands. "Hurry. Get the Captain."

"I . . ." Tears had welled up in her eyes, were even now blocking her vision.

"I am a dying man," he managed to say, his voice no more than a gravelly blur. "I do this because I must. You must be protected once you reach England and if I am not there, someone must do it."

"I . . . Uncle!"

"Estrela, please." He inhaled sharply. " 'Tis my last request. Can you deny me?"

All this time, she hadn't really believed it. All this time, she'd been certain he was play-acting. All this time, these, his last minutes on earth, she had wasted.

She gasped in reaction to what she had done, what

she had said. And to state she felt remorse was surely an understatement. As she knelt there beside him, she took his hand into her own and, silently, so that he wouldn't see, she cried.

"I love you, child," he went on speaking. "I always have. And I would never rest in my grave if I were remiss in seeing to your future. Please."

Estrela sat before him, then, realizing the extent of her loss.

"I have made you my life," his voice, as he spoke, ever softer. "All I have done, I have done for you, for your grandfather, for your mother, god bless her soul, the woman I have loved above all else. You must promise me you will marry whom I say. You must promise me you will never break this vow. Do you love me, child?"

And Estrela, unable to say anything, unable to do anything, simply nodded her head.

He sighed. "You must marry him, Sir Connie. Promise me you will. You will be safe with him. You must tell him about me, tell him who you are." The Earl tried to smile at her, Estrela saw it, witnessed the amount of effort the Earl expended on the simple gesture. "Promise me this, child. Promise me you will honor this marriage. Promise me you will find him."

And Estrela, unable now to stem the stream of tears did the only thing she could. She nodded.

She agreed.

"What was that, child?"

"Yes," she whispered at last, her throat constricting.

"Say it, child. Say the whole thing."

"Yes," she mumbled it. "I will honor the marriage. I'm sorry, Uncle, I didn't know—"

"There, there," he said and as he raised a hand to pat her, he added, "So be it."

*   *   *

Estrela rolled over onto her back and gazed up
now at the pink and gold headboard of the bed.
"Anna," she said, "I have no choice in the matter.
I never did. I must make Black Bear leave. For my
sake, and for his."

Anna said nothing.

Estrela drew a deep breath, then another. "But
come," she said at last. "I feel I need a ride." She
paused, sighing softly. "Yes, I need to ride. And
though 'tis still morning, the majority of traffic on
the horse path in the park should have died away
by now." She rose then and ever so slowly, so very
gradually, she paced over to her wardrobe before
saying, "Anna, you must come with me. I can dress
myself this morning. Please, I feel I need to get out
immediately. Go to the stable quickly, won't you,
and ask the groom to prepare a mount for me and
one for you?"

"Mistress, I couldn't," Anna exclaimed. "A ride
through 'yde Park is for me peers. I—"

"I have an extra riding habit," Estrela said it quietly, softly, yet she earned a smile from Anna all
the same.

"Ye drive a 'ard bargain, ye do." And then, still
smiling, Anna said, " 'Tis done." And with this
last, Anna hurried from the room, never fully observing, nor seeing that at that moment, her mistress cried.

Dressed in a bright-green velvet riding habit and
top hat with veil, Estrela coaxed her gelding into a
faster gallop, while Anna rode alongside on a
smaller pony. A groom from the Colchester House
followed behind the two women.

Estrela sat up straight in the sidesaddle and

gazed around her while the rush of air ruffled her hat and blew tiny whisps of blond hair back from her face.

Estrela rode well, having learned the basics of riding at an early age. She closed her eyes, luxuriating, if only for the moment, in the feel of the horse beneath her. She almost smiled, a sad, self-reflective smile.

She listened to the wind as it rushed past her, relishing in the flutter the air made, wondering if the wind would speak to her now, or if Black Bear might use it again as a medium, but she heard nothing, only the silent passage of air; no message. She pushed her gelding onward, not realizing till too late that she had left Anna and the groom far behind.

She pulled up on the reins, stopping her mount as quickly as she had set him into a run. She quieted him with soothing words while she deftly maneuvered him, bringing him under control. Stopped, the animal pawed at the ground in protest, but Estrela calmly sat upon him, in full control.

She gazed all about her, feeling her worries dissipate, if only slightly, in the stillness of the air, giving her enough space for the moment to think clearly.

And think she did. She knew what she must do.

She had to make Black Bear leave. She had to make him see that there was nothing here for him. Nothing. Not herself, not her life and as she must make him believe, not even her love.

It would be no easy task. For she knew she loved him still, loved him more than anything else, anyone else. Forever.

But she couldn't let him know. Not now. Not ever.

She had sealed her fate, never envisioning at the time that he might come after her. If only she'd known then; if only she could undo it now. But such things could not be. She was trapped, trapped by a pledge she could neither change, nor ignore. She closed her eyes and despaired. There remained only one course for her: She must shun Black Bear completely.

She moaned.

She wasn't sure she could do it. And yet do it she must.

Her eyes remained shut while she awaited her maid and groom.

Gradually the chatter of birds teased her into opening her eyes; the sight of herons, of bluebirds and robins combined in an effort to lift her spirits, if only for a moment. The thudding of the horses' hooves over the sand path as her maid approached, the familiar creaking of the leather saddles lightened her mood, if only temporarily.

Even the cool, moist air that clung to her skin seemed to conspire to raise her spirits. And as she glanced about her at the silken-gold and green beauty that was Hyde Park, she sighed. Off in the distance a man, probably a servant from the St. James's Palace, knelt on his knees in the dirt, placing bulbs in the ground and pruning flowers that ranged in color, from the shades of the bright, red roses to the more sedate, pale shadows of the violet mums.

She almost smiled, looking up. Street lamps were still lit even at this late hour of the morning. They hung aloft from the trees and cast a dim glow over the lush scenery. For a moment, for just a tiny space of time, Estrela experienced a sense of one-ness with the out-of-doors. And as though the park itself plotted to uplift her, she felt a sense of well-being wash over her.

She smiled at last. The park, all of nature, it was good.

Anna and the groom approached her and Estrela greeted them both with an apologetic smile.

"M'lady, Estrela," Anna said, out of breath. "I do not ride as ye do and I beg ye not ta take off like that again. Gave me ole 'eart a shake, ye did."

Estrela's grin turned a little mischievous, her eyes twinkling as she said, "Come, Anna, I'll race you."

"M'lady!"

Estrela laughed, the ring of it cushioned by the moist air.

And Anna, watching her mistress, grinned. " 'Tis a good thin', this ride? It 'as been too long since I 'ave seen ye smile."

"Yes," Estrela agreed. " 'Tis a good thing. Come, Anna," Estrela nudged her horse into a walk. "Will you ride with me a moment? I have a need to talk with you."

Anna nodded, and with a "Yes, M'lady," set her own pony into a walk.

Estrela glanced at her friend and maid for a brief instant before she turned her gaze once more to the front. "Anna," she began, "I need to ask if you will help me with something."

"I will try, M'lady."

"I need to ask you," Estrela said, "to help me convince Black Bear that he must leave here. I must prove to him there is nothing here for him. And I must make him believe I no longer love him. I am convinced that he must leave; I am sure this is the right thing to do."

"But M'lady, I—"

"If he stays here, you and I know I will eventually succumb to him. And he will hate me all the more for it. I cannot return with him. Ever." Estrela stared off in the distance. "No, I have decided. This is the best thing for him." She looked back then, glancing sidelong at her maid, before asking, "Will you help me?"

"M'lady. Estrela. I . . . I will do what I can ta 'elp ye, but I 'ope ye dunna think I agree w' ye. I still believe ye could find a 'appier solution."

Estrela glanced away. "I, too, wish it could be different. But such things are not possible."

Anna sighed before saying, "So be it."

And Estrela, looking over to her maid, nodded, remembering when the Earl had said much the same thing.

Without any warning, Estrela frowned, sitting suddenly still. She stared, her eyes widening. There, off to the side of Anna, hidden among the bushes, stood a man. A man with a gun; a gun aimed straight at her.

Estrela screamed.

At the same time, Black Bear shrieked out his war cry, the frightening sound of it shooting through the air. It blocked out Estrela's scream.

And while the would-be assassin hesitated, Black Bear reacted from pure instinct, sprinting toward Estrela.

One leap. He bounded atop Estrela's horse, landing behind her.

"*Hante!*" He kicked the horse forward into a run,

while he caught his foot in the leather strap of the stirrup and in a move, practiced and perfected by the American Indian, he heaved himself and Estrela over the side of the horse, away from the bullet.

Estrela almost fell. Black Bear, however, clutched her in his arms while spurring the horse on faster and faster.

A gun exploded in a loud blast, missing its target by a split second.

Black Bear whooped and hollered, taunting the enemy with his cry, while at the same time, he blazed the horse over the sand path.

He kept himself to the side of the animal until he felt they were out of the range of danger. Then, he righted himself and, pulling Estrela with him, crouched low on the horse, with Estrela seated before him.

Another shot. To the side. Again a miss, but only by a fraction. So the gunmen were moving with them.

Black Bear whooped again, tearing forward, oblivious to the screams and curses from other riders.

Oddly enough, no one thought to object to the gunshot, it being too common a sound; no, all cursed the Indian as their own horses reared away from him.

Black Bear, however, didn't care. He drove his mount over the path at a furious pace; his thoughts, his senses, all his efforts focused on one goal: Save Waste Ho.

He heard no further shots, but still he didn't stop or slow his pace. He had already surmised that the would-be assassins were also mounted. He just didn't know the caliber of their horsemanship. Would they be able to keep up?

He could probably outrace the attackers. Probably. Black Bear didn't like those odds. The attackers had the advantage: They were on their own territory. Black Bear needed advantage. He searched the unfamiliar environment for something, anything that could tempt fate more fully into his own favor. He saw it up ahead, to the right of the path—a small opening, surrounded by trees and bushes, and speeding toward it, he veered off the sand path at the last minute, guiding the horse into the cover provided there.

He comforted the horse, silencing any sounds it would make, and the horse, as though it understood the Indian's foreign words, stood still, making no noise.

Black Bear watched the road, waiting.

Two men, mounted, sped by, both armed, and Black Bear memorized their looks in one swift glance. Still he didn't move; he listened, he observed, he took notice of everything until assured, he turned the horse back toward the gate, in the direction from which they had just fled, but not on the pathway. He steered the gelding instead through the trees, in and around them, leaping over bushes, hurling his mount on as fast as he dared, until they were well clear of the trees. Then he urged the animal over fields of grasses and colorful flowers, leaping past pedestrians and couples who, out for a leisurely stroll, stood aghast at the sight of the half-naked Indian speeding his horse over the fields of the park, brandishing arms and carrying a white woman before him.

And if many a woman fainted at the sight, it was to be understood.

The sun chose this moment to come out of hiding and shone its brilliance down upon the couple, and Black Bear smiled at the omen. It was a good sign. And as he gloried in the feel of the sun upon his back, Black Bear knew he had acted wisely.

But he didn't slow his pace.

He cried, he screamed out warning to those about him as he fled over the grassy park, his half-naked body poised forward, his blue-black hair and Estrela's blond curls whipping back in the wind. And anyone who would have seen them would have agreed that they made a delightful, if somewhat savage sight; the Indian holding the white woman to him as though she were a prized possession and the white woman, in her turn, accepting her role as "captive" with a grace that would have instantly belied the term.

Still Black Bear couldn't resist counting coup as he passed by a trio of older ladies. Bending over in his seat, he touched all three ladies lightly on the shoulder while he sped past them, straightening back in his seat, whooping and speeding on forward.

That the ladies screamed and fainted didn't affect Black Bear, since he never looked back.

He shot the horse forward, as fast as he could, unaware that two bobbies were making quick pursuit behind him, as though the Indian, not the two assassins, were at fault for the disturbance to the park.

But neither policeman could match the horsemanship of the Indian, especially when the

Indian rode over unpaved ground, and soon Black Bear left them far behind.

He fled back toward Mayfair, galloping through the stately gates of the park, dodging the traffic over Piccadilly Street and on into Green Park, where, with its fields and tree-lined paths, the wilder environment of that park lent him more of an abundance of hiding places.

And there, among the trees and shaded paths, he discovered temporary sanctuary.

He reined the gelding to a stop beneath an enormous maple tree, and once there, jumped off the animal from the rear. He didn't look at Estrela. He didn't even speak. He began to pace, back and forth, Estrela still atop the horse.

Several moments passed. The horse grazed, Black Bear tread up and down, scattering golden leaves here and there and Estrela sat quietly.

At length, Black Bear approached her. "Where is your husband?" he asked, his words sounding sour, even to his own ears.

Estrela didn't answer.

She merely looked at him, and her gaze, as she stared at him, irritated him immensely.

"Why am I the one to save you?" he interrogated. "Is your husband a coward? Does he even now hide from danger?"

Estrela did nothing more than look at him in that way of hers that set his blood to boiling, and Black Bear found himself in need of a tremendous amount of patience, for he felt like shaking her.

At length, she opened her mouth to speak, hesitated, closed her lips; and watching her look away, he could see tears cloud her eyes.

His response, however, was not one of sympathy. No, it was more one of raging anger. And it was all he could do at this moment *not* to howl at her.

And so he resorted to a grunt and a groan, turning away from her to resume his pacing, up and down, back and forth.

"I intend to leave here before another new moon is upon us," he said to her, sulkily. "But I must leave you in the care of your husband, who should be here, even now, to protect you. Where is he?"

Estrela gazed back, again that sad look in her eyes. She shook her head slowly, uttering not a word.

Black Bear could barely contain himself. "What sort of man would leave you unprotected?" he railed at her. "How could a man leave his own wife to the guardianship of another? Has he no pride?"

"Black Bear," Estrela voiced to him at last, softly. "I must speak to you about my husband. There are things you don't know, about him, about me; things I need to tell you—"

"I will hear nothing of this coward you call husband," he interrupted. "I only seek the knowledge of *where* he is so that I can return you to him—no more."

"But I can't tell you that. I—"

"Cannot? Or will not?"

Estrela sighed. "Black Bear," she said as she gave him an odd look. "I feel a little funny."

That set him to gazing at her. His glance scanned over her, from the top of her head to the high black boots she wore.

"You are fine," he said. "I see no wounds."

Estrela nodded, but repeated again, "I still feel a bit odd."

He strode toward the horse then. "Here," he

said, reaching up toward her. "I will help you from this horse."

But it was too late. All he heard was a muted sigh before she slid off the horse, not because of his command, but rather because . . . Black Bear looked down at her. She had fainted.

He took a deep breath, unaware that in his glance, all his emotions toward her; his love, his admiration, his devotion, his anger shone readily there for anyone to witness.

They made an odd picture, the Indian and his woman, one, tall, bronzed warrior standing practically naked, holding the petite, blond Englishwoman in his arms. They were bound, these two and he clasped her to him amid the backdrop of golden, falling leaves, and the dark bark of trees. Her long, blond curls fanned back against him in the slight breeze, entwining with his own darker hair until one noticed that the blond and black strands blended together, forming a new color that shone as naturally and as grandly as the golden surrounds of trees, leaves, and grasses.

Had anyone observed them at that moment, he would have witnessed a powerful and compelling vision; for the two young people, together, united, became a part of and yet were more than the grandiose and expansive beauty exploding all around them that was Green Park, that was England.

And Black Bear, holding her, gazing down at her, suddenly realized that he would not run away from her. He could not. Not now. Not ever.

He loved her that much.

It was a startling and sobering awareness for him.

And Black Bear, completely honest with himself, despaired.

Chapter 9

King William and his sister-in-law, the Duchess of Kent, Princess Victoria's mother, had little love for one another. Truth be told, only a few short days before, at the King's birthday party, King William had risen, in response to a toast, and had wreaked vengeance upon the Duchess in a most horrible and public denouncement.

He had decried her, stating she had caused him great embarrassment; saying she was keeping the Princess, Victoria, from him; denouncing the Duchess as unfit to raise the Princess; calling the Duchess incompetent; and moreover, accusing the Duchess of listening to ill-conceived counsel, stating she was surrounded by evil advisers.

Evil advisers indeed!

The dark, shadowy figure of a man smirked, raising his glass in a mock toast to the dying embers of the fire, whose smoke billowed upward toward the small chamber's chimney.

Evil advisers!

Why *he* was probably the only one in all of England who had the foresight to advise the country's affairs correctly.

King indeed!

Hadn't that one's father lost the American con-

145

tinent? Weren't King William's British forces, even now, struggling with her other colonies? Wasn't England threatened with the loss of her powers if someone didn't act? And act now?

Ah, the Duchess of Kent. What was he to do with her? If she didn't handle her daughter prudently, if she continued to mock the King within his own territory, Her Grace stood every chance of losing her daughter's favor. And if she lost her daughter's trust, so would end her political influence over the child; so would end his.

He at least had noticed the Baroness Lehzen, young Victoria's governess, spreading her influence over the unwitting Princess, that Baroness taking up a camp in direct opposition to her Grace's own policies. And why had the Duchess dismissed Madame de Spath, the Baroness's ally? Because Madame had discovered the liaison between himself and the Duchess and had dared to speak of it?

He sighed. Such matters were trivial to him. Didn't Her Grace realize how attached the Princess had become to Madame de Spath? Didn't she understand that Victoria would only see her mother's actions as cruel? That the young Princess would ultimately condemn her own mother?

Evil advisers.

The King's statement could only apply to one man: Sir John Conroy, that pompous Irishman. It was he who had ill-advised her Grace, disaffecting the woman toward the King, accumulating His Majesty's wrath by encouraging her to flaunt herself in front of the English populous as though she, herself, were monarch, not the King.

Drawing a deep breath the dark, shadowy figure nodded his head. He knew he should be more lenient with the woman, but it was becoming difficult to do so. He tried to calm himself, tried to tell himself that he could not expect much from the Duchess, yet he was not successful in these attempts and with tremendous force, he slammed his fist down on the table at his side, causing the glass there to jump up before it came down hard, shattering into a hundred pieces.

Still, the man didn't move.

It couldn't be worse. Not even her Grace's brother, King Leopold of Belgium, could cause this much havoc.

Leopold? Belgium?

The man's stomach twisted. Why had he thought of that country? Why had he thought of that man? Such memories induced visions of another entire series of problems. It reminded him that he could not allow any sort of Belgian influence within the court of England, not in the past, and certainly not now.

The man tensed, the very shadows in the room echoing the strain. He could not fail. He could not allow England to unite with Belgium in her civil war against the Dutch. For if such an alliance ever occurred, all would be lost, for him, for his homeland, the Dutch Netherlands.

And to think, after all these years, he was still fighting Leopold's influence within the English court. He thought he had rid the country of that influence nineteen years ago when he'd stolen Leopold's own child away, the night the future Queen, Charlotte, died in childbirth. Leopold's sympathies, even at that time, aligned with Belgium in her disaffection with Dutch Patriots.

The man shook his head.

Was he to let all his efforts slip away then, simply because the Duchess of Kent kept overstepping her influence?

No, he could not. He had worked too hard, too completely, now and in the past, to achieve his present position of power through which he could advise England on her own foreign policy. He could not let such hard work go to waste.

The man smirked. He remembered all those years as though they had only happened, his fear of Leopold, his conviction that the child, Estrela, must never be allowed to ascend to the throne of England. For through her, Leopold would rule all of England, uniting England and Belgium.

But it had never occurred. He had ensured it.

It had been easy, in those early years to convince the King, George III, to requester the twin babe, his great-granddaughter, away. After all, the man had been insane. It had only required a few choice words spoken to a select group of people.

The Prince Regent, on the other hand, had proved to be more difficult to control; that one requiring strong counsel and proof in action. Thus, had been born the constant threats to the Princess's life, some staged, some real. For only in this way could the Prince Regent be persuaded to hide the child.

The silent figure of a man suddenly laughed, though the sound was hardly infectious.

Well, he'd done it. He'd forced the powers that be to do his bidding all those years ago. And if he had done it then, he could do it now.

It only required that he mend this situation between the Duchess of Kent and the King. He would need to talk with her, to convince her to cease her flamboyant ways. He could not allow Her Grace to lose influence with the Royal Court, with the Princess. For then what would his own position be?

The man sighed. Such was the matter of whim. He had no time for it. He had other problems to attend to, other things that required his attention, other matters to resolve—like that of the Princess Estrela.

What was he to do about her?

Rotten luck, that's what it was. Didn't he have enough to think about without adding worry of *her* to his already full itinerary?

He had thought the young Lady Estrela's quick murder would put at least one problem to an end.

It should have been a simple thing. He had hired good assassins. Twice they had failed. Twice they had blundered.

Something he could ill afford. Hadn't he just yesterday been forced to kill them both? For their knowledge of her; for their knowledge of him.

Foiled. How was he to know some wild Indian would rush to her assistance, twice, and, amid stray bullets, save the young lady's life?

He snorted.

His plans had been too-often thwarted of late. With everything else he had to worry about, he didn't have time to spend on a would-be Princess who didn't even know her own true identity. Her quick murder must be accomplished. And soon. He had too many other matters to which he must attend.

He must hire other assassins and soon.

Already the Duke and Duchess of Colchester suspected the Lady Estrela's aristocratic heritage.

Luckily the Duke's search for that young lady's identity would come to nothing, since there were no clear-cut records of her existence.

Hadn't he ensured that condition long ago? Hadn't he, himself, burned all records of her birth?

Still he worried.

The Duke of Colchester could be a determined man, the wild Indian an entirely unknown quality. What if they stumbled onto—

The dim, gloomy figure arose.

He hadn't considered her upbringing; the loyal Earl of Langsford, his staff, his household of long ago. The old Earl was gone now. But there were other people there, loyal servants who would remember her. Would any of them know of her royalty?

He must seek them out, each one; he must eliminate them all. He could take no chances.

He would have to set out to the country at once—there to hire assassins, there to eliminate anyone who had been with the Earl ten to fifteen years ago.

Ah! The duties he had to perform. Did no one else see it? Did no one else know? Was it always to be upon his own head that lay the exalted future of England? Of his beloved Netherlands?

He felt heavy with the weight of responsibility. What he would do he did as his patrotic duty. But he must act quickly. All must be quieted. All must be murdered. Only in this way could England be saved from herself.

There was no one else.

And as the Lord was his witness, no one would stand in his way

Rising, he advanced toward the fire, stirring the dead embers as though it were a cauldron pot.

'Twas highly symbolic.

And with this thought, he laughed, the evil sound of it carrying to every part of his small, sparsely furnished chambers. And even the fat, fearsome ravens outside took wing at the horrible sound.

Chapter 10

Estrela gasped. She stared; her eyes widened. She'd never seen anything like this. She'd never witnessed anything so—

What was the man about?

He sat upon a horse, his long hair, unbound, falling well below his shoulders, the blue-black strands of it fluttering slightly in the wind. His chin jutted forward, his face lifted proudly, his eyes watched everything about him.

But that wasn't why she stared. He . . . His clothing. She gulped.

He was dressed as . . . he was . . . where was his Indian clothing? His buckskin shirt, his leggings, his breechcloth? He wore no moccasins on his feet and the conspicuous absence of quiver on his back, bow in his hand seemed altogether strange. He looked more foreign now than he had ever appeared to her in the past. He looked English. He looked like a gentleman. Goodness help her, he could have been an aristocrat by the manner in which he now appeared.

At that moment, he shifted his gaze to look toward her coach, and Estrela ceased to think. She groaned.

It was the only sound to be heard in the otherwise quiet coach. Even Anna, seated across from her, who was watching the same thing, said nothing.

They were sitting, she and Anna, in the Duke of Colchester's carriage, a barouche that comfortably held four people. As was common for the English aristocracy, the Duke had spared no expense in making this carriage as beautiful and as ornate as possible. White satin curtains trimmed with gold hung at each window. The curtains could be pulled back to afford the person inside a view of the out-of-doors or they could be hung down straight, giving privacy to those inside.

Estrela chose the former, her gloved hand holding the curtain back while she peeped outside. She rested her cheek against the polished, mahogany wood that adorned the inside of the coach and lay in trim all around the window. The dark, red velveteen seat upon which she sat cushioned her weight in luxurious comfort.

"What do ye suppose t' man is up to?" It was Anna who spoke.

"I don't know except that I—"

He jumped off his horse at that moment, dismounting Indian-style, swinging one leg in front of him, up and over his mount, the action at complete variance to the manner in which he dressed. And Estrela in reaction to him, flung the satin curtain down and straightened away. She looked wildly about the carriage.

She heard the approaching crunch of boots —not the muffled sound of moccasined feet— against the cobbled drive, and she gulped. What was she to do? What could she say to him?

She hadn't seen him, hadn't spoken with him in

well over a week. After the incident in the park, she hadn't known what to do, so she took to her chambers. She did not come down for meals, for entertainment, nothing, no communication until now.

She had tried to hide, from him, from herself, from a would-be assassin. But it hadn't worked. During the past week, she'd become more and more certain of just one thing: She needed Black Bear. Now more than ever. And the terrible part of it was that she dared not do anything about it. For she must, must send him away from her—somehow.

She fidgeted. What was she to do? She'd been more content to live without him before . . . but now . . .

After the attempted assassination, something had happened to her and she didn't quite understand what it was. Yes, there had been danger there, a threat to her life, but it wasn't either of those things that plagued her now. Something powerful had taken hold within her, something forbidden. Something . . .

She moaned. Truth be told, she felt closer to Black Bear now than she had ever felt at any other time. He had stirred something within her, awakened something, something she had thought had died on a sea voyage long ago. And though she knew she mustn't, that she must fight whatever attraction he held for her, she sensed that from this moment forward, without Black Bear, she would be only half alive, a circumstance, she realized, she must learn to face. She—

The door to the carriage opened and, in response, Estrela's stomach plummeted.

"Ladies," Black Bear's deep voice rang out into

the crisp, early-morning air, causing spasms to run along Estrela's nervous system.

It was a simple word, really. It conveyed nothing but greeting, yet Estrela could not account for its effect upon her, nor for the change it bespoke upon Black Bear. Like the clothing he now wore, the word, the way in which he said it, was reminiscent of nothing of the Black Bear she knew.

Estrela sat, gazing at him. "Mato Sapa," she said at last, her lapse into Lakota unintentional, yet. . . .

He grinned back at her and Estrela almost swooned.

It was his smile, that lopsided, boyish grin that she knew so well. Its charm, set against the magnificent sight that he made, set her heart to racing, and she suddenly felt life coursing through her.

"I have missed your presence," he was saying to her, "at breakfast and at dinner this past week."

"Oh?" It was all she could manage to say at the moment, and even that was said softly.

"Yes." His eyes twinkled. "We have had so many things to discuss and I have entertained my friends with stories. Stories of hunting, of geese, of love, of—"

Estrela conveniently coughed.

And he laughed, saying after a moment, "Do you two women ride alone in this . . . carriage?"

Estrela spread her skirts over the seat as though in answer before she glanced up at Black Bear, saying, "I think so, but I do not know for certain. I have only just settled in here myself."

"Yes," he said. "I know."

That last had her squinting her eyes at him. What was he implying?

She saw him glance around the yard. "I will

speak to the Duke," he said. "You must have someone guard your carriage. If he has no one, then I will do it."

Estrela smiled politely. "Thank you," she murmured, "but I—"

He shot her a glance, his look alone silencing her.

"I must ensure your safety. Had I time, Estrela, Waste Ho, I would show you why it is I worry over you. I would finish what I had started so many nights ago. Despite your husband, I would—"

She gasped, glancing briefly at Anna, and catching the maid's gaze, Estrela blushed; she set her glance at once back toward Black Bear, but he merely grinned devilishly.

"Now, please do excuse me," Black Bear continued. "I must find the Duke of Colchester and see to your safety. I hope both of you are well-seated." And as though to further startle her, he bowed slightly toward them.

She couldn't help herself. "Black Bear," she said, detaining his retreat with her quietly spoken words. "Forgive me, please," she said. "I know that if we were at home, in Lakota country, I would never think to ask you this, but we are here in England and I . . . well, you . . . what I mean is . . . Black Bear, what has come over you?"

She expected anger, or at least a reminder as to proper Lakota manners. She *had* spoken out of turn. She waited, but nothing happened. She received none of it. No anger. No incriminations. Just a grin, a heart stopping, soul-stirring grin.

She set her gaze away from him, hoping to lessen the effect he had on her.

It didn't work. Instead, she became much more aware of him, of the clean, male scent of him, a combination of the smells of the buckskin and leather from his English trousers, of soap and water and a musky fragrance that was his, alone. She sighed, inhaling also the crisp aroma of autumn air.

He took his time answering her, too, as though he knew what he did to her. At length, though, he said, "I take it you have noticed the change in me, then?"

"Yes," she said, turning back to him, "pray believe me, it would be hard to miss."

He laughed. "I am merely," he said, a leer in his glance, "trying to show the goose all that she resists. Husband or no. He is not here. I am. And," he stressed his next words, "I am available."

"Oh!" She glanced briefly at Anna, but seeing the maid gazing discreetly out the carriage window, Estrela shifted her glance once more back to Black Bear.

He immediately placed a booted foot against the carriage floor and, leaning forward, brought into her vision exactly what he meant. And, this time, she could not look away.

But he wasn't finished. He continued talking to her, saying, "I have decided that if the goose is silly enough to entice more than one male to her nest, it would be a foolish gander who would not take advantage of such . . . whim."

"Oh!" she said again. And then for good measure, "Oh!"

And she looked exactly where he meant her to, exactly where—

Estrela moaned. But she did not avert her eyes. No, she watched his every move, his every flicker of sensitivity as he stood before her. Was the man flaunting himself at her? Or was it her? Was she irresistibly sensitive to him?

She shut her eyes. She shouldn't look at him in this manner, she shouldn't gape at that area of his body. She shouldn't.

She opened her eyes and stared all the harder. And as though she had forgotten all the teachings of the grandfathers and all the good manners of the English, she gazed at him as though he might suddenly take the view from her.

And while she longed to focus her attention there, she forced herself to look away, glancing back to his face.

What was she to do? Here was Black Bear, the man she loved, the man she worshiped, the man she would just as likely die for, but this man . . .

Well, this man wore a white, linen shirt with a cravat at his neck, not the beautifully ornamented, white-elkskin shirt that fell well below his thighs. On this man's legs were tights, a light buckskin that was popular in the more lofty English circles for its snug fit as well as its soothing feel to the skin. This man wore no revealing breechcloth, yet the outfit he sported so exposed his masculine form that her gaze was once more drawn to the juncture between his thighs.

Reluctantly, she looked away from that area, but not before she heard him snicker, the sound not at all pleasant. She met his eyes.

Her breath caught in her throat.

Black Bear was angry. His face, his eyes, the set of his brows, the way he pursed his lips as he stood before her, they all mirrored raw emotion.

What had happened? Only a few minutes ago the man had been teasing her, certainly it had not been a gentle tease, but it had not been this . . . this . . .

"You look at me as though you are hungry," he taunted her, speaking in Lakota.

"Black Bear, I—"

"Does Waste Ho," he asked, interrupting her, "have so little feelings for her husband that she would so easily . . . admire me? Have you no respect for him that you would act this way in public?"

She gasped.

"Did you think I would not see it? That I would not respond to such open admiration?"

"Black Bear, I am trying not to—"

"But then, Waste Ho," he went on in the same language as though she hadn't spoken, "is much used to seeing . . . men, though most likely without—"

"You go too far!" This from her in English.

"Do I?" he asked in Lakota, the subject seeming to make him ever angrier. "Why do you admire me like this? You act as though you have never seen a man . . . Can you say to me now that you have never seen your husband—"

"Black Bear!"

He straightened away, bringing his booted foot to the ground and Estrela watched as he visibly strove to bring his temper under control. She allowed him that time, glancing away, and wondering what it was that had come over her.

He was just a man, after all, and men were all endowed with . . .

She glanced back at him. She moaned.

He was not just any man. This was Black Bear, the man from her past, the man she loved. She could no more ignore him than she could cease her own breathing.

Estrela swallowed, a great effort, and closed her eyes; in truth, she was as scandalized as he was with her behavior. Not only did she admire him in the most exotic way possible, she had done it in such a manner that anyone could watch her.

"Black Bear," she began softly, speaking in their shared language, "I am truly sorry. I do not understand either what has come over me. You have every right to chastise me, every right to—"

"Halt!" He said it, his hands signed it. He leaned forward again into the coach, resuming his former position and bringing back into her vision all that troubled her. He smiled. "I will not hear you speak of yourself in this way. After all," he said, taking her gloved hand and placing it on his knee, "it is not so terrible. I—"

He inhaled sharply.

And Estrela, in reaction, glanced at him, herself gasping. He was . . .

He immediately replaced her hand to her lap, though when he looked up to her, he merely grinned. "You," he said, "have an interesting effect on me. One I intend to examine further in a more . . . private moment.

" 'Tis the way you dress," she said.

He peered down at himself. "I fail to see—"

"Before now I never noticed . . . I mean I was not so . . . you didn't . . . 'tis the vest and coat," she said as though with full authority. "See how the vest conforms to your waist? And the coat. See how it tapers down to a long tail in the back? Why the very effect emphasizes all that . . . that is to say it . . ."

Black Bear smirked. "Do all men," he asked,

"here in England have this same effect on you, then?"

"Of course not, I—"

She chanced a glance up to his face before shutting her eyes. "I didn't mean that—"

"Did you not?"

Estrela drew a strained, deep breath and opened her eyes. In truth, he looked magnificent.

But she could never tell him that.

She had never seen anyone in England who could compete with Black Bear. His very figure rivaled the perfection of a Greek statue. And the way he was now dressed merely emphasized the fact. No, the only difference in Black Bear's new clothes from the standard well-to-do outfit of the wealthy was that Black Bear wore no hat, having chosen to ornament his head with two feathers instead. They hung suspended from his hair on the left side of his head, held there with strips of buckskin, and reached well below his neck. He had left his hair free, the long splendor of it boasting the blue-black highlights which, she had noted earlier, gleamed and sparkled under the invigorating, autumn sunlight. And Estrela, gazing at him now, had to still her hand, for it appeared to have a will of its own, itching to reach out and touch his long mane as it fell almost to his waist.

On anyone else the outfit, along with the feathers and long hair would have looked ridiculous. But on Black Bear the clothes appeared handsome, stately, even imposing. And Estrela found the appeal of his masculinity magnetic, daunting, overpowering . . .

"Black Bear," she said, gazing back at him, her

eyes settling at chest level. "I think it is time for me to tell you about my husband. There is much you don't know. There is much I must tell you. You see, he—"

"Halt!" He said it loudly, and he signed it with the slash of his hand. And whatever control he had placed over his anger earlier must have been held there by the flimsiest of threads, for his constraint fled in an instant. "When I wish to know about your husband," he said, "I will ask." He drew himself up straight, folded his arms over his chest, and thrust out his chin. "But you see, I am not interested in him. I am only interested in how you act with me. It is that which tells me much about him . . . about you."

"No, you are wrong. I need to—"

"When I want to know, I will ask."

"Oh!" She glanced directly up at him then. "I think this has gone far enough," she said. "You hear only what you want to hear. Listen only to what you wish. And I think you purposely flaunt yourself at me. I think you intentionally entice me with no other purpose in mind but to . . . to . . . Well," she paused. "I think you should know that I am no longer interested." She, too, tipped her chin up. "You may go now."

If she had intended to "fob him off," she had certainly failed miserably. All he did was laugh, a good, hearty sound. One that had her staring at him again.

A mistake. He caught her eye and leaned forward again.

"Humph!" His voice sounded amused, his look angry as he asked, "Has Waste Ho taken to lying?" He still spoke in Lakota, his tone ripe with challenge. "You are no longer interested? In what? Certainly that doesn't apply to me. I have only to move my leg . . ."

"Black Bear! Don't!"

He laughed. "Does Waste Ho wish me to show her what would happen if I move?" He changed his position—only a little. Still her gaze came crashing down to his . . .

He laughed again. And bringing his head in toward her, he said, "Married or not, husband or not, people watching or not. It does not matter, does it, Waste Ho? You would still look. You would still ache. Tell me," he taunted her. "How long has it been for you? Many widows would gladly welcome me. Would you do the same? Husband or not?"

She opened her mouth to speak, closed it and self-righteously set her gaze to the mohagony wall of the carriage, ignoring him—or at least it was what she attempted.

Black Bear snorted in response and smiled, a smug, self-satisfied smile.

"Ah, Black Bear, there you are." The Duke of Colchester approached the carriage. And though Black Bear might have said more, he was cut off by the Duke's utterance of "Ladies," as the older gentleman stepped forward, making a slight bow.

And if the Duke noticed anything peculiar about Black Bear, about Estrela, he didn't say a word, even though Black Bear, with a wicked grin at Estrela, straightened away and turned his back to the Duke. "I say there, Black Bear," the Duke continued, not at all daunted by talking to the Indian's back. "I have come to ask you if you would prefer to ride in the carriage with this beautiful lady and her maid, or will you ride in mine? Was hoping you might come and keep us entertained, you know. All your stories and all. Ever been on a fox hunt? No, I don't suppose you have. Jolly good fun, my fine, young man. I must tell you all about it." And as Black Bear faced about to confront the old gentleman, the Duke said, "Well, what do you say?"

Black Bear paused. He smiled at the man, a gesture of respect. Then at last he said, "You are most generous, and I am deeply honored at your invitation. But you must know that it is my duty to ride out ahead of our party and ensure our safe passage. Please understand. In my country, I would bring dishonor to you if I sought my own pleasure by riding in the coach when there might be danger lurking ahead for our party."

"What was that? Dishonor me?" The Duke of Colchester scratched his bearded face. "I say, jolly good of you to think of it, but it would be no dishonor. None at all. I have servants, pray tell. 'Tis their lot to face the danger, my good man, not yours, and certainly not mine."

Black Bear appeared to register none of what the Duke said. Perhaps the concept was just too foreign. After all, Black Bear had been raised to fight his own battles, make his own decisions. Maybe the idea of paying others to face dangers that a man should confront himself appeared too cowardly to him or perhaps he just didn't like the concept of others stealing the honor of battle. Whatever the reason, Estrela sensed his bewilderment.

"Excuse me, sir." Estrela spoke up unannounced from within the carriage. "But perhaps, sir, I might be able to help." She looked at the Duke and so missed Black Bear's frown at her. "You see," she continued on, "in Indian society when a whole camp is moving, the men always ride out ahead of the women and the elders so that the men will face any danger to their families, not the women or children. Please, sir, Black Bear does not understand the system of servants and their 'betters.' And I believe he will be insulted if you insist that he ride in the carriage. He would do better riding out ahead."

"I believe," it was Black Bear who spoke, Black Bear who drew himself up to his full height, Black Bear who sent her an angry glance. "I believe that I know English well enough to speak for myself."

"But I was only trying to—"

"I think," Black Bear said, turning his back to Estrela and speaking directly to the Duke, "I think that although Waste Ho speaks truth, I am no longer in my own country and I think it would be wise if I follow your advice, after all. And in truth, your offer is too tempting to be ignored. However, if I am to ride in the coach, I would prefer to ride with these two women. They must, after all, have protection, and I am best suited to do that."

Estrela might have been struck, so silent and unmoving was she. In truth, it was shock that kept her so still, so immobile she didn't even hear the Duke's reply. But when the Duke, after a short bow to Black Bear and a tip of his hat to the ladies, walked away, Estrela could only consider that His Grace must have agreed to Black Bear's proposal.

And Black Bear, after saying a short, curt, "Ladies," paced around to the back of the coach, there to tether his horse and leave the two women to themselves, if only for a moment. And if his step was unusually heavy, neither lady within the coach noticed.

"M'lady?" Anna spoke into the silence Black Bear had left.

Estrela glanced up at her friend.

"What do ye suppose . . . ?" She sighed. "M'lady, it would seem that we 'ave a long ride a 'ead of us. A long ride w' . . ."

"Yes."

"Would ye prefer that I sit next t' ye, so that yer Indian canna—"

"Yes, Anna. Please."

Anna changed seats, sitting silently for a moment, before glancing toward her mistress and saying, "I dunna know what ye said to yer Indian, but I kin imagine. I 'eard what ye said to t' Duke, though. About t' Indians, about one's peers. M'lady, does t' Indian society not 'ave servants, then?"

Estrela shrugged. "All tribes are different," she said. "The Lakota have no slaves, no servants. If someone is captured from another tribe, they are adopted into the tribe, or sent home in our finest clothes. The Lakota have much pride and feel others also have pride and do not seek to take it away from another. No, my people have no servants, no slaves."

And Anna, ever observant, sat silently, saying nothing, not about Black Bear, not about his outrageous behavior, not even the observation that Estrela had just called the Lakota "her people."

Anna sighed.

Chapter 11

Black Bear sat in the coach across from Estrela and sulked. Beneath him the coach jerked and bumped over the dirt roads while outside the driver whipped the horses forward, the steady thumping of their hooves, the creaking of the wheels and of the carriage itself the only audible sounds.

Black Bear stared outside the window watching the scenery pass by amid the dust. His mood one of pure gloom, he steadfastly ignored the other two occupants of the coach.

Estrela, Waste Ho, had been right when she'd said he would be more relaxed riding outside. Out in the open air he would have had the sun upon his back, the breeze in his face, the chatter of the birds in his ears, and the boasting of the other horsemen to best. He would even now be mounted on his horse, a much more pleasant circumstance than this, no matter the ornate comforts inside the coach that proclaimed the Colchester wealth.

Yes, he would have been happier outside. Yet here he sat, inside, discontent and grouchy and he had no one to fault for the situation except himself. She had angered him and he had reacted. An unwise thing to do. So now while others rode out ahead to face any possible danger or enemy, here he was, stuck inside a coach as though he were a small child needing protection. Well, he was not a small child nor an old man. Neither was he fearful.

Yet, it remained true. Here he sat. Trapped in a spectacular, richly decorated carriage. Stuck.

He glanced toward Waste Ho as she began to speak softly to her maid, Anna, remembering that this one Waste Ho called maid was as observant as an Indian in matters pertaining to the household or to her mistress.

Hadn't he already had to deal with Anna when he had taken up guard inside Waste Ho's room each night this past week? He'd won the maid over to his side. Anna let him into her mistress's room each evening and understood he had to protect Waste Ho.

Damn! He cursed to himself as though he were English.

He had paraded himself in front of Estrela purposefully, strutting, fully intending to taunt Waste Ho with the sexuality of his body. He had done it to prove a point, to show her that she responded more to *him* than to her husband. She had seen through him, and he had painfully realized that not only she, but he, too, would fall victim to the attraction they held for one another.

Damn!

He had lost control.

He turned to gaze out the window, admiring the lush, carefully manicured countryside, yet upset with it nonetheless. Here he saw the forces of nature tamed into a most beautiful obsession, all natural growth controlled. He stared out at the rolling hills, the fertile fields bordered by the most magnificent hedgerows, the scattering of trees throughout the green and golden fields. He saw that autumn was wielding its influence over the landscape, some of the bushes here remaining green, some losing their leaves altogether while others transformed from green to the bright reds and yellows of fall.

And as Black Bear stared at the stately beauty of the borders of trees and trimmed shrubs, he listened to Anna explain to her mistress that the borders had not been planted for their beauty; that the hedges had formed a system of prickly bushes and trees, put there long ago by the large landowners and individual farmers to keep others out, when before this, men had worked the fields in unbounded peace; that the bushes, such as the hawthorn, the holly, the blackthorn, the briar rose, were all planted for their prickly nature, not their beauty.

And Black Bear, upon hearing this, understood now why he had perceived a barbed nature to the beautiful landscape. He also wondered idly if this might account for the extreme greed he had witnessed in the white-skinned American, this need he had observed in them to claim and fence in land, something he'd been hard-pressed to understand. For the Indian, the land, like the air, was free. And he speculated that these white people, these Americans, were, in turn, dramatizing an aberration that had been done to them here on this foreign continent. They sought to adversely control others as they, themselves, had been controlled.

He shrugged; an interesting thought, but unproductive at the moment and as Black Bear decided such things really didn't matter to him, he turned his attention once more to the landscape, to the window, unaware that the scowl on his face attested to his mood.

They traveled north and east through what the Duke had called the Midlands toward a place named Warwickshire where stood the Colchester's country manor, Shelburne Hall. Black Bear recalled his part in the family's sudden departure.

After returning from the park with Waste Ho, Black Bear had sought out the Duke of Colchester immediately.

He had demanded to know all that the Duke knew. Why was someone trying to kill Waste Ho?

But the Duke had known little, and unsatisfied, Black Bear had demanded that Waste Ho be taken elsewhere.

Black Bear smiled at the thought. He had actually threatened to steal her away to America if the Duke didn't act, and didn't act now.

But the Duke had remained steadfast and unyielding to the Indian's demands, at least until he had heard Black Bear's story of how he'd rescued Waste Ho in the park.

Black Bear narrowed his eyes. Even still, he knew the Duke held back from him, relating only those incidents to the Indian that the Englishman felt were safe. And truly, how could Black Bear complain? If he were the Duke, wouldn't he do the same thing? Wield the same protection over Waste Ho? No, the Duke's caution earned Black Bear's respect.

Yet one question remained unanswered: Why would the Duke extend such protection to Waste Ho?

Black Bear shrugged. It was a question he'd pondered ever since the night he'd spoken with the Duke. Eventually, he would discover the answer. It would require patience on his part; patience and the Duke's trust in him. He only had to bide his time.

But Black Bear had also learned much that night. He had demanded to know the whereabouts of Waste Ho's husband, learning an important fact: The Duke of Colchester had no knowledge of Waste Ho's marriage.

Interesting.

Not that Black Bear had enlightened the Duke as to Waste Ho's marital status. Learning of the Duke's ignorance on the subject, Black Bear had pretended no more than mild curiosity over her situation, explaining to the Duke that in his country, at Waste Ho's age, she would surely have been married by now. And then Black Bear had ceased speaking, listening to the Duke instead, the Indian on the alert, observing.

Nor had Black Bear attempted to make sense of it. He wouldn't. He merely noted the fact that something was quite amiss; these two details, both of them true, did not align. Waste Ho declared she was married yet she'd never been seen in the company of a man.

An odd situation for a married woman.

He shifted his position, gazing away from the window and back into the carriage, contemplating Waste Ho now as she spoke in quiet conversation with Anna.

The women's good-natured friendship irritated him irrationally so that when he spoke, his voice mirrored his disaffection.

"What is the name of your husband?" he asked in English, his manner grumpy.

He saw Waste Ho gaze at him, her glance guarded, and Black Bear watched her carefully, though he presented, for all appearances, a guise of indifference.

"Why?" she asked at last.

He shrugged, catching Anna's quick look at her mistress before that maiden lowered her lashes, looking to the floor. He smiled, a deceptive sort of gesture before answering, "I am curious."

Waste Ho peered at him for several moments and Black Bear stared casually back, waiting, noting her every reaction.

"I . . . his name is . . . what difference does it make?"

"None, I suspect," he said, pausing. "However, will you not enlighten me? After all," he said. "What difference does it make?"

Waste Ho caught her breath, endowing him with a strange sort of look. "His name," she said at length, "is Sir Connie."

Black Bear nodded but didn't say a thing.

He could tell by her direct gaze, by the fact that her pupils did not dilate, that she did not lie, and Black Bear became more and more interested.

"Where does he live?"

Again she caught her breath and her gaze, when she looked to him, had all the appearance of that of a trapped animal.

He waited patiently, staring at her, infinitely aware of every nuance of her mood, of her facial expression, even of the delicate scent of her body.

"I . . ." she said. "Black Bear, what are you about?"

He shrugged again, observing all the following: the pulse at the base of her neck suddenly raced; her coloring had changed from a vivid rose to a chalky white, her scent grew a little stronger; her eyes were guarded, unsure; her pupils had dilated at the mere mention of this Sir Connie's residence; her lips had thinned and her gaze darted about the small confines of the carriage.

And he knew, from just these small facts that Waste Ho not only did not lie, she did not know where her "husband" lived.

An odd sort of situation.

He let the subject drop, or so it would appear, saying to her, "Were I your husband, you would not know my absence."

She cast him a curious glance, but all she said was, "Oh?"

He smiled, then pretending ignorance, he asked, "Did you meet this Sir Connie through the Duke?"

"No, I . . . Black Bear, I don't have to answer your questions."

Again, he presented every appearance of nonchalance, saying, "Have you reason to avoid them?"

She gasped. "No, it's just that I . . . What is the purpose of all these questions?"

He grinned, saying only, "I am curious. How long have you been married?"

"I . . . I was married before I came to the Colchester House."

Black Bear nodded and glanced away from her.

She had married, then, he reasoned, just shortly after leaving the Indian camp. He had learned from the Duke that Waste Ho had been with his household for about five years; first as a servant, in much the same capacity as Anna, then only a short time ago, the Duke had discovered her working for him and had taken her under his protection. The reason: She had resembled the Duke's own mother so much Waste Ho might have been that other woman at a younger age.

Five years ago.

Black Bear fought with himself to contain his anger.

How could she have betrayed him so soon? Had she forgotten him, the love they had shared so easily?

"Black Bear?"

He shot her a stormy glance.

"Please forgive me my lack of manners," she said, her gaze shy, and as he stared at her at that moment, he thought, despite himself, that he would most likely have forgiven her anything simply because she smiled at him and looked so pretty doing it. And then she spoke, breaking the spell, asking, "Black Bear, why are you dressed like this?"

He looked away. "I desire it," he said curtly. "It is enough."

He sank back into a somber gloom as he stared out the window. He was not about to tell her what had happened to him, what he had come to learn about himself, about her. He wasn't proud of it, after all. He was attracted to a married woman. *Married!* And he would not, he could not leave her.

But he would never tell her. In truth, after he had rescued her in the park, he had needed to come to terms with himself. He had changed after that incident. For he knew now that no matter what she did, no matter what course her actions took, he would not abandon her. His feelings for her were that deep.

And so he had sought seclusion.

Within the gardens of the Colchester House,

there finding the peace and solitude he'd needed, he had faced his demons.

It had been a rude lesson for him to learn, this knowledge that no matter what she did, he would not desert her; yet Black Bear, ever honest with himself, could not ignore it.

He had thought long and hard, about her, about himself, about whatever power it was that drew them together, and lastly about her would-be assassin. He had used the forces, the very energy of nature all around him to help him decide what to do. He had asked Wakan Tanka, God of all, for guidance. So strong were his feelings, he had made a blood offering, cutting his arm and singing his courage-giving song.

He had sat through that day, the evening, and that night, fasting.

Finally the next day, when the sun arose to its zenith, he'd induced his vision, his guidance.

He knew what to do.

But he wouldn't tell her. And not just because a man would never discuss his visions with anyone except a man of medicine; no, he would not tell her because she already held too much power over him.

What would she say if he were to tell her that in his vision he had seen himself dressed in English garb, with her on his arm, happy and well? That the vision had related to him that only if he became as an Englishman, could he truly protect her? What would she say if he were to tell her that what he did, he did for her safety alone? Didn't she already hold the power of happiness over him? What would she do if she knew she held the power of life over him as well?

But there had been another part of the vision, that piece of it puzzling him. Sent to him in symbols, he could make no sense of it. An eagle, a nightingale, and a raven, all intertwined; what could it mean?

He pressed his lips together and narrowed his brow, wishing he could speak of it to a medicine man.

And as he stared out the window, so engrossed was he in this thought, he didn't see the other two occupants of the coach, didn't realize that one of them sat gazing at him quietly, grinning, until—

Clink!

The faint noise had Black Bear peering back into the interior of the carriage.

"Pardon, M'lady." It was Anna who spoke. "Forgive me, but I seem to 'ave dropped me knitting needle," she said. "Would ye mind picking it up fer me?"

"Of course," Estrela said, while Black Bear and apparently Estrela, too, remained happily unaware that a servant would never ask a true mistress to do such a task.

And as Estrela bent down, Black Bear was treated to a full view of Waste Ho's perfectly formed breasts.

He moaned. He shot his gaze upward, then away. But he couldn't help himself. He glanced back almost at once, centering his attention again upon the delectable sight before him, unaware that Anna sat watching him, a cool grin on her face.

"Sir Bear?" Anna asked after a moment.

Black Bear eventually tore his gaze away from Estrela to look at Anna, but not before Waste Ho had straightened up. She was studying Anna, repeating in what sounded like disbelief, "Sir Bear?"

Anna grinned. "Yes, M'lady. 'Tis what 'er Grace 'as instructed us to call t' gentleman now."

Estrela, Waste Ho, repeated again, as though not hearing her maid's explanation, "Sir Bear?"

Anna nodded, then said to Black Bear, "Sir Bear, would ye mind turnin' yer 'ead so that I can straighten M'lady's dress before we arrive at Shelburne Hall?"

Black Bear sat stunned that the maid would ask such a thing—and perform such an act in his presence, but he nodded his assent all the same. And though he made a pretense of turning his attention elsewhere, he looked discreetly back, watching Anna push her ladyship's skirt up, up, over the knee, up further to mid-thigh, Anna bent over her mistress's dress.

And Black Bear couldn't have moved away, couldn't have looked away had he tried, which he had no intention of doing.

Looking at Waste Ho, he was immediately assailed with all the things about her that he found intoxicating: the scent of her perfume mixed with her own earthy fragrance; the shape of her calf, her thigh; the hint of what lay further up from the thigh, beneath the dress and only just hidden; her breasts, which were almost exposed by the low neckline of her gown; the way they strained against the material as she breathed in and out.

And unbeknownst to himself, he groaned.

The action had Waste Ho straightening up, pulling her gown down and frowning at Black Bear with a most censorious expression.

"Black Bear?" she asked.

And Black Bear merely raised an eyebrow, meeting Waste Ho's gaze directly. He smiled then, sardonically, before saying, "Did you think, in truth, Waste Ho, that I would not look? After you so openly admired me?"

And to her gasp and her statement of, "A gentleman wouldn't . . ." Black Bear merely cocked up the other brow, meeting her stare, until, realizing that Anna had returned her ladyship's skirts to their normal position, Black Bear lost interest, resuming his vigil at the window.

"M'lady?"

"Yes?"

"I need to check yer shoes, but 'tis 'ard when ye are sittin' so close and next to me. Would ye mind," Anna asked innocently, "movin' across from me 'ere and sittin' next to Sir Bear?"

"I . . . of course," she said, and picking up her skirts she made to move across the seats.

Anna appeared to have misunderstood her own question, since she chose that same moment to stand, herself. And in the resulting confusion, Anna "accidentally" bumped into her mistress, sending Estrela stumbling toward Black Bear.

"Pardon, M'lady," the maid said, but it was too late. Estrela, caught off balance, landed on Black Bear's lap instead of the seat.

His arms came up immediately to steady her, to hold her and as he looked up to catch her stare back at him, all his hard-earned control fled. He felt lost, lost to the look in her eyes, lost to the overpowering force of all that she was. He moaned in protest, yet he strengthened his grip on her all the same.

She sat on his lap, one of her hands holding onto her hat, the other around his neck and Black Bear, inhaling the sweet fragrance of her, found himself unable to think of anything else but her—the feel of her skin beneath his fingertips; the look of her lips, rosy and ripe, begging for his kiss. Black Bear watched her in fascination as he brought her head down slowly to meet him, the movement toward him so gradual that his lips were on hers before he could help himself.

"Waste Ho," he heard himself moan just before he swept his tongue into her mouth, tasting the sweetness of her breath.

Ah, magic.

She groaned, whispering his name, and Black Bear thought he would quietly go out of his mind.

He brushed his hands over the expanse of her back, down to her waist, up again, over and over until his thumb traced over the top of her breast.

It was too much, he wanted her too much and he pulled himself away at the last moment, realizing just where he was.

He rested his head against her bosom while he let his breathing return to normal. And they sat, thus embraced for a very long time.

"Waste Ho," he said at last. "I cannot hold you like this, I cannot feel you like this." And though he meant his every word, his hands appeared to have a mind of their own, for they began their search of her body again, feeling her back, her stomach, her neck, until Waste Ho, herself wimpering, leaned all her weight on him.

And then he held her. Just held her, the feel of her so good, so natural, Black Bear thought there was nothing, not a thing so wonderful as hugging her close.

And he might have let her go. He might have.

But he didn't. Cradling her head against his shoulder, he refused to relinquish her, even when she sank against him in sleep.

And silently, to himself, he whispered all that he felt, his devotion to her, and at long last, his love.

He smiled and with the intoxicating feel of her body close to his, he, too fell into an exhausted sleep, forgetting and not noticing a curiously happy Anna, who gazed discreetly out the window.

Chapter 12

"**O**h, I say. He is the most handsome specimen of man I have ever seen."

"And so broad . . . so . . . Why, bless me, but I didn't know a man could look so good. I—"

"Well, I believe he quite fancies me . . ."

"You!"

Estrela, who was strolling past Shelburne Hall's breakfast parlor, stopped. She peeked into the parlor, inhaling the wonderful smells of breakfast before entering the room and as she did so, she wondered who these women were and who could be the object of this unusually gossipy conversation.

She had never seen any of them before. Not too unusual a circumstance, except that . . .

Estrela thought back over the last few days. The entourage of the Duke and Duchess of Colchester, their two daughters, Estrela, and Black Bear had arrived at the Colchester's country estate, Shelburne Hall, only yesterday.

It seemed unlikely that the Duke and Duchess of Colchester would already be entertaining guests, and yet the presence of these three ladies would attest to the fact that the Colchesters were, indeed, entertaining.

Estrela had always wondered at the specific lack of guests who visited the Colchesters at their country home, mostly because the estate lent itself so well to receive callers.

Built in the late 1600s, Shelburne Hall had been passed down through the family, one generation after the other until the Duke of Colchester had obtained it via marriage and dowry. Stretching over almost an acre of ground, the Hall could have fit at least three hundred two-bedroom cottages inside. It boasted of well over one hundred and fifty rooms, a three hundred square foot garden in the center of the home and over twenty-five hundred feet of corridor space. It sat in the middle of green, rolling hills and was itself surrounded by over a thousand acres of gardens, parks and sprawling, neatly trimmed lawn.

An unusual circumstance, indeed, when one thought of just how little the Duke and Duchess of Colchester entertained.

Estrela gazed again into the sunny breakfast parlor, studying each of the three ladies who sat around the wide, elaborately decorated table. The women were young, pretty, and dressed in the height of fashion.

Who were they?

Estrela stepped a foot into the room, her weight cushioned by the Chinese rug that spread from one end of the room to the other, the rug's lively hues of reds and blues and pinks imitating the sky at sunrise. On the sideboard a feast of hams of all varying sizes, eggs, sausage, and pheasant were set among the scones, crumpets, and breads.

On the east side of the room, floor to ceiling windows admitted cheery sunlight while all three of the other walls boasted paintings of recent and distant family members.

The ceiling was painted white with gold trim and as Estrela glanced around, she discerned that no one else was about except these young ladies.

"Well, I think he fancies me!"

"Don't be silly," another one spoke. "He fancies none of us."

"Why, I don't believe it."

"I think you're wrong."

"Well, I believe—"

Estrela cleared her throat.

Nothing. No reaction. No acknowledgment. Everyone still spoke, no one paying her the least shred of attention.

She tried again, this time louder, stepping into the room and gliding toward them as if her feet floated above the floor.

Again, no reaction and the feminine chatter took on a high-pitched whine that escalated almost to a shriek.

Estrela smiled.

Nothing. No change, the soprano roar quite grating.

"Ladies," Estrela spoke in an attempt to gain their attention, but to no avail. "Ladies," she raised her voice and when she still received no reaction, she stepped around the sideboard, quietly taking her place at the very head of the table.

That did it. Gasps burst from the table; no matter that breakfast was an informal affair, no one, but no one sat at the head of the table except the master of the house.

Estrela knew it, and had counted on thus obtaining a reaction.

She smiled at the three ladies now, having secured their attention and said, "Pray, do excuse my ill manners." She gazed about her. "But I couldn't help overhearing your conversation as I walked by and I was wondering who it was that you were speaking of?"

"Who are you?" It was the beautiful redhead who spoke.

"Oh," Estrela answered, "did I forget my manners again? Please excuse me. I am under the guardianship of the Duke and Duchess of Colchester. I—"

"Oh, you are the one. You are the one we've been dying to meet. Why, you are the one who owns the Indian, are you not?"

"Owns?"

"Sit down," one of them said.

"Here, beside me."

"Tell me about him."

"I've heard so much about you. You've known him awhile haven't you? Oh, you lucky girl. Please sit here with me."

Estrela leaned forward, wondering if her mouth had dropped open the required two inches to show her bewilderment. She attempted to speak, but truly, words seemed to have fled her and, "I..." was all she could manage.

"Did you grow up with them?"

"Did they try to scalp you?"

"Did you ever see anyone tortured? Here sit next to me. Tell me all the details..."

"Ah, well I see you have all met." The Duchess of Colchester, followed by her daughters, hurried into the breakfast parlor, creating a stir, enlivening the atmosphere around them, bringing with her more confusion. "Oh, you poor, dear girl," she addressed Estrela, "how are you feeling now that we've whisked you away from London? I do so hope you will find our estate here more peaceful and comforting than the trying atmosphere of London. Girls, take your places at the table," she said to her daughters, then turning back to Estrela, she said, "as you can see we have company. I must say your Indian is quite an attraction. And oh, don't we have so much to do? I do hope you've met the young ladies here, and there are ever so many more people expected to arrive today. And where is your Indian friend? So noble a fellow. He does plan to join us today, does he not? Why, already the Duke and Duchess of Cambridge have accepted our invitation to the ball I'm planning—they are so dying to meet with your Indian, don't you know, and I expect, dear, that at this pace we might even expect a visit from the King himself. Oh, imagine . . ." The Duchess here left off briefly, picking up her longish gown and pacing forward hurriedly. ". . . imagine, King William and Queen Adelaide coming here—to visit me. Why, I do expect I might become the most sought-after person in all of England. Here, dear," she said to Estrela, seeming oblivious to the fact that Estrela sat, unable to absorb most of what she said, "have you had your breakfast?"

It took several moments for Estrela to put her thoughts together, just the pause her Grace was awaiting, it seeming to give her permission to speak.

"Ah, but of course you have had breakfast," the Duchess continued. "You are an early riser, after all. But come, sit here next to me while we plan our day. I do so hope you can convince your Indian to join us and to meet all the wonderful people who will be visiting us."

"I . . ." Estrela did not rise from her seat, she did, however, answer the Duchess, saying, "I believe you must ask Black Bear this, yourself."

The Duchess looked contrite. "No, dear," she said. "I'm afraid I can't do that. You see, I have already asked him and he has declined. I was wondering," here the Duchess lifted her gaze to Estrela. "I was wondering if you might have some influence over him and if you could ask him to meet the people who are coming here. They are, after all, mostly visiting us in an effort to see him. He is in much demand, you know."

"He is?"

"Oh, yes."

"Why?"

"Why?" The Duchess looked as though the simple question might cause her to faint although luckily, she was seated and no such occurrence took place. "Ah, such a pretty thing you are, my dear," she said, recovering at once, "but such incomprehension of . . . why, bless me but there I go again, you poor, dear girl. I forget that you have not been with us long. Pray, forgive my ill manners. I do so pity your background, to know that somewhere you have a noble family, and yet to have been raised in the wilderness away from all this . . . this civilization. Well, it is no wonder that you don't see it. Why, my dear, your Indian is the most popular man in all of England after he made such a daring rescue of you last week on the mall and then in Hyde Park only a few days ago. Why, all of London is talking, you know. And oh, my, bless me, but it is my good fortune to have him living here in my home, under the protection and guardianship of my husband. Ah, what a handsome fellow he is—and so noble. How can you doubt that he is so popular?"

"I—"

"Here he is now. Come, dear," she said to Estrela, as the Duchess rose to step around the table and greet Black Bear, "won't you please help me?"

"Black Bear, please sit with me."

"No, I want him to sit next to me," one of the other women whined.

"You had him at dinner last night. I get him this morning."

"He's mine at the table, didn't I say so before we came down to breakfast?"

"No. I'd like him to sit with me."

Estrela thought her head might likely burst from the incomprehension of it all. Never had she seen anything like this. Never would she have expected such a thing. And as Black Bear stepped into the room, the clatter for his attention rose to such a crescendo, Estrela thought she might likely cover her ears. Courtesy, however, forbade her this small pleasure.

What was happening here?

How could Black Bear have made such a favorable impression on so many people and in such a short time?

She recalled again the journey to Shelburne Hall. It had taken them two days traveling time to reach the estate and on the first evening that they had spent at an Inn, Estrela had shared a room with the women, Black Bear with the men.

But Estrela hadn't slept much that night, had lain in her bed with her eyes open, pondering her predicament. Perhaps the reason for such unrest lay in the fact that she had spent a good part of the day traveling in the coach, being held in Black Bear's arms and sleeping, his arms around her, his presence a soothing balm.

But that night, alone, she had run over and over in her mind what was happening with her, with him, seeking possible solutions to their problems; for it was obvious that what she was doing was not solving her dilemma, not at all.

And so she hadn't slept.

But that next day had found Black Bear mounted upon his gelding, his ride in the carriage at an end, and Estrela had been unable to tell him what she had decided: that whatever was between them, whatever the attraction, must end.

No. Instead she had moodily watched him from her seat within the carriage, watched him ride up ahead, laugh with the men and the servants, and boast of his skill by sending arrows into the sky, as many as twenty at a time.

And Estrela had realized, quite unhappily at that moment, that there was no escaping him, no sending him away, no running away.

Even if she never saw him again the rest of her life, it wouldn't matter.

She loved him. She would always love him.

No matter where he was, no matter where she was, he would be with her. If not in physical presence, then within her heart.

Forever.

It had been a daunting, sobering admission.

And though the rest of the journey had been made in relative peace, within Estrela burned a fire, one that she intended to ignore, to bank for as long as she possibly could.

Truly, she had no other choice.

And so it was with great mixed emotions that Estrela greeted Black Bear now.

She gazed at him and her stomach plunged at the sight of him, her senses spinning. Rising tall and dark among the splendor of the English wealth, he presented an enticing picture of perfect staid, English dress with a complement of long hair, feathers, and beads. It was an enticing combination of continental elegance and backwoods, American charm. His chin bore absolutely no trace of whiskers and his black eyes, as he entered the room, looked everywhere, gazed at everything, the man memorizing his environment at a glance.

He appeared foreign, wild, and utterly male; the unrestrained quality of him barely tamed and Estrela recognized, for the first time, just what it was about him that was creating such a stir.

And she sighed; she, too, was a victim of his magnetism.

"Ah, Black Bear." It was the Duchess who spoke, interrupting Estrela's thoughts. "My dear boy, come and sit by me, won't you? I do so need to talk with you."

Black Bear acknowledged the Duchess with a quick glance and a nod of his head, but Estrela saw that his attention caught and held onto her. Black Bear did not even glance at the rest of the occupants of the room. And Estrela, shifting uncomfortably, wondered at his continued observation. She looked away.

But it was impossible to ignore the man, the

clamor for his attention alone bringing continued awareness of him.

"No, come and sit with me," she heard a high-pitched voice demand.

"Me first."

"I saw him before you did. Here, with me, Black Bear."

"What do you know? He's mine today. I claimed I would have him only this morning."

But Estrela saw that Black Bear ignored them all, saw that he watched *her*, observed his roguish grin at her, causing her to wonder what he was about when he all at once said, "I believe I will sit here," choosing a chair to Estrela's left. "And," he said into a silent room where each one present seemed to hang onto his every word. "I hope you are all well-settled."

"Oh, yes, quite."

"Yes, but I—"

"We are."

"Good, then," Black Bear said, and then after a moment, ensuring he had everyone's attention, he began, "I was wondering if you all might enjoy an old Indian story as we sit here in each other's company with this feast of meat and eggs."

Estrela shook her head slowly, glancing up toward the ceiling.

"Oh, how exciting!"

"Yes, please, pray tell!"

"Here, sit next to me and tell it."

"No, I—"

"Please," Black Bear held up a hand. "It is the custom in my village that when a person talks, others listen." And to the "oh's" that filtered around the table, Black Bear continued, "I have already been at the hunt this morning. I caught much game and I have found your land to provide much meat. But," he lowered his voice as he said, "this morning I found a beautiful goose—"

"Black Bear!"

"Oh, how lovely."

"Tell us more."

"Did you sacrifice it?"

He grinned. "And do you know," he continued, ignoring all the comments, "I found the goose to be without a single gander to protect her. And after she'd had so many. Do you suppose she did not learn from her mistake? A most unwise goose. For had I desired her meat, I could have made a feast of goose flesh for our supper tonight."

He turned his head then and stared directly at Estrela.

"Ah, Black Bear, please tell the whole story."

"Yes, please."

"Well, I'd like to know if you have ever scalped an enemy."

"Oh, you silly, no. Please, tell us the story."

He smiled and gazing about the table he said, "I entertained you last night with my stories. I believe it is time for Waste Ho to speak to you now about this particular tale. I think she could tell it better than I could since she has so much experience with it. Perhaps she can tell you why the goose is so silly that she cannot pick a mate and stay with him."

"Who's Waste Ho?"

"Oh, an Indian name, may I have one, please?"

"Is that Lady Estrela? Would you know any stories, Lady Estrela?"

"What does it mean, Waste Ho?"

"Did you ever torture an enemy? I'd like to hear about that."

Estrela shut her eyes, then opening them, she looked about the breakfast table, seeing everyone there except, of course, the person sitting directly on her left, to whom she was expending so much energy ignoring.

"Oh, I daresay, Lady Estrela, tell us a story."

"Yes, please."

Estrela cleared her throat and sweeping her gaze once more around the table, said at last, "I will tell a story, if you all would like it."

"Oh, yes, please."

"Pray, believe me, we do."

"Yes, well," she said, "have you heard the story about the silly goose who couldn't decide on her mate?"

"Yes."

"Oh, a truly great story it is, too."

"Is this a story about her?"

"Well," Estrela said, "it's a bit about her, but it's more about the pompous, arrogant, self-satisfied gander who didn't have the intelligence to listen to the goose."

"Oh, how wonderful!"

"Do tell us."

"It sounds a marvelous story. Do tell it."

"Is it an Indian story?"

"Well, it is a bit like an Indian story," she said, ignoring Black Bear's glower at her. "It goes like this. Once there was a gander . . ."

"Why should he listen to her?" It was Black Bear who spoke.

"Because," Estrela said, "she might have something to say to him, that if he would only listen, might make a difference to him."

"Would it explain," Black Bear asked, drawing everyone's attention to him where he sat next to her, "why she desires more than one mate?"

And though others at the table gasped, Estrela sat her ground. "Perhaps," she said, her chin thrust forward. "Perhaps she doesn't desire more than one mate, perhaps she only—"

"Then why does she flirt when she is already taken?"

"Taken?" It was the Duchess of Colchester who spoke. "I thought she couldn't make up her mind."

"Do you want to hear this story or should I tell one about the Trickster?" She glared at the Duchess of Colchester, who sputtered and Estrela was at once contrite. "So sorry," she said. "I forgot that 'tis only a mere story."

"What is this about Trickster?"

"Who is Trickster?"

"Oh, how lovely. Please tell us that story."

"Yes, it sounds fascinating."

"I'd like to hear about scalping and about . . ."

"Oh, do be quiet." It was one of the other ladies who spoke.

Estrela sighed. "Do you know who the Trickster is?"

"No."

"Please tell us."

"Well," Estrela said, "Trickster is a legend in Indian culture. He is part hero, part god, is human and animal at the same time. He can take any form and one has to be careful when dealing with him, because one never knows what he will do."

"Oh, how endearing."

"Yes, pray continue."

"Well, this story is about Trickster in the form of a coyote. Now, Trickster loved to play tricks on unwitting people and animals and so many a story has been told about him." She glanced at Black

Bear, but noticing he said nothing for the moment, she continued. "This story begins with the day Trickster took a walk along the Big Muddy."

"The Big Muddy?"

"The Missouri River, a wide, muddy river on the American frontier."

"Oh."

"Yes," Estrela said. "Now as he walked along, Trickster came upon an eagle with a broken wing."

"An eagle?" It was Black Bear who spoke, Black Bear who uncrossed his arms and sat forward. He frowned.

"Yes, an eagle," she said, sending Black Bear an inquisitive glance. But when he said nothing, merely gazed back at her, she continued her story. "Now Trickster was interested because Eagle just sat there. So Trickster said, 'Fly.' 'I cannot,' said Eagle, because Eagle's wing had been hit with an arrow. 'Then,' said Trickster, 'you will surely die, for I will eat you all up.' "

Someone at the table gasped and Estrela stopped, looking up.

"Pray, continue."

"Yes, please."

"Very well," Estrela said. "Trickster did not realize how smart Eagle was. Trickster had played so many tricks and had fooled so many animals that Trickster grew complacent and so when Eagle said, 'I am but one bird. I have little meat. But wait. I have many plump children. If you will only help me to that rock over your head and mend my wing, I will let you eat all my children.' "

Here Estrela left off to glance once more about the table. But her audience sat enraptured and Black Bear remained quiet and so she continued, saying, "Now Trickster thought about all Eagle said. And Trickster was hungry, his hunger making him think unwisely. So he said, 'I will help you but you must show me where your children are.' "

"Oh, do go on."

"Yes."

"Well," she said, "Eagle was quite a smart character and so he said to Trickster, 'They are in my nest, way up high, a place you cannot go, but if you will only help me, I will fly to my children and tell them to come down to you.' And when Trickster said, 'Fine,' he forgot to look deeply into Eagle's eyes. And so he said, 'But you must give me your word that you will send your children to me.' And wise, old Eagle agreed."

She darted a glance to her left and saw that Black Bear had sat back, was watching her with a smug grin on his face, and looked as though he weren't at this moment teasing her. But Estrela knew him, knew that he scoffed at her silently, and had she not had a point to make, she might have left off right there. But she had more to say and so she continued, "It was then that Trickster helped Eagle to the rock, mended his wing and Eagle flew away to his children. But once Eagle alighted onto his nest, he took his children and, laughing down at Trickster, he flew away, his children and himself safe. But before he flew away, Eagle looked down and said to Trickster, 'Oh, foolish one. You have tricked many. You have killed many. But you cannot trick me. Don't you know to never trust an enemy?' " She paused and looked carefully at Black Bear. "And so it was that Trickster, himself," she finished, "was finally tricked."

Silence spread about the table at first.

Then, "Oh, that was lovely."

"And so Indian."

"My, what entertainment."

"Do you know more?"

"I'd like to hear about scalping and looting and torture and—"

"Eagle was wise," Black Bear spoke up from beside her, "to protect what was his in the only way that he could. Do you mean to tell me that Eagle should steal away with all that is his?"

"I—"

"Are you suggesting," Black Bear asked, "that one should not honor one's word when the price is too high?"

That had Estrela gasping at him. "No," she said. "I—"

"Perhaps then," interrupted Black Bear, "you should know the moral of the story before you tell it."

"But I thought the story was simply about outsmarting the Trickster." It was the Duchess of Colchester who spoke.

"Yes," said another.

"I thought so, too. Why, bless me, but I thought it was about ensuring the safety of your children."

Estrela set her lips together and, ignoring the others, glared at Black Bear. "The moral of the story," she said, "is quite plain to those who have more intelligence than that of a stupid gander. Oh, so sorry, I didn't mean you," she said to the others, then stared back at Black Bear. Eagle is supposed to fly away. Don't you see? Any animal, when faced with the same situation would fly away. Once Eagle had mended himself, he had no reason to stay. He should *fly away*," she emphasized the words, "while the chance is still upon him. And," she sprung to her feet, "the sooner, the better."

Black Bear laughed, a good, hearty laugh that set Estrela's temper to boiling all the more.

"But Eagle . . . me," he said, himself standing, grinning, "is wise only when he protects those he has vowed to defend first. And then"—his smile turned to a leer—"never mistake him. He *will* fly, but not before he teaches Trickster a lesson. Did Trickster also have the morals of a sparrow? Or was he more like the goose who would give her favors to anyone who would ask?"

"Oh!"

Black Bear smirked, but Estrela, twisting away from the table, didn't see. She fled from the room as quickly as possible, with only an occasional "oh" echoing down the long, long corridor to prove that she had once sat at the breakfast table.

Black Bear stood and uttered a formal "Ladies". So involved was he in his own thoughts he didn't hear the Duchess exclaim as he left, "They seem to get so much more out of these stories than we do. Have you noticed this?"

And to the resounding agreement that flowed all about the room, Black Bear took his leave.

Chapter 13

Shelburne Hall's ballroom could have rivaled one of Almack's Assembly Rooms—its splendor was so great. Although unlike Almack's, the Duchess of Colchester imposed little or no rules of behavior upon her guests, which caused the party-goers to sense a certain feeling of freedom.

Laughter and music filled the hall, no one noticing that the polished, hardwood floors gleamed with a deep luster under several coats of beeswax, shining as though cast under a spell from the light overhead where hung at least a dozen crystal and gold-trimmed chandeliers. Likewise no one seemed to note the Grecian statues that stood beside each entrance, nor the elaborately framed eight-foot paintings that guarded each wall. In the paintings, had one observed them, were various pictures of balls, of people dancing, of men and women in each others' arms. But no one seemed to take much notice of this at all. Attention was focused men upon the women, women upon the men and all, of course, upon the wine.

The orchestra was situated on the minstrel's gallery at the top of the room, hidden by the balcony on which they sat, only the strains of the musicians' melodies a reminder of their presence within the room.

At the east end of the ballroom stood floor-to-ceiling windows, each draped with curtains. Interspersed among them were three different sets of doors which, opening inward, led out onto balconies overlooking the lush, carefully manicured gardens of Shelburne Hall.

It was on one of those balconies now that Black Bear stood, facing into the ballroom, pensive, silent, observant.

And he saw everything, from the tight, tight black trousers of the men to the long, white or pale gowns of the ladies, with only the toes of their shoes poking out beneath the flimsy materials of their dresses. Everyone, he observed, wore gloves and the women had adorned themselves in jewelry that gleamed and glittered under the shimmering lights. No beads, no wampum he'd ever seen shone such as this.

He watched as that drink he called spirit water passed from one person to another; he watched as men promenaded the room with their women after each dance; he observed the couples dancing in the middle of the floor. But most of all, he scanned every corner of the room, his gaze inspecting the people, the servants, even the orchestra members above for signs of weapons, of ambush, of possible danger.

He could find none. And while this should have comforted him, it had the opposite affect: Black Bear worried.

Waste Ho seemed to take no heed of her situation. He looked at her now as she stood inside the room, a circle of men surrounding her.

Someone had shot at her. Twice. Someone had reason to desire her death. Twice. That someone could be here and though Black Bear had memorized the looks of those two men in Hyde Park so many days ago, he had never seen them again. It worried Black Bear. He felt he was no closer to solving the mystery surrounding these attempts upon Estrela's life than he had been that first day he'd saved her.

He watched her now as she laughed and a familiar warmth spread through him.

It was good, the way she looked, the way she smiled, standing there in a delicate, practically see-through, white dress. Cut low in front, he had an enticing view of her full bosom before the dress fell away in an angled line almost to the floor. He had noted that the style of dress here concealed little, the flimsy material on the outside of the women's clothing doing a great deal more than just hinting at what lay beneath.

He continued to gaze at her. Her blond hair was pulled up onto her head in back, while in front she left ringlets of curls adorning her cheeks and falling over her ears, the curls turning to her shoulders. Her mouth, painted delicately, was curved into a smile as she laughed up at the men who circled her; her soft, white gown neatly conformed to her figure. Black Bear, looking at her now, understood why he had risked all to come after her, trouble though she was.

He remembered again the conversation he'd had with her maid and friend, Anna.

The maid hadn't told him much, only that Waste Ho had made a promise long ago and that he,

Black Bear, should not be "fobbed off" by Waste Ho's marriage.

He set his lips and narrowed his eyes.

Just what did that mean?

Did the sanctity of marriage mean little here in this foreign land? Was it a common practice to know another intimately? Another besides one's wife or husband?

Black Bear tilted his chin upward.

It would seem so.

In these past few weeks, since coming to the "country," Black Bear had received practically every invitation known to man from the fairer sex, whether that woman be married or not.

He had been passed notes, requiring the Duke of Colchester or Black Bear's own manservant to interpret. Notes of liaison, notes of passion. He had been propositioned; he had been waylaid. He had even come into his chambers to find a woman there—in his bed.

And through it all, Black Bear had steadily ignored them or carefully declined, though it was taking quite an effort to continue to do so. But he had determined that he wanted Waste Ho and if he couldn't have her, he wanted no one.

Still . . .

He saw her glance his way and he wondered what she thought. Did she love *him*? If she did, why was she married to another? If she didn't love *him*, why did she respond to him so completely whenever he held her? And why, he questioned himself, was he holding her when she *was* married? Where was her husband?

He shook his head, and deciding he would get no answers tonight, turned his gaze elsewhere.

The Duchess of Colchester's shrill laughter reached out to him and Black Bear found himself smiling. He glanced at the woman, all dressed in bright yellow; he was not in the least surprised to find her two daughters standing neatly behind her, both of them wearing various shades of yellow, too. They reminded him, the three of them, of a mother duck and her two ducklings and he had fallen into the habit of calling her *magaksica*, the Duck, and her two daughters *mahcinca*, the Ducklings. The women seemed thrilled with their new Indian names, not even concerned over their meaning, and Black Bear had found himself more and more amused.

And while he appreciated Lady Colchester's hospitality and her congenial manner toward him, he was not unaware that she used him—or at least she tried to. But Black Bear was not the sort of man to do others' bidding and soon a sort of "truce" had been made between him and the esteemed lady— a mutual understanding that Black Bear would do as he saw fit, that the Duchess of Colchester could pretend his ideas were her own and that as long as her plans did not interfere with his own, he would suffer her introductions.

The smile remained on his face as he continued to stare at her. And he realized that the lack of guests to the Colchester estate might likely lie in the fact that the Duchess, good-natured though she was, made others feel uncomfortable. Her prattle tended to bore.

But Black Bear couldn't complain. The Lady and her two daughters were most kind, and generally, they amused him.

"Ah, there you are."

Black Bear brought his gaze back and to his left,

where, looking through the tall shrubs, he espied the Duke of Colchester, standing on yet another balcony.

But the Duke wasn't talking to Black Bear, he was speaking to another, whom Black Bear could not see.

Black Bear crouched down. He listened.

"What have you determined?" It was the Duke who spoke.

"Not very much, Your Grace."

He heard the Duke of Colchester sigh.

"We look for the housekeeper. No one knows where that lady has gone. She might even be dead," he heard another voice say. "All others are gone or are dead—some very recently."

"Is that so?"

"Yes, Your Grace."

"And how did they die?"

"A knife, Your Grace. A bullet. A sword. The usual."

"And all recently, you say?"

"Yes, Your Grace."

There was a pause and Black Bear strained forward to hear.

"Jolly inconvenient, wouldn't you say?"

"Yes, Your Grace."

"Well, keep at it, I say. There must be someone left from the Earl's old estate who would remember her. Someone who might remember—what? A manner of address." Here the Duke paused. "Did they call her 'Lady' or did they call her 'Your Highness?' Do you see? Such a thing would hint at her heritage. There must be something."

"Yes, Your Grace."

"There, there, now. Just keep looking, keep investigating. Not a word to the others, now."

"Yes, Your Grace."

"Jolly good. You may go."

And as Black Bear looked over to the other balcony, he saw a dim shadow move toward and through the doors.

You may go. The phrase ran round and round Black Bear's mind. It was the same one he'd heard Waste Ho utter on many occasions. And what was a manner of address? *Your Highness or Lady?* What did it mean?

The Duke of Colchester knew something and Black Bear determined that soon, he too, would have that same knowledge.

It was a pledge.

What did she do?

Black Bear stared out onto the dance floor some time later.

There stood Waste Ho dressed in her white gown, looking good, looking beautiful. But she had paused in the middle of the room, in the center of the dancers.

Other dancers swirled around her in a circle, some looking at her, most ignoring her.

She didn't notice. She gazed around the room, but her glance alit upon nothing and Black Bear could only wonder what she did. Then he saw it.

A round, black box, in the middle of the floor.

She knelt beside it gradually, setting an arrow down along one side of it and a knife on the other.

And Black Bear could not believe what his eyesight demanded was true.

It could not be. It was not possible.

She was married. Hadn't she admitted it herself? What was she about? Was she trying to bring the spirits down upon her with her lies? Didn't she know it didn't matter to him? She didn't have to risk all to lie to him.

He took a deep breath.

This was for his benefit; no one else would understand the ceremony. He had best step forward and stop her now. It was either that or accuse her for the liar she was.

Or was she?

He took a quick glance around him to ensure that there was no danger to her, at least for the moment. And then, cautiously, silently, Black Bear moved out and away from the shadows.

Estrela was tired. She was angry and upset. He had accused her of harboring loose morals and of infidelity one too many times.

Well, no more; Black Bear would learn the truth. It was something she had decided after that breakfast so many weeks ago. Black Bear might not listen to her, he might think she spoke with a two-sided tongue, but he could not, he would not ignore the contest she held, the virgin ceremony.

It was a direct challenge to Black Bear. Estrela knew he would not be able to set aside what the ceremony proclaimed. For the contest she held, the virgin ceremony, was a solemn oath, a pledge of chastity. And no Lakota maiden participated in it lightly. It was believed that if she claimed she were pure and were not, disaster would befall her.

Estrela set the round box in the middle of the dance floor, the arrow on the right, the knife on the left.

She knelt before it and placing her hand in the box, she prepared to wait.

* * *

"Oh, Black Bear, do you dance?"

"I saw him first."

"Here, Black Bear, I have a note for you. Will you please read it in private and give me an answer?"

"Oh, my, but I would like to talk with you."

"Do you like English society?"

"However did you come to be here?"

Black Bear stopped at last, taking stock of the fact that he could go no further. He was surrounded by women, many of them. Not an uncommon occurrence of late.

He sighed. He had to reach Waste Ho before she did damage to herself unnecessarily. Did these women have nothing better to do but to cater to him as a novelty? It was becoming a wearisome, daily task to simply deflect their attentions without at the same time doing great damage to their pride. And Black Bear feared that he might, at some future date, be too truthfully honest, hurting beyond repair the poor lady to whom he might vent his frustration.

"Oh, here, sign my dance book, won't you?" A young lady shoved a book at him and Black Bear jumped back, out of the way.

"I cannot write," he said to the dear, young girl, giving her back her book.

"Won't you dance with me?"

"I cannot dance," he rejoined with a shrug.

"Come and speak with me, won't you?"

He smiled. "Forgive me, but I . . . do not . . . language . . . speak . . . not good."

"Well, won't you come and have some dinner with us?"

"I do not eat . . . no, I did not mean . . . I—"

"Do you women want husbands overmuch that you cannot leave my brother alone?"

Black Bear, startled, glanced up. And had he been anything but American Indian, he would have grinned. All he did, however, was stare, although in his eyes was a light of warm recognition.

"Oh, my!"

"Bless me!"

"Oh, tush!"

Black Bear heard the feminine gasps and its many equivalents repeated again and again as he watched the three men on the outskirts of the circle of females.

He smiled at last. There, directly before him stood his two Lakota friends, accompanied by the German Prince, who was waving and attempting, even at this moment, to shove his way forward.

"Excuse me, dear lady," he heard the Prince say. "Pardon me. I beg your . . . oh, dear me, aren't you a beauty?"

Prince Frederick, Prince of a small, but influential German duchy edged his way through the group, bowing frequently and coming to stand by Black Bear. "Took me a long time to find you, friend," he said under his breath.

Black Bear merely looked at the man, saying nothing, observing the necessary silence that was considered good manners among the Indians. At length he said, "I have been occupied."

Prince Frederick leered at the ladies before turning to his friend, to say, "So I see."

Black Bear might have laughed, but he didn't. Instead, he nodded to his two other friends over the heads of the ladies present.

"Oh, there's more of them, look!"

"I get this one."

"Do you dance?"

"Will you tell me all about where you are from?"

The crowd soon expanded, circling and enclosing not only Black Bear, but the other two Indians and one German Prince.

"However did you meet all these ladies?" the Prince asked Black Bear.

Black Bear grunted. "I did not want this."

"Shows what taste you have."

"Yes," Black Bear said. "It does. And, friend," he stressed the word and in the tradition of their easygoing bantering, said, "your comment tells me much about *your* love life."

"Ouch!"

"Pray, this one is more handsome than the other."

"I daresay, look at this fine fellow."

"Bless me, look at their clothes."

Black Bear glanced over to his friends and smiled. It was good to be momentarily forgotten and spared the attentions that *he* had been battling daily.

He Topa, Four Horns, the first of his friends, attempted to draw away from one of the ladies; he bumped into another. Wasute Sni, Never Misses a Shot, Black Bear's cousin, frowned, but it didn't daunt the young women he frowned at, not one bit.

Black Bear grinned, unsympathetically staring at his friends.

And he heard the ensuing battle, listened to one of his friends say, "I think you mistake me for someone I am not. I have no need of a wife."

"Oh! You are not married yet?"

"I . . ." it was He Topa who spoke. "Speak

not . . . language . . . not good. Not good . . . all."

Another lady laid her hand on Wasute Sni, saying, "Why, my dear fellow, you look positively kissable."

Wasute Sni had always been much more the rake than his two friends. He looked down at the lady now as she spoke and smiled, saying, "You may try it, if you like."

The young lady giggled. "Oh, my!"

She kissed him.

Another lady saw it and did the same, another and another.

"Ladies, ladies," Prince Frederick addressed the procession of women. "Can't you tell how tired these young fellows are?" And, in Lakota, to the two Indians, "Look tired both of you." Then to the ladies, "Have pity upon us, please. We have just arrived here from London. Must you ply them," he continued, "with kisses and hugs and pleas for their attention?"

The Prince glanced at a smiling Wasute Sni, who bore all the unmistakable evidence of rouge and lipstick smeared over his face. The Prince simply smiled, muttering, "Perhaps I should rephrase that question to the ladies."

"I want him to dance with me."

"I want to kiss him."

"Here, let me."

"No, no. Ladies, ladies," Prince Frederick interceded. "We are greatly fatigued. And we must go immediately to bed."

"Oh, I'll accompany you."

"Let me. I'll take you. I know where the rooms are."

"Ah, that was not my plan," the Prince said.

"Mayhap I should . . . ah . . . restate that." Prince Frederick looked around him. "Wasute Sni, get that grin off your face. He Topa, grab your friend. We must—"

"What does she do?" It was Black Bear who spoke, Black Bear who roared, "Does she not realize the chance she takes?"

Prince Frederick looked up then, Black Bear's questions being more command than question.

"What is it?" the Prince asked, abandoning the other two to their fate and retracing his steps back toward Black Bear.

"My friend," the Prince said, "have you found her? Was she the one who I hear you rescued? The one all the rumors are circling about?"

Black Bear nodded.

"Which lady is she?"

Black Bear merely inclined his head in the direction of the dance floor.

The Prince looked, squinted, looked again. "I am no more enlightened than I was before, my friend. You will have to be more specific. There are too many people dancing for me to tell—"

The Prince broke off. Black Bear wasn't listening. He was already moving away toward the middle of the dance floor and as Prince Frederick watched him go, he wondered what was wrong with Black Bear.

He looked as though he'd seen a ghost.

She saw his approach.

Her stomach plummeted at the sight and she almost lost her courage. Almost. But she had gone this far; she would go the entire journey.

He would know the truth.

She watched him as he came ever closer. She ignored the other women as they tried to pull him aside. They were not important here. This was between the two of them, her and Black Bear, alone.

He maneuvered between dancers, among people and their partners, coming ever closer and closer to the center of the room until finally he stood before her.

He stared at her. She at him.

A moment passed. Another.

At last, with her hand still in the round box, she picked up the knife. She put it between her teeth and looking straight at Black Bear, she bit it.

It was a highly symbolic gesture. With her hand in the hole of the box, she proclaimed she was a virgin; when she bit the knife, she vowed before all, even the spirits themselves, that what she said was true.

And Black Bear, barely believing what he saw, stared at her.

He Topa came up behind her.

He smiled and Estrela, seeing him, removed her hand from the box.

He Topa knelt, put his hand in the box and picking up the arrow, bit it. For a male, this too proclaimed his celibacy.

Estrela gazed at him and smiled.

She looked at the floor, then at the couples who continued to dance in the circle, and finally at He Topa.

It was quite a long moment before Estrela found the courage to glance up at Black Bear.

But at length, after taking a deep breath, slowly, so very, very gradually, she raised her gaze to meet Black Bear's.

He stood rigid, unflinching, his face carefully

masked to hide what he might feel, though his chin jutted out, and he looked at her as though she were stalked game.

Then at last, with a motion of his hand, telling her in sign exactly what he thought of her ceremony, he spun around, striding from the room with such intent, others gave way at his approach.

He never looked back.

And Estrela, watching him, wondered if the ceremony had been worth it.

He knew it now. He knew and yet he'd left her just the same.

Estrela lowered her gaze to the floor and picking up the box, the arrow and the knife, she prepared to leave the dance floor.

Is she available?

No! Black Bear answered his own question. *She is married!*

Or is she?

Black Bear stood within the shadows of the balcony and looked back into the ballroom with such an intensity in his gaze, it was a wonder the glass in the doors did not shatter.

Was she lying?

He didn't think so. Her eyes had been clear, her cheeks slightly flushed when she had bit the knife.

There were no signs of her lying and yet . . .

He thought back to what he knew about her. There was no man in her life now and no one could remember seeing her with a man—ever.

Anna had said that he should not be "fobbed off" by her marriage.

Was she truly . . . ?

Black Bear shook his head as though the movement might shake his thoughts loose. He had left her there in the middle of the dance floor, not because he was angry with her and not really because he didn't believe her. No, he had left her there because what she did, what she told him via the ceremony was too much for him to accept all at once. She was a virgin.

He needed to think.

Think. Wasn't it what he had been taught all his life? That a truly great man will think before speech, before action. Hadn't he needed then, as he needed now to come to terms with all that the ceremony proclaimed?

He thought back to it.

She had bit the knife. It was not something she would do if the facts were not true.

Which meant . . .

Black Bear's head spun and he felt lightheaded. His heart seemed to swell in that moment, though, and as Black Bear surveyed her out there on the dance floor, he ventured to think thoughts he had dared not consider ever since that day he had learned of her marriage.

If the contest were true then . . .

Among his people, the contest she had given was well-known. It was a statement of virtue, a contest given by virgins, for virgins, especially those whose chastity had been questioned.

When a woman bit the knife or a man the arrow, it was a sacred vow. No liar ever did it without severe consequences. No liar survived the test. It was a bold statement of fact; it said for the woman "I have never known a man intimately."

It must be true.

Was she available?

There had been no misfortune to her, no harm

to tell that she lied. To the contrary, He Topa had befriended her, himself biting the arrow.

She was married!

Or so he thought.

But if what she said were true, then . . .

He watched her as she participated in the dancing and as he did so, his heart raced so fast, he might himself have been dancing, he—

" 'Tis a waltz."

Black Bear darted a look around him.

Prince Frederick stood beside him, the light from inside clearly illuminating his tall frame, and Black Bear sighed.

He had been so deep in his thoughts, so intent upon contemplating Waste Ho, he hadn't even noticed his friend's approach until the man was right upon him.

"I tried to teach you that one," Prince Frederick said. "Do you remember it?"

Black Bear nodded. "Why does he hold her like that?"

"Ah . . . yes, I see it," the Prince said. "Look at them, Black Bear. Everyone is dancing the same way. I daresay, I suppose I forgot to teach you how to hold the woman when you waltz. You could do it. You hold the woman like this." The Prince held up his arms. "Do you see?" He moved around the balcony. "It's a three-step. One-two-three, one-two-three, around and around as though you are . . ."

Prince Frederick glanced around him.

He stood alone on the balcony.

"Black Bear?"

But there was no response.

And as Prince Frederick gazed back into the ballroom, he saw that Black Bear was already striding purposefully toward the dance floor.

The Prince shook his head. But not one to contemplate a situation for long, he shook the handkerchief from his pocket and opened the ballroom doors wide.

Chapter 14

Estrela watched his progress from the corner of her eye. He crossed the room, women gathering around him, but he ignored them as though they were mere distractions. He looked at *her*. He watched *her*.

She nearly swooned. And though it was what she'd hoped would happen, she still felt unprepared for it.

Did he believe her or was he coming to accuse her?

Would he publicly disavow her? Or . . .

"Black Bear," she muttered.

"I beg your pardon?"

"Oh, so sorry," she said to her partner.

She had forgotten where she was. She glanced up now, her gaze searching through the crowd for Black Bear.

She found him.

He stood against the wall, directly in her line of vision. As she looked at him, she thought she had never seen anyone more handsome, nor anyone so—what? *Angry?*

She gulped.

His glance held her own as though she were imprisoned and Estrela felt as though she could not look away from him without consequence.

He looked that determined.

He was dressed in black suit and tails. His shirt was of a thin white-linen; his pants, black. And as was fashionably correct, his pants were skin tight, leaving nothing to the imagination. His coat was double-breasted, cut to his waist in front and falling into a long tail in back. On his hands he wore gloves, on his feet, boots; but around his neck was the symbol of his heritage. He wore a beaded, bone choker that boasted a pink shell sewed carefully in front of the beads and the bone. The shell seemed to glow, presenting the only color upon him and creating quite a contrast to the constant blacks and whites that society demanded he wear.

He had pulled his hair together on one side and secured it with buckskin, while he had left the other side free. Two eagle's feathers dangled there.

His look was determined, proud and fierce, and his grace as she watched him walk, was as beautiful as the steps of any dance, as the notes of the music itself. Estrela beheld him, she stared at him; she could do no more than admire him.

He reached her at last, his gaze so powerful, Estrela lost her step.

Estrela muttered an apology to her partner, but it was unnecessary. The procession of dancers moved on in the continual, swirling motion of the waltz, her lost step forgotten.

Excitement raced through her at Black Bear's continued stare. He wanted her. She knew it by his simple glance.

Would he wait for her to finish the dance? Would *he* dance with her? Her heart tripped over at the thought as her partner whirled her around and around in the ever constant procession of dancers.

A swing, another one and she glanced to where Black Bear should have stood, but he was no longer there. She had but a moment before she would be swung around again, and she took that moment to search the room for Black Bear.

He was nowhere to be found.

Another swirl.

She looked up. Her heart must have stopped, then picked up double-time. There he was—right there, on the sidelines, watching her, watching their movements, his gaze following them.

Another whirl.

Her partner stumbled, recovering quickly and swinging Estrela back around to the intoxication of the constant motion.

And with each swirl, Estrela sought out Black Bear's gaze, until—

Where had he gone?

Her partner mumbled something, missing his step in his flurry to turn Estrela.

And with the next rotation Estrela saw it. Several steps ahead of them, Black Bear waited . . . waited for her.

Such was unorthodox behavior for the prim, English society and had an Englishman done the same, he would have been "cut" from the more dignified social circles. But not so Black Bear. Perhaps it was because he didn't care what was thought of him; perhaps it was because he was too foreign, too charismatic for anyone to find fault. Whatever the cause, no one seemed to care that he suffered a momentary lapse from correct, English manners.

And as Estrela danced closer to him, emotion

surged through her. She stared, she gaped.

He waited for her. He would have her.

With each gyration of the constant movement, she swirled ever closer and closer to him until at last Black Bear loomed before them, blocking their path.

To his credit, her partner tried to stop, but he couldn't; the waltz, as though endowed with a life of its own, kept the man going on, dancing. He had no choice, her partner, but to maneuver around Black Bear, not realizing that it was useless to do so.

And then it happened.

Black Bear shrieked, his voice raised in a high-pitched cry.

Perhaps it wasn't meant to startle. Perhaps. In truth it was how Black Bear would have responded to her contest tonight, to the dance he would have done in his own country, his voice raised in song, in pleasure. But no one in England was to know this.

For a moment the dance might have stopped. The sound of Black Bear's cry certainly had that effect upon everyone, if only for the moment.

The orchestra, however, apparently unaware of the disruption on the floor, played on, encouraging the dancers to continue the waltz.

And the procession continued, the couples swirling around the hall, their passion for the dance more powerful than their momentary fright.

But not so Estrela's partner. He now stood slightly away from the dancers and stared directly at Black Bear; the Indian blocked the path forward.

It didn't take the Englishman long, however, to make his decision. Without a word being spoken, the young man bowed to Estrela, nodded to Black Bear, and left the floor.

Black Bear was quick to act, and with one fluid movement, stepped forward. He encompassed Estrela in his arms and swung her back into the procession of dancers, continuing the waltz without falter as though he had invented the dance, himself.

As Black Bear swung Estrela around the floor, he stared down at her. She gazed up at him.

His hand captured hers. His arm encircled her waist. He held her closely to him, his movements against her erotic. And Estrela luxuriated in the feel.

He did not smile at her. He didn't need to.

He gazed into her eyes, instead, his look potent, inquisitive.

It was all that he did. He didn't try to woo her. He didn't say a word; he merely looked at her. But in his gaze was an emotion, something he even now tried to hide, but he couldn't. Desire, it said, passion, devotion as strong as the willow, as sacred as the cottonwood. For her.

And as Estrela gazed up at him, at his foreign, yet handsome features, she knew him, she knew his thoughts. His dark eyes held her own, his stare at her intoxicating in the constant, whirling motion of the dance they performed, his hair rushing back with their movements.

"It is true, then." It was no question he asked. And his whispered voice, so close to her ear, sent tingling sensations running over her skin, her neck, down her spine. And Estrela basked in what could only be seduction.

"Yes." It was all she could say. "Black Bear, I—"

"We will talk later."

She gazed up at him.

"For now," he continued, "I want only to feel you in my arms and to know it is true."

"Yes." She said, closing her eyes. She felt it, then, his being, the very essence of all that he was. The allure of it, of him encompassing her, cradling her. It was good, it was beautiful, he was beautiful and Estrela, caught up in the knowledge of all that he was, could only stare at him.

"I want you." It was Black Bear who spoke.

Estrela moaned in response. It was a soft sound, barely over a whisper, yet Black Bear seemed to lose himself to it for he groaned in return, the sound a deep growl low in his throat.

"I want you," he said again.

Estrela's stomach plummeted and her body responded to him as though they were alone.

She whispered back to him, "And I want you. *Ciksuya Canna Sna Cantemawaste*, when I think of you, my heart is happy."

She felt him sigh against her, although his arms stiffened around her and his step became more wooden. But she didn't say a thing.

In truth, she was struggling to keep her composure, for she felt swamped with her love for him. Her feet kept time to the music, but Estrela felt lost, lost in his gaze, lost in the magic that was Black Bear.

And as she looked up at him, she was bathed in sweet realization. She loved him, she *would* love him, she would let him make love to her. It was a daring thing for her to do, and yet it was right. She knew it. Nothing that felt this good, that brought her such happiness, could be anything but right.

And perhaps the Earl, wherever he was, could forgive her. Just this once.

Her life here, her marriage, her search for her family, the Duke, the Duchess, all of it was fading away as though all these things were nothing more than mere shadows against the overpowering love she felt for Black Bear. And she knew in that moment with full certainty that her life from this moment forward was irreversibly intertwined with Black Bear's.

Forever.

She would never tell him. She would never even pretend it was so. She would even let him go afterward. But it didn't change the facts.

She would always love him.

Black Bear looked down at her and she saw him breathe in deeply before he closed his eyes, if only for a moment. Perhaps he felt it, too. His dark eyes had fastened onto hers and he had smiled at her before he swirled her around the floor in perfect rhythm, holding her ever closer and closer.

Yes, perhaps he felt it, too.

And then, not even missing a step, her thoughts all jumbled, he kissed her, once, twice.

Magic. The moment was alight with sweet magic. Estrela clung to him as though he represented life itself, unaware that the dance had stopped, although the music kept playing.

The dancers, too, had stopped, every gaze within the ballroom turned their way. But the couple in the middle didn't notice and as Black Bear kissed her once again, sweetly, ever so reverently, many a sigh was heard from their audience, certainly no censure.

The orchestra began another song, the dancers moving again to the intoxicating rhythm of yet another waltz, swirling around the couple in the center who appeared to be unaware of anything in the room, save themselves.

And though Estrela did not see it, there were many people in the room who were not scandalized by what they saw, who smiled at them. Caught up in the whirling movements, the dancers moved on, the young couple in the middle protected from view by the ever rhythmic swirl of the waltz.

Black Bear touched her cheek, her neck, her hair. He brought her hand to his chest, over his heart and there, beneath the light of over a hundred candles, he kissed her. It was a powerful moment, a time of renewal, of reawakening; Estrela knew that despite all, no matter the future, her devotion to him would never die.

She might send him from her as she was bound to do, but it mattered little.

The fact remained. She loved him.

She always would.

It was a vow.

Chapter 15

The heavy drapes billowed in and out with the midnight breeze. Fresh, dewy fragrances from the courtyard below filtered in through the curtains and Estrela took an appreciative sniff of the succulent air.

A particularly strong gust of wind blew in at that moment, causing her to look toward the window, there watching the shadows sweep across the curtains.

She sat in her bed with the sheer drapes pulled back toward the high bedposts. She waited for him; she knew he would come.

She hadn't felt the need to say anything to him as they had parted from one another at the ball only a few hours earlier. She knew he would seek her out, in her room, tonight.

And so she waited, barely able to breathe, daring not to think.

The winds were high this night and another frisky breeze blew open the heavy curtains that hung over the doors, bringing with it the cool temperature from the outside and the fresh scent of aromatic grasses and bushes.

Estrela rose, her body naked beneath the sheer, silk of her nightgown. And as she paced to the doors, which opened up onto a balcony, the fragile lawn of her nightgown blew back, outlining the curves of her figure, the material flowing over and around her, moving with her body, the feel of the soft, flimsy cloth a heady sensation against her own body heat. She placed her hand over the sturdy linen material of the drapes, but before she pulled them closed, she gazed out into a sky littered with stars and boasting a full, golden moon.

A shadow flitted across the moonlight.

She gasped.

"Are you phantom or real woman?" The voice was low, barely above a whisper; the words spoken in Lakota, and close to her ear.

She turned just sightly, there confronting Black Bear. He stood beside her, a scant few inches away, dressed in no more than breechcloth and moccasins. She hadn't heard him come up beside her, but then, she shouldn't have.

"How long have you been here?" she asked, her gaze taking in all of him; his bare chest, his abdomen, the way the breechcloth fell over his—

She shot her gaze up to his eyes, a half apology in her glance.

But he merely smiled at her and reached out a hand toward her before he repeated, "How long have I been here?" He took his time answering, letting his own glance roam the length of her body until at last he said, "Long enough."

She turned in full toward him then, repaid for her efforts by his indrawn breath before he said, "So beautiful. So—"

He stared at her; he reached out a hand toward her, touching her lightly, gently; his hand, opened, outlined her hair, the silvery strands of which

gleamed as though with a life of its own, set off
from the light of the moon, the stars, the very heavens.

"Do you understand what it is I want of you?"
he asked and she nodded.

He groaned then before he wrapped her in his
arms. And Estrela sighed, comforted by the heavy
beating of his heart.

"I wanted to tell you about it, about me," she
whispered. "I tried to tell you in so many different
ways, but I—"

"Shh—" he said. "I know now. It is enough."

Estrela nodded.

"You are sure you are ready," he asked, "for all
this will mean to you, to me?"

Again she nodded and he sighed.

"Ah, Waste Ho, you are as potent as spirit water," he said, nuzzling his face against hers. "And
I want you."

"Black Bear, I—"

"Do you want me?"

She gulped. "Black Bear, I . . . please—"

Whatever she would have said was cut off as
Black Bear ushered her back into her bedchambers,
leaving the doors wide open. The small wax candle
by her bedside flickered with the draft that blew
in, throwing fleeting shadows over the couple
where they stood outlined against the dim light
from the moon.

"Black Bear," she said, "I do want you. I—"

It was all she was permitted to say.

His lips captured hers in a kiss that had his
breath mingling with her own, his clean scent fill-
ing her senses.

"Black Bear . . ."

She had never felt this good, she had never felt

anything like this and as he raised his head, his eyes still closed, he shivered.

Estrela felt it straight to the bone. What was between them was powerful, was good, was more than she had ever thought it could be. And she could never remember ever loving anyone more.

"Ah, Waste Ho," he said, raising his hand to her face. He inhaled sharply, letting his fingertips trail over her eyes, her nose, her cheeks, seeking the feel of her as though he were blind. "I have waited for you," he spoke to her in Lakota, "for this too long. I fear for my own control. Shh . . ." he said when she would have answered. "Just feel, Waste Ho. I think I have died these past few weeks thinking that another man has had you. And now that I know that you . . ." he shuddered, "that you have never been with a man, I want you to remember always this, your first time. I—"

"Black Bear, about my marriage, you—"

"Shh—" He smoothed a lock of her hair back from her face. "We have much time now, you and me. We will know all there is to know about one another, but not now, I think."

He kissed her again, only this time he brought up one hand to trail a path down over her throat, slowly—as if afraid he might miss some sensitive spot. The feel of it, the sensation was almost more than she could take and Estrela fell in toward him.

But it didn't seem to bother Black Bear. He simply held her more firmly. He gazed down at her as she looked up to him, but he didn't stop the movement of his hand. Down further and further he touched her, until at last he reached her breasts.

Estrela gasped and Black Bear, in response, brought his head back to gaze at her. He groaned then before he lowered his head, his lips touching her own.

Ah, the feeling. The exquisite feeling. And as shock wave after shock wave reverberated through her body, Estrela thought she would surely faint.

But he wasn't finished with her. First he nudged her lips open with his own, then his hand, where it lay on her breast, began to squeeze the soft mound of her flesh, first one, then the other breast, his fingers circling the rosy tips until her nipples became hard nubs pushing forward against the fine material of her nightgown.

And this time, Estrela's legs would not hold her.

She melted against him, her own body useless to her will, yet seemingly alive to his.

"Waste Ho," he muttered as he drew his own smooth cheek over her own. "You try my very control. Forgive me if you push me over the edge. I try," he said. "I will try to hold myself back."

Estrela nodded although she had no idea of his meaning.

He set her away from him, if only a tiny bit and she saw that he watched her. He gazed at the slight gown where she felt it fluttering over her skin; he touched her hair, the sight of his darker hand amid her long, pale curls intoxicating; he stared down at the pale patch of color there at the junction of her legs.

His gaze was potent, too much, and as if to add to the sensuality between them, the wind chose that moment to invade the room, blowing back the flimsy material of her gown, toying with the silky curls about her shoulders.

And he caught his breath.

She sighed, leaning in against him. The feel of the wind, cool against the heat of her body, was creating such sensation within her, she thought she would go mad if he didn't touch her again, and soon.

She moaned. And as though in slow motion, his gaze sought out hers. They stared, he scrutinizing *her* face now as he had earlier done with her body. And Estrela wondered which was more sensuous: the feel of the wind or the potent caress of his glance.

But Estrela, unused to the heady sensations of lovemaking, felt too shy.

She turned her head away, hiding her face under the silky curtain of her hair.

"*Hiya*. No," he said, reaching out a finger to gently touch her chin, bringing her glance once more to his. "Do not be embarrassed. You are beautiful and I have longed for this moment it seems for most of my life. Permit me just a moment longer."

Estrela looked up at him then, her embarrassment fading into a new feeling, a strange sensation that began at the junction of her legs, spreading upward and downward. A sensation that demanded her attention—and his.

She could stand it no more. She reached out toward him, though he stood a mere inch away.

It was all the encouragement he required. He reacted, seizing her hand in his own while with his other hand, he drew the nightgown over her head, permitting him a clear view of her. And this time his hands followed where his gaze explored.

Estrela took a sharp breath.

"*Waste Ho*," he said, "I hope you are truly ready for this, for I fear I can stop myself no longer." And with this said he touched her most feminine spot with one finger, there seeking out her intimate secrets, Estrela aware that her own body moisture welcomed him more readily than any words she could have spoken.

He didn't hesitate now. Watching her every re-action, he prodded her legs further apart with his knee, and at her acquiescence, felt her feminine need.

She moaned and strained against him as he held her in his arms.

"Waste Ho," he groaned in reaction to her. "I need you. I must have you. Are you ready for me? Waste Ho, do you want me?"

"Yes," she whispered without hesitation, the nod of her head telling him her answer, too. "Please."

He picked her up in his arms then, and with a few short steps to the bed, he lay her down on it, himself coming to his knees beside her.

She looked to his face and marveled at him, this dark, handsome man, whose touch sent fiery sen-sations over her body.

He held her hand. He didn't do anything; he didn't say anything. He just held her.

At last he lifted his gaze to hers. And there, as she looked to him, she saw his need, usually so carefully hidden, now etched into his features.

She reached out. "Black Bear . . ."

"Shh . . ." he whispered. "Just feel it, Waste Ho. Feel me, who I am. It is all yours tonight."

And then he began to touch her. Up and over her breasts, down between her legs, over her calves to her feet, up again to her head, down, over and over until Estrela felt she might burst with sensa-tion.

"Black Bear," she almost cried out. "I don't know if I can stand it. Please."

He looked up to her and Estrela saw him gaze at her intently before he rose to his feet, looming over her.

He removed his breechcloth and Estrela gasped. She had never seen anyone look so magnificent, nor anyone so—

"Black Bear," she said, "aren't you a little too . . . what I mean is . . . how can you fit?"

He smiled. "Do not worry," he said, a touch of humor to his voice. "We will manage."

"Oh." It was all she said.

She watched him as he leaned over her; she watched as he parted her legs, as he touched her.

And then, never looking away from her, he thrust into her.

She cried, but he was right there, easing her shock and her pain with a kiss.

He waited several moments while she accustomed herself to the feel of him. He lay on top of her, holding his weight away from her with his arms, himself still hard within her.

"I must do this now," he whispered in Lakota. And then he smiled. "It will hurt for just a moment longer, but do not fight it. I promise you, there is more to this than just pain." And then he withdrew, waited, thrust into her again, over and over.

Estrela gazed up at him as he lay atop her and marveled at his male perfection. She set her hands against his chest, now moist from his exertion. And with each drive against her, she, too, strained against him.

And then it began to build.

"Feel it, Waste Ho," he said, reading every sign within her body. "Let go, Waste Ho."

Her own skin became moist. Her own exertion crescendoed. And soon she was straining against him as frantically as he was with her.

"Come on, my love," he coaxed her. "Feel me within you. And know that from this night forward, you are my woman. Come feel the passion between us."

And though she heard him, his words, his meaning didn't really register.

It had no chance. She was beyond thinking.

The pleasure kept blossoming inside her, kept building.

"Stay with me, Ho," he urged her. "Feel me. Feel the pleasure I give you." He took her hand in his own as they strained against one another, carrying her hand toward his heart. And with his eyes staring into hers, he smiled before whispering, "Stay with me."

And Estrela thought she would burst.

She strained, she twisted, seeking a release she didn't understand.

And then it happened.

Eyes wide, pleasure exploded within her and she held onto Black Bear, he being her only salvation in a sea of swirling emotions.

And when she looked up to him, he smiled, saying to her words she never expected to hear.

"Now let us do it again."

And though Estrela could barely believe him, he proceeded to show her exactly what he meant, bringing her once more to the point of release. But this time, when she reached her peak, he followed her, the force of his pleasure driving into her again and again.

Expended, he collapsed against her and Estrela sighed in contentment.

Never had she known such pleasure.

She smiled and gazed at him. He already lay asleep in her arms.

She touched his back, felt the expanse of his long hair against her fingertips and she murmured, "I love you, Black Bear. I always have. And I hope that you will remember this." She sighed. "For when morning comes, I will still be married."

And with this discouraging statement, she adjusted his weight into a more comfortable position and holding him tightly to her, knowing, yet fearing this would be their only night together, she drifted off to sleep.

Black Bear, although not plagued by such a troublesome thought, dreamed nonetheless; a horrible, terrifying nightmare. And if it were vision; it was the part of his vision he'd not understood.

He tossed and turned, helpless within the dream, but he didn't cry out; nor did he awaken.

The raven swooped toward the nightingale. The nightingale flew, but she was no match for the black bird. No matter where she went, Raven followed.

Nightingale flew away home, across the sea; Raven followed. She stayed in England; Raven was there.

She could not escape and Eagle was powerless to help.

He even now heard the cawing of Raven as the huge bird plunged down, down toward helpless Nightingale.

He had her in his claws. He had her imprisoned. Her life drained away, until . . .

Black Bear awakened.

A cold sweat ran over his body.

He shook his head, his whole body.

And then, startled, he glanced over to where Waste Ho should have been.

He heaved a sigh of relief.

She was still there, safe, protected, asleep. But could he always keep her by him, safe?

He thought back over the dream.

Eagle had been there, way up high, unable to do anything. Watching, waiting. Eagle. Himself.

But who was Raven?

He didn't even question the identity of Nightingale: Tonight he had seen that Nightingale was female. And he was certain it meant only one thing: Waste Ho Win, Pretty *Voice* Woman.

Black Bear lay back down in the white man's bed.

He needed a medicine man to help him interpret the dream.

No other Indian was here except . . . Black Bear thought back to his two friends, both here in England. Both men were great warriors; neither, however, was a man of *woksape*, wisdom; he needed a powerful man, a medicine man.

No, he could not speak to either of his friends about this. It was his alone to resolve. He would have to draw on whatever *woksape* he possessed.

He only hoped it would be enough.

But of one thing he was certain: He could not yet leave to go home.

And though the thought plagued him, he would not, he could not show it in his manner. He must not yet return home. And not just because whatever trouble that pursued Waste Ho would follow them there. If he returned home now, he would never discover the identify of the enemy. Here, at least, he had the chance. Here, the enemy was close at hand, if only he could discover him.

He allowed himself one deep sigh before stoically setting his features to reveal nothing. Oh,

how he longed to see the familiar landscape of
home; how he longed to take Waste Ho there.

But it was not to be. At least for now. He would
first have to find the danger to her. He would have
to seek it out and confront it here.

There was no other way.

Rolling over, Black Bear sighed and cuddled up
toward Waste Ho where, taking her into his arms,
he fit her soft body to the hard contours of his own.
It gave him a momentary feeling of safety, though
he didn't fall back asleep for a long while, his troubled thoughts unwilling to be stilled.

And it was several hours later that Black Bear,
still awake, came upon a sudden realization, so
sharp, so unexpected, it had him leaping up in bed.

That was it. His vision, the one where he'd
known he'd had to become an Englishman if he
were to help Waste Ho, Estrela. He'd not had it
right.

He didn't have to *become* an Englishman. No, he
had to learn to *think* like an Englishman.

A subtle difference, but very important.

If he were to stalk this enemy and find him, he
would have to *understand* the Englishman, learn his
habits, his intentions. Wasn't it what the Indian did
on his own land? Wasn't he taught to think as the
animals did?

And so, too, did he need to learn the habits, the
aims and purposes of the English.

Black Bear lay back down. It would begin today.
He would watch and observe everything. And he
would do something he had been taught as a child
never to do: He would ask questions. He had to.
There was not much time left.

He took Waste Ho once more into his arms and
smiled, at last able to fall into a untroubled sleep.

*   *   *

Estrela awakened with a dire need to tell Black Bear something. What was it?

She looked over to him where he still slept and smiled at him. Then, she frowned with doubt.

What had she done?

She was still married, still as deeply bound as she had been before, only now there was a difference.

She was no longer a virgin.

Why? Why had she done it? Why had she told Black Bear she was a virgin?

Surely she had known the results of such knowledge upon him. Surely she should have envisioned that Black Bear would come to her, make love to her.

She frowned. Yes, she'd known and yet she had gone ahead and done it anyway. And if she were truthful with herself, she would admit to having wanted him so much, it hadn't mattered.

But she wasn't quite so honest and so she let herself believe, if only for a moment, that she'd done it because he had angered her. Angered her with his snippy attitude and insulting remarks.

The morals of a sparrow! Indeed!

She sighed.

What was the use? She was fooling no one, least of all herself.

She'd wanted him. It had been that simple. The rest, her anger, his teasing, her defense, were nothing but excuses.

She had wanted him. That simple.

In truth, she had little defense against him, and what bit of it she possessed, had been battered down by his needling, his sensuality and her love, her love of him.

But it couldn't go on. She had to make what had happened between them a one night incident.

She had given her vow to a friend on his death-bed.

Estrela frowned. Why did it matter so much to her?

Why couldn't she just take Black Bear and pretend the rest of this didn't matter? It didn't really—did it?

She sighed.

It shouldn't matter and yet it did. Why?

Honor? Trust? Duty?

The Lakota had taught her the value of these virtues, and now one of their own made her question her belief in them.

Estrela moaned and relaxed back into the bed.

These virtues were everything. No matter what she did, she had to live with herself. Yes, the Indians had instilled in her the importance of keeping her word, the value of trust. But there was more to it than just this; it was an ingrained sense of duty that was all her own. A feeling deep inside that her self-worth depended upon her ability to keep faith, to stand by her word, no matter the consequences.

She almost cried. To break her word would be as to break herself.

Could she do it? It was a testimony to the amount of devotion she felt for Black Bear that at this moment she even considered it. It would mean a lessening of herself in her own estimation.

Should she do it?

She gazed at Black Bear as he slept. He looked strangely vulnerable in sleep and it was more than Estrela could do not to touch him, an action that would assuredly weaken her resolve further, since it would awaken him.

But she reached out a hand anyway, needing to feel his long, dark hair where it lay against the silken sheets of her bed.

She shouldn't do it. She shouldn't.

It didn't matter. She touched a dark strand of his hair anyway, glorying in the sensation of such a simple action. She inhaled the musky scent of him, this early morning, the fragrance enticing and all his own.

She shut her eyes.

She could never remember such intense feeling for another person. Never.

What was she to do?

Black Bear would consider that she was his now. He would not understand her withdrawal. He would resent it and her.

But what choice did she have?

She grimaced. She shouldn't have done it. Hadn't she just told him via her story of the Trickster that he should leave—and that he had even agreed? Didn't she truly think this was best for him?

But Estrela, with a surprising insight, realized that maybe it was this that had caused her to do it. Much as she said she wanted him to leave, much as she encouraged him to do so, she also knew that if he left, so would end her happiness.

But wasn't that selfish of her? What could she offer him, after all?

An affair?

It would never work, one reason being that Black Bear would never allow it. Another being that she simply couldn't do it to him.

He deserved more. He deserved a wife who loved him and a family.

Something she couldn't give him.

Unless . . .

What if she found Sir Connie? What if he were already married? What if he granted her a divorce?

Yes, and what if he demanded the marriage be consummated?

Estrela caught her breath. She couldn't do that. She couldn't risk it.

At least living alone was better than living with a man she didn't love.

Oh, what was she to do?

Her doors still stood open from last night and a cool breeze filtered inside, calling to her, begging her to come outside.

Perhaps she should.

Perhaps she should go outside for a walk . . . or for her early-morning ride.

She stared out the doors, into the new day and though it was still dark outside, the pale shades of dawn were beginning to brighten the eastern sky.

Why not?

Why not go for her ride now? Yes, it was a little earlier than her customary morning ride, but what did that matter? Perhaps the exercise would clear her thoughts enough that she might see a solution to her troubles, which now eluded her.

She wouldn't be missed.

Black Bear still lay asleep and it would be several hours before Anna would invade Estrela's rooms, since most ladies in the country did not arise much before eleven o'clock.

Yes, that was it. She would go for a ride.

Her mind made up, Estrela arose silently, and pulling the nightgown over her head, she prepared to go out into the new day.

*   *   *

The view from Edgehill, which was only a short ride from Shelburne Hall, was spectacular.

It was early September and everywhere around her she sniffed the unmistakable scent of fall, the air crisp with the smell of fallen leaves and cut hay, the haystacks rolled and standing golden in most every field within her vision.

The sky was blue, the fields a mixture of different hues of browns, greens, and golds. The hedge in front of her stood heavy with blackberries and to her right were bright, red rowanberries. The leaves were brown, golden, or red depending on the bush and as Estrela looked out over the land of little rises and valleys, slopes and ridges, she felt alone and suddenly, very strange.

She had traversed over the countryside this morning, keeping away from the narrow roads and lanes, passing by small hamlets and sleepy villages, her journey on horseback always onward, seeking escape from her thoughts and, if she were truthful, for a solution.

She sat sidesaddle now and as she looked out over the landscape, a cold wind suddenly whistled and swept by her, spooking her mount and leaving her with a feeling of being haunted. And Estrela, as she calmed her horse, tried to remember what she had been told of this place, Edgehill, of the battle that had occurred here almost two hundred years ago, but she could remember little about it, except that it had been a civil war between King and Parliament.

It is said of most battlefields that they are haunted, and Estrela realized that this one was no exception. For she felt alone all at once, and yet in company, an odd feeling. And as she continued to gaze out over Edgehill, she thought that she could see the armies, hear the panicked whinnying of horses, the commands from officers yelled about the field, and the moans from the wounded, the dying.

She shook her head to escape the mood and gazed instead at the sky, the deep blue increasing by the moment and wispy clouds beginning to scatter in the sky.

It was then that she felt her saddle slip.

Startled, Estrela grabbed for her horse's neck. The saddle slipped further and Estrela realized with horror that her feet were caught in the stirrup.

She tried to ease her feet out but she slid further down and two things happened all at once: Her feet kicked her mount and her arms flailed backward, hitting the horse on the other side.

And her animal, already spooked, leaped forward, Estrela barely astride.

Estrela screamed, gripping the horse around the neck. She held on tightly, too tightly, for the strength it required only exhausted her arms. But she realized that her grip was her only salvation. With her feet trapped, if she let go she would either fall forward to be dragged by the animal, or she would fall under the horse.

Either way, she was doomed.

It was a dire realization. It was also a fact and Estrela, unable to do more than hold on, screamed.

Chapter 16

Black Bear tossed within the confines of the silken sheets.

He dreamed now and he couldn't awaken himself, so intense was the dream.

Nightingale lay dying, in pain, an object beside her that Black Bear had no way to identify. Small, the thing an earthen mixture of clay, it stood beside her, unrelenting, imposing, filled with . . . a potion.

And Eagle soared above her, unable to help her, unable to do more than look at her.

She implored him to help and he—

Black Bear awakened, automatically reaching for his weapons.

Something was wrong. Something had awakened him; a voice, the feel of a hand on his shoulder. Something.

He shot out of bed, glancing around, but he saw nothing. No one was here, and yet, he felt a presence in the room.

Spirit. A spirit had awakened him.

What was wrong?

He tied his breechcloth on around him and slid his feet into his moccasins in one swift motion.

He glanced at the bed; no surprise. He'd known she wasn't there.

Waste Ho was in trouble.

He heard her voice. At that very moment, he heard her screams as though she were right beside him.

He panicked. Somewhere out there, Waste Ho was in trouble—now.

He knew it. He didn't have to dream it, he didn't have to picture it. He knew it with utter certainty.

He was Indian. These awarenesses were not something he could ignore.

Her life was in danger and he had to find her—or lose her.

Terror filled him. Terror at the knowledge he carried; terror that he might be too late.

He panicked at first, rushing around the room, trying to think, and it was with tremendous effort that Black Bear forced himself to remember the grandfathers' teachings.

He must calm himself. He must think clearly. He must track her.

Track her. Where had she gone? Where would she go first thing in the morning? Think like a white man.

Riding.

Waste Ho had gone riding. Again certainty came to him.

Black Bear burst from the room, tearing through the house and blazing out into the stables.

He didn't ask for a horse, he knew at a glance which animal was the best and, ignoring the groom, he jumped onto it, trotting the horse out into the yard where, picking up Waste Ho's tracks, he shot the animal across the lawns and fields of Shelburne Hall.

And a thought occurred to him as he tore over

the landscape: the enemy stayed within Shelburne Hall.

Both he and the Duke of Colchester had sought to escape all danger by coming into the country.

Instead, they had carried it with them.

Whoever tried to kill Waste Ho, knew the movements of the family. And Black Bear, putting into action his decision to think as the English, realized that the enemy came either from the Duke's own household or the aristocracy itself.

Nowhere they went would be safe from the assassin.

It was a sobering realization.

Waste Ho was clearly out for a leisurely morning ride. And lucky for him, she had avoided the major intersections and paths.

Her trail was as easy to follow as if she had purposely led him here.

He came upon Edgehill and he shuddered, feeling the spirits of an age long past. A battle had taken place here. He could feel it. Ghosts haunted the grounds.

Was it a ghost that had spooked her horse? Was that what had happened to her?

He read all the signs of what had happened. She had sat here awhile, but something had happened. He slipped off his horse's back to study the hoofprints in the grass.

Those prints, he looked at the ground, were barely discernable in the grasses, while those a little further on were deeper and further apart, the horse at a run.

Something had startled her horse.

He knelt down to feel the clues left behind.

They were fresh. He might be in time.

And as Black Bear mounted, urging his horse across the fields, following her obvious trail, he wondered why he worried. Waste Ho was an excellent rider. She would never panic over this. She would easily bring the animal under control.

Why hadn't she done that?

It was then that Black Bear saw it, as though he had been there at the time. Her saddle slipping, Waste Ho trapped by her stirrups, holding on to the horse's side.

It was an odd phenomena, this knowing exactly what had happened, this being able to read the impressions left behind on the landscape. Yet he did it as easily as another might read a newspaper.

He spurted his horse onward, into a frenzied run over the countryside while he sent a prayer to Wakan Tanka, willing Waste Ho to hold on.

And with every ounce of his being, he tried to endow her with strength from afar.

Estrela slipped further and further down the horse until she was practically standing in the stirrups alongside her mount. Closing her eyes had somehow given her more strength to hold on, but the effort was almost too much. Already her arms shook under the burden of her own weight.

She didn't even bother to scream anymore, all her attention was caught up in holding on.

I can't do it. And she felt her arms slipping.

She cried, knowing the disastrous result of letting go, and though her arms shook and her strength ebbed, something wouldn't let her give up. She couldn't.

Her horse leaped across something—a stream. Up, up in the air; down, down, hard.

She lost her grip. She screamed, thrown into the air. But as she came down, she lunged forward, catching the horse's mane in one hand. It was all she had. She'd slid down on the horse even further.

Hold on. I am not far away.

What was that?

Was she hearing things?

Hold on.

"Black Bear." She actually said it through her sobs, then, "Black Bear?"

She heard another horse.

Was it Black Bear's?

She heard someone riding up beside her, she felt someone touch her, but the touch soon left her.

She heard a voice, Black Bear's. She felt the wind from his own mount at her side; she felt her horse begin to slow.

It was minimal at first, but gradually, her animal's pace eased into a canter, down into a trot, and finally the animal fell into a walk. And Estrela sobbed with relief.

She couldn't let go, though. And with her eyes tightly closed, even when she knew the horse no longer moved, she could not let go, her hands seemingly frozen into position.

But he touched her. He spoke to her in soothing tones. He complimented her and Estrela finally mustered the courage to let go.

It was a traumatic thing. She had to will her hands to open and when she did, she fell into Black Bear's arms.

He held her closely to him and she sobbed, she pummeled his chest, she laughed and then she sobbed again. And Black Bear did no more than stand there, holding her, whispering to her in his own language, in her own language, until at last,

Estrela fell into a quiet cry against his shoulder.

She'd heard him. When she'd needed strength, he'd been there. He'd saved her life. And she? What did she plan to give him in return? She cried all the more.

She couldn't do it and yet she had to. And this fear, added to the other trauma, could have been her undoing, but Black Bear shushed her, whispering to her in her ear, his grip on her ever tighter and tighter. Until gradually, so very slowly she didn't at first notice, her tears fell away.

She simply stood within his arms.

They made an unusual sight on this early morning in September. The dark, handsome Indian holding the pale blond beauty.

And as Black Bear held her body against his, he realized that he had received help from a highly unlikely place. From the very spirits themselves.

He smiled. So this was not a cursed battlefield filled with demons. Ghosts, yes. But certainly not demons.

And Black Bear, always one to acknowledge the actions of another, murmured a prayer of thanks.

She felt just right in his arms.

He shivered, but whether from the coolness in the air or from the yearning to possess her, Black Bear could not be certain.

He had almost lost her.

He didn't know why it was affecting him in this way. Since he had arrived in England, he'd "saved" her twice already, but this time . . . this time he knew her intimately and the thought of losing her . . .

It was not even a concept he wished to explore.

He felt her now as he embraced her. Her slight body fit into the grooves of his own hard contours, her velvet riding habit warm and soft against his skin. Her hair smelled fresh, clean, and as crisp as the autumn air; her skin, where she lay her cheek against his chest, felt smooth and delicate, her breath sweet, her tears a welcome distraction.

He breathed in deeply, relishing the scent of her hair, her skin, her perfume.

He loved her. He intended to have her.

He'd not told her in words; he wouldn't, but every action he took, every movement he made expressed his devotion to her more clearly than words ever could.

They stood on a rise overlooking green and golden fields and ripe hedgerows. Concealed beneath the trees, they had a view of the red-gold landscape below and anything that might happen there, while they remained, themselves, hidden and unnoticed.

The horses, tethered, grazed off to the side.

Black Bear pulled her in, if possible, more closely toward him.

He rubbed his hands up and down her back, lower still over her buttocks. He bent his head and nuzzled her neck, sweeping his tongue over every bit of skin there.

She tasted sweet, like nectar and his head reeled with the intoxication of her.

He lifted his head to caress her cheek with his own and then slowly, as though they stood outside of time, he brought his lips to hers, gently, a tender exploration.

At first.

But she was so responsive to his caress, Black Bear could not contain himself.

He deepened the kiss at once, his tongue invading the dizzying warmth of her mouth, and she returned his passion, meeting his every overture.

It was almost his undoing, but he held back.

He bent down slightly to rub her buttocks more fully and in doing so pulled her off her feet.

He held her with one hand while the other groped over the unfamiliar material of her dress, seeking buttons, ties, anything that would allow him access to her skin, before he became too frustated and thought to rip the material.

But she pulled away, still caught in his embrace, her feet off the ground.

"Oh, Black Bear," she said. "What do I do?"

Black Bear didn't understand why she said what she did, but he soon forgot to wonder. She was breathing heavily and her hands, of her own volition, loosened the buttons to her outfit, throwing off her jacket, her skirt, her chemise. Layer after layer, she peeled off clothes and Black Bear, unable to look away, smiled slightly to see the amount of clothing hidden beneath her outer garment.

But at last she stood within his embrace, naked, shivering in the cool, autumn air.

Ah, the feel of her soft skin beneath his fingertips. He set her feet on the ground. And while his one hand cushioned her bottom, holding her tight, his other hand reached upward to caress a ripe breast.

She moaned and threw her head back and Black Bear almost lost himself. He despaired, wanting her, unsure if he could wait.

But he needn't have worried.

Waste Ho was ready for him, her hands even now untying the strings that held up his breechcloth until at last, he stood firmly within her grip.

It seemed to excite her and he heard her breathing grow labored.

He pulled her up off her feet, then, spreading her legs around him and driving himself within her moistened sheaf.

Ah, the sweet warmth of her, the overwhelming strength of her response. She twisted her hips against him as he pulled her closer to him.

He didn't need to talk, to whisper or to coax her. She strained against him, seeking a pleasure to which she was no longer innocent.

And as he held her in his arms, he gazed into her eyes, seeking to witness the desire there in those blue depths.

She looked at him, her glance filled with longing before throwing her head back, exposing her neck to his kiss.

And he did kiss her, he embraced her, he rocked her where she rested on him, at the same time restraining himself, waiting until she had reached her conclusion.

He relished the moist film he felt on her body, he beheld her passion as she twisted against him.

And as she brought her head back upright, he gazed into her eyes.

"You are mine," he said, watching her heated response, witnessing her pleasure build and build. "You are mine," he whispered again. "Feel me. Tell me, Waste Ho. Tell me you are mine."

He heard her moan, he heard her sigh, but she didn't otherwise utter a word. He listened as her voice grew louder until at last he heard her scream; the silent, autumn atmosphere cushioning the sound. On and on it went, and just as she reached her climax, he whispered, "You belong to me, and

Waste Ho, sooner or later you will admit it."

And as he reached his own pleasure, Black Bear realized that all between them was not yet won. Waste Ho still held back from him.

But he smiled. Little did she know, it was not something he would allow.

It was a vow.

Black Bear gazed at her from over his shoulder.

He watched her as she dressed under the cool autumn sunlight, debating whether he should tell her what he'd discovered or not.

At length, he said, "Tell me about the aristocracy." He glanced at her. "How does it work? Why do some people have so much while others have nothing? And how," he asked, "can such people have power when they do not share what they have with others?"

Waste Ho, Estrela, looked at him and he stared back. "I am not sure," she said, at length. "I do know that it has been so ever since they were conquered by the Normans so many years ago. Or perhaps it could be that the English have been conquered so many times by so many different people that they no longer care about one another. All I know is that there is a central group of people who seem to have all the wealth and power and then there are those who cater to them. Why, I do not know."

Black Bear nodded. He was silent, studying the frayed saddle that he held in his hands, until he asked, "Do you come from the aristocracy?"

She hesitated. "The Duke thinks so."

"Humph." Black Bear glanced away. "What would be a good enough reason for someone to want to kill another? Power? Wealth? I do not understand. Are these things alone enough to make someone desire another's death?"

Waste Ho sent him a concerned look. She gazed at him a long while until finally she asked, "Why?"

He looked back at her. "I understand," he said, "revenge. I grasp why another would seek revenge if only to settle a wrongdoing. I understand the need to defend what is yours. What I do not understand is why someone would want to kill you."

He held out the frayed saddle for her inspection. He fingered the leather buckle there, the jagged edges where the leather had been cut. Deliberately.

He glanced over to her. "Your accident here today"—he motioned to the surrounding area, then to the saddle itself—"it was no accident."

She gasped, looking down, then away.

"Do you have any idea," he asked again, "who might be doing this and why?"

Waste Ho shook her head. "No."

He sighed. "Tell me, is power and wealth alone enough to have another want to kill?"

Estrela sent him a startled gaze. "Yes."

It was then that Black Bear smiled. "Tell me," he said. "Why?"

And as Estrela began to explain about wealth and land, estates and money, title and power, Black Bear began to understand little by little the thought processes of the English.

He might not agree, but at last he began to understand.

Chapter 17

"**Y**ou will stay in your room."

"I will not."

"You will."

"You cannot make me."

"Shall we see?"

Estrela stomped her foot. She knew it was childish, but she couldn't keep herself from doing it.

"You waste my time," Black Bear said. "I cannot stay here and guard you. There are others I must speak to this morning. There are other things I must do. Until I am finished, you will stay in your room."

"So, you do not allow me to go down to breakfast?" she asked. "You do not allow me to visit with friends? And how am I to eat?"

She knew she was being unreasonable. Anna could easily bring her a tray. And in truth, someone, just this morning, had attempted to take her life. She should be grateful to Black Bear.

Perhaps.

No, she supposed she should thank him and yet, why didn't he *ask* her to stay in her room? Why didn't he *consult* her, instead of just ordering her?

She gazed over to him where he stood, staring at her—one moment—another. And she looked back, their gazes dueling. Both knew what they were doing. Both knew that in Indian society a stare such as this meant certain insult, for a Lakota Indian will always avert his eyes to show respect.

At length he sighed before saying, "Waste Ho Win, you know it is not safe for you to leave your room. Must I remind you of where we have just been?"

"I have to eat," she said, "and I had wanted to visit with friends today. There are so many people staying in this house."

Black Bear shook his head. "Why do you argue with me about this? Is it not for your own good? I do not understand you."

"But I understand you, Black Bear. You think just because you have made love to me that you can control my life." She placed her hands on her hips, the action emphasizing her next words. "Well, you can't. You don't own me."

"I most certainly do."

She gasped. "What do you mean?"

He smirked. "Did you not give me your favors, not once, but twice? Did I not find you to be a virgin? Am I not the only man who has known you? Did you not tell me you loved me?" He placed his arms, crisscrossed, in front of him and scoffed. "No, Waste Ho," he said. "Make no mistake. You belong to me."

"Oh!"

She turned her back on him.

They stood in her chambers, having just returned to Shelburne Hall. Black Bear had followed her to her room, was even now standing here, making demands; had started doing so as soon as they had entered.

What was even more frustrating was that it was

still fairly early in the morning. There were only a few other people up and about, only a few people she could speak to at this hour. So why did he demand she stay here?

Besides, she felt safe within the house. After all, if she were truly in danger, couldn't the stalker just as easily come to her room? Wasn't she really safer among other people?

He might have his reasons for what he did, but it didn't matter to her, not at this moment. His orders, without regard for her own opinion or her own feelings, wounded her. It was as though she were some imbecile who couldn't think for herself. A degrading thought, a degrading feeling.

No, she would not do as he asked. She could not afford to submit to him.

She reacted instead.

"You do not own me," she said it quietly, turning around toward him. Then she looked away, presenting him with her profile. "The only man who owns me is my husband. And that man is not you."

From the corner of her eye, she saw him flinch.

"I disagree," he said, his voice deep, with no expression whatsoever. "I did not notice your objecting to me. You are the one who performed the virgin ceremony, otherwise I would have . . ." he didn't finish. "Who is this man?" Black Bear continued saying. "This man who marries you and then leaves you, who does not even touch you? I say he is no husband. I say you are not married." His voice became more emphatic. "You are mine now."

She turned her back on him. "I am not."

Black Bear sighed. "We argue for nothing. It matters little to me what you say. You gave yourself to me. You belong to me. You will stay in your room."

"No! And I . . . Black Bear." She spun around. "What?" Her eyes rounded.

He stood before her, a sheet from her bed in his hands, his knife slashing at the material, making it into . . .

"No!"

He sighed. "I dislike doing this, but you give me no choice. I have told you that you will stay here. I have tried to reason with you. I have tried to warn you. You are too stubborn for your own good. I think I will change your name to Stubborn Woman for all the trouble you give me." He gazed at her her. "But I mean it when I say you will stay here."

"You wouldn't!"

Black Bear didn't even deign to give her an answer.

Instead he moved with the silence and speed of a cat, catching her and lifting her off her feet.

"Oh! Stop this at once!"

For answer Black Bear threw her to the bed.

She scrambled away, but he was too quick for her. He'd caught her foot and he pulled her back toward him as she struggled.

"You can't do this to me. I do not will it. You will cease this at once."

She might have been talking to a stone wall for all the effect it had.

So she kicked out at him instead. She would have scratched him, too, but he deftly avoided her hands, grabbing her feet and tying them first.

"Anna will be here soon," Estrela complained. "She will untie me."

"She will," he said, "but not until it's too late. I

will tell her you are troubled and didn't sleep well and want to remain undisturbed."

"And why would she believe you?"

He gave her an incredulous look, grabbing her hands as she struck out at him. "Do you think she doesn't know that I have been with you every night, guarding you, since I first came to this land?"

"She never said anything to me."

"There is nothing that escapes her notice. She is as deft within this household as an Indian is upon the plains. No, she will understand that I have been here, that I have seen to you and that you wish more rest. Only later will she discover you."

"Oh!"

He laughed as he finished restraining her hands. He set about fastening the "rope," tying her hands to the headboard, her feet to the footboard.

"How can you do this to me? Not only do you tie me hand and foot, but you strap me to the bed."

"After all you have said to me, how can I trust you by yourself? If I don't bind you, as soon as I leave you will find a knife and cut through these straps. And then you will parade yourself outside where you are an easy target. No, Waste Ho, you will stay in your room as I have ordered."

"I'll scream."

He grinned. "I do not stop you."

She gave him a curious glance.

"Of course they will find you naked."

"You wouldn't!"

His only answer to her was a leer.

His job finished, he looked down on his handi-work, and Estrela swore that he grinned over what he supposed was his own brilliance. She didn't see the fire in his glance as he knelt next to her at the bed, his hands reaching for her.

He drew his knife, reaching for her clothing.

"No!"

"If I leave your clothes on, you will scream and escape and all my work will be for nothing."

"Untie me, then," she said.

He shook his head. "You will leave," he said, setting the knife toward her.

"No I won't," she said. "I will take my clothes off. It's all I will do."

He nodded then, sheathing his knife and leaning over to untie her hands.

She nodded to her feet while she rubbed her wrists, but Black Bear shook his head, saying, "One thing at a time, only."

She watched him closely before she ordered, "Turn your head."

And Black Bear laughed. "I think Stubborn Woman forgets," he said, "that I have already seen all she has to offer."

"That's different."

He merely smiled. He didn't say a word, he just looked.

But when she hesitated, he drew his knife and she immediately set her hands to her coat and, taking it off, to her blouse.

"You could look away from time to time," she complained. "You don't *have* to watch me."

"I think," he said, "that Stubborn Woman forgets that I still have knife."

"Oh!" was her only response as she stripped down to her chemise.

He motioned toward it.

"I have to take off my skirt."

He waved to her then, saying, "Proceed."

Estrela harrumphed before carefully pushing her riding skirt to her ankles, Black Bear removing the skirt completely and then retying her feet.

She sat then, in her chemise. It was her only remaining covering.

And he motioned toward it.

She removed it reluctantly, pulling the garment away from her in a lazy, slowed pace.

But at last the garment was off and as Estrela lay it aside, her gaze sought out Black Bear's in one, shy glance.

She looked away and Black Bear, taking her hands, tied them back together, then fastened them to her headboard.

But Estrela averted her gaze.

That's when it happened.

He started with her cheeks, caressing first one and then the other.

Estrela stiffened and tried to turn her head, but she couldn't avoid his touch.

"Don't," she said.

"Shh . . ." was his only answer as he trailed his fingers over her lips, down over her chin, to her neck, finding each and every pulse point along the way.

"I don't want this."

"I know," was all he said. "Please forgive me, Waste Ho. You are so beautiful, I cannot keep away."

Estrela groaned. And try as she might to pretend indifference, she couldn't stop the warmth that spread through her body at his touch, at his words.

He took his time. He stroked her, he fondled her, his fingertips tracing over her shoulders, her arms, her fingers, his palms coming close to but never quite reaching her breasts. And everywhere he grazed, Estrela felt the lingering warmth of his touch.

"So beautiful," he whispered as his fingers brushed the back of her neck.

"Please," Estrela said, "don't do this to me. This can't be right. I feel so wicked."

"Shh . . ." he said. "There is nothing wrong. Have I not said you belong to me? Is there anything wrong with giving what is mine a little . . . joy? Now, shh . . . Just feel."

He stroked her then, his touch, his every fondle as a kiss upon her heated flesh. She wanted it. She'd deny it if he asked her, but he didn't. And as she lay there, bound, unable to refuse him anything, she thought she would die if he didn't soon start to feel her in much more intimate places. She whimpered, she twisted and despite herself, as he caressed her shoulders and chest, she arched her back to him in quiet invitation. Black Bear moaned then, his only reaction as his hands reached out toward those softened mounds she offered him and Estrela sucked in her breath as he molded first one and then the other velvety breast in his hands, his fingers circling their rosy tips. Then gradually, so slowly she barely even noticed, his fingers dipped lower and lower, but still he didn't touch her in that special place at the junction of her legs.

Estrela almost screamed her frustration.

She wanted him. She wanted his touch. But, lord, she didn't want him to know it.

"Black Bear, please stop. I can't let you . . ."

"I wish," he said, "that I had tied your legs apart."

"No!"

He smiled at her, the warm smile of a lover.

"I mean no offense, Waste Ho. I only wish to see all of the beauty of you. With your legs together as this, I cannot view . . . you."

"Please," she said. "I don't want you to talk to me this way. I don't wish you to . . . see me."

"You do not?" he asked, his fingertips trailing over her skin to her knees, her feet. "Shall I prove you wrong?"

"Please."

"Please what? Please yes? Or please no?"

"Black Bear, I can't . . . You try my very patience."

He smiled at her and Estrela, despite herself, nearly swooned from the effect of it. This was not the smile of anger, of antagonism, or even a gesture of warmth. This was the look from one lover to another.

He kissed her then.

And although Estrela knew she shouldn't, she surrendered.

His mouth explored her own. The touch of his fingers passed from one breast to the other, down, down further and further till he reached that spot between her legs.

She bucked against him, her only attempt at protest.

He smiled, his lips close to hers. "So beautiful," he said. "I only hope that when I leave you, your perfume will remain with me, for I may never wish to wash again."

And though his voice teased her, these were still heady sensations he was sending her, heady words, and Estrela was becoming a willing victim to them.

At last, his touch fell to that area of her anatomy that proclaimed her need.

Estrela moaned. "Black Bear," she said, "this can't be right. You have me tied. I can't . . ."

"Shh . . ." he whispered. "If you were not mine, if you did not belong to me, I might agree with you. But there is much medicine between us." He brushed a lock of hair away from her face. "Do not worry. What is between us is good."

"No, I can't let you." She squeezed her thighs together, an attempt to thwart him. The result, however, was not the one expected and none was more stunned than she when a hungry desire began to build there between her legs.

Black Bear merely grinned at her.

"Just feel it, Ho," he whispered. "Not many people can claim so much medicine when they love. What we have is special. Even I did not know there was so much between us when I came in search of you. It is a gift, Waste Ho. Enjoy it."

His touch found her then, that exact spot that made her squirm with desire.

Still, she wasn't ready to give in.

She twisted, little knowing that the more she resisted, the more avid a pleasure built within her. And it was this discovery that was as unexpected as it was unintended.

She stared at him as he leaned over her, watching her. She was caught in his trap, in her own trap of sensuality and desire—for him. The spreading heat betrayed her. And try as she might, she could think of no way out of it. No matter what she did, no matter how hard she protested, the result was the same. The pleasure built and built within her.

She might protest being tied, she might object to

his method, but she was as much a part of it now as he was.

She gazed at him, her eyes pleading with him, but she knew she no longer pleaded with him to stop.

Instead she sighed.

He smiled at her and Estrela noted that all the mockery in him was gone.

"You surprise me," Black Bear said to her, his voice low, gravelly. "There is much more passion within you than I had ever hoped to discover. I am pleased. Come, Waste Ho, there is nothing wrong in what we do here. We are united, you and I. Let me give you one more pleasure before I leave you this morning."

This said, he pressed his lips to hers again and all the while his fingers continued to create that special magic within her.

"Feel it, Waste Ho. Feel it," he coaxed her as he lifted his head. He watched her and Estrela could no more help moaning and twisting, groaning and bucking than she could stop him from wreaking this havoc upon her body. On and on it went, Estrela twisting back and forth, no longer caring to protest. At length, the pleasure built within her until she could stand it no more. And still it crescendoed and crescendoed until she screamed, Black Bear quieting the noise by placing his lips over hers. Her body shuddered in pleasant reaction while her heartbeat raced and Estrela sucked in air, quickly, deeply.

He sat with her while her breathing quieted and her breasts ceased to heave. He still knelt beside her, his fingertips continuing to massage her. And only when he had assured himself that she had recovered, did he sit back, grinning at her.

After several moments he said, his voice teasing, "Tell me again, Waste Ho, that you are not my woman."

It was the wrong thing to say.

It reminded her of her exact position here.

It restored her anger.

She looked him in the eye. "I am not your woman."

He laughed.

"Your strength pleases me," he said. "But remember that I am your man, no matter what you say. And do not forget that I will always ensure that you follow my orders. It is useless to defy me. What I do is for your own good."

"Untie me," she said. "Only then will I believe you are my man. What good am I to you if you don't trust me?"

He laughed again and Estrela, despite herself, thought how pleasing a sound it was.

"I do trust you, Waste Ho." He grinned again and shook his head. "I trust you to disobey my orders, to run around all over this country where you make a fine target for someone. Yes, Ho, I trust you to ensure you get killed if I do not do these things to prevent it."

"Oh!" It was all she could think to say. He had spoken too closely to the truth.

"You will be fine here and I will be back before the sun sets," he pulled away from her and stood. "Until I return, I wish you only the happiest of dreams."

He stepped away from her, treading toward the doors in her room. But before he left, he stopped, hesitated, and looked back to her. "I will give you one last chance," he said. "Promise me you will not leave your room and I will untie you."

"I . . ."

"Remember that you are Lakota."

She hesitated, then, "Untie me, Black Bear," she said to him. "This is so unnecessary."

His smile was his only reaction. With a shake of his head he trod through the open doors and just like that he was gone, as swiftly and silently as a phantom.

Chapter 18

Hours later, Black Bear sought out the Duke of Colchester, whom he found pondering over stacks of papers in a room the English called the "study."

The Duke's manservant showed the Indian into the room and Black Bear rushed in amid a flourish of buckskin and hides, feathers and fine linen.

Black Bear had draped a buffalo robe over one shoulder and carried another in his arms, along with his own quarry pipe. Approaching the Duke, who sat behind an enormous oak desk, Black Bear threw the buffalo robe onto the floor.

He gestured toward the robe, then toward the Duke, saying, "This robe was made by my mother. It is finely sewn and carries with it pictures of the fights of my father and his grandfathers against the Pawnee tribe in my country." He gazed steadily at the Duke. "It is now yours."

"Mine?"

Black Bear nodded.

"Is there a reason you would so honor me?" The Duke stood up behind his desk.

Black Bear again nodded. But he didn't speak immediately; instead, he gestured to a chair directly in front of one that he claimed for himself.

He lifted his chin. "I seek counsel with you."

"I see." The Duke of Colchester came around his desk, seating himself in the chair the Indian had indicated. "Jolly good, then," he said, and Black Bear followed his lead to sit in the chair just opposite. "What can I do for you, boy?"

Black Bear didn't answer at once. He drew out his quarry pipe instead and, first offering the stem to the north, the south, the east and west and then to the heavens above, he took a puff. He inhaled the sacred fragrance of tobacco before he handed the pipe to the Duke, indicating that the Duke should do the same.

When at last this had been accomplished and the pipe restored to its owner, Black Bear began. "The sacred pipe is a symbol of wisdom and honesty among my people. In smoking it here with you, I am telling you that whatever you ask, I will answer. Whatever I say will be truth. And I would ask that it be the same with you. I seek knowledge that you have," he said. "I am a stranger to this land and there is much here that is unknown to me, much here that I must learn, quickly."

The Duke nodded. "Yes," he said. "I can understand that, and I appreciate your trust of me."

Black Bear acknowledged the Duke's words with a slight dip of his head. He stared intently at the Duke. "I seek to know what knowledge you have concerning Waste Ho, Estrela. It is imperative that I learn this now since I cannot seem to discover the source of these strikes upon her life."

"What do you mean?"

"There has been another attempt to murder her. It happened this morning while she was riding." Black Bear handed the Duke the frayed leather of her saddle. "Whoever this stalker is," he said, "he follows us."

The Duke examined the leather straps, the buckle, the jagged edges. At last, he looked up to the Indian.

"I don't understand. What do you mean, you seek my knowledge?"

Black Bear had known it would not be easy to pry the information he sought from the Duke, whom he could not fault for his discretion. Still, it didn't keep Black Bear from being impatient.

He took a deep breath before he spoke. "You know something about Waste Ho, Estrela, and the Earl of Langsford that I do not. I believe you know of her father and her mother. I believe this because, if you did not, she would not now be under your protection—"

"That is only because I believe that she—"

Black Bear held up his hand.

"It is not necessary to continue your pretense with me. I admire that you protect her. It is what I would do. But I notice you spend no effort looking for her parentage. You do, however"—here, Black Bear stared directly at the Duke—"seek knowledge of people who used to know her when she lived with the Earl."

"Why, I never—"

Again Black Bear held up his hand.

"It is customary among my people that when a man has something to say, no matter what it is or how long a talk it is, he is permitted to finish. Perhaps this is not the English custom, but I would ask that you suffer my speech until the end."

The Duke sputtered and grunted, but he otherwise remained silent.

And Black Bear continued. "The time has come

when I must know what you know. The time has come for you to seek what skills I have, also. The time has come for us to bind together to find this enemy. You misunderstand me, I seek not only your knowledge, but your wisdom of this country, this culture. I seek your assistance." Black Bear indicated the room with the sweep of his hand. "I need your help. You see, if I am to stalk this prey, I must learn to think, to act like a white man, like an Englishman."

The Duke hesitated. "My good man, do you ask me to teach you?"

Black Bear inclined his head.

"Why, how could I possibly? I daresay it takes years to cultivate the exact, correct manners. It takes breeding, education. Why you couldn't possibly learn it all in a short period of time."

Black Bear didn't even smile. "And yet I must."

The Duke arose from his chair and paced toward the windows until he stood before them, looking out onto the immaculate lawns of Shelburne Hall.

"Why do you do this?"

It was a question Black Bear had anticipated. "Waste Ho is my woman. I came to this country after her. I intend to leave this country with her. I cannot leave with this unsolved. The trouble will follow her even into my own country. I must, therefore, solve it here. But I do not understand why someone would want her death. And it is this understanding, these things an Englishman requires, the reasons he might seek to kill another which I must learn. Without it, I cannot find this enemy."

The Duke of Colchester lowered his head. "You know, young man, that if I tell you these things, you cannot relay them to another soul, not even the lady herself. No one else must know."

Black Bear nodded. "I realize this. You have my word."

The Duke sighed. "You have been honest with me and fair, and I must tell you, son, that if I am correct in what I believe, you could stand to lose Lady Estrela." The Duke hadn't looked back into the room as he spoke. He just gazed out at the countryside.

Black Bear frowned. "I stand to lose her now. What is the difference?"

The Duke breathed out a long breath and, turning back into the room, he retraced his steps toward the Indian, coming to stand behind Black Bear.

"I will help you, my good man," the Duke said. "I will help you because I trust you and because"— he placed a hand on Black Bear's shoulder—"because I need you. I, too, am bound to discover this plot. But beware, son. I believe you may find that if you solve this mystery you may be left with nothing."

Black Bear didn't move. "I do not understand. In all things there is this possibility. Why would this keep me from resolving this problem?"

The Duke hesitated. "Have you ever considered that the Lady Estrela might not be able to return to your tribe with you?"

Black Bear didn't answer and the Duke continued. "The old Earl of Langsford was a good friend of mine. His estate is not far from mine here in the country and so we often took to visiting." The Duke paused. "He had living with him at that time a young girl whom he insisted was under his care. Of course I thought nothing of it. His affairs were his own. But one night, here in my home, after having too much wine at dinner, the Earl confessed that the young girl in his household was the King's own granddaughter, unknown to anyone but a close circle of friends. If"—the Duke strode around the chair, until he was facing Black Bear—"if Estrela is that child, and I suspect she might be, she is a Royal Princess, heir to the throne of England. My son, she would never be able to marry you."

Black Bear did nothing at first. It appeared that he met this bold statement with nothing but stoic calm.

Only if one were truly observant would one discern a reaction, yet even then, only in the dilation of the Indian's eyes.

At length, Black Bear said, "Explain this to me. Do you mean she will change her mind? I have already considered this."

The Duke sighed. "It is more complex than that."

The Indian shrugged. "And I ask you a question. Have you considered that Waste Ho may not wish to remain here? Do you realize that she may decide on her own to leave?"

"She would not be allowed to leave."

Black Bear inspected the Duke's face and his manner in detail. At last, he asked, "Who would prevent it?"

"Why," the Duke answered, "the Royal Guard, the Dukes and Earls, Parliament. The only way she could leave would be to give up all claim to the throne, including all the wealth, the title, the power that comes with the monarchy. 'Tis not something that is done."

To this Black Bear merely smiled and, changing the subject, he said, "I will require you to teach me these things. And whether she can be my woman or not makes little difference. I am bound to protect Waste Ho, Estrela. Whatever the outcome, whether she comes with me or not, it is still something I must do."

The Duke seemed to find encouragement in what Black Bear said, for he smiled, and studying Black Bear's face, he grasped the young man's hand in his own. "I will explain it to you. I will teach you how an Englishman thinks. We have a pact, son. In the next few weeks, I will try to teach you what I know of our royal monarchy. And I truly hope for your sake, and for hers, that I am incorrect, that Estrela is merely a cousin of mine and has no royal connection at all."

Black Bear did nothing. He said nothing for a long time, giving nothing away in either his speech or his manner.

At length, he smiled at the Duke, finally saying, "I, too, hope for your sake that Waste Ho is merely cousin. For, my friend, you may find she does not wish to stay. And this"—he paused—"is all I have to say to you."

"I say, Ladies, are we all ready to go?" It was Prince Frederick who spoke, his dark head bent toward their carriage.

Estrela glanced out the window of the coach, observing that the man's clean-shaven face was unusually flushed, a result of the cool autumn air. The Prince stood beside their barouche, the man apparently engrossed in the act of putting on his riding gloves.

Apparently.

He kept tossing interested glances into the coach,

his gaze seeking out not Estrela, but rather Estrela's maid, Anna.

And Estrela thought it odd that her maid did not seem to notice. Even now, Anna gazed out the other window to the other side of the coach, her attention caught on—Estrela glanced at Anna's hands.

So. Estrela smiled. Her friend was not immune to Prince Frederick's attentions. Anna rubbed her hands together over and over nervously.

Estrela grinned and placing her face partway through the open window said, "How kind you are to inquire about us and yes, indeed, sir, we are ready to leave. Do you ride with us, then?"

She tried to inject just the right amount of disinterest in her voice and she hoped she had succeeded.

She needn't have worried. Prince Frederick noticed nothing awry. Instead he bowed, making quite a ceremony out of it. He smiled, toppling his hat to his hand as he said, "At your service."

Estrela grinned while her maid, Anna, groaned, that maiden gazing out the other window, her attention, it would seem, on some other happening.

But appearances could be incorrect and as Estrela watched her maid and friend, she noted that Anna cast many a furtive glance at the Prince.

Estrela looked back out her window, seeking, herself, a glimpse of Black Bear. She found him. Sitting atop a fine-looking steed, Black Bear appeared to be engrossed in the other activities in the yard. But as if he knew he were being watched, he turned his head toward her.

He saw her and tipped his head in acknowledgment.

Estrela, in response, looked away. But it was too late. Black Bear had already dismounted, was at this moment striding toward them and as Estrela glanced at him, her stomach performed a flip-flop.

She moaned.

How she wished she could deny the effect he had on her. How she longed simply to ignore him. But it was not to be. Every time she saw him, she swooned; every moment she spent in his presence, she treasured. He was like no other. And though she wished it could be different, she couldn't deny his influence on her, though she certainly tried. Since that horrible morning when he had tied her to the bed, she had gone out of her way to ignore him, to avoid him . . . and it was no easy task. It took quite a bit of effort to pretend that she noticed him not at all.

Not that she had seen much of him in these past few weeks. In truth, she hadn't spoken to him, not counting the few monosyllabic replies society demanded she utter in polite company.

And it was just as well. What could she say to him, after all? She was still recovering from the degradation of being discovered tied in her room—nude—to do more than mumble polite nothings whenever she had to "suffer" his presence. That Anna was the only one who had discovered her, and had enjoyed quite a laugh at her mistress's distress, hadn't mattered.

Pride demanded she prove to Black Bear that he could not treat her in such an improper manner although her heart pleaded that she put her shame aside.

But pride won, that and her sense of duty toward the late Earl, both providing reasonable excuses for her to ignore Black Bear.

And she had proceeded to do just that—no simple undertaking, especially when Black Bear gave every impression that he enjoyed her "nonattention," seeming to relish her attempts to "cut him," enjoying a quiet chuckle over calling her Stubborn Woman—not in Lakota, of course, but in English, so that all could share in his joke.

In truth, it was just as well she had seen little of him; the man was grating on her nerves.

He came upon them now and stared down at her, his features unreadable.

"I see," he said to her, to them all, "that you are ready to go. This is good. I have discovered that the Earl of Langsford's estate is not far from here. We should be there by evening." He placed a foot on the carriage steps and leaned forward to gaze at her. "And how is Stubborn Woman?" he asked, a slight grin on his face as she raised her chin upward. "I regret to say that since a terrible, fateful day a few weeks ago, I have not been able to witness *all*," he stressed the word, "of Stubborn Woman's beauty. Not that I couldn't, you understand."

"Humph!" It was all Estrela deemed to say to him and if she hoped to avert a confrontation, she was to discover it was not so easy.

Instead of ignoring her, he raised his voice, saying, "But then it has been so difficult to find you these past few weeks. I've heard you were 'tied' into doing other things."

Estrela tilted her nose a bit more into the air, while Anna grinned. But none of it tempered Black Bear. He just grinned while he sent a mild nod of acknowledgment to Anna in the coach and to the Prince, who still stood outside.

"It reminds me," he said, "that I should ride in

your carriage so that I might participate in your conversation." He glanced over his shoulder at Prince Frederick. "Do you ride in the carriage here with the women?"

"I had thought to do so, my friend."

Black Bear nodded. "You do realize that were we in Lakota country, you and I would be considered *winkte* to ride with the women."

"How true," Prince Frederick said. "How true. But"—the Prince swept his handkerchief from his pocket with the flick of his hand—"we are no longer in your country. And I might add, I am grateful that we are not."

Black Bear smiled. "Do I detect the wistful sounds of infatuation in your voice there, brother, or is there another reason you wish to stay in this country?"

Prince Frederick snorted. "You imagine things, my friend. But I say there, old man, do I detect a note of frustration in *your* voice?"

"No more than in yours."

Prince Frederick shook his head. "Were there ever two less likely specimens of *winkte* than ourselves?"

Black Bear glanced away toward the Duke of Colchester's carriage. "I will ride with you soon," he said. "But now I must see to the Duke and Duchess of Colchester before we set off. Ensure all is ready."

With this said, Black Bear strode away toward the front carriage, toward the Duke of Colchester.

And although Estrela marked Black Bear's progress across the yard, Prince Frederick had no such inclination; and with a click of his heels, a slight bow and a "Ladies," the Prince proceeded to climb into the carriage.

That he chose the seat directly across from Anna, was to be expected, although he didn't glance at the maid or say anything to her. Instead, he glanced out the window, his gaze careful to show boredom, though Estrela, by now, knew better.

He Topa and Wasute Sni chose that moment to ride up to their carriage and, looking inside, addressed the Prince, saying, "Do you ride in this coach with *women*?"

Prince Frederick looked mildly out the window. He sniffed the air, tilting his chin upward before replying, "Of course. And do you gentlemen, too?"

"Hiya! Do you seek to insult me?" It was Wasute Sni who spoke.

He Topa, however, bent down toward the window, and looking in, said, "Tell me why you wish to ride with women." He smiled. "Perhaps, my friend, you do not remember that it is *winktes* who stay with women. We have good horse out here for you, unless you wish to be thought of as *winkte*."

But Prince Frederick was not to be coerced. Instead of responding at once, he produced the handkerchief out of his pocket again and with the flip of his hand, he applied the cloth to his nostrils. "I say, my good friends," the Prince said, sniffing, "Perhaps you are unaware that we are no longer in your country. We are in England. Ah, England. 'Tis not done, my friends. 'Tis not the gentry who ride up ahead, but servants. And you," he didn't even smile. "You may ride with us, if you would desire."

The two Indians scowled at their friend. At

length it was Wasute Sni who, pursing his lips and shaking his head, said, "*Win-ni-yan!*" And with a flick of his hand upward, he signaled that this was all he had to say on the matter.

And with this, both Wasute Sni and He Topa turned their horses, galloping away.

Estrela laughed, as did Prince Frederick who said, "Well, I guess that takes care of that." And, with this said, he proceeded to glance back out the window.

At length, Anna leaned over toward her mistress, asking, "W'at did the Indians say, M'lady? What did t' Indian call t' Prince?"

Estrela gave Anna an amused glance. "Wasute Sni told the Prince," she said in a low whisper, "that he was acting as *wintke*, men who are women."

Anna gasped.

Estrela placed her white, gloved hand over Anna's unadorned one. "Do not be concerned. 'Tis only a good-hearted argument. The two Indians do not understand the English penchant for riding in the carriage. 'Tis not the Indian way. In truth, who could find two more handsome specimens of men than Black Bear and the Prince?"

And when Anna dipped her head in agreement, Estrela smiled.

Just as he had promised, Black Bear joined the two women and the Prince soon after the noonday meal.

As he strode toward their waiting carriage, he presented an odd picture, a strange mixture of English and Indian dress. He wore the standard English buckskin tights and linen shirt with coat, but at his neck he again had chosen to wear the Lakota

bone choker instead of the silk cravat, and on his
feet, he had traded the well-established black riding boots for his tall moccasins, which themselves
rode up high on his calf, almost to his knee. That
the moccasins were colorfully decorated with
beads and porcupine quills, plus a few items of
crystal and gold chain, only indicated that Black
Bear had produced these moccasins himself here in
England recently.

Estrela watched him approach and admired his
stately gait, with his toes turned inward, as graceful as ever, a trait that manifested itself as clearly
belonging to the American Indian. He had once
again left his hair down, but he had tied one side
together in front, positioning two feathers to dangle from the front lock. And there was one other
thing he had added: earrings. Long, beaded earrings.

Estrela gulped. She had never seen him look so
handsome.

His black eyes sought her out. And though he
didn't smile, Estrela could feel the warmth of his
glance upon her.

"Ladies," he said, reaching their carriage and
bending to climb into the seat. It was another odd
combination: gentle, English manners with stoic,
Indian charm. An intoxicating blend.

The barouche tipped as he leaned his weight
onto the steps and eased his tall frame into the
coach. Prince Frederick had scooted over until he
sat directly in front of Anna, a not unlikely maneuver.

And if the Prince were happy about being closer
to the maid, he never showed it. In truth, Estrela
might have been fooled by him if it weren't for the

Prince's fleeting looks at the young lady seated before him, those glances occurring much too frequently to be casual.

Anna sneezed and the Prince produced a clean, silk hanky for her disposal. Anna murmured a polite, "Thank you," and quickly looked away.

Black Bear, however, ignored them both and sat glaring at Estrela. His gaze seemed to take in everything about her and Estrela glanced down at her white gown self-consciously, wondering if she were properly "put together."

But the gown, though quite low-cut and pulled in tightly to emphasize her bosom, was still fashionably correct, her coat of the same color, worn for warmth, yet still accentuating her beauty. She had left her hair in the stylish ringlets at her ears, while the back of her hair was pulled up onto her head, though a few wisps were left to dangle in springy curls.

She glanced down to her feet where her slippers peeked out beneath her gown.

No, she was properly dressed, which meant Black Bear tried to intimidate, not an uncommon occurrence of late.

She stuck her chin up in the air and placing her hands carefully in her lap, she raised her gaze to his, glaring back at him.

But he was too much for her. He was *too* handsome, *too* imposing, *too* magnificent.

She looked away.

"How long has it been," Black Bear asked in his low baritone, "since you were last at the Earl of Langsford's home?"

Estrela glanced up at him, gazed away. "I wish I could remember," she said, "but I don't. Ten years, perhaps twelve. A little more, a little less."

"Do you remember anything of the house itself?"

She shook her head. "Hardly anything at all: a library, a door, books. Not much to talk about, I'm afraid."

Black Bear nodded, but all she heard was his "humph."

"I have been there already," he said casually. "I rode there only two days ago when He Topa stood watch over you. I wanted to see this place where you spent many years of your life. Do you remember the Duke of Colchester from your early days here?"

"No," she answered. "I recall little from that time, only dim memories."

Black Bear nodded. "My father used to tell a story about a very sad man who could remember nothing. One day, the man came upon a place where his wife and children had been killed. For several days nothing happened and then, all at once, the man remembered. Not just that incident, but all others. The man felt relieved, for at least now he could remember. It is said that our Grandmother, the Earth, healed him. And so it is legend among our people that if one is bothered by a loss or pain, he should ask our Grandmother, the Earth, to take him again to that place where it happened. And there she will ease his pain."

Estrela stared at him. "I have never heard that story. Is it true?"

"Yes."

"And then you hope that I will remember something?"

Black Bear shrugged. "I do not know. I can only hope for something, anything that will lead me to this person who threatens your life. Do you recollect any of the people who had been with the Earl when you lived there?"

Estrela shook her head. "That whole period of my life is unclear to me. I remember silly things. Like a doll. I had a porcelain doll. I recall that but little else. I was awfully young when we left this place."

Black Bear nodded.

"Am I to be guarded?"

Black Bear looked to her quickly, frowning.

"These past few weeks I have had no moments to myself. If it's not Anna with me, then it's He Topa or Wasute Sni, even Prince Frederick. I can't even have a moment's peace when I use the toilet."

"I understand," he said. "And yes, you are to be guarded."

Estrela scoffed at him. "Am I some sort of child that I must be watched continually?"

"Yes. It is for your own good."

Estrela sighed. "It seems I have heard these words from you before."

Black Bear leaned forward to whisper, "Yes, you have, I think. Would you like me to refresh your memory as to when?" He raised his voice. "I believe it was in your bedroom—"

"Black Bear!"

He smiled. "What I have done, I have had to do to protect you. I said that I would keep you safe and I will. But it is not easy when you fight me; pleasurable, perhaps, but not easy."

"Black Bear!"

He chuckled and sat back in his seat, his gaze lingering over her.

Anna leaned over toward them. She pointed out Estrela's window. "Look t'ere."

They had been driving along a tree-lined dirt

road, the oaks, the beech, the chestnuts all blocking their view. But as they glanced out the window now, there was an opening in the trees, admitting to a most beautiful view of rolling, golden hills, amid rising fog. The fall foliage touched each tree, each bush and seemed to scream with different hues in colors ranging from the bright reds, the shiny golds, to the yellowish oranges. It was the most beautiful sight Estrela could remember seeing.

"What's it called?" she asked, her voice just barely above a murmur.

" 'Tis Sun Rising Hill." It was Prince Frederick who spoke. "A most pretty place, I daresay."

Anna smiled at him. "I do believe, M'lord," she said, "t'at ye do understate."

The Prince grinned back at the young maiden and as Estrela glanced over to Anna, she saw her friend quickly look down, the maid's golden hair falling down to hide her pretty face. Estrela had always thought Anna a beauty, with her clear skin and golden eyes. And Estrela wished that Anna were not a maid, a position that allowed for no other life outside of that of a servant.

It was not fair, Estrela thought. Anna was too pretty and too kind to live the life of a mere servant. It was a pure waste. Anna deserved more: a husband who adored her, a family of three or four children, and a nice cottage somewhere in the country.

Estrela wished she could give it to her.

And as Estrela glanced at the Prince, she wondered if real-life fairy tales could come true.

It did no good to speculate, however, and shrugging her shoulders, she returned her gaze to her window and to the most spectacular scene that lay just outside.

She didn't know Black Bear watched her. She didn't know and didn't see his glance at her soften, and certainly when she looked back to him, she didn't see that his gaze had shone, if only for a moment, with deep emotion.

Now, as she glanced over to him, he only stared back at her and Estrela, frustrated, uncomfortable, looked away.

The castle rose high in a valley of manicured gardens and lawns, grassy hills and slopes, the Colchester party having come upon it as they drove along the narrow, winding lane. Estrela caught a glimpse of it now as their carriage lingered between the trees; she looked and she looked.

The sun had burned off the early-morning fog and the house sat, stately, shiny, its many chimneyed roof a design in Elizabethan architecture. Hidden behind the hedgerows bordering the road, its brick structure boasted so many different shades of brick; soft yellows, rich reds, muted browns and grays, that Estrela lost count of them all. It looked to her like a fairytale castle, a home built for princes, for princesses, and for dreams-come-true.

She couldn't help herself.

She stared and stared.

And as she looked, a memory jogged.

Estrela blinked.

She remembered something. Sadness. Leaving home. She'd seen this glimpse of this building before, but at night, late at night, and attached to the memory was a feeling of loss.

Estrela blinked again. She hadn't expected this. She hadn't really prepared herself to experience any memory boosts. It came as a shock.

"What is it?" Black Bear spoke to her.

" 'Tis nothing."

He didn't say a thing. He just stared at her, his glance stating more clearly than words that he did not believe her.

At length, he gazed out the window, but the view of the castle was gone, their carriage had moved forward.

Black Bear continued to gaze outside until Estrela, at last, could take his silence no more.

"I remembered something," she said.

He returned his gaze to her, but he said nothing, encouraging her with his silence to speak.

"I remembered the night we left here, the Earl and I. 'Tis all."

Black Bear nodded his head and gazing away, he said, "This is good, that you remember. Perhaps being in the house will enable you to recall more."

"If the present Earl will allow us to stay here the next few nights."

Black Bear acknowledged what she said by a quick tilt of his head and choosing to remain silent, he stared back out the window.

The men alighted from the carriage first, Black Bear striding away to face any hidden danger, as was Indian custom, Prince Frederick staying behind to assist the women, as was the continental fashion.

The estate's housekeeper, frowning, put up a long debate with the Duke of Colchester as their party stood outside, but at last, staring at each one of them in turn, she swung the huge, wooden door open to admit their company. The ancient door

squeaked and groaned as it opened to them and
Estrela, looking around, tried to find something familiar about the home.

There was nothing.

They entered into a hall and the same woman
who had recently frowned at them became suddenly polite once they entered the house. The old
housekeeper stared at Estrela, seeming to study
her, before she gestured for their party to follow
her down a long hallway, her steps and theirs echoing over the stone passage.

The housekeeper admitted them to a huge, darkened drawing room, the place where it was custom
to await the lord of the house, in this case, the new
Earl of Langsford.

The fire from the central wall was the only light-
ing in the room and in the late hour of the afternoon, it threw eerie-looking shadows against the
wood-paneled walls.

Estrela shivered as she studied the paintings
hung on the room's walls, paintings of long-dead
men and of tragedy, of wars and murders. A deep-
red, silk curtain fell down over, and completely
covered, one huge painting and Estrela wondered
what sort of image the curtain hid.

A memory stirred, was almost there within her
consciousness, then gone.

She stared at the picture again. *Odd to have the
painting hidden. Why?*

Estrela had no answers. She looked up then,
where she glanced at several different coats of
arms, which lined the ceiling. She didn't recognize
any of them, nor did the sculptured wood that lay
over each entryway into the room arouse any
memories.

She kept glancing around. A bouquet of flowers

drooped over their silver casing as the bunch sat on the central table, while a dark brown, Chinese rug lay in part over the floor, the entire effect adding to the dreary atmosphere that hung over the room as though it were a dark, smoke-filled fog.

Truly, it was an odd place.

The new Earl was quick to join them, however, and he begged them to sit, to relax, to enjoy their tea while his household servants and maids attended to their rooms and to their dinner.

He was a small man, this new Earl. A plump man, yet he was friendly and graciously entertaining and for this Estrela was grateful.

And as the company of three Indians, one Prince and one Duke sat, stretching out before the great fire and relating the adventures of their trip, the two ladies, each with their maids, sat quietly, the Duchess of Colchester asleep in her chair while Estrela looked everywhere, her gaze catching again and again on the picture hidden behind a red, silk curtain.

Chapter 19

It was only a matter of moments before the servants returned to the drawing room, there collecting individual guests from the arriving party and escorting each to his or her respective room.

The upstairs maid ushered Estrela to her chambers, announcing the usual dinner hour and the "rules of the house" at the same time. "Doors must be locked after midnight," she said, and "no reading in bed." The last an odd rule, Estrela thought as the maid departed.

Once inside the bedroom, though, Estrela glanced around her chambers. The walls were a dark, paneled oak, the floors a hardwood maple. A worn, faded rug lay over one end of the room and chairs were strewn through the chambers as though placed there in haphazard haste.

The sturdy, four-posted oak bed took up one entire side of the room and from its posts hung beige curtains, decorated with green and red flowers.

Again, as in the drawing room, dreary paintings hung over the walls and Estrela wondered at the history of the old Earl's lineage.

"Do ye wish t' rest before dinner, M'lady? Shall I postpone unpacking until t'en?"

Estrela looked over to Anna, whose room lay just

beyond her own. "A nap sounds wonderful, Anna," Estrela said. "Thank you for suggesting it. Perhaps you could rest, too?"

"Per'aps."

Estrela smiled and Anna, after seeing to the bed and pulling back the coverlet and linen sheets, retired from the room.

Estrela lay down on the bed, pulled up the covers and, sighing, closed her eyes.

"She cannot stay here," a tired, old voice said. "It is not safe for her."

"But Your Majesty, where shall I take her?"

"France? Germany? Belgium? No not Belgium. You must take her someplace where no one will find her. Someone knows of her descent, someone whose hatred for her grows ever stronger."

"It cannot be, Your Majesty."

The older gentleman sighed. "I am afraid it is so. Now, go, while it is still safe. Go before they know how you run and where. It is the only way."

Estrela awoke with a start. Afraid, her heart pounding loudly in her chest, she scanned the now-darkened room.

Who had spoken?

Was someone else in her room or were the very walls talking?

For comfort, she lit the wax candle next to her bed, the flickering light adding a hushed element to the already eerie atmosphere of the room. She glanced about the room once again.

The windows, directly in front of her were closed, the drapes covering them standing still, with no breeze to disturb them. On each wall hung paintings, the pictures carefully mounted in richly carved frames, their presence adding a certain depth to the room. And it was at those paintings that Estrela now stared, examining each one as best she could in the dim candlelight. Mostly the paintings were of men, dark men staring out from the canvas, though now and again, she caught a depiction of a war scene or that of an execution; no ladies, no children, no paintings of quiet, idyllic scenes, no family portraits. And despite herself, she shivered in the chill of the evening air.

Were these rooms haunted?

She had never envisioned that she would have such a reaction at just visiting a place, yet she could not deny that she felt afraid. And the strange thing was that she felt she should remember more about this house where she had spent several years of her life. She hadn't been that young when they had left here, five years of age, perhaps six.

But she didn't. She remembered very little.

"It is not haunted."

Estrela jumped.

And before she could assimilate the fact that it was Black Bear's voice she heard, he stepped out from a darkened shadow in the room.

"What?" she asked, her voice breathless. "Black Bear, what do you mean it's not haunted? This room or the house?"

"Both," he said, stepping more fully into the room and advancing toward her where she lay in the bed. "It was what you were wondering."

She gulped before replying. "Yes, but are you sure?" It was odd. She didn't question his presence in her room; she didn't ponder how he knew her thoughts. Such things had become natural to her, to him, to them both. "Why do I feel so odd here?" she asked after a moment.

He shrugged. "I do not know. I can only tell you that the gloom you feel, that I feel, too, is recent. The past does not haunt this place, only the present."

She glanced at him quickly. "What do you mean?"

Again, he shrugged. "I have been asking questions. I have learned just now that many of the old servants in this place have met with death—and recently."

Estrela drew back, her eyes widening.

"It was perhaps not wise that we have come here. But since we stay only the night or two, it may not be too bad. I have seen one thing here, though, that concerns me."

"What is that?" she asked.

"A raven."

"A raven? Why should this trouble you?"

He hesitated. "Because I have dreamed of a raven and of other things and I do not understand these visions."

"Oh." It was all she could think to say. She knew he would not share his vision with her. And it was not because she was female. No Indian ever spoke of his dreams to another person other than the medicine man. "Then do we leave here tomorrow?"

"Perhaps," he said. "I decided to come to this house, hoping that you might remember something. Because this house is so close to the Duke's, it was not a hard journey to make. But I did not know at that time of the danger that presently lurks in this place. Had I known, I would not have brought you here. However, now that you are here and you are recalling things, we may stay longer, if I can assure myself of your safety."

"Why is it so important that I remember?"

Black Bear smiled. "Because, Waste Ho, someone tries to kill you. No one knows who it is, not even you, and if we are to protect you, we must discover why someone would consider you dangerous. Then we can discover who it is."

"I still don't understand."

"Waste Ho," he said, "you hold the key. Your memories may be your protection. Besides," he smiled. "Would you want to keep this mystery unsolved and then despair that someone was trying to kill our children?"

She gaped at him. "*Our* children?"

"Is not a womanly virtue for you to bear children?"

"But Black Bear, I am—"

"Shh . . . You belong to me, no one else. It has always been so."

"No, I—"

"Enough!" He gazed at her where she lay in her bed. And with only her thin chemise for covering, Estrela shivered in the cool air.

The movement seemed to be his undoing. He bound across the few necessary steps that would take him to her side, and once there, he knelt quickly before her, his dark eyes staring straight into hers.

He smiled. "But I am silly to talk of these things now when you are still angry with me," he said, bringing a hand up to trail his fingers over her cheek to her neck.

"Yes, you are," she said to this handsome lover, throwing her head back to allow him more access to the sensitive spots that he was missing. "I am terribly angry with you."

"It is too bad," he said, tracing his touch over her throat, her shoulders, her arms, passing his hand further down over her breast. "If you were not so angry, I could make love to you."

"Yes," she murmured again, straightening her shoulders, and pushing out her chest.

"If only I had been more thoughtful," he said, his voice, his baritone caressing her as his lips followed the path of his hands, his fingers. "If only I had seen to your needs more that day, I would not now have to beg for your favor."

She shivered. "Yes," she whispered, "it's true."

"But," he spoke softly, his warm breath a delicious sensation as he gently suckled her breast through her chemise. "But I acted such a clod, and now I have nothing but your wrath to attend to."

"Yes," she muttered, barely able to speak.

"Take it off."

She didn't even pretend to misunderstand. Her whole body felt warm and a particular part of her anatomy on fire.

Without pause, she shrugged out of her chemise, the caress of his fingers over her naked skin feeling so good, so right, it was her undoing. "Why have you waited so long to make peace with me?" she asked at last. "Couldn't you have done this a few weeks earlier?"

He smiled. "Were you not angry with me? Were you not denying me your favors?" he asked as he trailed his tongue lower and lower, down to her stomach. "What chance did I have against your wrath?"

She sighed and had she the strength, she would

have answered him. His tongue, however, was working magic over her flat stomach, the touch of his fingers there against the inside of her legs an intoxication she could not resist.

"You are mine, Waste Ho," he said. "You belong to me and I to you. Say it to me, Waste Ho. Let me hear it from your lips."

She whimpered; it was her only response.

"Say it."

"I . . ." She twisted her head.

And then he slid down further, the touch of his tongue finding that hidden place between her legs.

"Black Bear!"

"Tell me you are mine," he insisted, pushing her legs back into place when she would have closed them.

"Black Bear, I . . ."

He brought his tongue more fully upon her there and Estrela's conscious thought ceased, replaced by raw feeling. Estrela could no more have thought logically than she could have stopped the sweet sensation.

It went on and on. He gave to her over and over, and Estrela, though she knew what he did was most likely indecent, her own reactions unthinkable, she had never experienced anything like this. These were heady sensations sweeping through her body and she had no will to deny herself.

The pleasure built and built until Estrela, instead of doing what would have been most femininely proper, opened her legs more fully toward him, her response a sweet surrender.

She moved to fit him. She couldn't help herself. It came as natural to her as talking. And just when the pleasure built so that she wanted it more fully, he removed the presence of his tongue.

"Say it," he said, gazing up at her. And as she shuddered, he repeated, "Tell me."

"Black Bear, I . . ." He lay a finger on her there. "Say it."

She gulped. "Yes, Black Bear," she whispered, "I belong to you."

And Black Bear, not even smiling, returned his attentions to her, where, only a moment later, he brought her once more to the brink of release; keeping her there, keeping her there until, just when she thought she couldn't take it, he tipped his touch within her and she fell over the edge, glorious sensation washing over her not just once, but again and again.

And while her body rocked in pleasure, Estrela seemed to float, until Black Bear, rising above her, pushed himself inside her.

He gazed down at her as he leaned over her and she returned the look.

Their eyes met and held, his body straining against hers and she twisting underneath his.

He smiled at her as they moved against one another, the pleasure between them building into a roaring crescendo in her ears, blocking out all sound, eliminating all thought and she tried to smile at him, but she couldn't.

It felt too good.

She groaned, she screamed, she gyrated.

Black Bear strained, his gaze never leaving her.

And as they struggled, their movements became as one, their gyrations in unison and amid all the whirl she thought she could feel his pleasure growing; it was as though it were her own. She heard him groan and then she felt it, the power of his release within her, and with one final twist of her hips she followed him, her own enjoyment so intense, she thought she could never have such pleasure again.

A silly conjecture on her part, she was to learn, for he proved her wrong within an hour.

They didn't sleep. They played with one another. They kissed. They laughed. They loved, exhausting one another until at last, both of them spent, they drifted off into a peaceful sleep.

Neither of them appeared at dinner that evening; neither one was greatly missed.

And somewhere in the middle of the night, Black Bear aroused her to start the lovemaking all over again, until at last, toward early morning, they slept, the two of them entwined together, so close in body and in spirit, Estrela knew his thoughts as easily as she knew her own.

She smiled, then, a self-satisfied smile of one who knows she is truly loved.

For she had learned something from the sudden insight.

Something of great value.

Black Bear loved her, not just loved her; Black Bear stood devoted to her. And just as she belonged to him, he was now a part of her.

He belonged to her.

It was a heady awareness.

She tiptoed down the stairs, the flickering of her shadow along the wall causing her more fright than comfort.

It was early morning, the time just before dawn and Estrela had left Black Bear still asleep in her bed upstairs.

She had to know. She remembered now the sensation she'd felt upon seeing this house, coming into the house and then, in the drawing room—the picture.

She had to know it. She had to see it.

If it was what she thought it was . . . No, she dared not consider it.

It was an odd sensation to come here again after what seemed a lifetime away. It was as though the house, perhaps this very location, stirred up old memories. Memories she'd not realized she'd had until now; a part of her life that had been lost to her . . . until she'd seen it . . . the picture, hanging on the wall, the curtain before it.

It hadn't occurred to her at first. She'd almost thought nothing of it. Except an idea of it kept coming back to haunt her again and again, ideas of what lay behind that curtain and a knowledge of just whose picture it was.

She had to know it and she needed to see it now.

Their visit here was not an extended one. Soon their party would return to the Colchester estate. Soon she would become again part of the Colchester family. But tonight, or rather this morning, she would discover the truth.

And if she were right, she would . . . She didn't know. It didn't bear thinking about.

She paced further and further down the stairs drawing closer and closer to the room, the drawing room, until at last she stood at the bottom of the stairs.

She had no light to guide her, the candle in her hand remaining unlit. No, she found the room from memory alone, her white nightgown floating out behind her as she passed silently forward.

She drifted through the sitting room now, ignoring the ghostly shadows that seemed to leap to life in every corner, sweep in behind every curtain. On she went, until she reached it, the drawing room.

She hesitated at the door, she sighed.

She opened the door.

It creaked.

She stopped and glanced around her, her breath coming in tiny gasps.

She pulled on the door again; it squeaked, it moaned, yet it opened enough to admit her.

She gulped, staring at the opening to the room in fascination, never remembering being more frightened.

She passed into the room, slowly, as soundlessly as her slippers would allow, their soles barely whispering over the hardwood floors and Chinese rug, as though to reinforce her ghostly appearance.

There it was. On the wall. The picture. The picture behind the red curtain. The one she'd seen earlier tonight.

She reached out a hand toward it.

She pulled back.

If it were true, what she thought was there, it would forever change her life.

She gasped, the fingers that she held over her mouth masking the sound.

She reached out again and, breathing deeply, snatched the curtain back.

She didn't faint. Life didn't suddenly stop.

In truth, she could hardly see the picture; it was too dark. And she squinted toward it until she remembered that she grasped a candle in her hand.

She looked at the candle, glanced at the picture, back at the candle.

Finally, drawing a deep breath, she moved to the

fireplace where, reaching out, she lit the candle's wick from a dying ember.

Then slowly she stepped back toward the picture.

She lifted the candle. She gulped.

The windows suddenly flew open, a breeze rushing in, the candle snuffed out by it and as Estrela glanced toward the window, her hand flew to her mouth.

There, by the window, silhouetted against the moonlight had been a figure, quickly gone now; a figure of a woman, a woman with something in her hand. A knife.

Estrela stifled the scream in her throat and spinning back around she came face to face with, stared straight into the eyes of . . .

She screamed.

Chapter 20

Black Bear awakened to the sound.

He felt beside him. She was gone.

Black Bear shot up and was out of the room, leaping down the stairs, his breechcloth tied haphazardly around him, his bow in his hand, his quiver on his back before even a minute elapsed.

He tore through the house. Where was she? What was she doing alone? And why hadn't he awakened when she'd left their bed?

He cursed himself a thousand times, an English habit he'd acquired, as he fled through the house. He'd been too exhausted, too spent.

Damn! He'd been taught all his life to sleep lightly, to anticipate trouble. He'd had protecting others trained into him from the time he could walk.

And for what good?

When he'd needed all that training most, he'd slept right through danger.

He shot through the house, checking each room, despairing.

Where was she?

"Your Royal 'ighness."

Estrela stared straight up into the eyes of the housekeeper.

"Mrs. Gottman?"

"It 'as been a long time since me eyes 'ave be'eld ye, child," the older lady stated.

"Yes," Estrela said, holding up the candle which she had relit to see the woman better. "I remember you now. I had thought you looked familiar when we first arrived here." Estrela's gaze trailed down from the woman's face to the knife the older lady still held in her hand.

"Oh, forgive me, Your 'ighness." Mrs. Gottman lay the knife aside on a nearby table. "There 'as been trouble 'ere this past mont' and I am nervous in this 'ousehold. 'as been a rash of murders, M'lady, and ye did but frighten me."

"Murders?"

"Yes, Your Royal 'ighness," the housekeeper said. "It would seem all t' servants from t' old Earl's 'ousehold are in danger. I be t' last one now who still lives."

Estrela stared at the older lady, whose younger image even now kept flashing into her mind. "Then you must have a care," she said, reaching out to touch the older lady's hand.

Estrela's gaze flicked to the painting.

"It was so long ago, it seems," Mrs. Gottman said, herself staring at the painting. "My, but ye were a pretty child. 'Tis you w' yer grandfather," she said and smiled, still gazing at the painting. "T' King."

"The King?"

Mrs. Gottman nodded. "Yes," she said. "Prince Regent, King George the Fourth, God rest 'is soul. 'E 'as been gone from us now seven years."

"He has? He was . . . Then that means I am . . ."

"Princess. Yes, Your Royal 'ighness. Did ye not know it?"

Estrela glanced over to the picture, a painting of a man, portly in his older age, and a young, blond-headed girl. Both smiled serenely, their images imbued with life and color there forever, the older gentleman wearing a jeweled crown and the long, red train denoting his station, the young child dressed in white gown and smiling happily toward the painter.

"I cried and cried t' night ye left us. Ye 'ad been w' us since ye were a babe and I remember feelin' as though me own child was leavin'."

Estrela glanced again at the picture, then back to the housekeeper. "Mrs. Gottman," she said, "tell me. Do you remember my parents?"

The older lady smiled. "I remember yer mother well," she said. "I was then servant in t' Royal 'ousehold. Princess Charlotte. Stubborn, willful, beautiful. She caught and 'eld t' eye of Prince Leopold."

"My father?"

Mrs. Gottman smiled. "Yes. Theirs was a love affair. A true love affair, not one of t'ose arranged things."

Estrela smiled. "What happened?"

"She died giving birth. It was a boy, a dead baby boy at birth a' all of England mourned at 'is loss. But then all of England thought that was t' only child she bore t'at night. No one knew about ye, about a twin. No one knew about ye because—"

The wind howled in through the open window as though in warning. It faded the older woman's words away and caught Estrela's attention.

Estrela looked away, then back to the older lady. "Because?" she prompted.

"Because yer grandfather feared fer yer life if it were known ye existed."

"Why?"

An image of a man flickered across the window, his shadow clear in the early morning dawn.

Both Mrs. Gottman and Estrela gasped.

"Who was that?" It was Estrela who spoke.

Mrs. Gottman turned wide eyes to Estrela. "It canna be."

"Mrs. Gottman!"

"Sir Connie."

Estrela spun around. No one was there. "Sir Connie?" Estrela asked quickly. "Mrs. Gottman, who is Sir Connie? Was he here?"

"It does na matter. It canna be. Come, Your 'ighness. 'Tis danger 'ere in this 'ouse, in this room."

She didn't say anymore, nor did she remain in the room longer than necessary to cover the painting, returning it to its anonymity behind the red curtain.

She ushered Estrela out of the room and they had no more than entered the sitting room when Estrela turned back toward the housekeeper. "Mrs. Gottman, do you know Sir Connie?"

"Yes, I—"

A window broke.

Someone threw a burning rushlight through the window.

Another window broke behind them.

Another flaming rushlight shot across the floor, a wooden floor in a room filled with wooden furniture.

It happened quickly then. The room went up in a blaze. The walls, the floors, even the furniture itself, all wood, set to fire as though these things were mere kindling.

Estrela grabbed Mrs. Gottman, who stood frozen and fixed, and threw herself and the older woman to the floor.

"Stay low," Estrela ordered. "You must not breathe the smoke. We will crawl out."

" 'Tis murder," Mrs. Gottman cried. "I was t' last of t' 'ousehold. A' now . . ."

"Nothing is going to happen to you," Estrela said, as though by her will it would not happen. "We will survive. Now crawl with me."

"No. I canna."

"Yes, you can." Estrela placed her arms around the older lady and by sheer will alone, crawled toward the door.

And then it happened.

A pillar broke loose from a wall.

It crashed to the floor, over Estrela, over Mrs. Gottman, effectively trapping them both.

The two lay pinned to the floor, underneath the pillar, while the fire blazed all about them, its flames licking ever closer and closer.

But Estrela could not give up. She would not. If not for herself, then for Mrs. Gottman.

It was in the front of the house, somewhere Black Bear would never have thought to look.

He smelled the smoke, he saw the flames, he heard the screams.

Waste Ho.

He rushed toward that place, his heart pounding loudly in his ears. And reaching there, he almost wept.

Fire raged everywhere.

It looked impossible and yet—Waste Ho was in there.

Black Bear hesitated not even an instant. He rushed upstairs, grabbing his buffalo robe, then back down, out into the morning air, to the side of the house where he had seen a water butt. And there dipping his robe into the water, he waited and paced. *Wance, nunpa, yamini.* One, two, three.

He lifted the robe out of the water and tugging it into place over him, he shot back into the house, back into the room.

Flames darted around him, boards and furniture falling before him, smoke making it hard for him to breathe.

He couldn't see her through the flames.

He hollered.

She answered back and Black Bear fled toward the sound.

He could see her now. Her foot was trapped, but she wasn't struggling to free herself; she worked over the pillar that had trapped another, a woman who lay unconscious beneath the weight.

Black Bear ran toward them.

He freed Estrela at once.

"Leave!" he ordered her. "I will help the woman."

"No!" Estrela cried. "She is an old friend. I will not leave her."

Black Bear didn't argue. There was no time. He set to work.

Wood crackled, walls creaked, plaster fell inward, flames whipped all around them.

The older woman awoke. "Go!" she said. "Leave me."

"Hiya!"

"No!"

The older woman gasped. "I kinna breathe. It is no use. Leave."

"We have you almost freed," Estrela cried. "You will leave with us."

Black Bear at that moment moved the pillar and Estrela, with a burst of strength, pulled the housekeeper loose. Then Black Bear and Estrela dragged the older woman across the floor.

He spread his buffalo robe around them and getting them all to their feet, Black Bear, holding the older woman up, guided them to a window where, crashing the glass with his foot, he lifted both women through it, jumping through himself last. He hit the ground, rolling over and over in the dewy, wet grass, coming to his knees in an instant.

He crawled over to Estrela, feeling her everywhere, satisfying himself Waste Ho still lived.

He sat back, watching Estrela kneel over the older lady, the lady he now recognized.

Estrela held the hand of the woman, who lay unconscious before her.

"Do not leave me," Estrela cried over and over. And as though in answer, the housekeeper opened her eyes. She glanced around wildly until, catching sight of Estrela, she smiled. "Doctor," she murmured. "Important . . . doctor."

It was the last thing she uttered, the last breath she took.

And Waste Ho, tears and soot running down her face, howled.

A raven chose that moment to take wing and fly,

Estrela unaware of the movement; Black Bear, how-ever, watched its motion, its path, the very flap of its wings, as it, a bird of prey, fled the scene.

Black Bear crouched down low, studying the boot prints left behind in the early-morning dew.

He followed the trail.

So, whoever sought to kill Waste Ho, Estrela, had not lived in this house.

The prints had originated from the bushes at the side of the house. Following them, Black Bear came upon more prints, though the boots were always the same.

One man. One horse.

And small feet.

Had Black Bear been anything but Indian, he would have smiled at this moment. But he didn't. He merely looked at the ground. This person walked with a limp, something easily discernible from the tracks. The print of one foot, the right, was more deeply embedded in the grass than the other.

This man would be easy to find. It might take time, it might take patience. But this trail, Black Bear could follow.

At last, Black Bear lifted his head, thrusting his chin forward.

And all at once, he smiled.

There were no other casualties in the house fire, though the Duchess of Colchester lost all her linens and fine clothing, which she had brought with her in a trunk.

But no other servant, no other person lay trapped beneath the burning fire. As those in the house-hold, a gathering of thirty to forty people, stood on the lawn, Estrela watched the flames devour the home she had only just remembered.

Black Bear had brought her here to help her remember. His plan had worked. Old images had been revived, the past recollected. But to no avail. As far as she knew, with this fire went all physical proof as to who she was.

She had found it, only to lose it.

Odd, too, she didn't mourn that loss. No. Not that loss; it was something else.

In remembering, she had at last recalled the presence of a friendly woman in her early life, someone who had been as a mother to her: Mrs. Gottman.

She sniffled and Black Bear pulled her slight body more fully into the warmth of his own. "What did she say?" he asked, his voice low and gravelly in her ear.

Estrela swallowed. "She called out for a doctor," Estrela answered quietly. " 'Tis all."

Black Bear nodded. *"Wanunhecun,"* was all he said. "Mistake." And to the Lakota, who had no word for "sorry," his expression related all the sorrow that he felt, and oddly enough, gave her all the comfort she needed.

It was enough.

Chapter 21

"**J**olly good to see you this morning."

Estrela pulled up on her mount this pleasant day in November and smiled. "So nice to see, you, too, M'lord."

Prince Frederick grinned at her as he met her on the pathway at Shelburne Hall, but he really didn't look at her. His gaze scanned the area around her. And at last, not finding that which he sought, he bestowed his glance upon Estrela.

Nearly a month had passed since that fire at the Earl of Langsford's estate; nearly a month Estrela fought with herself, with her feelings of guilt over her inability to save Mrs. Gottman. And though she tried to tell herself that there was nothing more she could have done, it didn't seem to help.

A horse whinnied, breaking into her thoughts, and Estrela glanced up quickly to look at Prince Frederick. She smiled. The man was holding his horse steady with one hand on the reins while he reached up to snatch a handkerchief from his pocket, and snapping the material in the air as was his habit, he brought the kerchief to his face.

" 'Tis so hard," he said, "to find good help these days. I do wish I had a manservant who was as good as your maid. And while we're on the subject"—he hesitated, as though to inject just the right amount of disinterest into his voice—"where is the maiden in question?"

"Oh," Estrela pretended surprise. "You mean Anna?"

"Yes," he replied, lifting his chin upward as he sniffed the air. "Rightly so."

"She will be along in a moment. Yet I must tell you that she quite protests my requiring her company today, though she used to join me every day without question. She suddenly seems to believe that her place is in the house, attending to my chambers, straightening my rooms, taking care of my clothes. I'm afraid, sir"—here Estrela gave the Prince a flippant look—"I'm quite afraid that Anna is turning into a prude."

"Lady!"

Estrela laughed. "I do believe that Anna suffers from the malady. She seems to believe that just because she is my maid, she is not allowed to enjoy a quiet walk with me, a leisurely ride, a picnic. She seems to believe only her peers are entitled to such things. Why"—Estrela lowered her lashes—"she may need someone to inform her differently. Someone besides myself, someone—ah, perhaps from the aristocracy. Someone"—she glanced all at once at the Prince—"like yourself."

"Me?"

"Yes," Estrela smiled. "Someone like yourself. Will you do it?"

"M'lady. I . . . well, I . . . "

"Shh! Here she comes now."

Anna rode toward them on a hack that looked more nag than horseflesh. The animal's back was swayed, her coat drab, her eyes glossy and she kept stopping to graze at the lawn while Anna sat quietly atop her, waiting.

Estrela chuckled. "Anna," she raised her voice to be heard. "Just jiggle the reins and click and she'll come here."

"I can't, M'lady."

"Of course you can," Estrela grinned. "Just—"

"I say," Prince Frederick spoke from beside Estrela, "may I be of assistance?" He was already trotting his horse toward the maiden, who, wearing one of Estrela's riding habits, complete with top hat, looked more lady than maid.

The maid smiled at him as he approached and patting her nag gently on the neck, she welcomed the Prince with softly spoken words that Estrela could not hear. Nor did she wish to listen. It was obvious to her that the Prince and her maid were attracted to one another. What was to become of that attraction depended on the two of them and their ability to battle society's insistence on the status quo of its aristocracy.

There was little Estrela could do about it besides provide a constant friendship and a willing ear, should the need ever arise.

In the meantime she escorted Anna on their morning excursions where they inevitably met Prince Frederick, Estrela providing the necessary chaperon, although in truth, it was supposed to appear that the maid furnished escort and chaperon for the lady.

It was an odd day for November but Estrela did not see it. As she rode up ahead of her maid and the Prince, Estrela hardly took note of her surroundings, her mind working over her own problems, which were considerable. But she looked up now and again and as she beheld the countryside more and more around her, her vision began to clear and Estrela suddenly noticed something. There was something unusual about this day.

It wasn't in the trees; they were still bleak. It wasn't in the grass, which was most commonly brown or golden, nor was it in the air, still seasonably cool and crisp. It was in the sky, the clear, blue, cloudless sky. The hour was early in the morning and yet the sky, which was normally overcast and dreary this time of year, was blue; even the sun, now risen, was strange for a November day. It felt warm upon her back, an unexpected sensation. And although its warmth was certainly not hot enough to heat the chill in the air, its presence upon her was invigorating.

She glimpsed a man out in the woods as she gazed off to the side, another. Ah, yes. The fox hunt season had begun as of last Monday, the first Monday in November and as Estrela glanced about her, she saw several more people up and out early this morn.

It was still too early for the sportsmen themselves to be about, the hunters not usually arising until late in the morning. All Estrela could witness now as she gazed about her, were the men sent out by the master of foxhounds to ready the area for the sport; stopping up the fox holes to ensure the foxes could not return to their dens.

One of the men saw her as she set her horse along the path and tipped his hat to her. Estrela returned the gesture with a nod.

Personally Estrela did not enjoy the sport. She did not see the point. Perhaps if she had spent more time in England, in the country, she, too, would enjoy the enthusiasm of it, but not having lived here long, she found herself sympathizing with the fox.

Besides, it seemed a bit of laziness on the part of the hunter. Up late in the morning, he depended on others to ready the sport for him. He did not really "hunt" the fox, the whole adventure more an exercise in galloping over the countryside in pursuit of the hounds. And given her Indian upbringing, she could not see the sense in killing something one did not intend to use for practical purposes. To her, to the Indian, hunting with no intent to provide food, clothing, or something equally useful, but carried on for the sake of sport alone, was utterly contemptible; perhaps it was this that colored her view.

Estrela looked back now to where the Prince and Anna rode behind her, but they, caught up in themselves, did not attend to her glance.

Estrela slowed her mount and sat straight in the saddle, glancing all around her. Every day since she had returned to Shelburne Hall, she and her maid would take this ride in the early morning. She had needed the excursion, the exercise after she had arrived back from the Earl of Langsford's estate. Shock and the knowledge that she had once again escaped a murder attempt, held her tense, kept her from feeling truly happy.

For she should be happy, or she should, at least, feel a shade of that emotion.

And on one hand she did.

She and Black Bear had never been closer. He came to her each night, performing as though he were husband. He guarded her. He protected her.

Even now, under Black Bear's orders, Prince Frederick furnished protection for her, a necessary part of Black Bear's arrangements. Black Bear did not allow her even a single moment alone. Between the Prince, the three Indians and Anna, Estrela had not one bit of privacy.

On the other hand, however, Estrela despaired.

Though she dared not tell a soul.

She felt more and more deeply entrenched on English soil as each day passed.

For one thing, she was still married, still bound by a vow, but now, even more so.

Before their visit to Langsford Estate, she had begun to believe that perhaps Sir Connie didn't exist, that maybe she had pledged herself to a phantom, that perhaps she was free to marry the man of her choice.

But no more. Now she knew her "husband" existed. The man lived. And it remained her duty to find him.

There was more.

She no longer wondered about her heritage. She knew it. And though she couldn't prove her royal connection, there remained yet a feeling of responsibility. A duty that mayhap was as ingrained as it was unwanted.

And Estrela felt more and more the need to "air" the truth, if for no other reason than she felt she had to express this newfound weight of duty and responsibility.

It was odd. The extreme wealth of her position, the riches due her, the power within her reach meant nothing to her. The only real riches in her life, the only things that meant anything to her at all, were her honor, her love.

Black Bear.

Without Black Bear, her life held little meaning.

And truly, he was the only wealth she considered valuable.

And yet he was not something she could have, the honor of her vow kept him from her.

Which left her what choices?

If she went with Black Bear, she lost her honor.

If she stayed here, and proved her honor, she lost Black Bear.

And what of her heritage? What did she do about that?

If she proved it, she still stood to lose Black Bear. For she realized that a princess had the duty to marry into other royalty. It was as much a responsibility of the position as was the power and wealth of the title. Plus, she assumed Sir Connie would step forward in such an event, himself most likely a part of the aristocracy.

If she remained unknown, she still could not win. Bound by her honor to find the man, Sir Connie, once she found him, she was duty-bound to the marriage.

Truly, she was damned on every hand. Caught by her honor, held by her love, she remained unable to set into action any plan.

And so it continued; yes, she was happy, no she was not.

An odd state of affairs, indeed.

She was still riding, Anna and the Prince still following her when, the sun almost at its zenith, she espied movement in her peripheral vision.

There—off to the right—the mad dash of the fox.

At once she heard the yelping of the dogs and turned her head to watch the pack of them in pursuit. In no more than seconds, the fox hunters came, dressed in scarlet-red riding suits with black caps, laughing and whooping with merriment, darting across the fields, jumping low hedges, splashing through streams in zealous pursuit.

It looked quite a fun sport—for people—and Estrela smiled to watch them as they dashed on past her.

That's when she saw them. The Indians, Black Bear, and his two friends.

Apart from the rest, dressed in their own native costumes of buckskin and porcupine quills, they burst across the fields, in pursuit of . . . Were they hunting the huntsmen, themselves?

Estrela thought so as she watched. The Indians galloped up beside each hunter, leaning over and touching each person with their bows, their coup sticks, their lances, even, in some cases, their hands, before spurting away, leaving the hunters behind as though those riders in red were leisurely cantering their horses.

What was occurring here?

The Indians were obviously not out fox hunting—or were they?

How curious. How curious, indeed. Estrela sat forward and adjusting her hat further down on her head so that it would not blow away, she gave a quick yell behind her to Anna and the Prince. Then, guiding her horse off the main road, she set her direction in determined pursuit of the whole party, fox hunters, Indians, and hounds, and with a quick kick to the horse's flanks, she burst away from the road, galloping across the fields as if she herself enjoyed nothing better than hunting down and watching the hounds devour a fox.

*　　*　　*

Estrela remembered the first time she had experienced a fox hunt. She clearly recalled watching the hounds corner the fox and then, when the signal was given, slaughter the animal.

She hadn't liked it then. She didn't like it now.

Mayhap it was her digression into her Indian mores that caused the disillusionment. Perhaps it was simply her belief that there should be reason to kill the animal. Or maybe she simply misunderstood the whole sport.

Whatever the reason, it made no difference. She did not like the game.

She watched now as, up ahead of her, the hounds cornered the wild animal. The yelping and growling of the hounds was almost deafening and Estrela experienced a moment of discomfort. She wished that she could . . .

What was that?

All three Indians seemed to swoop down into the scene out of nowhere. One moment no one was there, the next, the three of them looked to be everywhere, themselves whooping and hollering even louder than the hounds.

A strange occurrence to watch.

The hounds cried like young pups as they cowered beneath the warlike yelps from the Indians and the three of them, with buckskin bags held outward, raced around the scene, disbursing the hounds, each of the three Indians sweeping down, attempting to pick up the fox.

Black Bear became the proud winner in this match, his prize securely fixed within his pouch. And he tore away, across the fields, jumping fences and hedges and carrying away the most valued possession of the hunt—the fox.

Estrela sat stunned, watching, having reined in her mount.

She didn't even notice when the red-coated hunters joined her. She didn't even hear them at first, until the cursing began. And then—

"Damn! They've jolly well done it again."

"Damn nuisance is what they are! Oh, excuse us, M'lady, we did not see you here."

"Can't keep denying the hounds their treat, can we now? Must do something, we must."

At last Estrela took note of where she was, just who was surrounding her and she asked, none too politely, "What is it?"

"The Indians, M'lady," one of the scarlet-coated gentlemen answered. "Every time we have a fox hunt, I tell you the Indians beat us to the fox, and I daresay, they carry the animal away every time. Getting to be a nuisance is what it is."

Estrela almost laughed. And it was only with the greatest of efforts that she replied simply, "Pray, do tell."

"I have no idea at all," the gentleman continued, "what the savages do with the animals."

"Probably tear it to pieces themselves . . . with their teeth," one of the hunters volunteered.

Estrela gasped.

"I do say," another ventured, "the savage's bite is probably worse than the fox's, probably worse than the hound's."

And to the resounding laugher, Estrela lifted her chin, frowning.

In all fairness, the hunters had most likely forgotten her heritage. And perhaps had they realized the true effect of their bantering, they would have stopped.

Perhaps.

". . . I say the savages probably eat the animal raw."

Laughter.

". . . snap off the tail with their teeth . . ."

". . . savages probably wear it in their hair . . ."

More and more laughter.

Estrela raised her chin a tiny bit higher. And assuming a pose whereby she looked directly down her nose at them, she said, "Gentlemen," but to no avail.

". . . pierce it in their ears . . ."

"Gentlemen!" she put the exact amount of stress on the word. First one, and then another and another huntsman looked her way.

She cleared her throat. "Gentlemen," she said, a trifle more gently. "I must tell you that in my opinion, if there are any savages present"—she swung her gelding around to look at each and every man present—"*if* such people are anywhere nearby, I daresay I sit among those 'savages' right now."

No one said a word. No one even laughed. Every gaze at the moment had turned to her.

At length, Estrela grinned. She said no more. She didn't need to. She simply reined in her horse and, turning him to walk into and through the ring of red-coated horsemen, she spurred her mount forward, following in the same direction as the "savages."

It was some time later, finally catching a glimpse of the three Indians that she saw Black Bear loosen his pouch to the ground. He had set the fox free.

And as Estrela watched, leaning forward in her saddle, she smiled.

*   *   *

"Children, children," the Duchess of Colchester hurried into the breakfast parlor, where even now, the servants were setting up an informal luncheon. "Oh, I must say, I am beside myself. What do you suppose I have here in my hand?"

No one answered, the hunters still sulking, the Indians not in the least curious and the Prince distracted, watching the maiden Anna as she stood a good distance away with the other ladies' maids.

The Duchess waved the letter she held in her hand, saying, "Who do you suppose this is from?"

Black Bear raised an eyebrow and Estrela glanced up.

"The King," the Duchess promptly answered. "He is coming here. Here, mind you, to Shelburne Hall."

"The King?"

"Coming here?"

"To Shelburne Hall, you say?" It was the Duke who spoke.

"Yes," the Duchess replied, smiling now that she had everyone's attention. "It seems King William has heard nothing but rumor after rumor of the Indians and he wishes to meet them. He also desires a country visit and so he is coming here. Oh, my, what shall I do? I will have to hire more staff, more servants, and of course, our daughters and Lady Estrela must have new gowns, only the latest fashion, of course, and I must see to . . ."

"Well, I daresay," even the Duke seemed suddenly agitated. "Must invite more of my colleagues from Parliament here. Politics, you know. Must be able to talk the latest in politics. The King is coming here," the Duke commented. "We'll have to import more game, more birds, mind you—perhaps partridges. Not enough wild game here to make hunting profitable at the moment. I say, is the Queen also visiting?"

". . . and I will have to ensure the dinner is prepared by only the best chefs I can find, oh, I must send into town for all our help there . . . and that . . . what was it you asked?" The Duchess looked up to meet her husband's gaze.

"I say, is the Queen also planning to visit?"

"Well," the Duchess glanced at the note in her hand. "The letter is not quite clear on that point, but I would assume that the Queen will attend as well, Oh, bless me, my, but I am afraid we will never be prepared in time. He is due to arrive here in, oh my, oh my, in only a fortnight. So little time, so much to do, so many things to attend to . . . I must send into town at once for my servants, my . . ."

The Duchess sat down to the table, still muttering, but so much to herself it was hard to pay her attention until all at once, "Why I know what we'll do." The Duchess stood up suddenly, scattering food and dishes on the table, upsetting her chair. "We'll give another ball, we'll give a dinner party. That will be easy enough. Oh, it will a party, the likes of which no one has ever seen before and no one will ever see again. Why, we have the most beautiful ballroom, the loveliest of halls in the country, all the best hardwood floors, and . . . Oh, dear me, they'll need wax. Beeswax. Why, I must send for beeswax immediately. Oh my, oh my, so much to do. So much to organize. Pray, do excuse me." She turned around as if to leave, then spun back toward the table and, with a grand gesture of her arm, the Duchess swept up the letter in one hand, a napkin in the other and pivoted back toward the door. With determination, she strode from the room, beckoning over her shoulder to the servants, "Bring me my paper and quills at once and oh, prepare the carriage. We must send word to people at once. Oh, so much to do, so many people to tell. I must . . ." Her words faded into the distance, her voice quickly out of earshot.

Black Bear reached for a scone, the movement so nonchalant, Estrela was unprepared for his next statement.

He didn't even smile. "We go soon."

Estrela heard him, but as though realizing her worst nightmare, she did no more than smile at him.

Black Bear took note of it, ignored it, looked directly at her. "We go now," he repeated, speaking in Lakota. "Prepare your things and mine. We will leave here soon. We will stay to see the King, then we go."

Estrela sat stunned for a moment. She had been living on the tip of time, knowing this moment would come, avoiding it, hoping for more time, more space. And though she'd been aware that this would eventually happen, she felt unprepared for it. And so she stared at him, saying nothing for a very long time. At last, she ventured, "We?"

He nodded his head toward her, answering her instantly. "We go. You, my two Lakota brothers, myself, perhaps even my brother, the Prince. Do you wish to bring your friend?"

Estrela sat still a moment longer. She opened her mouth to speak, but not knowing what to say, she closed it.

Perhaps the moment had not yet arrived. Maybe

she misunderstood. And so, after several moments, she asked, "Where do we go?"

He didn't even look at her. He chewed on a bite of scone as he said, "Home, to the prairie."

Estrela choked on the tea she had just sipped. That a servant immediately pounced on her, pounding her on the back didn't help in the least.

And as she sputtered into her napkin, the servant still pounding her back, she heard Black Bear say, "We leave to go home soon. My brother, He Topa, brings me news from the great water docks in the town called London. He says there is a ship there that will sail to America within another moon." Here Black Bear took note of Estrela, her face flushed, her breath still coming in wheezes. "We will be on it."

He reached for another scone, placing it carefully in a napkin, along with other food, which he would then take outside to give to the poor.

He didn't look at her. He didn't look anywhere and Estrela could have sworn she saw the tiniest trace of a smile, but it was too quickly gone for her to be certain.

Did he merely play with her?

Did he only jest?

She prayed so.

She had come to hope after a month had gone by and he remained at her side, that somehow, without her speaking it, he had understood her problem.

She silently cursed herself now.

What had she thought? Had she really believed that Black Bear, against all personal mores, would agree to be only lover to her? She had never asked it of him, she had never explained it to him. She had simply hoped . . .

Pure foolishness.

And now what could she do?

How would she tell him she could not go with him?

He would not understand. She had been a virgin when he'd found her. And in bringing him to her bed, hadn't she insinuated that she had already broken her vow? Hadn't she effectively told him in deed that she was free? Of course he would believe that she was his to order, his to command, his to love.

He would not understand her motives.

What he didn't know, what she hadn't told him, what she hadn't explained was that her vow to the Earl was as binding as if she were truly married. She could not break it.

And so she sighed. She tried to smile. "Have you planned this long?" she asked at last.

"This has been my intention ever since I first decided to come to this country. I told you of it when I found you. So, yes, I have planned this long."

"But I thought," she ventured, "that you might have decided to stay here."

He gave her a long, considering look. "In what role have you envisioned me?"

"I—" she choked.

"Did you intend," he still spoke in his native language. "Did you have marriage in mind?"

She swallowed.

"I . . ." she gazed away from him, and then, "Black Bear," she said. "I'm already married."

He merely raised an eyebrow. "Then I suggest," he said, his voice calm, clear, "that you decide

what you will do. For Waste Ho, you are married
to me, too."

"We never—"

"We most certainly have, you most certainly did.
Did you not state to me that you belonged to me?"
He stared steadily at her. "You must decide now
which husband you want more. One you do not
even know . . . or me. The choice is yours."

"I have no choice. You ask me to break a vow.
You must know I cannot do this."

He tilted his head back. He stared at her. "I do
not know this," he said at last. "You broke a vow
to me. You did this freely and of your own will.
What am I to think?"

"Black Bear, you know that I . . . I . . ."

He waited. He watched. He set his lips together.

"I had no choice in that. The Earl of Langsford
was my guardian, my friend. He was a father to
me at a time when I had none. He saved my life,
and not just once. I owed him. I could no more
have denied his demand on me than . . . But you
know this. Why do you do this now?"

He waved his hand, making signs as he spoke in
Lakota, "Understand, Waste Ho. This land, these
ways here are foreign to me. I grow hungry to see
my family and friends. I have little to do here except make love to you. And while this is pleasant,
it is not enough. I feel I grow less a man each day.
I provide nothing here. What I do here is more easily and better done by others. It is my duty to return home where my strength and my skills are
needed. Just as you say you are bound here, I am
compelled to return. We go soon. You make choice
now."

Estrela could not look at him. She blinked away

tears. What could she say? She couldn't ask him to stay. Not now. She couldn't go.

She gulped. And turning back to him, she tried to smile, but the gesture came out wobbly. "When do you leave, then?"

"We stay for the King's visit. Then we go."

"I see." She glanced away again. "I will tell you my decision then." She bit her lip. "Couldn't you just—"

"Does the goose forget that the gander has a duty to his flock as well as to his mate? True, he mates for life, true, he will love his mate all his life, but he also cares for others in his flock. Does the goose forget that this very protection he provides is his strength? That to take it from him would be as to take away his life?"

"Black Bear, you are no bird."

"The point is the same."

She gazed down, stalling. "Perhaps," she said, at length, "the gander misunderstands. Is it possible that the gander does not realize that he might not be gander at all? Could it be that gander might be Eagle instead? That his strength comes not from the flock, but from himself, his mate, his family? Could it be that Eagle could make his own way in life, not depend on others?"

"Waste Ho," Black Bear said, signing his words in the language of gestures as he spoke. "You misunderstand. True, Eagle does not draw strength from the group, but you see, Eagle gives the group strength. There is a difference."

She closed her eyes. She nodded her head. And though she felt a sob well up inside of her, she kept her composure. "I will tell you before the King leaves," she said. "I . . ." Her voice broke. "I promise."

He nodded, and then, because she couldn't see, he said, "*Hau, hau*. Good, it is done."

He rose from the table and Estrela, her eyes blurred with tears, could not even lift her gaze to watch him leave, his action a mimic of what was to come.

That she didn't see his departure, however, was no consolation at all.

Chapter 22

The transformation of Shelburne Hall from a mere beautiful manor to a spectacular castle was nothing short of a miracle. Lights blazed at each window, floors gleamed in the candlelight and each piece of wooden furniture shone under many coats of wax.

The dining hall, where all the guests were now gathered, stood a masterpiece in tall windows and Grecian architecture.

There were five huge windows on just one side of the long hall. Each began with a golden arch at its top which rested on white pillars at each side. Heavy red curtains hung luxuriously over the windows and were pulled back at the sides to provide a spectacular view of the landscape. A fire blazed at the head of the room with a fire screen set in front of it to shield those who had the misfortune to be seated close to it.

Over the black and white marble floor was an enormous red, Chinese rug and upon the rug stood the long dining table, which currently sat what must have been at least fifty guests.

Servants, twenty in number, each dressed in gold and red, stood to the left of the room, each presiding over a portion of the table.

The tantalizing smells of roasted lamb and of beef, fish, and game permeated the room, along with the delicate scent of roasted potatoes and vegetables.

Wine passed from one person to another freely, including sherry, champagne, and Madeira. At least four servants were on hand to do no more than replenish the wine for the obviously thirsty guests.

Black Bear, having left the table early, stood at the back of the room and stared. He had never seen such a feast as this, and he watched in awe as course after course was served. It had begun with a soup, followed by red mullet and cardinal sauce. Before one was able to finish one dish, the next was served.

There were servants carrying round platters of lamb cutlets, fish, duckling, roasted turkey, stewed beef, and venison followed by other servants carrying peas, beans or asparagus, desserts of chocolate creme or truffles, tart-tasting ices and, once again, the ever-flowing supply of fine wines.

Black Bear frowned. This fine culinary display could not distract him from the future.

Should he continue his efforts to persuade Waste Ho to come with him? The question kept surfacing over and over within his mind. Should he demand that she leave here after experiencing wealth and abundance such as this? he wondered.

He hadn't truly meant it when he'd said they were leaving immediately. He had offered it up to Waste Ho as a challenge. He knew he could not leave until he discovered the plot against her life.

That didn't, however, keep him from seeking to make her his own.

Now.

But as he watched the feast taking place before him he wondered: Was what he asked of Waste Ho the best for her? Should he continue to pressure her to return to his country where, while there was no shortage of food, there was the ever-constant threat of death from either the elements or hostile, enemy tribes?

He could not provide this sort of luxury for her. He, while wealthy in his own country, did not possess anything like this.

Which meant what?

He could not stay. He must not. Much as this life offered security, the longer he stayed here, the less a man he felt. And how he longed for the thrill of home, for the friendly faces of his relatives, for the familiar quiet of the land.

This was not his home.

It also was not hers. Or was it?

As he watched the dinner progress, he was becoming more and more afraid, more and more aware of just what he was asking her to leave behind.

Was what he demanded the best for her?

He had come here, knowing he was right, convinced she needed him. And he'd been right. She had needed him. She needed him still, but not in a capacity that fulfilled him.

He must return.

Did it mean he would have to leave her?

Could he?

He was gambling with her now, gambling that she loved him more than the wealth that surrounded her, more than the vow that bound her.

It was an all-or-nothing game.

If he lost, he lost all, even himself. For life with-

out Waste Ho would be no life at all. Hadn't it been
so before?

Wasn't it Waste Ho who even now brought him
happiness? Light?

But he could not relent.

Bored, unable to continue in this foreign environment, he had made the gamble.

And now he had to stand by it.

He sighed.

He'd come to this land thinking that she was still
one of his people, that, once he had wooed her back
to him again, she would want to return home, to
the prairie. But he had reckoned without realizing
what wealth existed here. Even he was tempted by
all that he saw. How could he ask her to leave it,
when she could have it all?

Was he doing the right thing?

He didn't know anymore. He just didn't know
and the uncertainty of it was as unusual as it was
an unpleasant experience for him.

He glanced around him.

Waste Ho had not yet arrived to the dinner. He
didn't understand why this was. He had thought
at first that she might be sick, but upon questioning
Anna, he had learned that this was not the case.
He could make no sense of it. Waste Ho strove to
make others feel comfortable and yet being this
late, even to the Indian, was considered ill-
mannered.

In view of the fact that their English sovereign
sat here in this very room, this did not make sense
to him.

Black Bear had, himself, been correctly on time
although he had chosen to eat very little. If he were
to meet the King tonight, he might need his

strength. And because he had been trained all his life into warring, he knew that too much consumption of food could weaken the mind and slacken the body's reflexes to a point where it made one act as though dispirited. And so, he had refrained.

Black Bear gazed down at himself as he stood to the side of the crowded room. He still dressed in the style of the English, wearing black tights, black boots, and a white, linen shirt under a black coat. Tonight, especially, he had worn his best, adorning that best with his usual bone choker instead of a cravat, beaded earrings at his ears and a fur-wrapped braid on one side of his head. The other side of his hair he had left hanging loosely to his waist, his attempt at pronouncing his duality in culture.

Black Bear stood against the wall of the room with his two friends beside him, who, themselves, had also chosen to watch the dinner party rather than participate. Their observations alone would make for tales that would enlighten many an evening when they returned home.

As the evening wore on, however, Black Bear despaired more and more.

He loved Waste Ho more than life itself. But if she stayed here, he still had no choice but to leave. It was a possibility he had never, not once, considered. He had always, even during his gloomiest mood, known he would somehow take her home with him.

This was the first time he had truly been uncertain.

And Black Bear didn't like it.

He didn't like it at all.

* * *

Estrela sat in her room, unwilling to go down to dinner, yet unwilling to stay where she was.

She sat at her vanity, wearing the finest clothes she had, a white frock of thin muslin with only a chemise beneath. She had tied a pink satiny sash beneath her breasts and wore a white pelisse over the dress. She had left her hair down, the long splendor of it sparkling in pale curls down her back.

White satin slippers covered her feet, and as Estrela sat at her dark, mahogany vanity, she stared at the reflection of a girl she no longer knew.

Who was she, really?

Was she truly a Princess? She didn't feel it.

Was she Indian?

She could find no trace of the culture in her appearance.

She felt neither, outside both cultures. And it wasn't a good feeling.

She didn't belong—anywhere.

Duty demanded she stay. Her heart begged her to go.

What was she to do?

Could she live without Black Bear?

No. She could not. She might exist. She could not "live."

Could she break a vow?

She could, but again, she would merely exist. Without self-worth, what did one have?

Black Bear, her heart answered, and Estrela closed her eyes.

Why not go with him? Hadn't fate pushed her in that direction since he had arrived? She had tried to deny him, but at every turn, circumstances had brought him closer to her, not further away.

No, she demanded of herself. She could not do it. She had promised the Earl. And not just any promise. It was a vow he had taken with him into death. It was a vow she could not lightly break.

She dropped to her knees before her vanity and with her head lifted to the heavens, arms open wide, she prayed, but whether to the English God or to Wakan Tanka, God of the Lakotas, she didn't know. And in her prayers, she begged the Earl to forgive her.

Tears fell softly down her face as Estrela at last came to see the truth: She could not leave Black Bear. She would not.

It was a startling thing to learn about herself: that Black Bear, his happiness, his well-being meant more to her than her own self-respect.

As she glanced upward, her gaze catching on her wardrobe, she knew what she would do.

It was an odd feeling.

Her mind suddenly cleared. Able to take direction now, she knew her only course of action.

But before she rose, before she readied herself to go down to dinner, she closed her eyes, begging the old Earl to release her from a vow that had almost destroyed her happiness, her life.

Tears streaming down her face, the wind suddenly chose that moment to push open the doors.

And as the breeze brushed past her, jostling back her hair, ruffling her frock, she could have sworn she heard the old Earl forgive her.

At long last, Estrela stood released.

A hush fell over the assembled crowd. No one stirred. No one spoke. Not even the sound of tinkling silverware marred the silence.

Estrela stepped a foot farther into the dining room and as she did so a gasp was heard as loudly as if it had been shouted.

Black Bear glanced over to the entrance.

He gazed. He shut his eyes, unable to mask the emotion in his expression. In truth, as the moments flicked by, he stood, eyes closed, one single tear welled-up in his eye.

He barely breathed for fear he was hallucinating. But at last he opened his eyes and looked.

She stood, there at the entrance, her glance lowered in quiet, Indian modesty.

She stood dressed in all the splendor and wealth of the plains Indian. Her gown, which he remembered from years ago, was fashioned from the finest of elkskin, the dress decorated from top to bottom with elk's teeth and ending in beaded fringe at the bottom of the selvage. Among the plains Indians, this was the most prized of all dresses. On her feet she wore blue and red beaded moccasins, white quills adding definition and further accenting the colors there.

She had wrapped a beautifully quilled and designed buffalo robe around her shoulders and her hair was braided neatly at the sides of her face. Blue, red, and yellow beaded earrings fell from her earlobes and in the part of her hair, she had painted the flesh there red, as was the Indian fashion.

Black Bear moved forward. He stopped.

Tears marred his vision making his passage difficult, but at last, Black Bear strode to her, and there, in front of the whole assembly, Waste Ho threw her robe, Indian-style, around him.

It was the way of Indian courting. She knew it. He knew it.

And as she wrapped the robe around him, he bent his head toward her, his lips finding hers, gently at first, and then, as the kiss wore on, he slipped his tongue into her mouth, tasting her, feeling her, loving her.

The robe slipped to the floor, neither she nor Black Bear noticing. In truth, neither of them caring.

Neither was aware of anyone else in the room.

No, this was between them. This was the fulfillment of a vow, the original vow made by them before any other being had come between them.

"I love you," she said, whispered, and he nodded his head. In truth, Black Bear couldn't have spoken at this moment had he tried.

And so Black Bear didn't try. He just looked, he admired, closing his eyes against the overpowering emotion that coursed through him.

At last he said to her, "I will care for you, love you always. I will give you all of me." He gulped. "This I promise."

And Estrela couldn't help it.

She cried.

Right there before the King of England, before the Queen, before all assembled, she cried.

He cried.

And if there were many in the crowd who felt the power of their emotions, no one said a word.

Chapter 23

"**O**h, that's quite another thing! That's quite another thing!"

King William watched the proceedings from his position at the head of the table with something akin to glee. "I say, are they all Indians?"

"Yes, Your Majesty, and no." It was the Duke of Colchester who spoke up beside him.

"Ah," His Majesty said. "Exactly so, exactly so. I do so like such definitive answers." The old gentleman, bubbling, his round eyes even wider, suddenly squinted and laughed. "What do you mean, yes and no?"

"Well, you see, Your Majesty," the Duke of Colchester tried to explain. "The three dark-haired gentlemen there, two of them dress like Indians and are Indians, and the other—well, he, too, is Indian, though he doesn't dress as one. But then you can see that for yourself. And then the blond, well, she's not truly Indian, though she grew up with them, but she's dressed like one, although she isn't really, although she was with them, but she's not really . . ." The Duke cleared his throat. "Now do you understand?"

King William, although not known as one of the greatest Kings of England, was not cruel. He had

a natural enthusiasm about him that could endear
him to most people and he enjoyed a good laugh,
even at his own expense.

He sat now, watching the Duke of Colchester
and without much warning, he suddenly burst out
in laughter. "Well," he said, "now that I understand absolutely nothing, won't you tell me what
it is that you mean?"

The Duke of Colchester removed the handkerchief from his pocket and applied the cloth to his
lips, then to his forehead. He watched as the two
young people stood at the door and did nothing
more than gaze at one another. At last, he ventured
to say, "The three dark gentlemen there, close to
the door are the Indians you have come to meet.
The girl, or rather the Lady there, the blond Indian,
is not Indian, but she isn't really white, well, she is
white. What I mean to say is . . . she's . . ." Here the
Duke of Colchester leaned over to speak confiden-
tially to his Majesty. "I think she is related to our
family, Your Majesty. She looks exactly as my
mother did, your sister. Grew up among the Indians, she did. Brought there by the Earl of Langsford
and brought back by the same. She doesn't know
her heritage."

"Ah, rightly so, rightly so," the old monarch replied. "Well, bring her along, bring her along. Let
me see her. Let me decide."

And to His Majesty's request, the Duke of Colchester said, "Yes, Your Majesty," and with the assistance of a servant, the Duke went to collect
Estrela.

"Your Majesty." Estrela bent over in a curtsey
while the three Indians stood behind her, arms
folded over their chests.

"Well, come forward, child, come forward," the King motioned her to him. "Here," he said as she approached. "Come, put your little paw there in my own. There, you see," he said, smiling at her as she took his hand, "that was not too difficult, was it? Not too difficult at all. My, but you're a pretty thing." The King squinted his eyes at her. "Come closer, now, come closer." And when she did, the bubbly, old gentleman smiled, staring at Estrela for an indefinite moment. "Well," he said at last, "I am not at all hard put to see the resemblance, not at all hard put. Do you remember anything of your mother at all?"

"No, Your Majesty," Estrela replied.

"Your father?"

"No, Your Majesty."

"And you say the Earl of Langsford took you to the Indians?"

Estrela hesitated. "He did not exactly take me to them. We were running away from trouble when the Indians rescued us."

Here the King leaned over toward her. He studied her, looking at her in minute detail before he requested, "Bring me another chair, there." He motioned to a servant. "Yes, there you go, bring me another chair. Now, here, young lady," he instructed Estrela as the servant produced a chair and placed it beside the monarch. "Ah, here now, exactly so, exactly so. Now, come sit here next to me and tell me how you came to be rescued by Indians."

Estrela sat while the King motioned to the Duke of Colchester to bring the Indians forward. "Must hear their side of it, too. Now, what do you say?"

Estrela hesitated before she began. "We left England," she said after a moment, "when I was quite young. I do not remember much of this country at all. But we were chased, Your Majesty, that I do remember vividly."

"Chased? I say. By whom?"

"I don't know. The Earl never told me, if he even knew himself."

"Ah, rightly so, rightly so. Please continue."

"We escaped to the new world and even there, we could never rest long. I remember fleeing into the west. I remember avoiding towns, any sort of civilization. I remember starving. And then we were found, by the fathers of these three Indians you see here. We stopped running. From then on, as long as we remained with the Indians, we were safe."

"Well," the old King muttered. "That's quite another thing, now, that's quite another thing. And tell me," he leaned toward her. "How did you come to be back in this country?"

Estrela gazed at the King, taking her time answering his question. As many as ten people from court stood around her, all listening avidly to her words. And though she was reluctant to tell it in front of them, there was little she could do, short of asking them to leave. And so, after a time, she answered, "The Earl returned to the Indian camp after being gone for several years and when he came back, he demanded I return with him to England."

"Ah," the King said. "And what did the Earl tell you?"

"He said that my grandfather had died and I was needed at home. He said I could stay with my father's people if we were not welcomed back into this country at once."

King William stared at her, squinting his eyes so that he might see her better. At last, he asked, "When was this?"

"Oh, it was several years ago," Estrela answered. "Probably as many as six or seven years ago."

Old King William rubbed his chin. He motioned one of his ministers forward, "Why," he asked the man in question, "have I not been presented with this young lady before now?"

The dignitary gave the King a blank look and said, "Moment," to confer with the Duke of Colchester and returning, bent back toward his King, and murmured, "The lady was presented a few months ago, Your Majesty. You were ill at the time and Queen Adelaide received the lady."

The King nodded his head. He brushed the man away with the wave of his hand, then motioned him back. "Go awaken and bring to me at once Lord Chamberlain."

"But, Your Majesty, he—"

"At once!"

The dignitary nodded and backing away, signaled two servants toward him.

And old King William patted the young lady's hand, saying, "Sit right there now. You so closely resemble my dear niece, Charlotte, it is a pleasure to behold you. Here now, what was that? We will receive the Indians and then we shall talk some more."

And when Estrela murmured, "Yes, Your Majesty," the King simply smiled, muttering, "Exactly so, my dear, exactly so."

A raven landed on the stone ledge just outside the darkened room. Its cawing grated on the nerves of the room's only occupant, the man whose willowy figure shadowed the wall.

Damn nuisance is what they are, damned birds.

He paced over to the window and throwing it suddenly open, knocked the bird from its perch.

A cawing protest was heard in response and then nothing.

The man chuckled, but the laugh didn't sound in the least infectious, there being a deep menacing quality in it.

Foiled. Stopped at every turn. Damned Indian. If it weren't for the Indian, the girl would have been dead long ago.

The man drew a deep breath. Oh, what he did for England, for his precious Dutch Netherlands.

Was there anyone as patriotic as he?

And what had he seen tonight?

The girl talking with the King?

The man paced back to the table where he stopped to pull on his gloves. Then, he began the chore of meticulously measuring out the white substance it had taken him so long to concoct, being careful not to spill any of the powder on himself. Finished at last, he emptied the whole thing into the small earthenware bottle, where he shook it with wine, smiling to himself as he sat back, admiring his work.

He wasn't sure why he hadn't thought of it until recently.

This was so much simpler.

It would be easy.

It would be effective.

And no one, not this simple slip of a girl, nor her Indian friends, could interfere with him. At long last, he need never worry about the merger of Belgian and English forces again.

The man laughed, only this time there was no raven remaining outside to echo the sound. Not a caw, not even the sound of flapping wings. Nothing.

The raven had fled.

Chapter 24

Black Bear came to her.

The hour was late, the party having lasted well into the night.

He stood in the shadows of the room, hidden from view, watching her as she went about her nightly toiletry. He stared and he stared. Dare he believe it? Was she truly his at last? He shut his eyes, then opened them wide. Yes, what was between them was good.

She looked beautiful in her white, flannel gown, which flowed out behind her as she moved. Her pale hair shone as though with its own light in the darkened room, the candlelight from her bedside table accentuating the silvery strands of it. She bent now to unbraid that hair and Black Bear swallowed, the action sounding loud to his own ears. Yes, their love was good.

He took a heavy breath.

He had spent the remainder of the evening with her, together with the King. That man had talked to Waste Ho endlessly while Black Bear had stood off to the side, listening.

The King had tried to speak with the Indians, but after a few words, with little between them in common, the King had once again turned to Waste Ho, and the two of them had talked endlessly about her early life, about her life with the Indians, about the long, lost Earl, whom the King had known personally.

The evening had gone quickly.

His attention was pulled back to the present as she stepped across the room. She flounced into bed, lying still for a moment until she straightened up and grabbed a fluffy pillow. "Well," she said, speaking toward the shadows, "are you just going to stand there and watch or are you coming to bed with me?"

Black Bear didn't respond.

"Black Bear, I—"

"M'lady." It was Anna at her door. "Please excuse the late hour. The royal physician is here to see you."

"Physician? I didn't ask for a physician."

"I know, M'lady. He is here to give you medicine to sleep. The King has ordered it."

"The King has ordered . . . I see," Estrela said. "Well, as you can tell, I am not fit to receive anyone at the moment. Please ask him to give you the medicine with instructions and let him understand that I will be happy to take his medicine before I retire."

Anna nodded. "Very well, M'lady."

Estrela watched the door close and then stared at the entryway for a moment.

And Black Bear, too, stood and stared.

Odd.

He was just about to emerge from the shadows when the maiden, Anna, returned. "M'lady?" she asked.

"Yes?"

"M'lady, the physician says he must see you tonight. He is attending to everyone this evening. There has been some stomach upset and he has been asked to relieve it."

Estrela stared at her maid. She paused, then said, "Anna, tell him that I have no such upset and that I—"

The physician suddenly burst into the room.

He limped.

"Forgive the intrusion, M'lady," the white-haired gentleman said. "I have so many people to attend to and I . . ."

Estrela didn't respond and so the physician didn't finish.

But Black Bear watched from the shadows, he listened. He stared at the man's boots.

He started to step forward, but pulled back when he heard the noise dimly in the background; a sound, somewhere outside the window, a bird, cawing, then silence; sound again, silence, then the flapping of wings.

A raven.

Black Bear nodded his head. He hadn't needed the raven to know the danger. Black Bear would have recognized the man immediately from his boots, from his walk.

But Black Bear was not prepared to fight. He silently cursed himself. He had grown lazy in the English environment. He had come here tonight with nothing, no weapons, an oversight he had never made before.

Damn!

With one last look into the room, watching the willowy figure of the physician bending over Waste Ho, Black Bear saw the man place something onto the table next to the bed. An earthenware bottle. The same one from his dream.

Black Bear knew what he had to do. Hurriedly, while the physician strode away to a far wall, there to wash his hands, Black Bear stepped out of the shadows and into the room. Estrela looked the other way, allowing Black Bear to creep to the table and, taking the object there, he stole silently away to retrieve a weapon—any weapon.

Quickly.

Estrela had recognized the doctor when he strode into the room. He had attended her once before, just after the parade earlier in the year when she had suffered the minor gunshot wound.

She smiled at the older gentleman now, saying to him, "Ah, I remember you."

The doctor returned her grin, but there was something about the gesture that made Estrela nervous. Something about it wasn't right; something about this man wasn't right.

Perhaps he was nervous.

"My maid tells me," Estrela said, "that there has been a rash of stomach aches since the meal tonight. How kind of the King to send you along, but you must be tired yourself." Estrela grinned at the gentleman. "If you would kindly leave me the medicine, I will take it and you can then attend to your other patients. I'm truly sorry you have to be up at this hour ministering to others instead of indulging yourself in sleep." She sat back against the pillows. "Did you enjoy the party tonight?"

The doctor looked at her before he replied, "Well enough."

Again, that grin. It set Estrela to shivering.

"The medicine will help you to sleep," he stated. "Have you a cup?"

"Surely," Estrela returned. "In the corner of my room." She pointed it out to him.

"Pray, excuse me a moment."

Estrela nodded and watched the doctor. He fetched the cup and returned to the bed.

"I trust that you will forgive the inconvenience tonight, M'lady," the physician said, reaching for the earthenware bottle.

An odd look came over the man's face.

"Did you see the bottle?" he asked, his eyes flashing with panic before turning his attention to the nightstand.

"Pray, I—"

"What have you done with it?"

"What?"

"The bottle."

Estrela gave the man an incredulous look. "I daresay, my good man," she said, "I have done nothing with the bottle. But I believe our conversation is at an end." She waved her hand. "You may go."

The physician stood up beside the bed. "No." It was all he murmured.

"I beg your pardon?"

The doctor drew himself up, standing straight, until he loomed over Estrela. A look of resignation crossed his face before he sighed and said, "No, I will not leave. I did not want to do it this way. I sought to save you anguish. But I see I cannot. I will not allow you to escape me this time."

Estrela turned wide eyes to him. "What do you mean?"

"Poison."

"Poison?"

"Yes," he said. "I had hoped to spare you the anguish of knowing you will die. But the poison is gone. What you did with it, I do not know, however—"

"You!" Estrela looked wildly around her. Where was Black Bear? He no longer stood in the shadows. Where had he gone? She turned back to the doctor and gulped. "You! You are the one who—"

"Yes, my dear." The doctor extracted a pistol from his bag, placing the cold metal at her temple.

Estrela stared up at him, oddly calm. "Why?" It was all she asked.

The man sighed. "Why?" he repeated. "Why?" He shook his head. "Because, my dear, I am the only one who can save all of England from a disastrous decision. Does no one else see what must be done? Is it always to rest on my shoulders, this burden of responsibility? It is nothing personal, you understand, Your Highness," he said. "It is only that you must not rule England. You with your Belgian influence. Such would be a disaster for my own country. Now, don't worry, my dear. It will be painless. It will be over in a matter of—"

Estrela screamed.

It startled the doctor.

He fell toward the bed, throwing a hand over her mouth, but it was too late. She screamed again and bit his hand, his bellow echoing her own.

He was struggling off balance and Estrela took advantage, heaving her arms upward over her head, pushing the pistol away from her, grabbing for his arm so that he pointed the gun elsewhere. She screamed again.

And the doctor reacted. The pistol fired.

But the weapon blasted harmlessly into the air. It had only the one bullet.

Cursing, the doctor threw the weapon away. He lunged at Estrela.

Estrela screamed and rolled in a somersault over the bed, but he caught a slender foot and using it as leverage, he pulled her back onto the bed.

"Damned nuisance!" he cried. "Look at the trouble you've caused me. But no more."

She beat at him, pummeling him with her hands, her arms, a pillow.

"Augh!" he grabbed the pillow away from her. He crushed it down over her face. But it lasted no more than a second.

"Hiya!" A war cry split the air.

The doctor froze, the pillow falling from his hands.

Black Bear, leaping across the room, knocked the doctor to the floor, jumping onto him at the same time.

The two men rolled over and over. Black Bear, the winner, remained on top.

Black Bear pulled his knife, the only weapon he'd been able to find, but the doctor had one also and he slashed out at the Indian.

Nothing. Black Bear merely dodged. Another stab. Another. But it was useless. The doctor was no match for the Indian. Black Bear easily knocked the knife out of the doctor's hands, but he didn't slash at the doctor or even make a stab. Instead he pressed his knife at the doctor's neck, just drawing blood.

"Now," Black Bear said, his teeth bared. "If you wish to see another day, you tell me why you try to kill Waste Ho, Estrela."

The physician tried to laugh, but the effect was lost. He only choked.

Black Bear sent the knife deeper into the man's neck. "Do you think I will hesitate?"

"You stupid Indian. You damned Indian. Don't you know that by harming me, you harm all of England?"

Black Bear smiled, and taking hold of the man's hair, he banged the doctor's head against the hardwood floor.

"You misunderstand. You think that I care," Black Bear howled, then, raising his knife—

"She should be Queen," was the rush of words.

Black Bear only laughed, banging the man's head again. "Why have you tried to kill her?"

The man didn't answer.

Another bang, and this time Black Bear pulled at the hair.

The doctor screamed. "If she were Queen she might unite England and Belgium against my own country."

Black Bear's grip loosened, but he said, "More."

Silence.

Black Bear gripped the hair.

"She is the daughter of King Leopold of Belgium and Princess Charlotte, King George IV's only daughter. The Princess Charlotte bore twins. I destroyed the records of her birth. Had she grown up here, she would now be Queen."

"No!"

The exclamation didn't come from Black Bear, nor Estrela, nor the doctor. Looking up, the doctor howled.

Estrela glanced behind her and gasped.

There stood the King. There stood his Queen, Adelaide. There stood the Duke of Colchester.

"Let the man up." It was the King who spoke.

"Hiya!" Black Bear protested, but then acquiesced, though not before he banged the doctor's head against the floor again. Springing to his feet, he pulled the doctor up at the same time and held the man by the hair.

The King paced forward, giving Black Bear the opportunity to check on Estrela.

"Are you hurt?" Black Bear asked her under his breath.

"No," she said quietly, "but where were you?"

"I had no weapons. I left to get some, but before I left, I saw that he had bottle. The bottle from my vision. I knew what was in bottle. I took it to get the Duke and the King and to get weapons. I wanted them to be here to witness what the assassin had to say." Black Bear shook the doctor, while the King paced right up to the accused.

"So," the King said, "this is quite another thing. The royal physician betrays me."

"Not you, my King," the physician stated, earning himself another shake from Black Bear.

"Let the man go," the King ordered and Black Bear, after hesitating a moment, relaxed his grip.

"What do you say, my good man?"

"I do not betray you," the royal physician said. "Only that"—he pointed to Estrela—"that girl who should have been dead long ago. Look at her. Should she rule England? Should she take your place?" The doctor spit on the clean Chinese rug. "No, I say. No, so would anyone say. What I do, I do for England."

The King hesitated. He glanced at Estrela, he glanced at Black Bear, then back to the physician. At last he said, "Well, this is quite another thing, indeed. Oh, she does resemble my niece, Charlotte, so well. Why, even the good Duke here could see it." The King smiled at the Duke. "Why, my good man, I do believe all of England is indebted to you."

No one was sure at first just who the good King meant until—

The physician gasped. "Your Majesty!"

"No," the old King said. "She belongs to the Royal Family, she does. Here, Popin," he said to Estrela. "Give an old man your paw, now. That's a good girl."

The King fell to his knees and kissing Estrela's hand, said simply, "My Queen."

The doctor howled.

Estrela gasped, and Black Bear let go of the Doctor completely.

In truth, Black Bear didn't see it, hadn't anticipated it, didn't notice that he still held his knife, blade outward in his hand. Had he known, he still might have wielded the weapon against the fiendish man, but he didn't have the chance.

The doctor saw the blade and with one last shriek, the man plunged himself into the knife.

Estrela screamed.

The physician dropped to the floor.

And all present, including the King, knelt over the man.

The physician sighed up at them, then he laughed. He stared at Estrela. "Ah, what trouble you are," he said to her. "I should have killed you when you were just a babe, then I would have avoided this now. But I couldn't do it then. No," he said, "I had to wait until you were fully grown and back in the country with Indians to protect you. Ah, such is my luck."

He coughed and Estrela stared at him in disbelief.

He laughed, the sound of it a mockery. "You win. I am beat. I, who stole you at birth from your mother's side. I, who have kept you unknown even to your own father. I, the man who has kept England and Belgium apart. But it is over now."

He glanced over to the King. "What a fool you are. Just like your father. Losing your colonies. If you had only taken my advice. It has been a war," he said, glancing once more to Estrela. "What matter that I kill others? Don't soldiers kill in war? Why can't I? Was my destiny, it was. I had to attend to anyone who stood in my way, even the Earl's old household staff. For it is only I who knows the best path for this country." He smirked.

But too quickly the physician seemed to realize he was truly dying and for a moment, his eyes mirrored his fear. And as he looked down to his wound, he scoffed. "I would have thought I could have chosen a more painless death."

He drew a deep breath, then looking to Estrela, he said, "Do you not know me?"

Estrela nodded her head.

The man closed his eyes and sneered. "You once commented I looked familiar, and so I should to you. Lord Wilburne, Court Physician and Doctor to His Majesty the King and Queen. It has been nothing personal, m'dear. Only the necessity to keep you from the throne. Couldn't have you ruling England; couldn't afford the risk to my country in these unsettling times. The Earl of Langsford was my best friend, but . . . such a naive man. Loved your . . . mother, he did. Charlotte. He was . . . he . . . I used to tell you bedtime stories, child. The old Earl never knew . . . Was . . . I . . . who forced him to . . . flee . . . was . . . I who . . . I . . . who . . ."

Estrela glanced up to Black Bear.

"Sir Constance Wilburne . . . would be ruler of all England . . ." the physician murmured. "Sir Connie . . ."

Estrela gasped. "Sir Connie." She drew away. And her voice barely a whisper, she said, "I have looked for you, Sir. I have tried to find you. Did you truly not know it, Sir? Did you not know that the Earl married me to you?"

"No!"

But Estrela nodded. "Sir Connie, you could have had it all."

"No!"

It was the last thing he said, the last thing he would ever say.

And Estrela, lifting her face to stare at Black Bear, whispered, "At long last I have found him. And," she said, her throat constricting, "I have found him dead."

Black Bear held her gaze. He didn't say a word, he didn't make a move, until, at length, he murmured, "So be it."

Chapter 25

"**W**ill Your Royal Highness stand still, please?"

Estrela fidgeted in spite of the request. The dressmaker tried to smile, but Estrela could feel the woman's frustration. In truth Estrela couldn't be still. She was too worried, too confused.

Where was he?

She surveyed the room around her, a room that could have fit an army into it. Delicate scenes were painted on the ceiling, trimmed in gold. Not golden paint: gold. A pink-and-blue designed Chinese rug cushioned her feet in pleasant comfort as she stood upon it while the rug also ran the full length and breadth of the room. There were five different chandeliers hung from the ceiling, each one alight with burning candles, with intermittent wax dripping down to the carpet below, only to be cleaned up immediately by a maid or servant.

Parlor maids, the maid of the robes, the keeper of the jewels, the seamstress, the maid of the gowns, and more hurried about the room. Servants seemed to be stationed everywhere, rushed everywhere. Ladies entered now and again, kneeling and bowing, speaking to her in soft voices.

It was, in all, a mass of splendor, of confusion.

Where was he?

She examined each shadowy corner. She attended each person who filtered into and out of the room. She stared around her. She could find no trace of him and she hadn't seen him in almost forty-eight hours.

She felt surrounded, surrounded by maids and a circus of servants, duchesses and ladies. All of them busy, if not with chores, then with gossip.

And as Estrela continued to scan the room around her, she began to lose courage.

Ever since that evening at Shelburne Hall, only two days ago, Estrela could not claim a single moment to herself. She had been whisked into the whirlwind of the Royal Court, had been transformed from M'lady to Your Majesty, from fugitive to future Queen, and all in a matter of minutes, her world changing from that of quiet order to massive confusion, just that quickly.

No sooner had Sir Connie confessed his misdeeds and confirmed her heritage than the old King and the Royal Court notables had swarmed her, hurrying her away from Shelburne Hall and hurling her into London, there to meet lords and ladies, ministers and bishops, dukes and duchesses.

And in all that time she hadn't seen Black Bear. Not once.

Where was he?

She had asked for news of him several times and with each asking she was told that she would see him soon. Still time elapsed.

As soon as she had reached London, she had been deposited at St. James Palace where she had been taken aside, schooled in the proper behavior for a future Queen, told the duties of her position and informed in a not-so-gentle fashion of the current affairs of Britain. She had been read to, lectured, and instructed, all in the matter of forty-eight hours.

She was tired, yet she was to meet tonight with Lord Melbourne, Prime Minister, before she was officially announced to the dignitaries as the new Princess, the next in line to the accession of the throne of England.

She had been told that her father, Leopold, King of Belgium, whom she had never met, was en route to meet her. She had even been informed that a Belgian ship lay in harbor, a tribute to her.

She discovered, much to her surprise, that there was rejoicing in the streets of Belgium. For her accession to the throne meant a possible uniting of Belgium with England, a political move that might bring about an end forever to the strife between Belgium and the Dutch Netherlands.

Estrela stood overwhelmed by it all. And all she could think of was Black Bear.

Where was he?

The Duke of Colchester came to escort Estrela to the waiting assembly of bishops and lords, generals and dukes, notables and ministers.

He approached her as she stood in her chambers, surrounded by what seemed to be a hundred servants and maids.

Estrela dismissed them all at once and taking the Duke of Colchester's arm, she directed him out of the room.

He smiled at her gently. And Estrela, looking at him, asked, "Did you always know?"

The Duke of Colchester snorted, he puffed out

his cheeks, he coughed. But at last he said, "So right. So right. I suspected."

"How so?"

"The Earl of Langsford told me something of his situation long ago, over a bottle of ale, it was. But, I daresay I couldn't remember it straight. Had to make nothing of it, you know. Couldn't arouse suspicion. Been grateful to the Indians, I must say. Grateful, indeed."

He escorted her down the long, curved staircase, the last leg of which lay carpeted in red.

They passed through a sculptured, arched doorway, and proceeded down the stairs, where waited what must have been several hundred people.

"Your Grace," Estrela said, as they hesitated at the top, "might I ask you a question?"

"Of course, Your Majesty," the Duke responded. "How might I assist you?"

"Your Grace," she said. "'Tis a delicate question I must ask you. Will you, Sir, keep this inquiry of mine just between the two of us?"

He bowed his head graciously. "Yes, Your Majesty."

Estrela glanced over to him and smiled. "As you know, more than anyone else, I have been long away from the court. I have no real knowledge of my station, outside of what I have learned just these past few days. And I have no knowledge of the . . . circumstances of marriage as due my position." She paused while the Duke of Colchester cleared his throat. "Sir," she asked, "might I ever be given permission to marry an Indian?"

The Duke of Colchester, a man with old age closing in upon him, had long been known for his light and gentle handling of situations and of men.

He might appear bumbling, but it was appearance only. He was an aristocrat well-trained. And it was this training that stood him in good stead now.

Without so much as a glimmer of emotion in his countenance, he said, "I think not, Your Majesty. I am sorry."

Estrela was silent. Then, "I thought not." She stared down into the crowd. "You know that I am in love with Black Bear."

"Yes, Your Majesty."

"You are sure about the marriage restrictions?"

"Yes, Your Majesty."

Estrela tried to smile, but the result was merely a weak, unsteady grin. She sighed instead.

"I'm sorry, Your Majesty." It was all he said.

Estrela offered him her gloved hand and murmuring a quiet, "Thank you," she allowed him to escort her down the stairs, into the majestic, painted hall, a solid gold handrail beneath her touch, a velvety red rug beneath her feet.

Black Bear stood toward the back of the hall and watched.

Princess, Queen, Estrela, Waste Ho.

He'd been told politely, but firmly, that he had to go. He'd been told he had no place in her life now. Someone had informed him that she didn't even want to see him. Someone had arranged his passage home and he was even now supposed to be on a ship.

But he wouldn't go, he couldn't go; he didn't believe it.

He'd come here to witness for himself what Waste Ho thought, what she felt, and if it were not her own wish that he leave . . .

And so he stood at the back, watching her, observing, listening. He caught her eye.

He looked at her. She stared back.

Their glances held; he didn't even dare breathe.

Stay, her eyes said.

Come, he answered back.

And then it happened.

She glanced away.

It was a deliberate move. And as he watched the profile she presented to him, he knew it: She stayed.

She stood surrounded by red, white, and black. She wore white, her train was red. His Majesty stood beside her in black.

But she didn't care about any of it.

She watched *him* in the back of the room.

And as she stared, she thought she died a little. She didn't dare to breathe, she just looked.

It was over. It was gone. It was impossible. She was to be a Queen. He was Indian.

She had responsibilities—to her heritage, to England, to everyone assembled here.

And he? He had his tribe, his people. He must return, for there could never be more between them than a love affair.

And as she gazed at him, she pleaded, *Stay here with me.*

He looked back. *Come.*

And Estrela, unable to change what took place all around her, the dukes, the duchesses, the barons, and court notables, her heritage, her coronation, her responsibilities, she gazed away.

* * *

"Your Majesty?"

Estrela placed her gloved hand over that of the old King. "Please," she said. "Take me away."

"But Your Majesty, the assembly, your Court, your . . ."

Her hand tightened over his own and the old King followed her gaze.

He sighed. "Ah, to be young again," he said under his breath. "But that's quite another story."

And with all the ceremony of the Royal Court, he turned the young Princess around.

She almost left. She almost walked away, out of Black Bear's life without a backward glance.

But it is said on the Indian plains that one should always take a second look. Always.

She did.

She turned. She sought out his gaze. She stared.

And that's when she realized: She didn't have to do this. She didn't know these people. She hadn't grown up among them. She wasn't really a part of this society, not anymore.

She gazed at the old King.

Why take his throne away? Why?

He could do it. He could still be King, and there was the young Victoria, who had been groomed all her life to this position.

She wasn't truly needed here.

She didn't have to do this.

She wanted Black Bear, had wanted him all her life.

She swung back around. "Black Bear!" she cried at the same time a shot fired from the crowd.

The old King ducked down, unharmed.

Estrela screamed, but she screamed a name, "Black Bear!"

Black Bear was at once in motion, blazing forward through the crowd, his two Lakota friends behind him.

He was beside her in an instant, and as he gazed at her, picking her up and taking her in his arms, he smiled, "Here we are again."

And then he ran.

Out of the assembly.

Away from St. James Palace.

Out into the streets, the two Lakota Indians at his heels, protecting his lead.

Toward the docks.

And as he ran, he asked, "You are sure?"

Estrela almost cried. She could barely speak. "I am sure, my love," she said. "What is my life without you?"

He whooped then. He hollered. He almost swung her around, but he couldn't.

Instead, he ran on to the docks, his precious possession pressed tightly to his chest.

And Black Bear couldn't help it; he tried but he couldn't help it.

Black Bear grinned.

Prince Frederick stood by the gangway of the ship.

" 'Tis a Belgian ship," he said. "Compliments of my Uncle Leopold, King of Belgium." He looked at Estrela. "Cousin," he said. "You are my own cousin, and I never knew it. Go now," he said, "before they find you. It was a Dutch Patriot, an enemy of Belgium, who shot at you. If you stay, there will always be strife. 'Tis better that you go now. But hurry, no one is looking for you here . . . yet."

Estrela smiled at him. "Thank you." She gazed at her best friend, who stood beside the Prince. "Anna," she said, her voice breaking. "I will miss you."

Anna smiled at her. "Why does M'lady cry," she asked, "when I be a boarding t' ship w' ye?"

"No!" It was Prince Frederick who spoke.

"Why would I want t' stay 'ere? My life 'ere as a servant would never allow me t' marry or t' 'ave a family of me own. Why not go w' 'er? 'Tis freedom there."

"No," he said, but he couldn't stop her.

She was already boarding the ship, along with her mistress, out of reach.

"Come with us, my friend," Black Bear shouted down to Prince Frederick from the side of the ship.

Black Bear stood with Estrela in his arms, Anna at her side.

And Prince Frederick, watching, waiting, suddenly ran, away from restrictions, away from a tiny German duchy, away from money and all the pitfalls it could possess, and jumping aboard the Belgian ship, he took Anna in his arms.

But before the vessel pulled away from the docks, he said to her, "Marry me. We will go to the New World. There we can start a new life. Just marry me."

"But—"

"I love you. 'Tis all that matters."

And Anna, smiling at him, whispered, "Yes."

The ship sailed that night, its precious cargo of three Indians, a Princess, a Prince, and a maid all safely stowed aboard.

And as it sailed out under a midnight sky, the happy sounds of laughter could be heard on the breeze, it is said, a full continent away.

At last, Black Bear and his Princess were coming home to the people, to the Lakota prairie, to love.

Truly, it was cause for great celebration.

Epilogue

A FABLE

A Tale Told In Many A Lakota Lodge

*T*hey came back to the Americas, it is said, the Princess and her handsome husband.

They were welcomed back by the people for we all loved them and we were much pleased to see them.

They lived long and prospered, their love a vibrant, real thing. And all who would see them would come away with happiness in their hearts, for there is nothing so potent as love.

They had many children, so it is said, some who live even to this day.

The old woman, sitting in front of the fire in the lone tepee, stirred the bright fire as she said these last words. She glanced up at the young faces of her grandchildren.

"Is it true, Grandma? Is the story true?"

The old woman just smiled. "Some say it's true, some say it is a mere fable. You will have to decide what you believe yourself." The old woman smiled. "Now come, your parents wait outside."

Everyone filtered out of the tepee, save the lone child with the strange combination of blond braids and dark, dark eyes.

And as she sat around the fire, a wind swept into the tepee, sparking the fire, sending smoke everywhere.

And for a moment, just one tiny space in time, there in the smoke, the youngster saw two lovers embrace and when she listened, she could have sworn she heard the happy sounds of laughter, of love.

And the little girl, her eyes wise for one so young, smiled.

Author's Note

Dear Reader:

If your curiosity about the interaction between the Europeans and the Native Americans has been piqued, I encourage you to obtain a copy of a rare old book entitled *Eight Years' Travel and Residence in Europe* by George Catlin. You may share my surprise in the discovery that the manner in which the English accepted the Indian, especially the women's reactions to them, is just as I have described them in *Lakota Princess*. As a matter of fact, Catlin records (albeit a little dryly) the romance of one of the traveling young Indians with "an English black-eyed beauty," their eventual marriage, and their ultimate acceptance into British society.

This makes for entertaining reading, and if you can obtain a copy of this account, even if only in microfilm, I would highly recommend it.

Avon Romances—
the best in exceptional authors and unforgettable novels!

Avon Romantic Treasures

Unforgettable, enthralling love stories,
sparkling with passion and adventure
from Romance's bestselling authors